Werewolf Tale

A minute seemed to pass. Nothing.

The raccoon scratched at his paws, its claws barely slicing his skin, but he could feel his grip loosening from it squirming around. When the paw over its face loosened to reposition, the raccoon went on the attack, biting into the flesh of his paw. With a dull snarl of pain, Alex pulled the raccoon off and sealed its mouth again, his paw now wrapped around its neck as well.

With it now at his mercy, how gigantic his paws were compared to its body made his pulse weaken and his blood run cold. He couldn't.

His grumbling stomach told him otherwise.

Days after he and a friend discover the victim of a werewolf, Alex Stryker is attacked and bitten.

As his wounds heal, his senses sharpen, and his anxiety around strangers mounts, he prepares for what he sees as a frightful transformation during the next full moon.

And what he may have to explain if his family or his friends ever find out what he is.

Werewolf Tale

Author – Adam Gulledge

Cover Artist – Katie Hofgard

Editor – Sean Gerace

- Renegade Publications -
2018

First Printing: 2018

ISBN: 978-1-7325210-2-5

www.werewolftale.info

Contents

Acknowledgements

Since I'm no fan of flowery language or long speeches, I'll skip both and go right into the acknowledgments of those who have helped make this, my first novel, a reality.

My cover artist, Katie Hofgard. Her art-style and depiction of Alex's Crossing the Threshold moment never ceases to amaze me. Without her art and unique typography gracing this novel, the visual flare would not exist.

My editor, Sean Gerace. His input on Werewolf Tale was invaluable in shaping the final narrative and pointing out the weaknesses in the prose and style of the older drafts.

My beta readers: Birgance Boyce, John Miller, David Pospisil, and the others who wished to remain anonymous. Along with Sean's input and that of the many readers of my work over the years, theirs was helpful in spotlighting further flaws in the narrative, helping iron out every wrinkle possible.

Last, but certainly not least, a personal shout-out and thank you to the creators of the Sad and Rabid Puppy campaigns, Larry Correia and Vox Day, as well as the many who've supported creative rights and individuality during the ongoing situation of #GamerGate. A movement based in the pursuit of ethics, yes, but this same movement has also spotlighted the intimidation and smear tactics used against creators under the guise of criticism and "social justice." Something that everyone, creators especially, should be aware of and willing to fight against.

To every one of you, thank you for everything you've done.

Preface

Werewolf Tale is a product of 2011, though it has a history with me going back a little over a year before then. Because it is a product of 2011, the most important events related to its creation all took place within the last three months of that year. The first was a Halloween themed contest on DeviantART, and the second was NaNoWriMo in November.

Before the news of either event reached me, my writing style was being shaped through participation in forum RPGs, and from reading the handful of YA horror and fantasy novels that were holding my interest at the time. Works from authors like Christopher Pike and Alan F. Troop. Then came September, when I learned about both events; the amount of writing I was already doing for entertainment helped push me to take a shot at NaNoWriMo and use the Halloween event to get some ideas onto paper before it started.

What resulted was a non-canon 1-Year-Later short story for Werewolf Tale that established Alex, his condition, and some of his friends. As a way of coming up with ideas without writing any part of the actual story, it worked.

As for NaNoWriMo, while I can't remember most of the fluxes and laxes of that thirty-day period, I do remember the final four days when, four thousand words away from the goal, ideas were running dry. I kept my laptop close, squeezing in what I could where possible.

And then came Day 30, where an evening crunch in my college computer lab got me past the finish line by 570 words. The following year, in June, was when the first draft was finished.

Though it was left aside with the approach of the 2012 NaNoWriMo, a suggestion from a fan in 2013 lead to a work-spanning revision and a chapter-by-chapter posting of the new draft on FurAffinity like what I had done on DeviantART with the first draft.

That same year was when I approached Katie about doing the cover art for Werewolf Tale. My signing of a contract with her, that business agreement, was when the idea of this story becoming the real deal was cemented. Now it is, and I couldn't be more pleased.

So, with that, read away and enjoy.

Prologue - Hunting in Pairs

Saturday, August 13th, 2011 - Sugar Land, Texas
Moon Phase – Full
11:03 p.m.

Angela relaxed her tense posture after a moment of nothing but cricket chirps. If not for how clean the evening breeze was of strong human scents, the startled animal snorting she'd just heard would've prompted a retreat; a rethinking of her decision to follow Shane out here was already several minutes old.

He continued moving before she did, drawing her attention as he passed. When he came to a stop near the edge of the brush patch, everything went quiet again.

"Ready?"

Shane's growl-laced, rumbling voice didn't catch Angela off-guard. "Which one? That doe?"

"The calf."

"That much meat…seems like a waste."

"Between us, it won't be." Shane resumed closing in on the stable after another stretch of silence, Angela tailing him. With every few steps, a handful of the crickets in the brush around them stop chirping, as though they were tiny alarms hidden in the grass.

A pair of animal cries came again as they reached the edge of the brush patch, this time from the mare and the doe. After glancing at Shane, whose expression and attention hadn't changed, the sound got Angela to hurry ahead of him. Within two seconds, she was diving from the steel bars into the calf's enclosure like a wrestler.

The calf sprung to life when she landed, her claws snagging its ribs and shoulders as it tried to stand and flee. The fearful cries it made as Angela wrestled with it left her ears ringing, and her attention distracted from the calf's thrashing hooves. She could hear them hitting and scraping concrete, the clacks not masking Shane's entry behind her, and then one of her legs was shoved. For half a second of adrenaline-fueled tension, Angela felt nothing besides the shove.

Then the pain hit, with needle-like stings from pulled fur, building heat around the impact spot, and the feeling that her femur had been bashed through her muscles. Angela rolled aside, her claws slipping from their hold on the calf.

Shane then rushed forward, tackling the startled animal into a corner of the enclosure before wrestling it to the ground by its head. His claws dug behind its skull as he held it down and in position for Angela.

After a second of no action on her part, Shane's head tilted up. Her muzzle was hanging open, and her posture was rocky, as though her confidence was gone.

"Well?" he demanded. When Angela tried to move, a wince replaced her drained expression, and one of her paws went for her thigh. A spreading red stain in her fur was what Shane saw next, and how slowly she was gathering her composure pushed him to act first.

With a grasp of the calf's right shoulder, his claws punching into its flesh, his jaws spread and closed in on the animal's neck. His fangs went through the skin and muscle before something hard stopped them. He put more pressure into his bite. No leeway, and very little blood was meeting his tongue. He'd struck bone. With a loosening of his jaws and a twist of the calf's head, his bottom fangs hit bone again while his upper ones cut further in. The calf's blood was quick to flow over his fangs in response to the punctured vessel, and his jaws once again relaxed, his tongue lapping the fluid on his teeth.

Angela, meanwhile, was holding back the trembling in her gut brought on by Shane's mauling of the calf. How strained its cries had suddenly become made it tougher, and then the many scents that composed fresh blood reached her muzzle. The familiar sensation of something akin to a bubble expanding within her stomach emerged, in stark contrast to how tense the many animal cries, and her injury, were leaving her.

As Shane got the calf's neck in his jaws, Angela at last glanced away, toward the enclosure's door. Its top was five-feet high, at most, short enough for someone to see over it easily. The sound of rigid tissue crunching then started and stopped. It repeated once, then again, with the calf going silent after the first repetition.

When Angela's attention returned to Shane, the calf was still pinned under his paws. His front teeth and fangs were tearing at a piece of muscle on the bovine's shoulder. With the previously panic-stricken animals calming down, she heard nothing that could mean an immediate threat to them, but offered a suggestion as she came closer anyway. "Let's move this out of here."

"Later. We'll be fine." Shane's head didn't rise as he replied.

Although Angela wanted to be assured of that, with their catch so close, a moment to reflect was all the incentive she needed to not protest. After picking her feeding spot, her fangs dug into the muscle, making a sizeable chunk to be pulled at.

Seconds later, Shane was growling.

Certain that no one had approached them, Angela glanced over to find him glaring at her, his teeth showing, his tongue flashing, and his ears erect and stiff. The noise and his stare sent a shudder down her spine and around her chest, and she released the chunk she had.

Shane spoke when his growling relaxed. "I said we're fine."

"Not in here we're not."

"Then take the deer and go, if you're that scared of being seen."

Angela growled in response, to which Shane resumed feeding. Until she was sure his attention was fully on the calf, she didn't move closer. Her fangs found a new spot on the calf's right leg, but Shane's growls began again, making her yank on the piece she had.

A sharp snarl during her second tug snapped her attention back to Shane. She almost missed the moment he lunged at her, backpedaling in response. The pain from the gash in her leg almost forced her back down from the standing stance she'd stopped in.

Shane followed suit, standing over the calf, his attention not swaying from Angela's turned head. "You had your chance. Get your own or wait." Until he began pacing backwards, the growling that had accompanied his demand continued. Angela refused to meet his gaze until he was back on all fours.

With her heart racing from the lunge and retreat, her attention changed to the rest of the stable's interior. She saw no one else, and no other animals. Just stored feed, empty enclosures, and what looked like a locked main gate on the far-right side. A check of the other side followed, with a similar closed door on display. She couldn't bring herself to feel apologetic with the discovery, however.

And the sound of sirens in the distance enforced that feeling.

Angela tried not to worry when first hearing them, but as the siren volume rose, her sense of safety rapidly waned. It was when the sirens sounded less than three streets away that it vanished completely, and she made for the calf's legs. Taking one in both paws, she noticed Shane stop feeding and meet her gaze, his growls starting again. "Not the time. Let's go."

Shane's lunge a second later slammed her into the enclosure's wall, rattling her already racing heart. She snapped her jaws in response, Shane backing up just enough for her to swing an arm under one of his. When her paw found his shoulder, she dug it in, now snarling herself.

Shane mimicked her jaw snap, missing the first time before gauging his next strike. His jaws closed on Angela's muzzle, cutting off her snarls.

The needle-like pain from the bite pressure and Shane's teeth on her muzzle got Angela to reach for his head. She slapped her free paw down near his eyes, sparking a growl from him as her claws raked at his face. That was when her arm was snagged and held down, with Shane's other paw pressing her left shoulder into the wall behind her. Angela tightened her grip on Shane's shoulder in the hope of getting him off. His resultant snarl and the increased pressure on her muzzle killed that hope.

When her attention shifted back to the sirens, they sounded closer than before. Remembering the closed, and likely locked, stable doors didn't help calm her fears. Her breathing quickened when the siren wail sounded within a street of them.

And then the intensity dipped. No relief came to her in turn. Only frustration and anger.

Shane wrenched Angela's paw free of his shoulder when her grip loosened, his muzzle remaining clasped over hers for some time after. "After this, what I kill is mine," he said once he'd released his jaws. Angela huffed in response, refusing eye contact in favor of nursing her muzzle.

When Shane didn't return to the carcass, she inched her way towards it, her paws balled into fists. The gesture didn't escape Shane's notice, and his attention stayed on her while they fed and hid the carcass.

Her defensive posturing and elevated pulse, both of which remained as they left the area, was evidence enough to him to be wary of her.

Chapter 1 – Of Comics and Company

Tuesday, August 23rd, 2011 – Sugar Land, Texas
Moon Phase – Last Quarter
3:05 p.m.

As his potential new boss read over his resume, the hand that Alex Stryker was stroking his chin with moved to adjust his tie. He tugged at it twice, shifting in his seat afterward. *If he asks what I can offer him, or the shop... What can I offer?*

His attention wandered to the comics tacked to the walls, the issues that didn't depict superheroes keeping his attention the longest. Gaming knowledge was the first thing he thought of; the shop had plenty of those products on offer. *How well do those sell versus comics?*

The sound of paper rustling and a thump against wood pulled his attention back to the man interviewing him.

"Alex, I've got a proposal for you."

A proposal? "What kind?"

"What say we skip the interview, and I just say, 'You're hired'?"

Alex shielded his mouth after a chuckle got away. "Just like that?"

"Yeah. Just like that."

"I wasn't expecting that."

"Very few of my employees were."

"Hmm..." As Alex pieced together the rest of his sentence, a shot of horror mixed with his elated mood. His boss's name was escaping him. *Oh, boy.* "If there's no need for an interview, then..."

"We can talk for a while. That does the job better, I think."

"Sounds good." *Gah, what's his name?*

His boss nodded, then glanced at his resume. "From what I read, I take it games are your specialty."

"PC and console games, yeah. My tabletop list is...kinda small."

"I wouldn't say so. Most role-players I know stick with one to three games they like. Of course, there are the miniature war games, board games, card games, etc."

"Do the gaming nights cover all of them, or just role-playing?"

"Only role-playing currently, but they'll expand to board games soon."

Alex nodded in response.

"Speaking of boards, I've noticed you always have a skateboard with you when you're here."

"Yeah. Been riding since I was nine."

"Ten years?" Trevor's surprise remained after Alex nodded again. "Impressive. You know any tricks?"

"Quite a few. Flip tricks and grinds, mostly. Truth be told though, I spend more time riding around than seriously practicing."

"That's better than me. The last time I rode a skateboard, I couldn't keep my balance on it."

"Those days I barely remember." When he was met with silence, Alex changed the subject. "About the position though, anything I should know before my first day?"

"When your first day comes, you'll be walking the floor and getting a feel for where everything is. Most of our regulars know their way around, but you will get the occasional question, or be asked to find something."

"And if I'm not sure about something, ask you or one of the guys for help."

Trevor nodded. "Exactly. That's pretty much everything you really need to know."

"I'm anticipating a few comic discussions on that day already."

"There's some big changes coming from DC soon, but don't worry about trying to memorize everything coming out. Much as I enjoy their stuff, even I can't keep track of every issue and plot-twist they publish. Still, it goes without saying that working with the public will be part of your job, so the more you know about what's going on in the comic industry or in the stories you like, the better."

At that, Alex thought over the comics he'd been reading during his store visits for the last three weeks. Only one DC series was keeping his attention versus a few more between Image, Archie, and Marvel. "Right now, Deadpool and Sonic are what I read most."

A smile grew on his boss's face at the latter name. "How much of it have you read?" After Alex answered, his boss began detailing some of the very early issues and related plots, allowing the minutes to slip by without either of them noticing.

At least until Alex's phone sounded its ringtone, cutting their discussions short.

He fumbled for the volume control, nerves chilled from embarrassment and shock. "Thought I turned that off. My apologies."

He got no comment from his boss about the interruption, but rather the time. "Three-forty already?"

"Something need doing?" Alex asked.

"No. Just surprised that much time got away from us." As his boss got up from his seat, Alex followed suit. "I'll be back in a minute, unless you need to leave right now."

"Nah, I'm in no rush."

"In that case, if you want, you can head out into the store while I get a few things for you."

"I'll wait here. Thank you for your time, Sir." Alex held out his hand for his boss, hoping, as it was gripped and shaken, that 'sir' was a professional enough stand-in for not knowing his name. Once he was alone however, his hands went to work, digging around in his pockets for the shop's business card. He located it in his back-right pocket. *Trevor Young. Damn it. How did I forget that?*

The still-present tightening of his flesh and chill around his back lingered until he was out on the sales floor with the stuff Trevor gave him: two company T-shirts, a sheet of paper with company policies and rules, and a lanyard with his nametag.

As he approached the front counter, Marcus, one of his longtime friends, turned to face him, setting aside the trade he was reading in turn.

"So, how'd it go?" he asked.

Alex held the T-shirts as though they were victory flags. "Looks like you and I are co-workers now."

"See? Told ya," Marcus replied, his expression barely budging.

"Yeah, it wasn't all flying colors. I completely forgot Trevor's name in there."

"Don't sweat it. He doesn't care that much, and there's worse things to forget during an interview."

Alex shrugged. "I guess. Anyway, thanks for recommending me to him."

Marcus nodded once in response. "You're welcome, man." He glanced around the store once before continuing. "So, you heading home, or sticking around?"

With the time still fresh in his mind, Alex answered with the latter, then headed for the role-playing section of the shop. Bailey had been sleeping soundly when he left the house hours ago, and his folks would be home by six.

After recovering the rulebook he'd been reading before the interview, he leaned into the shelving and thumbed to where he'd left off: a pair of pages with columns of rules sandwiched between two opposing pieces of magic-themed art.

Every so often as he read, Alex checked his phone for updates. Another IM beep drew his attention as 5:15 came around.

Catherine W.: 6:30. Don't forget.

"That from Catherine?" Marcus asked from the register.

"Yeah," Alex said as he put the book back and pocketed his phone. She and Marcus had pitched the idea of a get-together several days prior, to plan some activities for their last college-obligation-free week. "Man, am I gonna be sad when summer's over."

"Not me. I'm ready to get back to class."

"Because you graduate in a year. I've got three of those left."

"Enjoy the easy years while they last, man," Marcus said as he stepped out from behind the counter to get another trade.

"Yeah." After fingering though the trade-in box he stood next to, Alex headed for the counter, asking for his backpack and helmet as he came close. "I'm going on ahead, so I'll see you guys there," he said as he stuffed his backpack with what Trevor had given him.

"I can't interest you in a comic or two before you leave?"

Alex noticed the smirk on Marcus's face when he looked up. "Nice try."

"Alright then. Later."

With a wave to his friend, Alex headed for the entrance, the glare of the setting sun forcing him to squint once outside. The sounds of vehicles driving on the nearby highway, and the lone, blaring horn drew his attention as he walked toward his motorcycle.

Except for the days when it was raining profusely, or the wind was cold enough to bite through his choice of jacket, the bike had seen use throughout and since his final two years of high school. It wasn't until his first year of college that his folks began suggesting a move to a sedan, for safety and insurance reasons. Alex resisted the idea; he'd owned the bike for years, and riding it was more enjoyable than driving a bulky four-wheeled vehicle. Plus, it already did the job of getting him from A to B.

After checking his backpack for anything left unzipped and buttoning up his jacket, he turned the ignition key, cranking the bike's engine with a sharp revving. He was the first to arrive to the restaurant, and picked out a table before ordering a soda and some water.

The next several minutes passed with his attention drifting between the darkening view outside and the subtitles on the restaurant's lone TV before he pulled his phone out. As the browser was opened, the first tab to load was a week-old news article detailing the discovery of a mauled and gutted calf carcass near his old high school.

Alex skimmed it before switching to another tab. The event had come to his attention thanks to his father, but how gruesome and unusual it was kept the article among his open tabs.

As 6:00 drew closer, Alex was feeling the urge to skate around outside. No cars had come or gone from the lot in the last fifteen minutes, but after detaching the board from his backpack and standing up, he spotted Nathan's sedan entering the lot.

"Hey," Nathan said as he came close and laid his jacket over one of the chairs. "Did the interview take that long?"

Alex shook his head. "Nah, just didn't feel like going home and getting changed."

"Alright. I'm getting an appetizer. You?"

"Nothing yet. Just got a refill."

Nathan nodded in response, returning soon after with a glass of soda and a receipt. "So, how'd the interview go?"

Alex's response was delayed thanks to the grin creeping over his face. "That's the thing. There wasn't one."

Nathan raised both eyebrows. "Really?"

"Yep. My boss read my resume, then hired me on the spot. Everything else was him and me chatting."

"Huh. Interesting."

"Yep. Suited me just fine, though."

Nathan smiled back, then pulled his own phone out, remaining silent until his order was ready. "Oh, question," he began as he returned. "Any updates from your dad about that calf from last week?"

"I haven't asked him about it since last time, and he hasn't said anything else about it."

"So, the official story is still wolves?" Nathan asked after chugging a bit of his soda.

"Yeah, unless something comes up that changes things. By this point though, that's probably the story."

A brief silence followed Alex's response. "Kinda hard to believe wolves would come around here."

"There is that park across the highway from our high school, don't forget."

"True, but that park isn't that big."

"It's big enough to hide a few wolves. As for them living around there, yeah, that's hard to believe."

"I keep thinking coyotes did it. Those I have seen around here."

Alex shook his head after recalling the day he and Bailey encountered one. "Makes sense, but coyotes tend to feed on bugs and rodents more than livestock."

"Still possible though."

"Yeah, it is."

An IM beep interrupted them a second later. It was Marcus, saying he and Catherine were on their way.

As he and Nathan waited for them, their attentions back on their phones, Alex couldn't shake the calf from his thoughts. His father's rank of lieutenant in the Sugar Land Police Department meant numerous stories and happenings had come to his attention over the years, the more unusual or gruesome ones never failing to pique his friends' curiosity.

Once Marcus and Catherine arrived, the event was pushed out of Alex's thoughts in favor of small talk and planning. No local events were coming up, allowing Nathan to suggest some LAN gaming.

Alex grinned in excitement as Catherine responded, "With what?"

"There's always DOOM." Marcus chimed in. "Wouldn't be hard for me to set up four systems for LAN play."

"I don't think so. You three would massacre me."

"Aw, c'mon, be a sport," Alex said, his growing smile seeming to bleed into Catherine's lacking one.

"Some other time."

"Alright, fine. Your idea?"

"Why not something simple like chilling at the mall or something?"

When Alex glanced at Marcus, he gave a hum. "There's that. Any other ideas?"

"Let me think…" Nathan then pulled out his smartphone. "Are there any good movies out this week?"

"None that I can think of," Marcus said.

"Then… Yeah, there's a few we could see… Not that one, though."

Alex leaned over to check the title. "Yeah, I wouldn't watch that one either."

The silence afterward lasted a few awkward seconds. "I've got nothing," Marcus said. "The mall and a movie are plenty for me, though."

"Same here." Alex admitted.

"Hopefully I won't get a last-minute fill-in call that day," Nathan said.

"You and me both," Catherine replied.

"Speaking of fill-ins, that reminds me." Alex glanced toward Marcus. "Does Trevor call in new hires mid-week, for training and all that?"

Marcus shook his head. "If someone calls in, which is rare, he may, but otherwise, no."

Alex let out a reassured breath, and his friends continued chatting as he let his thoughts drift to his soon-to-be-former vet tech job. At first, Dr. Galliard and some of the staff were the only things he'd miss. The longer he let his memories of the place, both good and bad, stew however, the worse the twinge of discomfort in his chest grew.

Chapter 2 – "We have a 10-67."

Tuesday, August 23rd, 2011
Moon Phase – Last Quarter

Despite the good company, the discomfort lingered and kept Alex more reserved until it weakened, by which time half of everyone's meals were gone, and the conversations had started petering off.

When he felt Nathan tap his shoulder, he glanced aside at him.

"How late are you planning on staying at the park?" he asked.

"Uh…not sure. Why?"

"My camcorder battery was almost dead, so I'll have to pick it up on the way over."

"Ah, okay," Alex replied before returning to his meal. The skatepark he and Nathan had planned to film in was open until ten every day, and with a glance at his phone's lock screen, he could tell they'd have plenty of time to spare.

As the get-together began to wind down, Alex's attention moved to his ideas for tricks and camera positions. It was as Marcus and Catherine departed that something else struck him: an urge to visit his old high school. The calf was gone by now, but with Nathan saying he needed a quick detour…

He was several streets away from the restaurant when he decided to wait until after they were done.

* * *

Alex arrived at the park to find no other vehicles in the parking lot, the dead street lamps allowing the moonlight to illuminate the lot. As he removed his helmet and gripped his motorcycle's ignition key, a noise louder than his bike's rumbling engine reached him. It was brief, and unclear, but it drew his attention regardless.

After killing the engine, Alex sat quietly and listened. Was the noise from someone screwing around in the neighborhood further west? After several seconds of nothing, he shrugged and got off his bike, figuring that was the case.

Then the noise came to him again, as brief as before, but much clearer. It was a scream. How close it now sounded chilled his flesh and glued his feet to the ground, his pulse building by the second. The only movement he made before the sound of car approaching from behind stole his attention was the inching of his hand into his pocket for his phone.

"Hey, what's up?" Nathan asked as he pulled up close, his window down.

"Thought I heard a scream..." Alex pointed towards the end of the street. "Over there, somewhere."

Nathan replied after a few seconds of glancing around. "Think we should get the police?" Before Alex answered, he continued. "Actually, I've got an idea."

As his friend put his car into a new gear, Alex's attention jumped between the supposed location of the scream and Nathan backing up and turning to the right. Another gear shift sounded, and the car began moving forward.

Good thinking, man. Alex trailed the car on foot, relaxing a bit with each step. His attention remained on the spot he thought the scream had come from, until his second glance inside Nathan's car showed his hand resting on the horn.

His friend then leaned into his horn for almost three seconds, after which Alex felt numerous invisible eyes looking their way. Nathan honked once again before pressing the accelerator, Alex jogging to keep up. They both stopped at the end of the street's cul-de-sac, with Nathan keeping his car in drive.

"Around here, you think?" Nathan asked, keeping his voice low.

"Could be... I'll check that field behind the pool." Alex stepped away after adding that he'd wave if he saw anything, his initial walking speed slow and cautious. Hearing only his footsteps against the concrete eased his nervousness.

When the field was fully in view, Alex's attention locked on a girl lying in the grass. Her legs and arms barely moved, but her position was enough of a hint that she'd been crawling away from something. He signaled to Nathan, and then went in closer.

As he did, the foot-long blood trails in the grass caught his eye, and then the extent of the injuries on who he'd found. The girl's chest and abdomen were bleeding under the tears in her clothing. The arm she was wrapping her wounds with was lined with gashes, puncture wounds dotting her left shoulder and face. Her expression was hopeful, though hiding a lot of pain.

Nathan's phone was in his hands two seconds after he stopped next to his friend. "Keep her company."

"Yeah," Alex replied, though in his head he didn't think that was enough. He lowered himself into a crouch, the trembling in his legs making staying balanced tricky. All the while his attention stayed on the girl's wounds, and how much they were bleeding. The lacerations on her arm were the most obvious, though the oozing there was minimal. *How bad did her chest get hurt?* Unable to tell beyond the existing red stains, Alex checked her shoulder.

Despite minor bleeding there as well, the pattern of damage—punctures and multiple tears on a sharp curve—got his attention. *How the hell'd she get bitten there?* Alex glanced around the area. Had Nathan's honking scared the animal off? And if so, where had it gone?

A sudden increase in the girl's breathing pace snapped his attention back to her. "What's wrong?" he asked, his voice shaking a touch.

"Noth…" The girl was cut off by pain, and her expression showed it.

Alex reached halfway out to her before stopping and pulling his arm back. "Don't strain yourself. We'll have an ambulance here soon."

"No, I'll heal. I'll be fine."

Alex didn't acknowledge the statement verbally, his mind writing it off to a phobia. Behind him, Nathan was listing off the details of her condition to the dispatcher. An ambulance wouldn't be long in coming.

The girl's breathing quickened again, this time punctuated with a bloody cough. Alex recoiled, but didn't stand up. *Fuck. Not good.*

"Anything yet?" he blurted out.

"Almost," Nathan replied. Alex heard him mention the cough in turn.

"Help'll be here soon." The girl's breathing didn't slow over the next few seconds. "If you can though, can you tell me your name?"

She struggled with a few breaths before giving her first name. "Angela…"

"If it hurts, don't force it." Alex said after a bit of silence. "You'll be fine. If anything happens, we're here." Angela soon turned her attention toward a dark area to Alex's right. He followed suit, though saw nothing of note. "I can handle that dog if it comes back."

Angela's reply came several seconds later. "He won't… He'll stay away."

He? "Was it a dog you knew?" Alex got no response; Angela kept looking in the same direction. Grass crumpled beside him, and he looked to see her clenching her free hand before closing her eyes, forcing a pair of tears from them.

Nathan broke the silence that followed. "They're coming."

"Good," Alex said. The start-up of sirens in the distance helped ease his chest tension.

Nathan then returned to talking on his phone, with a few acknowledgments to the dispatcher. "They're saying we need to keep her from bleeding and keep her warm."

Alex nodded, and began removing his jacket.

"The bleeding's not bad..." Angela cut herself off.

"You don't sound good, though," Alex noted before he hesitated. *Wait a second. That chest injury.* "Can you pull your left arm away for a second?"

"...don't want to."

"Just for a second. I'll be quick." Angela clenched her free hand again, and didn't respond. Alex didn't want to force her, but his instincts were telling him that was the injury he had to focus on. When he thought of the bloody cough, and then looked over her surface wounds again, a chill ran through his skin. Was she bleeding internally, or into her lungs?

He had no chance to act on that suspicion before Angela's shallow breathing worsened. "Nathan?" Alex's weakened voice went unanswered. "Nathan!"

"What?"

"She's not breathing well." Alex tossed his jacket aside before his right hand went for Angela's free one, taking it by the wrist. The cold feeling of her flesh, how embedded it felt, stood out immediately. Her pulse didn't, raising Alex's again. *Shit, what do I do?*

Stopping the bleeding became his snap priority. "Lie down, Angela." He got no response, and she stayed in place. "Nathan, I need a hand."

Nathan kept his phone close as he hurried in, the two of them helping Angela down onto her back. Alex then wrestled his tie and shirt off, folding the shirt until it was four layers thick. His taking of the arm that, for all he knew, was keeping blood from gushing out of Angela's chest, put pressure on his stomach.

The newly exposed wounds, four in total, were covered as best as Alex could. What pressure he applied didn't feel like enough; Angela's now noticeably rapid heartbeat worsened that feeling.

"She needs her legs elevated," Nathan suddenly said.

Alex shot his friend a glance, catching him looking towards his shoulder-couched phone. He tilted his head towards his backpack.

C'mon, Angela, stay with us, Alex thought as Nathan made for the pack. Though the sirens continued to draw closer as her legs were propped, her shallow, gasping breaths dug the fear of her giving out into Alex's head.

"OK... She's gasping almost... No. Uh, Alex?"

"Yeah?"

"Are you CPR trained?"

At that question, Alex's shuddered. How close was Angela to something worse? "For dogs, not people."

Nathan repeated what he'd been told to the dispatcher, then kept quiet, nodding and acknowledging several times at something they were telling him. "They're saying chest compressions only if she stops breathing," he soon said.

With these wounds? Alex imagined Nathan having to do them before shaking his head at the thought.

A new, rapid wail sounded and stopped a second later. The ambulance had reached a highway intersection several streets away. *Not much longer. Hang in there.*

When Angela's arms then reached up and toward his own, the unease that Alex had been holding at bay came rushing forward. The pressure he had on her stomach lapsed for a moment when she grabbed him, and the intense cold of her flesh became apparent.

He ignored Nathan saying his name in favor of glancing at Angela, then to his right. No flashing lights yet. *Fuck. Hurry.*

Several gasps later, her breathing strength weakened.

Alex heard Nathan swear out loud in response. His response lodged in his throat until he forced it out. "Start them, now."

His friend hesitated before inching into position, the trembling of his arms remaining noticeable until he was several compresses in. By then, Alex had glanced away from the scene twice. The third time let him spot the first flashes of red.

It felt much longer than it took for the ambulance to close in, stop, and for at least two paramedics to exit. Alex called to them as they reached the grass, and within seconds, the two he'd heard and one more were nearby.

The several steps up and backwards he took as the professionals took over allowed the emotions he'd been holding back to rush into his face and limbs. As he massaged his throat, his eyes darted to and away from the scene. Angela was swarmed by the medics, leaving him unable to tell if she was stabilizing or getting worse, and Nathan seemed unable to reign in his trembling lungs.

When the blue and red flashing lights of a police cruiser appeared, another paramedic came close with a gurney, upon which Alex swore he saw a white sheet. He couldn't help picturing Angela's lifeless face being covered by that sheet, even after telling himself it was needed to keep her warm. More massaging of his throat followed, until he noticed an officer heading Nathan's way.

He forced a swallow and wiped his eyes at the sight before making his way closer to them, his attention drifting from the medics and Angela to the officer, and the sergeant insignia on her uniform.

The sergeant—Hill by her nametag—was quick to speak up as Alex approached. "You both okay?"

Nathan responded with a shaky, "Yeah." Alex only nodded.

Hill continued after a few seconds, keeping her tone as calm as possible. "Would you guys follow me, please? I just need a few questions answered, and then you can leave."

Alex nodded to Nathan before the two of them did just that. They stopped near the sergeant's cruiser, and once Hill had produced a notebook and pen from her chest pocket, and introduced herself, the questions began.

It was the usual gauntlet at first, and then came others unique to the scene.

"You found her around 9:05. That correct?"

"Yes," Nathan said.

"Was anyone else around?"

"No. Just us. She looked like she was crawling away from something, though."

Hill glanced up from her pad. "Any idea what?"

Alex took over after Nathan shook his head. "From what I saw, probably a canine."

After a glance over Alex's shoulder at the ready-to-depart ambulance, Hill asked, "How could you tell?"

"Worked at a vet for a few years. She had a bite pattern on her left shoulder, from a large breed, I think."

"Did anything else stand out?"

As the ambulance departed, sirens wailing, Alex recalled the wounds on Angela's chest. Those had been unusual, in spacing and number.

"I thought I heard her say whatever attacked her would stay away."

Nathan's jumping in drew the sergeant's attention, and redirected Alex's response. "Yeah, she did say that."

Hill stayed quiet for a few seconds, glancing once at the scene. "Are you both sure you were alone when you found her?"

"Very. I didn't see anything," Nathan replied.

Although ready to agree, Alex recalled Angela's behavior from before she'd made the claim. "Me either, but she was looking past me before and after she said that."

"In the direction the animal ran, I'd assume," Hill noted.

"Yeah, that what I was thinking."

"Anything else?"

"No, Ma'am." Alex said with a shake of his head.

"Okay." With a few more notes, and another glance at the scene, Hill continued. "One last thing. I need to get some contact information from both of you."

"What for?" Nathan asked, glancing at Alex shortly after.

"We're witnesses," Alex said. "If what happened to Angela leads into a legal case, the prosecution may need testimonies from us. Or they might have more questions."

"I haven't seen something like this go as far as the courts, but yes, this is in case it does." Hill flipped to another page in her notebook. "For now, I need your names, your addresses, and a phone number we can reach you at, and then you're welcome to head out." Alex went first, expecting the mention of his last name to draw a comment from the sergeant. When it didn't, he stepped aside and waited for Nathan to give his info, after which the sergeant thanked them. "You two stay safe."

"We'll do our best," Nathan replied as Hill got back in her cruiser and shut off the flashing lights. She was halfway down the road when, without a word between them, Alex and Nathan decided to abandon their old plans and head home.

"Think she'll be okay?" Nathan asked after they reached his car.

"I hope so, man. That bleeding was bad."

"You okay?"

"More or less," Alex said after a short delay. "You?"

"Still kind of shaky."

Alex nodded. "Then, guess I'll see you later."

"Yeah. You too."

Alex walked off after a sturdy fist-bump, his drive home leaving him questioning what his folks would do if he told them what had happened. His throat tensed a bit as it lingered in his head, but as his motorcycle rolled into the driveway and the ignition was shut off, saying nothing about it won out.

Chapter 3 – First Day on the Job

Tuesday, August 23rd, 2011
Moon Phase – Waning Crescent

Despite a light being on in the living room, Alex heard nothing at the front door in line with his folks still being awake. Bailey, however, was keen to rush for the door when anyone was unlocking it, and within the first inches of it being swung open, Alex saw him sitting at attention, his tail sweeping the front rug.

"That's my boy. Stay." Bailey stopped listening and came close before the door was closed, zeroing in on one of Alex's arms and sniffing at it. "Sorry, boy, don't have any leftovers," Alex said before rubbing Bailey's head and making for the restroom. Once in front of the mirror, what his dog had really been interested in became clear: the dried bloodstains that dotted his arms and palms. Fighting back the image of Angela reaching out and at him, he washed his skin until no evidence of the event remained.

Bailey continued to tail him as his blood-stained clothing was mulled over, soaked in stain-remover, and then dumped in the wash. The first chance his dog got, he was up against the washing machine, working to get his muzzle closer to the source of the unfamiliar scent.

"Hey. Bailey, no," Alex said as he heaved his pet's paws off the washing machine. Although Bailey didn't jump back up, his attention didn't divert. "C'mon, boy. Leave it," Alex said as he stepped away, stopping only to slap his leg a few times.

When Bailey at last followed his lead, a lack of tail-wagging and an unblinking stare came with him. *Nothing gets by you, does it?* Alex scratched his dog's ears and head until he was ready to retire to his room.

Wednesday, August 24th, 2011
Moon Phase – Waning Crescent
6:43 a.m.

The next morning, Alex slipped into the bathroom for a shower while at least one of his parents was busy in the kitchen. What he could say if the bloodstains were brought up had survived the night, though the tone of his mother's first sentences didn't hint that she'd noticed them.

"Did the interview go well?" she asked as Alex guzzled a glass of milk.

"Mmm… Yeah. First shift should be next week."

"Did you get any uniforms or clothes that need washing?"

"Yeah. Just a sec."

As Alex approached the hallway, the door to his parent's bedroom swung open to reveal his father, dressed in his dark blue SLPD uniform. "Morning, Son," he said as he slid his smartphone into his shirt pocket.

"Hey, Dad," Alex replied as he slipped by him and into his room. The hint of surprise in his father's tone hadn't escaped his notice.

After recovering the tees from his backpack, he turned around to see his father standing in the doorway.

"You have a minute?" he asked.

"Yeah," Alex said as his backpack was set aside.

"One of my sergeants told me about the call-in you were involved in last night." Despite the concern in his father's tone, Alex hesitated too long on a response. "You didn't do anything wrong, Son."

A slight shake of his head was the first half of Alex's response as the emotions from that night leaked back into his head and face. "I know…" When his mother chimed in with a 'What call-in?' response, how close she sounded urged him to not show any emotion.

"Alex and one of his friends called dispatch last night, reported someone who'd been mauled. One of the sergeants I work with left me a message about it."

"Well…" Alex glanced to his left during the pause in his mother's sentence; she didn't continue until she could see him. "Do you want to talk to us about it?"

Alex shook his head again, letting out a sigh instead of talking.

"You sure?"

"…Yeah."

"Later, maybe?"

His father then chimed in. "He'll be okay, hun."

"But…"

"I know, but he'll be okay."

Alex waited to be left alone before making any moves to wipe his eyes or move from the spot where he'd been standing. Bailey had stood nearby the entire time, doing little beyond stare. As Angela's well-being returned to his thoughts, Alex crouched down to rub his dog's head and ears. He couldn't see his folks letting the incident go unquestioned for long, even if his father explained what he could to his mother, and in turn he sighed quietly.

* * *

It was nearing 7:30 when his father came to his door again; Alex heard his footsteps and turned from his desktop screen to find him leaning against the doorframe. "Can I talk to you for a minute?" he asked.

"Yeah," Alex replied, staying in his chair as his father made his way to his bed and sat on the head of it.

"About yesterday..." His father paused, as if to watch for a sign of discomfort. Alex didn't allow any beyond a glance away. "Before Sergeant Hill arrived, did you get any sort of feeling that you were in danger, or being watched?"

Alex took a second to consider it before shaking his head. "No, but we found her right after Nathan had tried to scare off whatever was there, so..."

"How so?"

"He drove his car towards where we thought something was happening and kept honking his horn and revving his engine when we came close."

"Makes sense."

"We didn't see anything, though."

His father nodded. "Hill told me the same. Probably for the best."

"Yeah," Alex said before his head filled with thoughts of a botched rescue, and of the animal returning.

"Are you okay otherwise?" his father asked after a bit of silence.

Alex gave a quick nod. "Wish I knew how Angela's doing right now."

"I figured. Chances are she's recovering in intensive care at wherever she was taken."

"Hope so."

"If Hill or one of my other officers update me, I'll let you know. For now though, try not to let it weigh on you too much. You both did what you could while you were there, and that's most important."

Alex nodded. "I know."

After another bit of silence, and a check of the clock on his phone, his father stood up from the bed. "I have to get going. Congratulations on your new job."

"Thanks, Dad," Alex said as he got up and hugged him. Not long after his father left the room, Bailey came and sat next to him, once again doing little beyond stare. "I know, boy. Let's go for a walk." Bailey's tail immediately started wagging.

As their second lap of his block started, Alex's phone rang. Seeing Blue Moon on the caller ID, he answered to find Trevor on the line.

"Our two to seven guy just called me," Trevor said after a bit of small talk. "Said he got food poisoning last night. If you want his shift, it's yours."

Guess he does call new hires in. "Sure. I'll be there."

"Great. See you then."

* * *

That afternoon, Alex arrived to find the shop more crowded than he thought. Of the customers there, most looked to be in their early to mid-twenties, many of them reading or fingering through shelved trades. A sole child of four or so running around near the RPG boxes then pulled his attention.

Oh, great. As the kid kept jogging about, one of the less than encouraging stories he'd heard from Catherine of children being let loose in the bookstore where she worked came to mind. *Hope no one's expecting us to watch him.*

At the front counter, an employee he'd never seen before set down the comic he was reading, exposing the name badge hidden behind it—Daniel was his name. "Hey. Are you Alex?"

"Yeah, that's me." Daniel then offered his hand and Alex shook it as his coworker introduced himself. "Pleasure. Kinda busy in here today, isn't it?"

"Not really. This is the day new comics go out for sale."

"Oh, right. Marcus did tell me that before."

"Did he also tell you about the secret room we have?"

Alex smiled as he heard that, even though he knew it was a setup for a joke. "No, he didn't."

"You'll find out about it soon enough, I'm sure."

"Probably by leaning against a switch on the wall."

Daniel's face didn't budge. "Yeah, we've lost a few employees to the lasers that way. Anyway, Trevor's in his office, but I can show you some of the basic stuff if you need."

Alex agreed to the suggestion, and Daniel was quick to start showing him where everything was that he would need for the day: the employee time-clock at the rear of the store, the storage room for the boxes of new inventory, the gaming room for the daily RPG sessions, and the restroom, which Daniel was quick to remind him was for employees only.

"It being that close to the storage room, we can't risk people sneaking in and making off with our inventory."

"Makes sense, but why would anyone try and steal from storage if the front counter is, like, twenty-feet away?" Alex asked, even though he already knew the general reason for the first part.

"All sorts of reasons," Daniel replied. "Anyway, Trevor usually clocks new hires in on day one. He should be in his office."

"Thanks," Alex said before making his way there. After two knocks, the door was opened, and Trevor greeted him before letting him in, with a word that he needed to file some papers before anything else.

The comics along the walls drew Alex's attention again as his boss continued working. At the same time, he tried to recall some of his employee duties. *Help customers, keep things in order...what else?* Without the paper he was given, he was left guessing at the rest until Trevor told him he was done.

"You ready to start your shift?"

"Yeah, I am. Do you want me working the floor or the register first?"

"For today, I just want you walking the floor and getting a feel of the store's layout. You read over the paper I gave you, right?"

"Yeah, I did. Keep the displays tidy, help the customers when necessary, and...uh, replace any comics or books that don't belong somewhere," Alex replied, counting with his fingers each duty he listed.

Trevor was pleased. "You got it, except for one thing. You're also responsible for getting backstock if we need it. Once you've gotten a few days with us, we'll train you on the register."

Alex nodded before being led back to the time-clock, where he was punched in. Over the next half-hour, the shop filled up with mostly window shoppers, a crowd of around six people in various locations. Only one person by that point had asked him for any assistance, leaving him little else to do.

While he made another check of the RPG and board game sections, his hand went for his phone before he pulled it away. Once Daniel was in speaking range, Alex got his attention. "I know it's my first day, but does Trevor mind if we use our phones on the clock?"

"Sometimes." Daniel looked around the store. "Right now's not a good time; it looks bad. When we've got, maybe, two people in the store, then it's fine."

"Thanks. I'll keep that in mind." Alex found the temptation to pull his phone out anyway, if only to quickly text one of his friends, hard to resist. Once his break came at the halfway point of his shift, he wasted no time texting Marcus.

> *Alex S.:* Hey, man.
> Trevor called me in for a shift already.

Marcus's response came a few seconds later.

> *Marcus A.:* That was quick. How are you
> liking the place so far?

> *Alex S.:* It's nice, but there's
> not much to do.

> *Marcus A.:* Unlike your old job?

> *Alex S.:* Yeah.

> *Marcus A.:* That'll happen a lot.
>
> My advice: read some of the new inventory
> and get familiar with what the store sells.

> *Alex S.:* Will do. Thanks.

As his break came to an end around five, his phone vibrated with an incoming call tone. Seeing Nathan's name in the caller ID, he hesitated on putting the phone away for a few seconds; chances were his friend was calling to find out if anything had come to light with Angela. Figuring his friend would also text him if that was the case, Alex pocketed his phone and got back to work.

His phone remained silent, even in that aspect, for the rest of his shift.

* * *

Back home, Bailey was quick to rush him as he opened the front door, his nose hovering around his clothing before attempting to leap up at him. "Hey, boy. Missed me, didn't you?" Alex said as he rubbed his dog's head and ears.

Once Bailey relaxed, Alex coaxed him inside and made for his room. His folks were already eating, but didn't say much until he returned for a plate for himself.

His father was the first to ask how his shift went, to which Alex responded with muted enthusiasm. "You miss your old job?"

"Some, yeah," Alex replied.

When he was pressed about why, he chocked it up to an uneasy gut feeling. The differing interpretations put forward by his parents took over the table talk until he was ready for a second helping.

"Are you still upset about yesterday?"

"No," Alex said after a light sigh. To his relief, his mother didn't push the topic.

As dinner wound down however, the event bore its way back into his thoughts, especially Angela's condition. His father's silence on the subject felt less worrying the longer he thought on it, but the nagging feeling of her not making it refused to go away.

The calf also returned to his thoughts as he cleaned his plate in the sink, but as he began to imagine Angela as a victim of the same animals, doubt rushed in to sweep at the idea.

Wonder if Nathan was calling about that... Alex felt for his phone, but remembering the lack of follow-up correspondence, left it in his pocket.

Friday, August 26th, 2011
Moon Phase – Waning Crescent

It wasn't until Friday afternoon, during an extended ride around the neighborhood, that Nathan called again and brought the subject up with him.

"Dad hasn't said a thing about it since Wednesday," Alex said after taking a sip of water.

"Hopefully that's a good thing."

"I'm pretty sure it is." Hearing his friend hum in response, Alex broke the silence that followed with a suggestion to hang out at the comic shop.

They arrived to find Marcus on shift reading another trade, and the rest of the afternoon, plus some of the early evening, blew past as their time was split between chatting with him and browsing the shelves. What happened with Angela stayed off-topic for several hours, and until there were few customers around.

When it did come up, as he and Nathan went back and forth detailing the event, what remained of Alex's bottled emotions never surfaced to his face.

"And then she said, 'He won't. He'll stay away'."

"What was she describing anyway?" Marcus asked.

"She didn't say, but it had to be a canine," Alex replied. "Probably one she knew, too; she had a full bite mark on her shoulder."

"Damn." Marcus's low tone vanished as soon as he spoke again. "Wonder if she told the police."

"That's what I'm hoping," Nathan said. "Last we saw, she was bleeding pretty bad and going into shock."

Alex waited for a pause following Marcus's brief response to speak up. "I'll ask Dad about it on Monday, if he doesn't update me before then."

"Fingers crossed for good news, then," Marcus said.

Chapter 4 – The Beast of Sugar Land

Friday, August 26th, 2011
Moon Phase – Waning Crescent

As 8:00 approached, Alex closed and replaced the role-playing book in his hands. His urge to get back to skating had overtaken the reading binge he'd been lost in for the last half-hour. After some small talk with Trevor and Marcus, he departed the store, finding several cars maneuvering around the better spots of the parking lot.

Though Alex gave them a minute to find spots and park or move on, the lost density was taken up by other cars nearly as quickly, and he soon abandoned the idea of skating the lot. The skatepark he and Nathan had planned to visit days ago then came to mind, and he made his way there, arriving to find just one skater inside—a low turnout for what he knew to be a normally busy night and hour.

After sparing a glance towards where Angela had been found, Alex passed the park's turnstile and his board was back under his feet. His first few minutes were spent riding around versus attempting any tricks, and once the other skater departed, the crickets in the grass around the park were all that competed with the noise his board and wheels made.

The empty park also got him thinking about getting some filming in. While setting up his phone to capture the shot angle he wanted, Alex picked a few tricks to try off the nearby incline. The foot and a half worth of height at the ramp's middle was enough to allow the extension of a few.

Once atop the quarterpipe opposite the incline, Alex set his board in place on the lip before shifting his weight over the edge and dropping in, holding a crouch until the incline's edge was close. The ollie off the ramp left his lead foot open to sweep the side of his board and force a center axis spin. He gave the board more time to spin than normal, before thrusting his legs and catching it a foot from the ground.

As he landed, the sound of wood snapping and cracking overpowered the clack of the board's wheels and bearings. His legs stuck to the spot and his feet forced his upper mass forward, the sudden jolt to his system leaving his hands and arms no time to do anything beyond try to slow his fall. What Alex could muster was enough to stop his head from hitting the concrete, with his chest and arms taking most of the impact and leaving him sliding a few inches.

As he shook off the fall and resultant trembling with an open swear, checking himself to see if he was bleeding, his attention went to his board. It had broken not only in the center, but also at the tail near the truck bolts, the grip tape all that was holding the three segments together. *Well, shit. Time for a new one.*

Once his board was recovered and the dropped splinters swept under the nearby ramp, Alex retrieved his phone and waited for the recording to process. He'd been in frame throughout the bad landing, making where the double kickflip went wrong easily viewable. His busted board was then strapped to his backpack, and until he was out of the park, his phone didn't leave his hand.

As it slipped into his pocket, he noticed something moving near the benches in the distance. A large, furry body with a canine-shaped head and ears. His pulse crept up as it stood, and his pace quickened, one hand going for his keys.

With his second glance towards the animal, he couldn't help but focus on how large it was, even on all fours. The sound of steady growling that then reached his ears made him turn to keep it in sight.

As it closed in, everything else wrong about the animal began to stand out. Its posture was off, as though its legs were too long. Its body looked too long. Its front paws were huge, and they motioned more like hands.

Torn between wondering what the hell he was looking at and the urge to run, the animal took two more steps before the lights of the park reached it. Its pelt was pitch black, tan in rare spots, its eyes a dark amber, and its front paws were more like clawed hands.

Its growling then snapped to a snarl and Alex recoiled backwards. His left shoulder hit the park's fence, causing a rocketing of his pulse. As though the creature saw his attempt to retreat as a challenge, it charged.

Alex's first instinct of a side-step didn't work. The creature shifted its direction and lunged at him, the immense weight of its body knocking him backward into the grass.

An open jaw hovered over his head for but a second before trying to bite at him. Alex got an arm under the beast's throat to hold it away, the quaking of his arms making grabbing at its jaw difficult.

The grip he did get didn't last a second. The beast grabbed his arm with one of its clawed hands and yanked it away, holding it down in turn. Its other clawed hand went over his face and mouth, almost keeping him from breathing.

As he grappled with the arm over his face, trying to get it off, he felt his right arm get taken in the beast's grip. Its hot breath blew over the flesh of his forearm barely a second before its fangs punctured his skin.

The searing pain that ran like wildfire down his arm and into his chest drew a scream that was muffled by the fur and pads of the beast's paw. Jerking his head around to try and free himself, Alex grabbed the paw over his face again and wrenched open his own mouth. His teeth went into the rough pads, the pain from the bite and the bitter taste of the beast's skin and fur both giving him incentive to bite harder.

He heard it squeal in pain, and his head was released. Alex slammed his left fist into the muzzle that had just let his arm go, feeling it impact and push away the beast's head. With his punctured forearm withdrawn, his body trembling in shock and fear, he struggled to get back to his feet and keep his eyes on his attacker.

The beast recovered in seconds, but instead of charging him again, stood up on its hind legs, its snarl still going. Alex's eyes widened at what he saw. It stood taller than him in that stance, even with a hunch and canine-like legs. His blood was coloring its fangs and muzzle, and it was bracing for another strike.

The terror Alex felt from the first attack intensified as the werewolf swung to try and grab him. He didn't think about which direction he went. He just went, ducking to avoid the massive paw as he did.

He got barely two steps before the werewolf got ahold of him, its paw snagging the neck of his T-shirt. The claws tore into the fabric as his collar jerked him to a stop. Feeling himself being pulled back, before he could scream again, the werewolf had wrapped its other paw around his neck, the claws pushed against his throat, above his jugular.

Breathing rapidly with tears running from his eyes, Alex tried to keep it together as his head was jerked to the side. When the werewolf sunk its massive fangs into his shoulder, he could feel them pass through his muscles but stop at his clavicle, his shoulder and head burning from the pain.

Suppressing his screams to fight the pain, Alex wanted more than anything now to have some kind of lucky break. To get away from this thing. Despite his hands jerking in reaction to the pain, he reached behind himself and grabbed two tufts of fur, from what felt like around the werewolf's hips. He couldn't tell how strong his grip was, but he twisted his hands nonetheless. He could feel the werewolf's skin moving as he pulled, making it produce a growl. The pain in his shoulder intensified. He was doing something right.

Lifting his foot, he swung it backwards and it hit nothing. The second time, he felt it hit something furry. Pushing down as hard as he could, he felt his shoe grab more fur, and then smash what felt like the werewolf's hind paw. It released him again, and his still-clenched hands yanked at two handfuls of fur. Alex barely saw it rubbing the affected areas before he started to run.

With every muscle in his body shaking, he made for his bike, only to stumble upon reaching it. Swearing out loud several times, he heard the clicking of claws behind him and then the werewolf was on top of him, pinning him down against the seat of his bike, one paw on his head and the other on his back, both with their claws digging into his skin.

Gasping in pain, Alex expected this to be the end. He'd fought back and lost. He'd only pissed it off instead of managing to get away. Hearing the beast breathing next to his ear, how Angela must have felt against this thing became clear, and he let his emotions rule his words, regardless of whether it could hear him or not.

"I knew you were a fucking coward." The claws in his back moved like the paw was clenching, and his words halted for a moment. "Yeah, fuck you too." After a sharp snarl by his ear and feeling the hot breath of the werewolf against his neck, Alex shut his eyes and stopped talking.

Then the seconds passed, and nothing seemed to change. Quick breaths ran over his shoulder wounds, and then the claws that were sunk in his back and head were pulled out. He again heard claws clicking on concrete, this time moving backwards.

Turning himself around with his motorcycle as a temporary crutch, he saw the werewolf backing up. It did so until it was about five feet away, and then stopped. It produced light growls and glared at him, but didn't move, as if it was taunting him. Sniffling once, Alex didn't try and anger it further, even though he wanted to. If it was just going to stand there, he had a chance to run for it.

He swung a leg over the seat of his bike, then reached for his keys with his bloodstained, quivering fingers. As the engine started up, he nearly forgot to pull up the kickstand before punching the throttle. He glanced back twice as he sped down the park's access road, both times seeing the werewolf not trying to follow him.

The evening wind whipped his uncovered face, and his muscles continued to twitch as he flew down the road, trying to maintain his composure and keep himself upright. His nerves were slowly cooling, but every little jostle made him fearful of overcorrecting and crashing.

As the first street into his neighborhood came up, Alex turned wide into it and pulled over near Nathan's place. He held the shoulder of his shredded arm until his breathing lost its shakiness, then wrestled his phone from his pocket. Though at first spurred to call his dad, as he found his number in the address book, he couldn't bring himself to start the call.

What was he supposed to say about his attacker? He knew what the thing was. He'd seen it clear as anything, but even on his best day, his father would never believe the use of 'werewolf' for an animal attack report. The idea of lying to make it something more believable came to mind, but if he made up a story and others died as a result...

With his heart sinking at the feeling of being wedged between two bad outcomes, Alex pocketed his phone and made for his house. For now, this was his problem to fix. If someone found out, then he'd consider what to do.

As he pulled into the driveway and shut off the engine, he heard his phone beep with a new text, but ignored it and went straight for the front door. Inside, Bailey was quick to run up to and greet him, but when the scent of blood stole his attention, he gave a weak whine.

"Quiet, Bailey," Alex whispered, hoping he wasn't dripping blood on the rugs and carpet. He then darted to the bathroom, locking his dog out behind him. Once there, even before he removed his torn and blood-stained T-shirt, the mirror made it clear how much damage the werewolf had caused.

On his left shoulder were two large piercings from the werewolf's fangs, with shallower punctures in the skin near his clavicle bone. His right forearm was lined with torn flesh and punctures in the shape of a massive canine jawline. Running down the length of both of his arms were drying trails of blood. The puncture wounds on his back didn't look as bad, though his spine and ribs still stung when he moved them too much.

When Alex found the store of medical supplies under the sink, he ripped a square of gauze free of its packaging and dabbed the area around his forearm as lightly as he could. His arm still seared at the slightest touch, but as he cleaned the spot, something caught his attention: few, if any, of the wounds were still bleeding.

His heart rate, which had begun to slow down, rose again; he knew deep animal bites didn't clot that quickly.

With a new gauze square in hand, he pressed it down over the deepest of the punctures on his shoulder, despite the searing pain. When it was pulled away, the once-clean square was stained with blood, but none that came from the exposed muscle. His pulse rose again, enough that he could feel it in his neck, yet still no blood leaked from his wounds.

What followed was a slow constricting of his throat, the building of a sick to the stomach feeling in his chest and lungs, and a closing of his eyes, tears dripping long before he could no longer see. As the image of the werewolf, its snarling face and massive frame, dominated Alex's mind between flashes of the attack, the first of his fear-laced questions surfaced: if he was already healing this fast, what else was going to happen to him?

Then more came.

Would he start acting like an animal in public? Drive his friends and family away? If they found out what he was, what was to stop them from turning him away?

Every possibility and every thought made him more upset and nauseous, though the silver chain necklace he had on confirmed, at least, one thing: he wasn't suddenly allergic to the presence of the metal.

Chapter 5 - Uncertainty

Friday, August 26th, 2011
Moon Phase – Waning Crescent

The torrent of emotion and physical tension brought on by the discovery and questioning was slow to lax, with Alex fighting the urge to sob every second it all lingered. Even by the time he'd relaxed enough to resume cleaning up, the quivering of his arms made cleaning off the blood and dressing the wounds he could reach difficult.

For what felt like hours he stayed locked in the bathroom, ignoring Bailey's sniffing of the gap under the door and only opening it after the lights were off and he was certain his mother was still asleep. Though his pet went straight for him at first, his attention quickly diverted to the overflowing pile of bloody medical supplies nearby. Instead of telling Bailey off, Alex snuck into the kitchen and dumped the pile, shoving it as far down the kitchen trash bin as it would go. His shredded, blood-stained T-shirt went in next, with a thick layer of already discarded trash covering the last of the evidence.

Once he was back in his room with a fresh T-shirt on, Alex sat against his bedside drawers in complete darkness, trying in what felt like vain to relax even a bit. Bailey was right behind him and went to lick his face when he came close, something that Alex allowed only because he didn't feel like pushing him away; some love from his pet was a welcome contrast to the last few hours, and how drained and heavy his mind and body had become.

It was when Bailey started sniffing near the dressings and sparked a shot of pain though his arm that Alex climbed into bed. His pet followed suit, staying focused on the injuries and strange scents above everything else.

Ow. Stop it, Bailey. Alex nudged him back, but he closed the distance right after, and almost got a lick to connect. *No, boy.*

It took Alex forcing Bailey to lay down to make him stop. As he did the same, the spread of damage to his torso and arms made resting comfortably, or in a way that would keep Bailey from being nosy and exposing the dressings, difficult. When he at last settled into a marginally comfortable position, Alex eased himself to sleep between strokes of Bailey's fur.

Saturday, August 27th, 2011
Moon Phase – Waning Crescent
7:22 a.m.

When he awoke the next morning and began to sit up, the sight of his helmet and backpack, the shattered deck still attached to it, laying near his closet gave him pause. The first thought he had was his father had found it, or been informed of it, followed immediately by worry that he'd seen the dressings, or something else related to his injuries, and what sort of questions he was in for.

With the coffee maker grinding in the kitchen, and footsteps coming from the same location, Alex slid out of bed and crept back to the bathroom. His injuries resumed stinging when he moved his limbs again, while the audible crinkling of the dressings sounded louder than he knew they should've. He faked a shower with just his head being washed, and his denim jacket hid the lumps the dressings created underneath his T-shirt.

The pressure in his chest grew as he approached the kitchen, more so when he found both of his parents up and giving him suspicious looks from minute one. As soon as he sat down, the questions started coming, his father going first.

"Why did you leave your things at the park last night?"

Alex's struggle to answer let his mother take over. "Were you doing something there last night?"

"Just skating…until my board broke."

His father resumed the questions. "Why did you leave your stuff there, though?"

Taking a breath and making a fist under the table, Alex's pulse picked up. The seconds kept rushing by with him saying nothing. He knew the longer he stalled, the worse it looked, but he didn't want to tell them the truth. Any of it.

"Alex, what happened last night?" When his father asked that question, the implications of it shot panic into Alex's head, and his gaze broke from his parents. As he tried to think of something, anything to say, he gripped his arms to stop them reaching for his injuries.

What felt like an eternity went by. *Is that all he knows?* That question sat in Alex's thoughts, and then something clicked. He didn't have to tell the whole truth.

"Someone tried to jump me," Alex blurted out shortly after that point crossed his mind.

The look on his mother's face snapped to panic-stricken at those words. "What? Who?"

"I don't know. Someone trying to get my wallet, or something."

The exasperated, possibly disappointed look that came onto his father's face was reflected in his tone. "And you didn't think to call me and report it?"

"I should have, I know." Alex held off on saying any more, and things went quiet for a time again.

"Do you remember what this person looked like at least?"

"No," Alex said with a shake of his head. The silence that followed pushed him to add more. "I ran back to the park entrance and then looked back, but they were gone."

"Any idea why?"

Alex shook his head again. "I guess they didn't want me seeing them."

"And then what happened?"

"I waited a minute, then got out of there."

"Then, I still don't understand why you left your stuff there, much less never called me. You had all night."

It took little time for Alex to answer, though the fear that his fib would fall apart at any minute continued building under his skin. "I didn't mean to. I panicked and wasn't thinking about it. The first chance I thought I had, I ran for it. In case they were nearby." His father's silence after his answer, and the suspicion and inquiry throughout his face, only made the feeling worse.

"Look, Son," his father began after what felt a full, tense minute. "Don't keep things like that to yourself."

Despite the tone and expression of his father hinting that he wasn't fully convinced by what he'd been told, a mix of relief and sadness hung in Alex's head as he replied. "I know, I know."

After another stretch of silence, his mother spoke up. "Was that park where you found that girl?"

Alex pulled his gaze up in response. "Yeah, it was." As what he thought his mother was implying with that question crossed his mind, his father spoke up.

"It was an animal that did that, hun. Not a person."

"Still, that's twice in five days he's been involved in something dangerous."

"Yeah…" Alex's father looked in his direction before lapsing into thought for a few seconds. "If he was older, I'd say a concealed handgun license would be worth his time to get."

As the thought of what he could've done with such a weapon crossed his mind, Alex faked a lean on his hand to feel the dressings on his left shoulder. The absence of the more severe stinging he'd felt the night before and as he'd woken up was obvious, even with an increase of pressure on his skin. A fact that caused a chill along his spine.

Even after breakfast was over and his folks had moved on to other things—his father typing away at something in the study and his mother getting ready to meet a friend—the tension that chill had brought on hadn't fully faded. When he saw his chance, Alex made for the restroom, locking the door behind him before stripping his jacket and tee off.

What he saw with the continued removal of the dressings made his previously relaxing pulse give way to the same fearful pace of the night before.

The most severe tearing and puncture wounds were at least a quarter smaller versus what they had been, with the smaller wounds already scarred over or nearing such a state, a pace of healing in line with months of time versus barely twelve hours.

Then something else about his wounds caught his attention: the absence of redness, bruising, and scabbing, all things that he knew followed animal bites and similar skin-breaking injuries. The sight stiffened his body and delayed his redressing of the worst of the wounds, but once his tee and jacket were back on, his handiwork was as good as invisible.

Bailey, however, wasn't fooled. As soon as Alex opened the bathroom door, his pet closed in and got to sniffing at his jacket pockets. He paid it no mind until after he'd gotten rid of the used dressings and retreated to his room, at which point his pet closed in and continued to sniff around where his wounds were.

"Hey, Bailey, stop," Alex said as he pushed his dog's massive head away. Even after getting him to sit, it was clear Bailey didn't want to give up on the idea. "I'm okay, boy. Thanks, though."

Monday, August 29th, 2011
Moon Phase – New

After the rest of Saturday went by, with Alex doing his best to focus on the time with his friends versus everything from that morning and Friday night, he allowed Sunday to pass with little activity besides playing with Bailey and breaking in his new board.

By Monday morning, only the deepest of his wounds was still healing, though the scarring the bites had left would be a constant reminder of what caused them. Throughout his quick breakfast that morning, Bailey sat quietly by his side, and Alex soon spared a hand to stroke his head.

When he arrived at campus, the parking lot was partially filled, and a mass of students were heading for their classes. Helmet and backpack in hand, Alex came in behind a group of them heading toward the main entrance. He followed them for barely two seconds before a twinge of nervousness ran through him, slowing his pace. A glance both to his left and right gave him no clue as to what caused it, but as he came closer to the main entrance, the twinge intensified.

It was when a pack of five students left through the door he was heading for that Alex near backpedaled and made for the path on his left. The tightening of his flesh and jumpstart to his pulse didn't relax until he was fully around the corner, where far fewer students were coming and going. He slipped inside with his head turned down, bought a soda from one of the vending machines, and then made his way upstairs.

The nervousness continued to build as he stood outside his classroom and sized up where to sit, as though he knew he was at risk of being jumped from behind and loudly declared a monster at the slightest hint. His skin tightened as he made his move, and once he sat down, Alex balled a fist over his leg and tried to relax, barely glancing around while he held his quivering arms.

No one knew what had happened to him. He had no reason to worry, but the feelings didn't subside, even with the thought of Bailey by his side. Twice he thought to leave the room and retreat to the closest bathroom to pull himself together, but that would mean walking back into a classroom where, once the door opened and he walked in, every eye would be on him. Instead he kept frozen to his chair, moving only when he needed to.

As soon as class was over, Alex wasted no time leaving the room, his anxiety diminishing as he watched the other students leave as well. He scanned their faces for signs of increased attention, seeing nothing to confirm his fears. With an exasperated exhale, he headed downstairs to the commons area.

His bad gut feeling came back as he found a spot to sit. He unzipped his backpack and pulled out one of the comics he'd bought the week before, though every few panels he looked up and around. None of the students from his previous class were nearby, but he noticed others looking at him, albeit briefly.

After a few minutes he gave up on sitting where he felt so exposed, gathered his stuff, and headed back upstairs, sitting in front of the room of his next class. With no one around besides the rare, lone person walking by, his anxiety eased at last.

What the hell's wrong with me?

Alex wracked his brain for an explanation, the werewolf's bite being the only thing that made the most sense. He'd never felt this uneasy about being on school grounds, or around other people, before he was bitten, and the area around the skate park had been empty that night.

He soon returned to reading his comics and finished one just in time for the professor to arrive. While sitting in class with only her around, Alex still felt normal, but as the class filled up, the cycle of building tension repeated.

"Hey." Hearing Nathan's voice, Alex looked up just in time to intercept his hand with a shake. "We're sharing a class again this semester, it seems."

"Nice," Alex replied. His friend took the seat next to him, getting his laptop out and resuming typing something on it. With him nearby, the unease Alex had been feeling up to then weakened, and remained so throughout the hour-long class.

His focus however returned to what he had feared the night he was bitten, that more than just his body had been affected. How long would it be until someone noticed it? His friends and family were around him the most. They were the most likely to notice something.

After class, out in the parking lot, Alex sat on his motorcycle for several minutes, doing nothing but thinking. Had any of his other mannerisms changed? If they had, when would he find out? In class again? At work? He shook his head and tried to push those thoughts aside. He knew Trevor and Daniel a bit already, and his shift was only four hours long. After that, he was free to go home.

He arrived to find just three customers browsing around, his boss greeting him from the register.

"Should I keep working the shelves, or..." Alex began as he shook his hand.

"You'll be working the floor for the most part today, but I'll let Daniel know to show you how to work the register."

"Sounds good." Alex didn't feel the unease returning as he began his shift, much to his relief.

* * *

After some time straightening the shelves, Daniel called him over to the register counter. A single customer about Alex's age was waiting there with a stack of single issues, the words 'Tampa Skateshop' printed on his tee.

"New guy?" the customer asked, his tone making it clear that Daniel was to answer.

"Yeah," Daniel replied. "Started last week."

When the customer nodded, but didn't speak, Alex jumped in. "I've used a register before. I won't screw up."

"One like this one?"

"Sort of."

"That's a start."

As Daniel stepped him through some basics, Alex waited for a chance to ask the customer about the skateshop. Before he could, the question of where he'd worked before came up.

His answer got both the customer and Daniel to express surprise. "Why'd you leave a vet job for a comic store?" the customer asked.

"I got tired of treating so many injured pets, and hearing owners getting upset at bad news," Alex replied.

"Yeah... That would do it."

"It was generally nice, don't get me wrong, but... Yeah, some time away from that was what I wanted. And if this job doesn't work out and nothing else comes around, I can get my old position back pretty easy."

"I highly doubt you'll get fired from a job like this," Daniel said. "Unless you try to, or you find that switch I mentioned."

Seeing Daniel and the customer smirk, Alex quipped back. "I'll have a mirror handy for that, man. Trust me." He finished the transaction shortly after he finished talking, handing the customer his receipt and sending him on his way.

It was when the doors began to close behind the customer that he remembered the question he wanted to ask, and kicked himself for not doing it. Noting the name for later, he burned through the rest of his shift and was quick to return home.

Neither of his parents' cars were in the driveway, leaving Bailey the only one to greet him.

"Hey, boy. You miss me today?" Alex asked as he crouched down to pet him. His dog attempted to lick his face in response.

As he tried to keep from laughing at Bailey's tongue repeatedly missing, he didn't immediately notice his pet's attention moving to his arm. Seeing no reason to hold him back, Alex stayed kneeled as his Bailey's nostril breaths swept over his skin.

Then his pet let out a whine.

"Bailey, what is it?" Instead of a vocal response, his dog looked him in the eyes, then turned back toward his scarred arm, nudging it with his muzzle before licking his skin—something he'd done for years in response to hints of injury.

"A werewolf did that to me, boy." After so many hours of unease and tension, Alex felt no shame at letting that sentence get away from him, or at allowing a bit of emotion into his face afterward.

Chapter 6 – New Scents

Monday, August 29th, 2011
Moon Phase – New

Later that night, as dinner came to an end, Alex filled a bottle with fresh water for a ride around the block.

"Alex, before you leave," his father said as he came close to the dining table, "can I talk to you in private for a minute?"

At first curious why, when Alex thought of the blood-stained dressings he'd been throwing out, his pulse jumped. "What for?"

"It's about that girl you and your friend found."

The slight bit of relief Alex felt was quickly replaced with concern, and then defeat. His father's tone wasn't the kind that meant good news.

"She didn't make it, did she?" As his mother looked in his direction, his father got up and nudged him towards the hallway leading to his room. He remained silent until the bedroom door was closed.

"No. She died while the ambulance was en-route."

Alex closed his eyes and blew a lengthy exhale at hearing that. Although glad to finally know what happened, sadness and anger welled in his chest.

Then his father continued. "That's not the whole story though, and that's why I wanted this said in private."

Whole story? After Alex's first thoughts of what that meant came to mind, that enough evidence had been found to lean towards 'werewolf', or that Angela had tried to warn the medics of something before dying, he almost couldn't signal his father to say what he needed to.

What he was told made his eyes widen, and halted his response for several seconds. "Her body was stolen, before any exams were done."

"Stolen? But...how the hell did that happen?"

"From the reports I have, someone set off the fire alarm at the hospital she was taken to and got away with her body and personal effects while the staff was distracted." As Alex held his drooping head up with one hand, his father placed a hand on his shoulder. "We're looking into who may have done it, but I thought you deserved to know."

"Thanks, Dad." His father gave him a minute, likely to let it all sink in, before he left his room. For the remainder of the night, Alex didn't leave the house. The news had made going outside and skating around lose too much of its appeal.

Tuesday, August 30th, 2011
Moon Phase – Waxing Crescent

As his classes drew closer the next day, despite his wounds being fully healed, his unease from before began to take root. Writing off the three hours he needed to stay as not that long didn't suppress it, nor did reminding himself that he'd done this once already. It was still three hours, and he'd be around strangers for almost all of it.

When he arrived, Alex took a few minutes to sit outside the side entrance before walking in. The unease continued to build, and then peaked when the professor closed the classroom door. He did his best to listen and ignore the feelings throughout the seventy-five minutes of class, but once that time was up, he bolted out of the room and split off from the other students.

He found a spot away from the packed hallways and sat down, leaning against the wall. Was this how he was going to go through his remaining years of college, or the rest of his life? Constantly in fear of people who barely knew anything about him? He covered his face with both hands, breathing a heavy sigh. He had to be able to control or relax these feelings somehow.

As his next class went by, he tried to think positive, imagining Bailey, his friends, anything uplifting, by his side. He ended up watching the time until class was over, barely noticing what the professor was saying. Upon leaving the building, and feeling his unease weakening, he began to wonder if something else was helping drive his anxiety. The idea of being caught in class, around so many people, if something more noticeable happened to him was what came to mind first, the coming full moon shortly after.

Wait a second... I wasn't bitten on the full moon. As he dug out his phone and found a lunar calendar app to load onto it, Alex was quick to doubt that was a factor. The reveal of the next full moon as the 12th of September, a Monday almost two weeks away, clenched it. That date he could prepare for; unexpected changes to his body in inconvenient places he couldn't.

The fact that the date fell on a Monday sparked some other worries, however. When would he transform? At night? At noon? Being anywhere near campus on a day like that... *I'll just skip that day. It's early in the semester anyway.*

Along the way home, and while stopping to buy some fast food, the number of police SUVs he was seeing versus the week before tugged at his thoughts. Were there more on patrol, or was he just running into their patrols more often? Being careful not to go over the speed limits around them, as soon as he was home, he checked what sites he could for information. None of the usual ones gave a reason, and his father hadn't left any messages about it either.

* * *

That same night, as he sat with his parents at the dinner table, Alex felt his chest grow heavy. Thirteen days until the full moon. That was all the time he had to tell them the truth, before he'd have no choice. Or maybe worse.

"Something wrong, Son?" his father suddenly asked after a period of silence.

Alex looked up at him, his mother looking at him for a second in turn. "No. Just thinking."

"You've been really quiet since last Friday," his mother said.

"Eh..." The first excuse Alex could think of never left his mouth. He felt a push toward breaking the news now, but didn't follow through. "Just wishing I'd paid more attention to that lunatic before."

"You can't change that now, Son. Don't dwell on it."

"I'm trying not to."

Friday, September 2nd, 2011
Moon Phase – Waxing Crescent

As the remainder of his class week grinded by, with no sign of relief outside of his class with Nathan, Alex kept trying to think of something that would help his unease. The ways he'd seen canines make themselves feel safer were mulled over along with other ideas, but none of them felt subtle enough, leaving him to continue imagining Bailey by his side and hoping things would change.

His shifts at Blue Moon after work offered a bit of relief thanks to the periods of low customer numbers and his freedom of movement, but until he was home, around his parents and Bailey, he never felt truly relaxed.

* * *

As his second class on Friday ended, Alex waited for Nathan to get up before doing so himself. After rubbing his nose, which had begun running the day before, he waited until they were out of the room to pitch the idea of a hang-out, and another attempt at filming at the skatepark.

"Can't do it. I've got some errands to run in a while," Nathan explained.

"No worries. Marcus and I are off-shift today. I'll see if he can help."

"Good luck." They were halfway down a flight of stairs when Nathan spoke again. "Oh, have you noticed the increase in police patrols around here lately?"

"Yeah, I did. No idea why it's happening, though."

"No word on anyone else getting attacked?"

Alex shook his head.

"What about Angela? Any word?"

Alex glanced around, then guided his friend to a quieter spot. "Yeah… She didn't make it."

Nathan responded after some seconds went by, giving Alex enough time to lean towards leaving out the body theft details. "I had a feeling."

"She didn't tell anybody anything about what attacked her either."

Nathan responded with a slow shaking of his head, and Alex held his breath. "So, we'll never know what killed her?"

"Don't think so. I still think it's a dog she knew."

"Makes the most sense, I guess. Or that wolf."

A chill touched Alex's nerves. "Would be a hell of a coincidence if it was."

"Yeah… Anyway, I gotta go. Catch you later."

"You too," Alex said after a quick handshake. Once he lost sight of Nathan, he pulled out his phone and dialed Marcus's number. A meeting was soon set for 3:30, and Alex set out for the skatepark after getting some lunch.

When he arrived, seven other people were filling the park, five of whom were skaters sessioning different rails and structures or just relaxing. As he waited for an opening in the roundabout of riders, Alex tried to relax his anxiety and ignore the few eyes he knew were on him. When it spiked, he pulled out of the grind he was in, anxious to return to simply riding around.

As he steered around one of the ramp structures, the familiarity of one of the skaters near the entrance caught his attention. After a second to think, Alex recognized him as the guy he'd rung up earlier in the week.

"Don't I know you from the comic shop?" he asked when he saw Alex coming.

"Yeah. I'm Alex." He held out his hand to his past customer, who returned the shake. "You?"

"Cameron."

"You skate here very often?"

"No, not really."

"Let me guess, things are too cramped here?"

"Yeah," said one from the group near Cameron. "Like that quarterpipe you were riding on a second ago."

"And the fact that we're too cramped just standing by this thing," Cameron added, slapping the ramp structure he stood next to.

"Looks it." Alex glanced away as his anxiety crested, his attention now on the parking lot. The time he and Marcus had agreed upon was still half-an-hour away.

Several seconds went by before his phone began to ring, shaking him out of the fantasy of Bailey sitting by his side. It was Marcus, and Alex answered, only to be told something had come up.

"That sucks."

"Sorry, man. Can't help it."

"It's okay," Alex said as he glanced around the park. "Thanks anyway."

"No problem. Later."

"Was he coming over here too?" Cameron asked as Alex hung up.

"Was, yeah. I was hoping he could do some filming with me, but something came up with his folks."

"Ah. You doing a sponsor video?"

Alex shook his head. "Nothing serious right now. It would be fun to be sponsored, but I'll let that come on its own."

Cameron nodded at that. "Believe me, that's always better."

"How so? You ride for a company?"

"In a way, yes. You ever heard of a place called Tampa Skateshop?"

Alex jumped on the question. "No, but you were wearing a T-shirt with their logo the other day. Forgot to ask you about it back then."

"Ah, cool. I need to meet with the owner about a video segment I'm doing for the shop in a little while. I can show you where the shop is, and I think you'll like what we have there."

Alex accepted the offer, and once on his motorcycle, followed Cameron toward the south side of town.

* * *

They pulled into the lot of a massive storefront building, the logo leaving Alex wondering how a place like this had escaped his notice. After slipping his helmet off, he rubbed at the growing pressure around his nose, and then followed Cameron inside.

Like Blue Moon Comics, the shop was large and the stock on display varied. Both walls to his sides were lined with new decks, parts, and clothing, with a mini quarterpipe and rail near the back of the shop. While it was currently occupied, what he saw behind the black walls and chain-link fence to his right was even more grin-worthy: a skatepark.

"Dude, you weren't kidding," Alex said, his smile not shrinking.

"Yep. We've got everything here. Have a look around."

As Cameron headed toward someone who looked to be in his late forties, Alex did just that. The case to his right, closest to the door, was his first stop. Most of the items on display were wheels and bearings, both blank and professional designs, though the multitude of designs and brands on display drew him closer and into a crouch.

Feeling the need to wipe his nose again, seconds after he did so, it felt irritated and warm, as if something had been rubbed inside his nostrils. While massaging the skin there, he caught the scents of sweat and heated rubber from his motorcycle handles on his palm, and two other mild ones he didn't recognize. A quick inhale to try and clear his nose brought several more scents with it. Mild ones he didn't recognize, and sharper ones that he did.

The irritation didn't stop. It bore deeper, into the roof of his mouth, past his skull, toward his throat. *Oh, shit. What's happening?*

His heart began to race as he freed a hand to cover his nose. Though he tried breathing strictly through his mouth, his nose kept picking up the smells on his hand and the many others around him. He closed his eyes and tried to relax, but despite not moving or pulling his hands away, he started smelling the products from the glass cabinet: the lubricants, the waxes, the urethane of the wheels, the fresh plywood, the glass cleaner...

With each new breath, his nose pulled in more scents. Alex lost track of how many as the irritation continued to affect him and burrowed deeper into his head. He then held his breath to try and collect himself, but his racing heart didn't allow it for long.

His first recovery breath drew the same scents as before, but how, what felt to him, fractured they were snatched his attention. What had been a single wooden scent from the plywood had become one of shredded wood and two aged adhesives. The glass cleaner, once a single, sharp, sterilized scent, was now reeking of four different compounds, then five, then seven.

With another breath, more of the scents fractured, and then the irritation reached his brain, leeching into his sinuses once it did. With his focus split, Alex kept his eyes closed and turned his head away from the case. The scents coming from it didn't weaken, and the sinus irritation changed into brain pressure, the kind that felt no different from a dehydration headache.

Alex then squeezed his forehead and bit his tongue, trying to reign in his now-quivering breathing. His breaths were directed to his nostrils in turn, flooding them with what felt like over a hundred scents with the first open breath.

That was all it took for him to wrap his nose and mouth with his jacket. The foreign smells quickly weakened, replaced by the familiar ones soaked into the aged denim of his jacket, before he pinched his nose shut.

Alex then forced himself to stand, the shakiness of his limbs leaving him leaning against the counter. Once the pressure on his brain weakened, he opened his eyes to relieve them from being squeezed so tightly shut, letting tears drip from both.

After wiping them, he glanced to his left, seeing no one paying attention to him. His breathing eased and the pressure in his sinuses continued to lax until he felt better. Though his head and face remained warm, the lingering shakiness throughout his body changed into a biting chill as he thought about what had just happened to him. About how quickly it had come and gone.

As Alex released the hold on his nose, despite not breathing through it, it was flooded once again with the scent makeups from the aged denim of his jacket and aged cotton of his T-shirt, as well as everything those two pieces of clothing had absorbed since their last washing. Every scent tested his brain's focus until he pinched his nose shut again.

After another wipe of his eyes, he heard footsteps to his left. An employee was approaching from behind the counter.

It didn't take him long to notice something was wrong. "You okay?"

Alex released his nose before he replied, trying in vain not to breathe through it. "Yeah. Something made my nose run all of a sudden. Don't know what."

"Hang on a sec." The employee reached behind the counter and produced a box of tissues. Alex thanked him and grabbed a handful to cover his nose. The sharp scents of the chemicals in the thin, sterilized paper overpowered everything else before he blew his nose. "Nose decided to screw with you, huh?"

More than you know. "Yeah. Ugh."

"Were you looking for anything earlier?"

"Not really. Just browsing. Really nice selection, though."

"Thanks. If you need anything, just let me or Walter know."

The employee departed, and Alex held his hands to stop them from quivering, pretending to look over the decks behind the counter. *Okay, calm down. He didn't suspect anything.* With a few spare tissues over his nose to block the weaker scents, he pushed himself away from the counter and moved towards the most open space that he could stand in.

He then relieved his nose and got a full breath before noticing Cameron heading his way, his board tucked under his arm. "Hey. What do you think so far?" he asked when he got close.

"Really nice place," Alex replied as he pocketed the tissue and tried not to focus on the new scents wafting from Cameron's clothing, or his breath.

"If you want, you can go ride around the park for a minute," Cameron said, thumbing toward it. "Just be sure to say hello to Walter, that older guy over there." Cameron thumbed towards the man he'd been talking to. "He's the shop owner, and the guy you'll need to impress if you want to ride for this place."

Alex nodded, glad that Cameron didn't notice what the employee had. "I'll keep that in mind. Actually, what was that video part you were talking about before?"

"It's for the store's promotional video," Cameron said as he spun the wheels of his board. "We're considering making shorter ones for more online promotion."

"Looking forward to seeing it once it's done."

"Thanks. One of our guys is editing it right now, so check back in a few days. It should be done by then."

After nodding again, Alex thanked Cameron for showing him to the store, and wrapped his jacket around his face again once he was out of his view. A few stray scents wafted up the gaps between his jacket and his chest, his exhale to blow them away taking their place. When he at last began heading in Walter's direction, his mouth was doing all the breathing, though he kept a hand at the ready in case he had to fake a yawn and block his nose.

Despite the exchange of a handshake, Alex felt his unease coming on as he started talking to him—not only from Walter's unfamiliarity, but how easily he could draw attention to himself in the position he was.

For a time, their chat went similarly to Alex's introduction to Trevor: he gave his name, then elaborated on how long he'd been skating versus gaming and reading comics. When Walter mentioned his arrival with Cameron, Alex pointed out how he'd shown him the directions to the shop. "He didn't say how long you've been open, but I'm guessing this place is fairly new."

"A few months, in fact. Not many regulars outside of the people looking for a good skatepark."

"I see. Uh...do you mind if I ride in the park for a while?"

"Not at all, and I can keep your stuff back here if you need."

"All right. Thanks." As he pulled his backpack off, Alex recalled a ledger saying there was a five-dollar per-hour charge for the park.

Walter got his attention as he reached into his pocket for some bills. "I'll give you a few hours on the house since this is your first time here." After thanking him for the offer and handing over his things, hoping they wouldn't smell too much once he took them back, Alex headed for the entrance gate.

With his hand by his nose, ready to block it if his olfactory sense started overwhelming him, he was five feet from the gate before he had to do it. Upwards of fifty scents, from he guessed thirteen to seventeen cores, made it around his hand. Most were clothing scents, and the stains and cleaners from the fabrics. Someone had been rubbing wax on a board, and he could pick out meat and cheese.

Once past the gate, the size of the park itself slowed his pace, his attention going everywhere. It was at least eight times the size of the one in his neighborhood. To his right was a towering halfpipe, the staircase leading to its top connected to a raised area above his head which ran along the left wall. Along that wall, and the one directly opposite the entrance, were a series of quarterpipes, inclines, and rails, with a funbox built into the middle of the park.

Grinning at the sight of it all, Alex made his way to the halfpipe first, standing on the higher lip and gauging the drop for a minute. Although he picked up more scents during the climb, giving him a laundry list of things that had recently been there, as soon as he dropped into the pipe and the air began rushing past his face, the intensity of the scents weakened.

Within minutes, he was working up a sweat from keeping up lines of ollies, grinds, and flip tricks. Though he would stop to wipe his face every so often, he was on the move again within seconds to keep his head from processing any set of smells for long.

After nearly half-an-hour, he felt like his legs needed a rest and headed for the viewing area. As he caught his breath and turned his attention to the skaters below, Alex wrapped his face with his jacket again. The slowing of his pulse helped him shift his concentration to understanding how much different his new nose felt.

With each breath, he felt the extent of his olfactory mucosa working to catch scent traces. He could feel its extent further back in his throat and nasal passages, even within his sinuses, the spots where the irritation had affected him. And unlike before, where only two or three intense smells would catch his attention while the weaker ones all meshed into a defining whole, nearly every unique scent makeup that was strong enough to linger in the air was fighting for his olfactory attention. Breathing through his mouth did offer relief, but only so far as slowing the air flow to his nose.

As he kept the fabric of his jacket over his face, some weak scent traces began leaking through. How quickly his brain processed the new scents meant that with each new breath, he'd lose track of some and find new ones.

When he heard more skaters enter the park, a chill touched his skin and a hand went over his heart. Suddenly, he didn't feel safe being in the park, in public and around strangers. Looking down and out into the park again, though he saw no one paying attention to him, the idea of going home to recuperate felt better than sticking around.

As he left, Alex bought some fresh wax and a set of blank white wheels before exchanging another handshake with Walter. Faking a yawn as the front door was opened, the late afternoon winds slipped past his hand and up his nose. Along with them came scents from cooked and fast food, the exhaust from the cars on the nearby highway, and hundreds more he couldn't identify before he lost them.

He squeezed his nose shut as his brain went to work, releasing it only once his breath was held. Once his helmet was on his head and the visor pulled down, the wildly varying urban scents around his head became overpowered by his recirculating breaths. Some leaked in from the heat vents and the cracks around his neck, but not enough to overwhelm him.

As he reached his motorcycle and sat on it, Alex shivered under his jacket. Why had his sense of smell changed so suddenly, and why now? The full moon was ten days away. Too far away, in his mind, to make his body change like this.

But then, his body had become exponentially faster at healing within minutes of the attack a week ago, and his animal-like fear of strangers hadn't fully shown until two days later, well after the day he'd been with his friends in a heavily-populated mall.

For a moment, Alex thought there might be a pattern to the changes, but even with a minute to consider it, he couldn't identify one. Even if there was, every change was showing without warning, and he had no idea what else would next prove true about his lycanthropy.

His eyes began to mist and his throat constricted as the more upsetting scenarios ran through his head. For all he knew, he would grow a tail before the full moon came, have his canines lengthen into fangs in a few days, or go completely feral once he shifted. No one was there to tell him what was coming or how to prepare, and if something happened that exposed him or put him in danger, where was he supposed to turn for help?

He'd not seen hide nor hair of the werewolf that attacked him since that night, but doubted it would be hospitable in any way if it was attacking people outside of the full moon. And his friends? What would he tell them if they were caught in the middle of something he caused because of this?

With a labored swallow, Alex tried telling himself that things weren't as bad as he was fearing. He could take solace in the fact that no one had deeply questioned him about some of his new mannerisms yet, but even with that, he feared it was only a matter of time.

Once he was back home, the sight of his father's truck in the driveway made him hesitate with opening the front door. He'd been working the graveyard shift the night before, and would likely be awake. If a strong scent caught him off guard in front of him…

After a few more seconds of staring at the door, an idea hit him. He pulled out one of the spare tissues, covered his nose, and then looked around. No one was walking the streets, but a car was coming his way. After it drove by, Alex exhaled, removed the tissue, and leaned towards the crack, feeling his ears warm up as he did so.

The closest outdoor scents were the strongest, but after two sniffs, a familiar scent of fur reached him. Bailey was nearby. The rest of the scents he noticed faded too quickly to identify.

After replacing the tissue, he unlocked the door and let himself in. Bailey jumped up to see him from where he'd been sitting, tail wagging and tongue lolling. The scents within his dog's pelt and breath registered immediately in Alex's head, along with the weaker ones he'd noticed within the air. Most were mild, but all were familiar, preventing his head from spinning.

"Good boy, Bailey. I missed you too," Alex said as he rubbed his pet's head and ears.

His father got his attention as he walked through the front room, letting him know dinner was coming once his mother was home. Almost on cue, Alex's stomach grumbled.

* * *

"Whoa, Son. Leave a bit for us." Alex looked over to his father as he returned with his third dinner plate, avoiding sitting in turn.

"Oh. Sorry."

"No, no. Sit down," his mother said as he stepped back toward the kitchen. "We've got enough."

"You sure?" Alex caught the hint of humor in his father's voice. "He's eaten maybe half the lasagna in fifteen minutes."

Alex shrugged. "I was hungry."

"No kidding. You spend all afternoon skating?"

"Yeah, but not at the park this time. I met one of my customers from the comic store there, and he showed me a new skate shop south of here. Only been open a few months but wow, this place…" Alex stalled to stop himself from gushing too much. "Can't believe I never heard of it before."

"What's it called?"

"Tampa Skateshop. It's a skate store with a built-in park."

"So, you can ride there instead of at the park?"

Alex looked toward his mother after she spoke, at first wondering why she suddenly sounded so unsure.

"Yeah," he began after recalling his and Angela's maulings, "It looks like a nice place to hang out and ride, but it's a bit of a drive, and I have to pay to use the park." His folks both showed hints of confusion at that statement. "Still, it seems worth it."

"Pay to use the park, you said?"

"Yeah."

"What for?"

"Maintenance costs. There's a lot of stuff in that place that could wear down and break."

When his third plate was finished, even though he could've gone for dessert, Alex passed on eating any more before holding back a few burps. Unsure of whether it was another of his wolf-like mannerisms surfacing or just hunger that had gotten away from him, he let the appetite spike stay confined to his father's brief comment.

Chapter 7 - Reasonings

Friday, September 2nd, 2011
Moon Phase – Waxing Crescent

With the end of dinner, Alex's attention was picked away from the scents of his mother's cooking back to the sensory changes. He'd already noticed several scents from his parents that detailed something about their days—a trace of reefer from his father's uniform, and hints of a toner spill from his mother's shirt and jacket—but his first step inside the walk-in pantry for some plastic wrap slapped him in the nose with several dozen new, and wildly contrasting scents. Until he pinched his nose shut, all of them fought for his olfactory attention, the few that stood out most leaving him questioning the source.

His room, though not as much of a kick to the senses, was quick to remind him of things he'd long forgotten about and newer things he'd been unable to smell in detail. Several old memories came jogging back as the scents reached him, and Alex found it hard to keep away from everything setting his brain off. His attempts to focus on something else didn't help, even once some time had passed, and what remained of his night was spent testing his new nose on a few of his belongings, and unwillingly on Bailey when he settled into bed with him.

You're getting a bath tomorrow, boy.

Saturday, September 3rd, 2011
Moon Phase – First Quarter

The next day, Alex tried to control his breathing when his parents were close, huffing his nose clear when something caught him by surprise. At the same time, he began to form a scent-map of the house, taking special note of what upset his senses the most. The scents that contrasted greatly from what was around him—spices, paints, cleaners, and things like them—took longer for him to stand being around, and sometimes made him reel from their source at a greater distance.

Outside, what he expected to be cleaner air was instead an invitation for more odd scents to reach his new nose. With some effort, he could smell the animals that had recently passed through the front and back yards, and the occasional bird in the trees. The lingering scent-markings from other dogs stood out as well, and were no less repulsive than before.

Unlike his new sense of smell, his appetite remained mostly the same: two or three meals between all the riding around on his skateboard. After skipping breakfast Saturday morning, he wrote off gorging himself on Friday to not eating much the entire day and having it catch up to him later.

Sunday, September 4th, 2011
Moon Phase – First Quarter

With both Blue Moon and the Tampa shop closed on Sunday, Alex stayed close to the house, getting in some time skating on his personal grindbox while throwing balls for Bailey.

As the afternoon came, so did a text from Catherine.

Catherine W.: I haven't heard from you in
a while. Something up?

Alex held his phone for a moment before texting her back.

Alex S.: No. Just not a lot is
going on.

Catherine W.: Okay.

Her next text came after a short pause.

Catherine W.: I'm thinking of getting us all
together for a hangout next weekend. Are
you off Saturday?

Skateboard in hand, Alex considered his response. Saturday was two days from the full moon, six from the current day. Any of those six could be a day that something more obvious than a sensory change could happen to him.

The closer to the full moon, the more drastic, he feared, such a change would be.

> *Alex S.:* I think so, but I'll get
> back to you on that.

Catherine W.: Okay. Later, then.

Alex then pocketed his phone, only to remember that such a drastic change could just as easily happen around his parents, and his old fears of what they would do, or say to him, if it did came back. The idea of telling them the truth weighed on his mind, but as he came inside and walked past them, he couldn't bring himself to do it.

* * *

When he kept his head down throughout his first plate of food that night, his mother took notice and spoke up. "You're awful quiet tonight."

Just get it over with. Alex shook his head after staying silent for almost too long. "Just thinking about stuff."

"You haven't said much about your first week of class."

"Nothing special about it so far."

"So, everything interesting is coming around November?" his father asked.

"Looks like it."

The benign topics from his parents eased Alex's drive to tell them the truth, though the lump in his chest didn't go away.

Not today. Tomorrow. *I still have time.*

Monday, September 5th, 2011
Moon Phase – First Quarter
Days until the Full Moon - 7

As Alex arrived at campus and made his way towards the main building, the same onset of anxiety crept through his chest and head. Inside, the swirling mass of new and familiar scent makeups rushed his nose, their wild variations making his head spin until he covered and then pinched nose shut.

Being on the second floor weakened many of them, and his classroom being empty gave his head the space to clear.

Then the other students began arriving.

With each body that strayed close to his seat, the collections of scents grew. His jacket once again served as a quick shield at the first hints of sharp or nasty ones. Then the air conditioner started up, sending a wave through the scents in the room, disturbing ones that had pooled on the floor and adding more from the network of vents.

Alex's urge to move to another seat lost to how unwilling he was to give anyone in the room a reason to pay attention to him. Until the professor arrived and asked for the homework he'd assigned, he didn't move beyond adjusting his jacket.

It was as his papers were removed from his backpack that some of the air from the pocket followed, reaching his nose before he sat back up. Among the collection of scents were some he recognized from Bailey's fur, and his anxiety laxed within seconds of noticing it.

Alex wasted no time pulling his backpack up onto the desk after that realization. With each fake search for stuff, the scents wafted by his face, keeping him calm for the rest of the class. Now with an idea of how his heightened senses could help him, Alex repeated the process with Nathan nearby, keeping his backpack close in case he needed it.

His friend's jacket was laced with paper and ink scents common to role-playing manuals and trade paperbacks, plus fresh plastic and shipping supplies in line with console game cases. The familiar scents helped for a time, but then a mild one he couldn't identify sent a chill through his nerves.

The hell was that?

Nathan didn't notice him shudder or wrap his arms around his gut. Whatever that scent had been, the feeling it gave him, a feeling as if he'd been publicly shamed, stuck with him until he left for work.

* * *

Alex arrived home after his shift to find his folks relaxing in the living room, and Bailey running for him.

"Hey, boy. I missed you too," he said as his pet circled him, his wagging tail bumping his legs. After coaxing him back to his room, Alex dropped his stuff onto the bed and sat down against the foot of it. Bailey then came in close, licking his face until he suddenly seemed to lose enthusiasm.

"Something wrong, boy?" Alex asked as he reached for his pet's furry neck. His fingers ran through Bailey's fur until he heard a soft growl that urged his hand away. Unsure of what had caused his pet to do that, Alex locked eyes with him as he lowered himself to the floor and rested his head on his paws. *Wish you could just talk to me...Wait. Is something about to happen to me?*

As he turned that thought over, Alex recalled something he'd read just before leaving the vet, about dogs being able to predict seizures and smell cancer cells. He kept still and waited, wondering if the same idea applied to physical alterations in werewolves.

All he felt was his pulse slowing down over the course of the next minute, and then when he brought his hand close to Bailey's muzzle, his dog lazily sniffed it but did nothing else. Even when he resumed stroking his head and neck.

Despite the inaction, Alex couldn't help thinking he'd noticed something. It had to be subdermal if nothing about his outside appearance was changing, but what? That was when he imagined his skin ripping and falling off when the transformation happened to make way for a possibly blood-caked pelt underneath.

He swallowed hard and squeezed an arm as the thought faded. As much as he wanted to forget the very idea, for all he knew, that was what he was in for. And then he imagined his parents catching him just before something like that. His eyes closed and he let out a sigh as a biting, terrified chill ran through him.

When he heard Bailey stand back up and take a step toward him, his eyes barely reopened before his dog's warm tongue contacted his face. How suddenly it came left Alex chuckling under his breath as he scratched Bailey's neck and ears. By the time his pet stopped, the things he'd pictured had lost much of their original impact. What remained tore him between telling his parents what happened and hoping for another option.

If he did tell them, the scars would be easy to point to, but if that wasn't enough... His olfactory sense alone wouldn't do it. *Am I any stronger?*

Alex got up and faced his bed. The individual wooden parts were heavy enough, but once he'd hooked his hands underneath the front of the frame and attempted to lift it, it was clear nothing about his strength had been affected. *Okay. What else could I try?*

The next idea he had was his speed. With one of Bailey's tennis balls in hand, he coaxed him outside, pitching it as soon as he stepped onto the porch.

It rebounded off the young oak tree in the front yard, straight into his dog's jaws.

"Bailey, bring it." Alex said after a few seconds. Once the ball was back in his hands, he led Bailey into the front yard, and then faced south. "Ready?" Alex asked, prompting a bark from Bailey. With that, he hurled the ball down the yard's length as hard as he could. As his pet took off after it, Alex followed with as heavy a sprint as he could manage. It was no use; Bailey was still faster than him, and retrieved the ball before he ran past the impact spot.

As he slid to a stop in the grass, feeling assured that at least those two things about him hadn't changed, he waited for Bailey to bring him the tennis ball again. No further ideas of what to test came to him while he continued tossing the ball around the yard, but the sight of a shadow on the bay window curtains got his chest to tighten.

He'd let it slide yesterday. Only seven days were left. The more time they had to process things...but what if they stayed nearby and he went feral during the shift?

When the front door opened, his father stepped out onto the front entry, his hair messy from the cushions of his recliner.

"Hey, Dad." Alex said as he came close, Bailey close behind.

"Hey, Son. How did your shift go?"

"Alright."

"You staying up a while?"

Alex nodded before glancing past his father toward his mother. Maybe his folks wouldn't be as upset or scared with sleep so close. Maybe he could convince them to leave the house when it happened.

"You look bothered. Did something happen?"

"Eh...some guy was short with Marcus," Alex said after looking back. "Got me angry."

"Yeah, you'll see people like that no matter where you work."

"Yeah."

"That reminds me, are you working next Sunday?"

"No, the store's closed on Sundays. Why?"

"I need you to watch the house for us that day."

"Okay. Something going on?"

"Officer Baker just got promoted, so your mother and I are going to a celebration for him."

"This an all-day thing?"

"Yeah. We'll be leaving in the morning and coming back Monday afternoon."

Oh, no. Alex's heart began to race. If he didn't tell them and went feral... "You working second shift Tuesday? I can watch the house Monday too."

"I don't think you'll need to." As Alex tried to think of something, anything, to add to that statement, his father continued. "Well, I'll see you tomorrow. Goodnight."

"You too." As his father closed the door, the news redirected Alex's thoughts. If his parents would be gone for at least one day, how could he convince them to stay away for another?

They weren't party animals, but if they were staying somewhere overnight, that likely meant a long drive and alcohol. Likely no shifts to hurry home to either. Did they both have those two days off? *Mom usually works weekdays...*

Eventually, the fear that his transformation wouldn't come until early evening on Monday became too great to ignore. The full day was the outcome he needed, with no risk of them coming back at a bad time, or at least enough time for him to find a place to shift and get away.

As sleep drew closer, Alex began to form his pitch. Casual, but insistent. That was the goal.

Dad, I insist. I'll watch the house Monday. If you guys have that day off, go have fun.

Tuesday, September 6th, 2011
Moon Phase – Waxing Gibbous
Days until Full Moon – 6

When he awoke Tuesday morning however, it was 6:53 and his dad was already off to work, his mother close behind. After waving her off, Alex slammed a fist into the wooden framework of the threshold once she was out of sight. He had to work after class, meaning little casual time with his folks tonight.

Returning to his room with one set of fingers running through his hair, he looked around for something thick with Bailey's scent to bring to class. After settling on the tennis ball, he brought it into the kitchen and set it down on the tabletop. It took a few seconds for him to notice the scents leaking from it, but bringing his head closer to the tabletop intensified them. *Perfect. A quick wave of air should do the trick.*

When he then glanced at Bailey, who was watching him like he was planning to go outside, Alex obliged him until he had to leave.

* * *

The tennis ball proved useful as a counter to his anxiety, and Alex grinded through his classes and his shift at Blue Moon. The customers he had to help provided only brief distractions from rehearsing his pitch, which he almost said out loud twice.

It was walking into the house that night that truly made his chest tighten. He had his words in mind. but if he couldn't convince his folks...

"Did you already eat?" his mother asked when Alex entered the kitchen.

"No, but I'll get something." While shuffling by his father, Alex found the scent collection of burnt gunpowder hanging around his uniform. "What rank is Baker at with his promotion?"

"Sergeant," his father replied.

Okay, good. Keep it up. "He enjoying the position?"

"Hard to say. He's got more work to do, but he hasn't complained to me yet."

"Sounds like he'll be celebrating as much as he can Sunday." Alex said.

"I wouldn't doubt it," his mother replied.

Bingo. Alex kept his smile reserved, but his pulse rose at the tone of excitement in his mother's voice. "If you guys want, I'll watch the house Monday as well. I don't mind."

"Uh...I don't think we'll be gone that long," his father said.

Damn it. "You both have that day off, right?"

"We do, yes, but we don't need to stay out all day."

Alex held off immediately responding. *Don't push it yet.* As he avoided eye contact with his folks and headed for the microwave, his mother spoke up. "Did you make plans for that day?"

"Sort of." He stalled for a moment to think of an excuse. "Might have Marcus or Nathan over."

"How's he doing, by the way?" his father asked.

"What... Oh, Nathan? He's doing fine."

"That's good to hear."

As Alex waited for the microwave to go off, he struggled to find something to continue the route of persuasion. "We'll likely be here, so I don't mind watching the house for a second day." His parents didn't respond to that.

During the silence that followed, whether it was his gut or his heart telling him not to say more, Alex did just that.

Chapter 8 – The Company of Friends

Wednesday, September 7th, 2011
Moon Phase – Waxing Gibbous
Days until Full Moon – 5

The next day, with his mind set on enjoying a few more hours at the skateshop after class, Alex rushed out the door ahead of most of the students. Though their scents were becoming more familiar, it did nothing to his desire to get away from all of them at first chance. Nathan was close behind, and Alex only had to veer left to direct him out of the student crowd.

"What was that you were saying before class?" Nathan asked once he'd caught up.

"One of my customers from last week showed me to a new skatepark. Damn nice place."

"Sounds like it. How's the comic store treating you, by the way?"

"It's fun. Already seen my first angry customer though, which was not."

Nathan laughed. "When people ask you about their sick pets and how they're doing, they're usually a lot nicer, aren't they?"

"Yeah." As Alex followed his friend to the first floor before splitting off to leave, he was reminded of the get-together, but didn't say anything about it. Phone in hand and IM app open, he couldn't bring himself to begin typing as he walked to his motorcycle. He didn't want to say he couldn't come, but was it worth the risk otherwise? *Nobody's seen the scars yet... I wouldn't have to hide them for very long.* He labored on that thought before giving it over to how close the full moon would be that day. That he couldn't look past.

* * *

When Alex arrived at the skateshop, he kept his helmet on with the visor cracked for a few seconds to let his nose and head adjust. At least two skaters were in the park versus the three window-shoppers on the sales floor, the lack of familiarity in the scents near the door leaving him assuming Cameron wasn't around.

Though Walter acknowledged him as soon as he took his helmet off, Alex kept his distance, pretending to look through the nearby rack of T-shirts and parts in the cabinet, until he would be the only one standing near him. It didn't take long, but even once he got to talking, keeping from glancing at others when they moved or paying attention to the scents that kept wafting up his nose proved difficult.

"Sorry," Alex said as he pulled a tissue from his jacket pocket. He pretended to wipe his nose to give it relief from the sudden discovery of a customer's rank scent. "Of all the weeks to get a runny nose."

Walter chuckled at that. "At least it doesn't keep you from skating."

"Uh huh." *Hope this guy doesn't track that smell in the park.* Alex shot a glance at the customer who'd left the scent trail before he put forward a question to Walter. "On that though, when did you start skating? The seventies, or…"

Walter cut him off with a negative-sounding hum. "Around eighty-six, actually."

"The decade when Rodney Mullen was making waves."

"Yep, and thankfully long after the kids your age were taking apart roller skates to make skateboards."

"Whatever works, I guess."

"It was clever back then. Would still be, I think."

"Yeah… Something like that would've been better than the 'Wal-Mart board' I had at first."

"Oh," Walter replied as though he had heard that story many times before. "I take it you noticed it was bad pretty quickly."

Before Alex answered, he heard a customer come in. Seeing a mother and her son, a board tucked under his arm, Alex spotted the straight contour of the deck in seconds. After Walter acknowledged her, and the mother said she was just looking around, he continued.

"Sort of. An older kid noticed me riding it and showed me how cheap it was. And it looks like this kid has one of those boards."

Walter took a second look. "Yep. Good eye."

"Hope he hasn't had it long." Alex then watched the kid and his mother walk over to the parts counter, the trucks on display seeming to be their focus. *He's a newbie, alright. Probably got that thing as a toy somewhere.*

Alex then pushed away from the counter and followed the trail the two had walked, stopping when the kid's mother asked if he worked for the store.

Though Alex shook his head, he spent the next fifteen minutes detailing to them the poor quality of the board. The kid's reactions to what he said was a near parallel to when he'd been in his position: interest, then disappointment as he was told, however indirectly, that what he had was a waste of money. The mother's was what he expected: confusion at first, then shock and surprise.

The result was the two leaving the store, saying they would be back once they'd gotten a refund for the junk board. The smile Alex gained was shared by Walter when he looked back at him.

Once inside the skatepark, and past the patch of repulsive scents he'd found before, Alex followed the same routine from the day his olfactory sense changed. He kept on the move to make it harder to focus on aerial scents, and stayed high up, either in the viewing area or atop a ramp or quarterpipe structure, when he wanted to relax.

When his thoughts returned to the meet on Saturday, the idea of skipping it continued to build until something occurred to him. His parents had begun to show suspicion about his behavior. Would his friends do the same if he skipped the meet after so long a time of not saying yes or no to it? He and Marcus were both off that day, and no believable excuses otherwise came to mind.

Where's she thinking of holding it? Alex pulled his phone out, got his IM app up, and pulled up the old texts between him and her. If it was at the mall, a theater, or anywhere else that was usually crowded, he'd skip.

> *Alex S.:* Catherine, is everyone coming on Saturday?

Alex's pulse rose a few beats as he hit send. Catherine's reply came around a minute later.

> *Catherine W.:* So far, everyone except you.

> *Alex S.:* Where are we meeting?

> *Catherine W.:* Nathan's place.

Seeing that response calmed Alex's nerves; Nathan lived just a few blocks from his house. *OK, good.* To be certain, he sent a follow-up text.

Alex S.: You thinking of seeing a movie or something like last time?

Catherine W.: Nah. Figure we'll just order a pizza and game for a few hours.

More of Alex's unease melted away. He could afford a few hours of that.

Alex S.: I'll be there. What time?

Catherine W.: 6:30.

Alex S.: Alright. Thanks.

Catherine W.: See you then.

* * *

Saturday, September 10th, 2011
Moon Phase – Waxing Gibbous
Days until the Full Moon – 2

As the days leading up to the get-together with his friends ticked away, Alex's focus returned to his parents. He was almost certain he'd not said enough to convince them to stay out an extra day, but when the chances he had to nudge them on the subject arose, his words would freeze in his throat and his skin would tighten, as though his confidence was being drained out of him. Or his gut was telling him to not blow what chance he already had.

Then Saturday came, and Alex awoke to crushing pressure behind his eyes. As he massaged his eye-sockets, the pressure held and then began to fade, his phone serving as the first clock he checked once his eyes opened.

4:47? His concerns about how bad the pressure had to have been to wake him up so early were soon replaced by him realizing how bright his room was becoming, despite his blinds being shut and barely any moonlight getting in.

Alex switched on his desk lamp after a moment, the bright yellow tint making him squint and shield his eyes until he shut it off again. At first, all could see were the black and dark blue outlines of his furniture and other large objects, but as the seconds ticked by, the black faded in favor of a steadily lightening blue, and the fine details of the objects he could see, including where colors began and ended, soon became clear.

Alex laid a hand over his chest as his room continued to brighten. Was this the last permanent change until Monday? That question, and the fear it revived, kept him awake and resting his eyes past the moment when he heard his parents start to stir.

What he found after the sun rose was no change to his color-vision or the color of his irises, which left the insides of his eyes as what had been affected. A point that brought on a shiver. Canine eyes shined in direct light.

Wait, will my eyes even do that? After recovering his bedside flashlight, Alex returned to the bathroom, shutting and locking both the hallway and shower room doors before taking a breath and clicking on the flashlight. The LEDs produced a crisp, white beam, which he slowly maneuvered in the mirror towards his eyes.

As the weakest parts of the beam reached them, Alex's hands started to quiver; the insides of his eyes shined a faded yellow, even with weak direct light. *Oh, shit.* He swallowed hard, and his limbs continued quivering after he tried to convince himself that not every light source would cause that.

* * *

6:00 came quicker than Alex wanted. As his skateboard propelled him down the streets, the streetlights resetting his night-vision every so often, he snuck a few glances at the rising moon, hoping nothing would happen to make him leave early.

He arrived to find only Nathan's sedan in the driveway and rang his doorbell. The sound was quickly replaced by the barking of Ginger, his yellow labrador.

"Hush, girl. Sit." Nathan's commands were followed by him opening the door. "Hey."

"Hey, man," Alex replied. With the scents of the house already swarming his nose, he was quick to find those of Ginger's pelt. Though it wasn't unfamiliar, the anxiety the scent brought out got his head to turn away and delayed the rest of his sentence. "Where's Marcus?"

"He said he had to get something. Not sure what."

"Oh, okay."

"C'mon inside."

As Alex crossed the threshold into the house, a chill gripped and tensed his skin. Ginger's scent was even stronger inside.

"You thirsty?"

"A bit. Just water is fine."

While Alex followed his friend into the kitchen, he noticed Ginger trailing them, but keeping her distance from him. As they set out the snacks and drinks on the living room table, he continued to keep his eye on her, just in case she reacted to him more noticeably than Bailey. Instead, Ginger made it apparent through the lowering of her head, multiple licks of Nathan's hands, and how close she stayed to him, that she wanted her owner's attention, and likely protection.

"Wonder why she's being so loving all of a sudden," Nathan said as he stroked her. Alex shrugged in response, but with Ginger's reaction, he now had a better idea of what Bailey had seen in him before.

Marcus and Catherine's arrival produced the same behavior with them.

"You bought it, didn't you?" Nathan asked after the front door was opened. Alex looked towards him and then Catherine, seeing a large black device with a couple of wires in her hands, along with an XBOX game case.

"Yep," Catherine said, smiling while holding up the game. "Figured we'd all get some fun out of it."

"Dance Central, huh?" As Alex took the game case and looked over it, the amount of movement the game required got him to rub his right arm. An inch of slack was all he had. He shifted his T-shirt a little in response.

* * *

"Almost there, Marcus," Catherine said as he began to finish up one of his dance routines. From the couch nearby, Alex and Nathan watched, laughing as their friend flailed his arms and legs around, trying to keep up with the moves that were coming. He missed some throughout the last chorus, but made up for it in the last few seconds.

Pumping his arms in success, Marcus stepped back from the TV and turned to Nathan, his face and short black hair wet with sweat. "You're up, Elvis."

Alex let out a short laugh and smiled as his friend replied. "If you think I'm shaking my hips for this thing, you're nuts."

"Fine. Do a Lady Gaga song then."

"Not much better, man," Alex said. With his friends and himself buzzed on soda and an hour of gaming, the fears he'd been harboring throughout the day had considerably weakened.

"Actually, I know just the one," Nathan said, walking in front of the TV. Picking one of his favorites, he maxed out the difficulty and got himself ready to start.

When he finished, Alex was next. He'd heard a song during the last rotation he liked, which became his choice. With a stretch of his back, and a check of Ginger's location, he set the song's difficulty to the second highest.

"Good luck, man," Nathan said. "Don't get your legs twisted."

Alex scoffed, then replied in jest, "Just watch me."

The song started off with a long set of up and down body moves, and as it went on with more and more arm-flailing, Alex grew more and more absorbed in what was in front of him. Knowing his friends were watching him as much for screw-ups as good play, his stiff movements eased.

As the song wound down, he followed the pose cards on screen as best he could, trying to stay ahead of each move that was coming. With the end in sight, he followed the last side-to-side movement, ending with his left arm flying back and his right in front of his face.

"That was fun," Alex said, straightening up and wiping the sweat from his face. "Catherine, I think you're up." Letting her take the player spot, Alex sat back down on the couch. When he reached for his soda, he felt Nathan tap his shoulder; the look of worry on his face was clear. "Something wrong?"

"No, but when did you get those scars on your arm?"

Alex's pulse jumped. *Oh, crap. When did...* He had to have seen it during his last routine. His throat locked up as he clenched a hand and the seconds went by.

"What happened? Those looked pretty bad."

Alex felt trapped. He could've kicked himself right then. No lie would help him now.

With Catherine's song nearing the halfway point, Alex reached for his tee sleeve, with as steady a hand as he could muster, and pulled it back to reveal only half the scar's whole. Nathan's wince at the healing job came before a fourth had been shown.

"Holy shit." His voice was barely carrying over the loud music from the game.

Alex nodded as best he could, anticipating another question to follow that statement. Instead, he heard Catherine exclaim something in shock, and his attention drifted to her as she paused the game, the house turning silent in turn.

"What?" Marcus asked.

Catherine pointed him towards Alex's exposed arm. "When did that happen?" she asked, leaning on the table.

As he was surrounded by his friends, Alex felt his anxiety rush back, as badly as it had been during class. He wanted to back away, get out of this cornering, but his legs felt loaded with lead. *Not here. Damn it.*

"About two weeks ago," he finally replied, dropping his sleeve in turn.

"Two weeks ago... That night you stopped in front of my driveway?" Nathan asked.

Alex nodded, and then blurted out the first thing he thought of. "I'm fine. Wasn't too deep a bite."

"That didn't look like surface damage to me," Marcus replied. "That looked pretty serious."

Alex cursed to himself as Catherine followed up. "What did that? Did you see it?"

"The pelt, mostly. Black, maybe dark grey, and tan."

"Was it a wolf, or you not sure?"

Alex's answer hung in his throat at first, his heart still racing. "Had to be."

"Oh boy."

Marcus broke the silence that followed. "If you stopped outside here that night..."

Alex jumped in to cut him off. "I didn't go any ER. I went home, patched it up on my own."

"Are you serious!?"

"If I'd gotten sick, I'd have done that. I've patched up bites before." With expressions of worry lingering on the faces of his friends after saying that, Alex's throat locked up and he turned his eyes away.

The silence remained until Nathan spoke, asking what everyone wanted for pizza. Thankful to have a different topic brought up, Alex felt the weight on his chest lax. As the night wore on however, despite the pleasant company, he couldn't help feeling that his choice to come was a huge mistake. How often he saw his friends glancing at his arm with barely a word made the feeling worse.

Chapter 9 – The First Transformation

Sunday, September 11th, 2011
Moon Phase – Waxing Gibbous
Days until the Full Moon – 1

The next morning, as Alex stood under the warm stream of water from the showerhead, the approaching departure of his parents kept his thoughts on what he needed to do if they came home before he transformed on Monday. He couldn't stop imagining his parents refusing to leave him alone, or freezing in fear, when the time came, or his father pulling his gun on him if he did go feral. The mental image of him with jaws agape and lunging for his father before taking a bullet and frenzying or being crippled drew a gasp and a hand over his throat.

His attempts to combat those fears by remembering that he and Nathan had been alone with Angela that night, and that the werewolf had let him go, went in vain. Restraint had been shown both times, but not until damage had been done. For a moment, Alex saw reason to think he wouldn't go feral, but then questioned why Angela had been killed and he spared but bitten.

Had the werewolf planned to kill him, but then backed off at the last moment?

Its snarling face flashed back to mind, and along with it, the worried expressions of his friends from the night before. Nathan's stuck in mind for longer, and as a realization about that moment clicked, Alex covered his face in shame. Of all the people he should've warned over the last few weeks, and yet didn't…

The patter of water disguised the few sounds that escaped him as he held his rushing emotions back. He could take solace in the fact that his friend hadn't been attacked, but he, Marcus, and Catherine were still under the impression that wolves were responsible, not something more.

Once out of the bathroom and back in his room, Alex tried to pass the time reading or gaming. The guilt that had been left by his recent train of thoughts kept him from enjoying them for long.

* * *

With the arrival of 12:47, Alex noticed his father, dressed in uniform, standing near his door.

"I thought you had the day off."

"Your mother and I are going to a remembrance service before we meet everyone."

"Where? In First Colony?"

His father nodded. "You want to come?"

The bad gut feeling that resulted from thinking about how many people would be there, and where such an event would take place, got Alex to shake his head. "I'll watch it on the news."

"Alright. We'll see you tomorrow then, Son."

After exchanging hugs and goodbyes with his folks, Alex closed the front door behind them, watching through the glass part of the door as they drove off. Bailey sat down next to him before he moved again, his tail wagging as soon as Alex looked at him. "Outside?" Bailey's tail wagged faster. "Thought so. C'mon, boy."

Despite the fun he had throwing Bailey's tennis ball across the yard, and showing him some love between each throw, hints of his earlier thoughts continued to resurface and pull at his heartstrings, going feral chief among them. Though he didn't believe he'd be murderously feral, he'd still be without control of himself for who knew how long.

"C'mon, let's get inside." Alex said as he took a breath to steady his nerves. Some good food felt in order right about then anyway.

As he opened a roll of salami, Bailey, who'd since sat down next to him, started sniffing at the air and lolling his tongue. After noticing it, Alex took part of one of the sliced circles of meat and held it near Bailey's nose, watching him follow it without jumping to bite it from his hand. "Good boy." Bailey then snatched the meat from him and resumed his at-attention stance after eating it.

"Okay. Lay down," Alex said, and his pet listened, going to his chest and front paws. "Good boy. Can you speak for me?" A quick bark followed, and Alex handed the rest of the treat over before rubbing his pet's ears. "Atta boy."

After he knelt to continue petting him, Alex began to wonder how Bailey would react to seeing him as a gigantic wolf. He'd been noticeably worried several times before, but would that eventually mean he would run and hide or try and fight him? The longer the idea of going feral and slaughtering his dog lingered in his head, the tighter Alex's throat got, to the point where he had to start massaging it.

As tears surfaced in his eyes, Bailey started whining as if he knew something was wrong. When Alex looked him in the eyes, he coaxed him over and then wrapped his arms around his pet's furry neck. "You'll be fine, boy. No matter what happens to me." Bailey was quick to shuffle from his grip after that, but then closed in and licked his face. "Thanks. I needed that."

With no urge to stop Bailey from licking him, Alex used the good feelings the gesture gave him to clear his head and think of a way to safeguard his dog. Locking him in the garage came to mind first. He'd whine after realizing he'd been tricked, no question, but having a sturdy door between them was far better than simply leaving him outside and hoping for the best. *Yeah, that'll work.*

Alex went back to stroking his pet after the plan was settled, and then retreated to his room. For a while, one of the fantasy novels he'd been reading held his attention, then his XBOX and the game he'd been playing before his parents left took over.

His pulse picked up a while later as he approached what he thought was a powerful enemy, and then lined up his rifle's scope for a headshot. The shot he made took off less than half the avatar's health, the sounds of suddenly alerted creatures around him making him grip the controller harder. He then switched to a machine gun and unloaded its belt of rounds at the coming swarm of mutant geckos. Less than three went down before his character went with them.

He tightened his grip on the controller in frustration, hearing something scratching the plastic, and feeling a strange tingling in his fingers. Before he could think too long about what was causing the numbness, he began tasting something slick and warm, with an aftertaste of iron. When his tongue ran across his teeth to his canines, he nearly froze stiff. The tooth he felt was longer and sharper than before. Fang-like.

"Shit." Alex dropped the controller and reached for his mouth, only to be hit by another shock when he saw his hands. Bone-white claws were sprouting from under his fingernails.

His heart-rate skyrocketed at the sight. *What the hell? The full moon's tomorrow.*

Swearing repeatedly, his breathing going ragged, Alex tried to maintain composure despite trembling like he was caught outside in bitter cold. He paced around his room, unable to look away from the horror show his hands were turning into.

The muscles throughout them were thickening by the second, the tips of his fingers reshaping for the still-forming claws. Patches of skin on his palms and fingers ballooned and thickened, the pigmentation of those spots darkening in turn. Torn between fear and sadness, Alex held his hands still as best he could, to no avail.

It was the sound of Bailey's whimpering that at last ripped his attention away; his dog was shirking back toward his bedside bookshelf. *How much longer do I have?*

"Bailey. You're going outside. Now." As Alex closed the gap, Bailey retreated further, his tail tucking and his ears and head dropping. "Bailey, I said..." Alex's speech was cut off as the muscles and organs in his chest constrained. He let out a painful groan, almost a growl. Bailey backed up again until he was pressed against the wall and his bookshelf.

With his hands over his chest, Alex could feel his muscles shifting and tightening with every breath. The same sensation moved out to his arms and legs. To him, it felt like someone was digging under his skin and manually moving his muscles around. As he fought the sickness rising in his stomach from that feeling, one paw came close to his mouth in case his stomach started to empty.

As his clothing became tighter, Alex switched his priorities to removing everything from his waist down. His tee came off afterward, with an effort bordering a complete rip-off. With just his necklace left, his claws and pads keeping him from working the clip; the thought of what might happen if he cut his skin with it kept him from tearing it off.

With his muscles continuing to move in ways he wasn't telling them to, Alex felt his head get hot, and the pressure on his sinuses and brain came back. With the taste of his blood still in his mouth, he made for the restroom, ignoring the mirror with every ounce of restraint he had, and opened the cold faucet.

Seeing his newly-formed paws in brighter light as they cupped for the water worsened the trembling around his body. His claws were pale—for all he knew, they had been made from the bones of his fingertips—and his palms were now dotted with blackened, tense skin, the stubs of white fur strands appearing where his pads had not formed.

When his face came close to his cupped paws, his nose bumped into his hands before he got a drink. It was softer and flush with the front of his face, rounded like a canine nose. Once he got to drinking, the water went down nearly as fast as the sink produced it, his still-growing fangs making him wary of biting himself, and the visible streams of red leaving him fearful of how much blood he'd lost through his mouth.

As his headache weakened from the continued drinking, Alex began to catch his breath, though his pulse refused to slow down. Feeling his chest with his new massive paw, he barely counted ten beats before he was struck with pain throughout his calves and thighs—the kind of pain in line with a rod being shoved through his muscles. Though he tried not to scream, Alex fell to his knees in front of the marble counter, his breaths coming erratically, and his sweat-drenched skin making the stone feel colder.

When he got back to his feet, his heart still beating hard and fast, Alex returned to his room, finding Bailey inching towards the door, his ears still folded back. His pet whined and backed away the second he saw him, into the same frightened pose. Alex got out only half of Bailey's name before he stopped talking. His voice had deepened considerably, and what little speech he'd heard was underlined with a rumbling. Something almost growl-like.

With another glance at his pet, Alex gave up on trying to coax him, hoping instead that he wouldn't pass out and wake up to find Bailey's flesh in his mouth.

As he felt his ears start to move up the side of his head, their shapes and size changing all the while, a jolt ran down the length of his spine to his tailbone. Alex reached back, feeling the bone pop out and a column of flesh grow past his fingers. When the jolt ran back up his spine, an itching akin to ants crawling out of and across his skin was right behind it, starting from his spine and going outwards, around his chest and hips, down his arms and legs and up his neck.

While he rubbed what part of him itched the most with his massive paws, he watched the growth of fur strands spread outward, down his limbs, and toward his paws and feet, white, grey, and brown making up their colors.

His breathing eased as the itching lessened, but along with the pace of his heartbeat, and the growl-laced breaths he took, his new ears were catching something else: bones cracking and popping.

The tiny movements around his face and jaw were the first he noticed, and tears ran from his eyes as his uncertainty and fear rooted him to the spot.

When he did move again, Alex remembered the look of the werewolf's legs too late.

The bones in his feet gave after one step with a loud set of crunching cracks, forcing him to his knees after he caught himself with the foot of his bed. Hot, crushing pain radiated out from his feet, running up his legs to his head. An unhindered yell of shock, a roaring growl, escaped before his breathing became rough and uneven again, the pain drawing out his memory of breaking his leg years ago.

As his eyes clamped shut, despite one a paw covering his face, his pained growls kept sounding. With his arms starting to tremble again, Alex then let himself down onto his back. How cold, frightened, and alone he felt as he lay there spiked, the thought of his parents seeing him like this making it worse. He soon pulled his injured limbs closer, fearing he'd crippled them. The lack of warmth from running blood on his skin didn't help ease that fear.

Now worried he was at risk of another broken bone shock, Alex tried to focus on the werewolf and what he knew of canine skeletal structures—the metatarsals in his feet, the sternum and ribs in his chest, and his skull and jaw. All of those canine bones were different from human shapes. With his metatarsals already broken, but his skull and jaw growing numb, he assumed one of them would change first and braced himself.

He lost track of how long it took for the first part of his skeleton to take a new shape, but he felt it first in his feet, the claws growing out before the rest shaped into a set of hind paws and pads. Though the hot, stinging feeling of the muscles around his recently broken bones wasn't as intense as he'd feared, the sensation of his flesh being stretched by a force he couldn't see ran up his spine, making his skin crawl under his fur.

His sternum and ribs came next, with his ribs snapping free of his sternum in pairs, and pushing outward behind his muscles, his chest cavity swelling in turn. His sudden fear of breathing too much for fear of further injury was tested with each second, and only when he no longer felt his ribs moving did he attempt to take a full breath.

With his eyes still closed, Alex let them open a little. The pooled tears watered his vision, and his only attempt to move an arm went nowhere, the whole of it feeling at least twice as heavy as he knew it should've been.

He hadn't blacked out yet, though he feared the moment was close.

As the once-subtle popping sounds from his skull and jaw bones grew louder, Alex opened his mouth. Seconds later, with a final pair of snaps, he felt his jaw go slack. What followed was both that bone and the front of his skull pushing outwards and shaping into a longer muzzle. As his jawlines reformed to match, his tongue lengthened and his fangs and teeth gained more mass.

Though he felt every movement and change, Alex was too wracked to do anything but moan. He tried to ignore how animalistic his moaning sounded, and the blood he could once again taste around his fangs, hoping that this would be the last thing he'd have to suffer through. As much as he'd gone through already, he had to be approaching some kind of end.

And it wasn't long before he felt his face stop reshaping. A few final snaps from bones resetting followed, and then everything was quiet again.

As his muzzle closed and he got in a swallow, the damp-with-sweat feeling of his skin and undercoat stood out as sharply as the head-to-paw soreness around his body and joints, and how much heavier his limbs, much less the rest of him, felt.

But as he kept breathing, it became clear he'd made it. No more itching, no more breaking bones, no more puppeted muscles, no more constant, battering pain.

With a lick of his lips with his now-longer tongue, Alex took a few breaths through his nose. He smelled Bailey along with some new scents from the carpet, but when he opened his eyes and turned his head up, he couldn't see him. He had to still be cowering near his bookshelf, but thinking about his pet watching his transformation made his heart clench. He didn't want Bailey to see it any more than anyone else he cared for, but there was nothing he could do about it now.

As his head relaxed and his eyes closed again, Alex heard the links in his necklace jingle against the floor and each other. Though he couldn't see it with his new muzzle blocking his view, he could feel it around the fur of his neck. It hadn't snapped off, despite how much thicker his neck felt.

The sound of Bailey's footfalls on the carpet sometime later got him to reopen his eyes. His dog offered only a glance at him as he left the room, but his fully-tucked tail and lowered head and ears said it all. *I'm sorry, boy. You didn't deserve that.*

Alex continued to lie on his bedroom floor for a while longer, a smile to himself eventually coming on. He was still in control, even this long after the transformation was over. Breathing a great sigh of relief and feeling more upbeat, he soon moved to get off his back and pick himself up, stopping briefly when he saw the massive hand-like paws he now had. His fingers felt a bit shorter, as if to make up for the length of his claws, but his thumbs had remained opposable.

As he moved onto his paws and knees, the wobbliness left over from the shock of the shift, his breaking bones, and how much heavier his body had become, had him spread his limbs out to help him stabilize. When he at last did, he reached for the top of his bedframe and pulled himself up. Despite his muzzle blocking most of his lower view, as he found his footing, he noticed the most dramatic changes immediately.

He wasn't standing as tall as he felt he could, but he'd gained at least a foot of height versus his human form. His steps were heavier than his human form, with all his weight concentrated in his hind paws versus his feet and ankles. The lack of feeling from his big toes, as though the other eight had taken over for them, also got his attention. *Did they turn into dew claws, or...?* He didn't want to look to find out.

As the AC turned on, the cold air from the vent in his room blew over his new pelt, ruffling every strand down to the finest ones and relieving his trapped body heat. His sore jaw was then cupped in one paw, his new teeth and fangs closing neatly around each other as he closed his muzzle. The muscles he could feel working and holding it as it opened again, and the thought of what he could do with such a muzzle, made him shudder.

When Alex at last checked the time on his desk clock, he panicked as he saw it was 3:56. With no idea how long the shift had taken, the question of why it had happened now instead of Monday stuck out most. How much noise he'd made when his bones broke left him somewhat thankful that all the windows were closed, but then his thoughts returned to his parents. If they hadn't left when they did... And what if his self-control was only temporary? Shaking his head at that thought, Alex decided to try once more to get Bailey outside.

His first real steps with his legs in their new canine shape were wobblier than he expected, forcing him to use his furniture, the walls, and then the doorframe for support as he headed for the living room.

When he emerged from the hall to find the bay window's curtains open, Alex swore to himself and dropped back to all fours, spotting the top of Bailey's pelt before he did—he'd taken to lying down near the couch. Once the windows were blocked, he turned around and approached his pet.

Bailey went back to his feet as he came close, lowering his body and ears and tucking his tail as he had before, but also curling his lips back from his teeth and fangs. Alex froze for a moment when the first of Bailey's growls sounded, lifting and holding out a paw for him when he felt he could. The growling deepened to a rumbling snarl as it came close and Alex withdrew his paw, his heart clenching at the sound, along with his throat.

When Bailey refused to stop snarling, at a loss for how to calm him down, much less get him to go anywhere, Alex took a step back. Three of them put an end to the noise, though Bailey's defensive posture didn't relax.

Chapter 10 – What Does It Mean...

Sunday, September 11th, 2011
Moon Phase – Waxing Gibbous

With silence returned to the room, the sudden growling of his stomach pulled Alex's attention away from Bailey. The growling persisted for nearly five seconds, the movement radiating into his chest muscles, and into the paw he laid over his abdomen.

The snack cabinet was his first stop after that, the scents of everything inside prompting a lick of his lips. The first thing he grabbed, a wrapped granola bar, proved a hassle to open with his pads, forcing him to use his claws. The scents the wrapper had contained rushed his nose once it was punctured, but after his first bite, the piece fell out of his mouth. He tried again and eased the piece back towards his molars with his tongue. Too far back, and he coughed it back out.

After a moment to consider how Bailey would eat his food, Alex tilted his head and took another bite. The piece settled into what remained of his cheek and he ground it down, finally swallowing it with a lick of his teeth.

Three bars later, his stomach was no longer growling, though his hunger was still going strong. Thinking some water would help, he went for a glass and filled it from the fridge dispenser. As awkward as getting a glass of water as a werewolf felt, he quickly found that not only was his first choice of glass too small for his new muzzle—the rim of it kept bumping into his nose and fangs—but that trying to drink like a human was a prelude to the liquid going up his nose, dribbling out of his muzzle and splashing over his pelt.

As he wiped himself off, Alex noticed Bailey's half-filled water bowl on the floor behind him. A chill ran through his nerves as he thought of lapping at his drinks. *Is that how I have to drink when I'm like this?* Seeing no other way, he refilled his glass to the brim and held his muzzle close, letting his tongue slide from between his jaws. His first lap with as good a cup as he could make with his new tongue did little but splash water outside the glass and over his paws, his second and third attempt ending the same way, each one building the feeling that he was wasting his time.

With an open sigh, which sounded close to a rumbling growl, Alex set the glass aside to think. Something had to be able to bridge the muzzle he had. Straws eventually came to mind, and he searched out a box in the pantry. With one placed between his front teeth, he got mostly air with his first attempt. He then repositioned the straw to one side of his jawline and tried to seal his lips. The water came in a steady stream once he managed it, prompting him to add two more to increase the flow.

Two glasses later, the fridge was his next stop, his fur keeping the cold air off his body effortlessly. The leftovers of the last few days were what he found first, but what was in the meat drawer almost made him salivate: two packages each of hamburger patties and hot dogs.

Ripping the plastic from the first package of patties, he almost took a bite before he stopped himself. He couldn't eat this stuff cold and raw. Or could he? Deciding not to tempt it, he set one on a plate and in the microwave on its highest setting for three minutes, hoping that would get the slab warmed up enough. That three minutes without food made his stomach start growling again, but it turned out to be too short a time; the core of the patty was still ice-cold.

Tearing the slab into eighths before deciding on breaking them into even smaller chunks, Alex tried again with four minutes. This time it was enough, and he took the first piece in his paws, trying not to flinch at how hot it was, or wrinkle his nose at how undercooked and laced with sodium the meat smelled. After just one of them, the hot dogs were zapped in clusters of three, each one eaten in less than a minute until only half of the second package was left untouched.

The chunk of lasagna that followed gave the meat and fillers enough time to settle and relax his hunger, but with no idea how long it all would last, Alex went for some soda to finish his impromptu meal, the carbonation filling what space was left in his stomach.

After putting up what he'd not eaten, Alex was left wondering what to do next. It was still bright outside, though the time had jumped to a quarter to five. How sore and fatigued he was soon made a nap feel like the best plan, more so when he let a yawn slip by. His lingering fear of going feral resurfaced as he headed for his room, though the fact that it hadn't happened because of the shift, or the passage of time, helped reign in his unease.

At the doorframe of his bedroom, Alex found Bailey sniffing at the carpet, his heavy steps drawing his dog's attention. He lowered himself to all fours after his pet's stare held for a few seconds, and moved closer to offer a paw again. This time, Bailey pulled his lips back and growled, but didn't shirk back, fold his ears, or tuck his tail. *Better not risk it.*

After his paw was withdrawn, Alex climbed into bed and laid back with an arm over his chest. As his eyes closed, his breathing relaxed, but not his mind. His phone going off, the front door opening, or a running engine coming up the driveway—he remained alert for any of the three until his mental lights went out. The sole dream that followed, which would push him to wake, shifted to him fleeing from his parents and the sound of gunshots, to a moment where something took over him and he began stalking his father, the one who had threatened his life.

Alex felt his heart as soon as his eyes opened. It was racing from the nightmare, making his growlish breathing uneven. The soreness he'd been wracked with before, however, had weakened considerably, and a few stretches helped even more.

When he checked his desk clock and saw that two hours had gone by, the many questions he'd been asking himself before he dozed off came back to mind, the first being how the shift had been triggered in the first place. He hadn't been doing anything strenuous or abnormal. Was it because he'd been bitten outside of the full moon? Was the day prior to the full moon, and the time the shift had started, what he had to be ready for from now on?

And why was he still sentient? Was it a trait all werewolves shared? Something only he was privileged with? If so, what was granting him that? Remembering his necklace, Alex held it in his paw, his thumb pad rubbing the bullet. As insignificant as it felt at first, he couldn't recall any silver jewelry on the werewolf the night he was bitten. It seemed in control at the end, but it still behaved like a monster otherwise.

Is this thing keeping me sane? Alex gripped the bullet at that thought. It hadn't taken much force to break the necklace's hook in the past.

With no idea how long he would stay the way he was, once he was out of bed, Alex walked the house, checking for curtains and blinds he could close and thinking about what he could do to pass the time. He had his desktop PC and his XBOX, but the keyboard, mouse, and controller all felt too small for his paws. He then gave one of his skateboarding magazines a few minutes, but found himself glancing at his window every few seconds.

After peering outside through the glass top of the front door, sneaking out once it was late and dark enough came to mind. If he stayed in the backyard or the garage, no one would see him, but as he continued to peer across the street at the vacant, tree-filled lot directly across from his house, that location became just as appealing.

That lot's not far... Streetlight's still busted too. Alex kept watch for another minute, seeing few hints of activity beyond the odd car going past or pulling into a driveway. What his father had told him about the precinct being on the lookout for large, loose canines sat in the back of his thoughts throughout. So far he'd seen no hint of any cruisers, making reaching the lot feel doable.

When he felt he'd seen enough, Alex headed for the guest room. The room's window was little more than a sliding pane of glass, but getting one of his new canine legs to fold up and rest comfortably on the windowsill proved more challenging than he thought. Some of the soreness resurfaced when his knees or hip or ankles were too sharply angled, and how much muscle mass and height he'd gained made anything less than a fully-open window look unfeasible.

For the next half hour leading up to 7:50, Alex did what he could to keep from pacing the house, his checks of the streets outside continuing to show few cars driving down them and even fewer people walking them. After hearing no one nearby at the guest room window, his claws and pads did little more than slide along the glass as he tried to slide it open. A few tries at the metal rim got the glass to inch over—with little noise to his relief—enough to where he could see his digits doing the rest of the work.

As he came close to the other side, the scents he'd let in with the cold evening air were drawn into his nose. It took less than a full breath for the wildly contrasting wave of scents to fire up his brain and olfactory senses, to get his head to swirl and drive him to block his nose.

The scents that got past as he struggled to do so, and then backpedaled from the window, didn't let his brain relax. Four scents, then eleven, then nineteen, then twenty-eight, then forty-one, and then more were processed within a second. All ones he recognized, even if the scent was weak, and for every one of them, several others went unrecognized or lost to the rest.

Alex huffed to clear his nose as he slipped out of the room, just missing smacking his shoulder and head against the guest room doorframe. Though it worked, what the event had revealed to him left him shaking. Not only was his nose even more sensitive than what it already was when he was human, but he'd noticed refined sugar in the scent-ocean, a scent from a refinery over a mile away from the house.

As he took a few breaths to clear his head, his phone began ringing. With it out of his jeans pocket and in his paw, Alex saw 'Dad' on the display.

Why's Dad calling me?

After a second to question it, his pulse rose. Had the celebration been called off? Were his parents coming back for something, or coming home early? First Colony was barely a fifteen-minute drive, if they were still there.

When the call tone stopped, the voicemail tone that followed it didn't erase his fears. He tapped at the screen with his claws, then his pads, neither letting him bring up the security screen. He then tossed his phone onto his bed and rushed for the guest room window. The mess of outside scents flooded his nostrils again before he blocked his nose and pulled the window open a few more inches.

Once his right leg was propped up on the sill, and the soreness was looked past, Alex gave the window another push. With the height of the window track forcing his head and upper chest to curl forward, further strain was put on his folded leg until the sill was no longer beneath it. It uncoiled as the air conditioner kicked on, the whirring of the steel fan blades masking his stumble into the fence and resultant growling grunts.

As the window was pulled closed, Alex hesitated on the last few inches. Would his parents lock the window? They usually didn't, and even if they did, he knew where the spare key to the front door was, but if he walked in on them like this...

Alex tried to forget that thought. As easy as it would be to wait for his folks to fall asleep, they'd never recognize him like this. He rubbed the bullet on his necklace again, feeling how much slack he had in the chain. *Can't risk it... Shit, fifteen minutes. Where can I hide?*

After dropping to all fours, Alex went for the garage door first. Locked, and the key was inside. Hiding by the air conditioning unit was his next thought, but the possibility of his parents letting Bailey outside, where he could easily find and possibly corner him, was quick to cast doubt on that idea. Moving towards the side gate, Alex looked out past the gaps in the wood, towards the wooded lot across the street. His night-vision, and the uncovered moon above, made most of what he saw deceptively bright, but his nose and his view through the wood planks for a bit gave him a good sense of being alone.

With his mother's sedan parked outside the garage and close to the grass, Alex made for the fence behind the garage. The edge of the lawn on the other side was lined with bushes, and the driveway wasn't far.

The top of the fence was almost level with his eyes, making a climb over it seem easy enough, but the shape of his legs once again worked against him and his attempts at finding a foothold. Wondering if he could jump it, Alex backed up a few steps and crouched, one front paw reaching the ground as his knees bent. After one step forward, the jump he attempted put his paws and shoulders in the right spot to throw himself over, but as his legs cleared the fence, he realized he'd overshot and tumbled over, landing on his back on the other side. The thump forced the air from his lungs and rattled his ribs and nerves.

Once back on all fours, Alex sniffed the air again. The scents in the grass had been disturbed by his landing, but otherwise there weren't any standout, risk-attached scents, and he heard no one walking around. After a stop near his mother's sedan, he made his move towards the porch, the sound of a car coming from his right getting him to hurry.

As he made it to the bushes lining the porch, he huddled down, ready to jump behind them as soon as the car came close enough. His pulse slowly climbed as it came closer, and the first signs of headlight reach became visible. What caused it to suddenly jump, and ice to touch his veins, was the sound of a police radio beep.

Oh, crap. If he sees me... Alex watched the light intently through the leaves, the fender grill the first thing to appear from behind them, then the tires. He shuffled sideways before he saw any hint of the officer inside, hoping, as he dropped flat to the pebbled texture of the porch, that they hadn't seen him.

When the vehicle stopped, Alex held his breath and fought the urge to cover his head.

A second passed, then another.

No doors opened. Just more radio beeps.

With the glance he managed at what was ahead of him, he saw the wooded area get lit up by what he was certain was a searchlight. The beam swept to the right, then the left, and finally turned off, the cruiser moving again afterward. The next sweep of the searchlight beam went over the bush he was hidden behind, a handful of light streams getting past and into his eyes before the cruiser drove away.

Shivering from the close call, Alex didn't move, instead fingering his necklace once again. *Maybe they'll understand...* He sighed and covered his face when his hope about that gave out.

After getting back to all fours, and feeling reasonably certain he could get to the lot without being seen, he went for it, trying to maintain more than a trot towards the street. Both his legs pushing forward at once seemed to help, and once past the sidewalk, he made for the closest tree and circled it, peeking back towards his house. Though it wasn't far away, he already felt like he was leaving the place far behind.

Finding a spot further back to lie down again, Alex watched for any sign of his parents. His heart was still beating rapidly, encouraging slow breaths through his mouth. The odd new scents leaking between his digits slowly joined the many he'd already processed, with one that he was certain belonged to decaying tissue getting him to glance around. *What's that coming from?*

Smelling it best on his right side, he inched that direction, the direction of the breeze continuing to move him towards the source. With a few glances up and around, Alex noticed an elevated patch of dirt coming up. Wondering if it was concealing the source of the scent, how weak it became after he moved his muzzle upwind of it was enough to tell him it likely was.

Seeing no obvious openings or gaps in the mound, he picked at it with his claws, eventually unearthing signs of a buried white mouse, the disturbing and popping of the pocket of decay making his paw cover his nose again.

For a moment after, Alex did little but stare at what he'd just found. This was how sensitive his olfactory sense was? If it was this precise...

He thought back to the werewolf that attacked him. Was it still in his hometown somewhere, or had it fled after biting him? If it was still here, where was it roaming, or hiding? The area near the city skatepark was his first guess, but the thought of traveling that far to check for scent traces felt like too great a risk. He'd been lucky just now with the officer, and didn't want to risk that again so soon.

* * *

As the minutes went by, Alex continued to roam the wooded area, looking back toward his house every so often. With no way to track the time, he breathed an easy sigh after what felt like thirty minutes went by with no sign of his parents.

Now what? When his thoughts returned to the other werewolf, where the past killings happened followed suit. Kempner's stable, the skatepark... *Is it using the creeks to move around?* At that, Alex recalled the creek two streets away that ran south through his neighborhood. The drainage ditch it connected to was just north of the skatepark, and his high school was almost directly north of the same location.

After inching forward to get in a glance down both streets, despite seeing nothing, Alex's legs grew heavy. Two streets. The creek wasn't far. He hadn't seen any police since the previous encounter, but the moon was giving off a lot of light, and one wrong move or curious pedestrian and he'd be exposed.

It was then that he wondered why he was seeing fewer people than usual outside this late. Or was he?

Was Dad calling me about a crime around here? The first thought he had was a manhunt, which would've explained the cruiser with the searchlight, but he'd heard no hint of helicopters since going outside, which he knew the police would use in such cases. A lot more cruisers would've driven down his street in such an instance too.

After another few minutes with still no sign of activity, Alex was left to assume he was overthinking things. How quiet the streets were also built a bit of hope that he could make it to the creek without being seen. If the werewolf was still around and using one of the creeks, or another off-the-road route, he'd no doubt find a hint of it by using them himself.

It was what he could, or would, do if he encountered the werewolf that kept him in place for a minute. The mass and curve of his claws left him picturing fighting the other werewolf, though his paws made it clear how much the white and grey of his fur contrasted the dirt and grass. He huffed once to calm his racing heart. He didn't have to let it get to that. An idea of where this thing might be was enough.

If I stay low, maybe...

Alex took a few slow breaths before moving back towards the roads, watching for any headlights or people. One car pulled into a cul-de-sac halfway down the road going south, but the eastbound road, the one he needed to use, stayed silent. Once his confidence built up enough, his first step eastward, away from the tree-line, was taken. Almost immediately, his skin tightened and he felt the urge to lower his stance, as though the moon was a spotlight focused solely on him.

Every few steps, he glanced up to check the road, weaving from trees, to bushes, to behind cars, to the closest shadowy patches in his path as he went, speeding up as best he could when there was a massive gap between spots he could duck into. The extended walk on all fours also helped him find the best method of moving his new legs, the scents near the ground helping him quell the thought of getting back to his hind paws and running like he felt he could.

As the four-way intersection drew closer, relief started to well. *One more street. Doing good so far.* He then took a few more steps, past the driveway of the last house on the corner, only to notice something bright coming his way from the north. The white shine was all the hint he needed that it was a headlight and his pace quickened, his body dropping and ceasing to move once behind a thick holly bush.

As the headlight came closer, the rumbling of the engine it was attached to sounded in line with that of a truck. Only after he heard it turn east, and drive down the street directly ahead of him, did Alex pick himself up. He kept watch of the intersection for a bit, and after hearing no more cars coming, made for the creek.

Another two streetlamps beamed light down on the sidewalks, getting him to start running again. He didn't stop after he passed them. The quicker he was out of sight, the better.

Within a few yards of the creek, the raw scent of stagnant water rushed his nostrils, making him slow down and cover his nose again before he slipped over the edge and down the creek's bank enough to duck under the bridge. After finding his upright footing on the grassy incline, he began his trek south, crouching every few yards to see if any scents stood out to him.

On approach of his neighborhood park, Alex dropped to all fours and inched towards the top of the bank to peek over it. With a few seconds glance, he spotted two people and one dog—a husky, by the build and fur color—walking the trails among the trees. The sight of the dog made him step back and move further down into the creek, with one free paw over his nose. He was upwind of it, but with Ginger and Bailey's reactions to him fresh in mind, the last thing he wanted was to do was spook it. Hoping the creek would contain enough of his scent, he continued his trek south, listening for a hint of barking.

* * *

Eventually, the creek started to give way to a deeper mouth, and Alex climbed out and stood near the corner of a fence. The bridge leading over the drainage basin was brightly lit by the moon, along with the soccer, tennis, and baseball fields of his old middle school on the other side.

With no hint of a large, black mass anywhere in his field of view, Alex took to identifying the ways he thought the werewolf would've traveled in the relative darkness. The drainage ditch had sidewalks along both sides, which ran east behind rows of houses. Their lengths were unlit and ran alongside fences at least seven-feet high. The other ways he could think of—the parking lot of his old middle school, the rear exits near the tennis courts, and the areas around the pool and skatepark—were all lit up in some way, but if the traffic was as barren around here as it was near his home…

He soon settled on a few areas that he couldn't see the werewolf avoiding, and after lowering himself to all fours, started across the moonlit bridge, the nagging feeling of being watched digging into his skin again. Once on the other side, Alex put his nose down and sniffed at the concrete. The breezes had since shifted eastwards, bringing out scents lodged in the pavement from, he guessed, twenty feet away, none familiar. With an eastward sweep of concrete and grass, which ended at a fence corner, he found nothing that stood out.

Maybe it hasn't come around here yet. Alex then hugged the fence and traveled along its length going south, for a few feet. Several rank canine scents got him to backpedal and shake his head in disgust. After moving aside until he could no longer smell them, the east length of the field produced nothing also, and he changed directions, this time going west.

It was as he approached the corner of the wall of his old middle school that a pair of scents—one skin, one fur—slowed his pace. Within half a breath, they sparked the terror he remembered from the night he was attacked.

As his pulse jumped from the discovery, Alex zeroed in on the spot where the scents were coming from, then swept his nose left and right. The second spot was to the west, and the trail the spots began to form led him behind his middle school and, to his concern, towards a lit rear parking lot. Despite no cars parked there he kept his distance, now wondering where the werewolf could have gone and how far behind it he was.

When a clank of metal sounded in the distance, he was reminded of the skatepark. Had it passed near there? After a second to think on it, Alex made his way there, his muzzle keeping close to the ground in case another scent trail presented itself.

As the area where he and Nathan had found Angela drew closer, another one did, this time going north and south—south towards a tiny but unlit park, and north around a spot-lit section of grass. Alex followed it as it wound a path towards the baseball park nearest the skatepark, but when the scent pooled and then went cold just before the entrance to the field, he was left looking behind him and wondering what it was even doing here.

The question turned over for a few seconds before the sounds of skating, and his relief at not finding the werewolf, pulled his attention towards the park again. With nothing else to do, he slipped inside the baseball field and found what he thought was the darkest spot before laying down on his chest. Though the three skaters inside the park were mostly riding around, whenever one of them attempted a trick, the urge Alex felt to skate, even for a minute, grew stronger. The mental image of standing on his board with his new legs and paws, doing a few, simple pushes to gain some speed, brought on a slight grin.

He later winced when one of the trio attempted and failed a transition into a Frontside Tailslide, his body flinging forward after the board slipped from under him. Alex almost inched forward in response to the others asking if he was alright.

Sometime later, the sight of headlights coming down the access road to the park got his attention. Thinking it was another skater, as the headlights turned away from facing his direction, the police lights on the hood and lettering on the doors became visible. The eastbound breeze also brought with it a new scent of fur.

Alex made for the open gate as soon as he realized, dropping low and stopping only when he heard the cruiser door open. Why the police were showing up here was answered as soon as the lone officer passed the turnstile.

"Hey, guys. This park is under curfew. You need to leave."

Was that what Dad was trying to tell me?

At first, the skaters asked if they were in trouble, to which the officer assured them they weren't so long as they left. When the curfew was questioned, the response the officer gave made Alex's head run wild with questions.

"Because we've had several animal attacks around this area over the last month."

Several? Since when? Angela was the only one before me, and that calf was just one kill. Alex swallowed hard. He'd been keeping an eye on the news since the day Angela was attacked, but now was unable to shake the feeling he'd overlooked something.

"You haven't seen any odd animals around here, have you?" the officer soon asked, making Alex grumble about the completely wrong use of 'odd'.

"No. Nothing's come around here," said one of the skaters.

"I see. Even so, you boys need to head home."

With crickets chirping around him, Alex stayed still until he heard the door of the cruiser once again open and close, making his move towards the creek bank as fast as he could go after that. The news of the park under curfew, and the thought of more places like it under the same rules, sat in his thoughts until he was halfway home. If he hadn't come that Friday night...

Ignoring the tightening of his throat, he continued towards the bridge and where he'd exited from the creek. This was enough exploration for one night. He'd seen pretty much everything he wanted to, and hunger pangs were starting to surface.

* * *

Back at home, as he worked to reopen the window, the start-up of the air conditioner pushed the inside scents out past his nose, a new collection of them drawing an old mix of concern and disgust. *Oh, man. Bailey.* With his dog nowhere in sight, Alex climbed inside. The spot his dog had marked was the wall below the windowsill, and even with the window open, the musts within the room were being overpowered by it.

Hoping his room had been spared, when Alex approached the doorway, he spotted Bailey resting atop his bed. The sight of his werewolf body made his dog's head shoot up, as though he'd been startled.

Relax, boy. It's still me. Alex inched closer while trying not to stare after the reaction, but within two steps, his dog began growling. Alex then backed off just as slowly and headed for the kitchen.

Does he really not recognize me like this? As he made a meal for himself and figured out how far Bailey's marking scents had drifted, he couldn't bring himself to believe that was the case. His werewolf scent overpowering what remained of his human one made the most sense. How he could get Bailey off his bed, and if possible outside, with that in mind became his next question.

After another glass of water and plate of warmed up hot dogs, an idea came to him: trick him with a doorbell ring, then a knock on the glass door in his parent's room to lead him there and outside. Alex couldn't help grinning as the plan went into motion, and once his pet had dashed outside, he slipped back in and shut the door behind him. *Sorry, boy. Not having that happen again.*

Once the spot had been cleaned, enough that the scents were drastically weakened according to his senses, and he felt enough time had passed, Alex let Bailey back in. His pet was quick to settle down on the futon in the guest room, leaving him an opening to get into his own room and reclaim his bed.

His parents stayed in mind the most as sleep approached, along with the hope that he would wake to see his human skin again.

Chapter 11 - ...To Be A Werewolf

Monday, September 12th, 2011
Moon Phase - Full

That hope was dashed when he woke the next morning to a still heavy body and the feeling of fur coating his skin. What time it was dominated his thinking as the shock from the realization began affecting his organs and breaths.

6:21?

Alex gripped his chest, feeling the necklace and bullet, and tried to calm down. His parents wouldn't be home this early...but they were coming home sometime today.

As he reached for his phone and then held it in his paws, he thought of sending them a picture and asking them to come back to let him explain things. The idea made him sick to think about, and the longer he lingered on it, the more he questioned their reason to believe him. Even if he recorded himself, they could write it off as just an elaborate fake-out.

As his throat tensed up again, Alex slid off his bed and set his phone aside, trying to breathe easy. He couldn't stay this way forever. Something had to change him back, but what was dictating that? An action from him? A length of time? If it was time, what had been the trigger, and how long was he supposed to remain this way? It had already been fifteen hours.

Until he felt something touch the fur on his leg, Alex stayed lost in his concerns. When he spun around, Bailey took a step back. He seemed curious, but ready to flee if spooked again. Alex held still for a moment in response, then lowered himself into a crouch as steady as he could. The discomfort at being wedged between his pet and his dresser built as Bailey closed the gap, but as he did, Alex started hearing an alternating double-thumping and single-swushing sound. Within two sets, he realized the noises were making up Bailey's heartbeat.

One...two...three...four... Good, he's calm. Alex took a second to meet Bailey's gaze, then raised and held out a paw for him once again. Bailey inched further forward, to within sniffing range, and ran his nose over the spread of Alex's paw, his sniffs ruffling his fur. When he stopped, a warm lick was quick to follow, then another.

"Good…" Stopping himself after that one word, the rumbling, growl-laced tone of his voice made Alex shudder. Bailey stopped licking him when his paw shivered, then looked him in the eyes. "It's still me, Bailey." The awkwardness of speaking with an elongated tongue and canine muzzle caused a slurring of his words, and Bailey's head tilted in response.

Whether it was because of his voice or his speech, the fact that his dog was recognizing something about him got Alex to curl up the back of his lips, as best a smile as he could manage without flashing his teeth. He then inched himself and his paw closer, causing Bailey to woof at him and lower his head away.

"It's okay." Alex held still until his pet sniffed his fur again, and then let his paw touch his pet's neck. "I won't hurt you, boy." Alex said, but after half a stroke of his pelt, Bailey had begun whimpering and Alex pulled his paw away, giving his pet the opening to step back.

With a deep sigh, Alex went back to considering his options with his parents. They would find him when they came home, and without warning them, he'd just be a monster to them. The thought of hiding soon came to mind, and his attention went to the guest room. The closet by the window was large enough to hide him, both upright and sitting down, and it was only a few feet from the window. With the room door closed, he could easily hide and then sneak outside when it was safe.

Remembering the loud cracking noises his bones made during his transformation made him question the idea, if briefly. Once he was outside, he could run for the garage. It wouldn't take but a few seconds, and he could shift back in peace there.

Getting back to his feet, Alex made for his parent's room and found the garage key. Outside, hints of yellow were showing in the sky. He had to be quick. Once the sliding door was open, he dropped to all fours, the key head ringed on a thumb claw, and unlocked the garage door. After slipping inside, he checked the rear storage room—spare fence planks, trash bins, and other junk were inside, but it felt big enough.

Better get some clothes while I'm at it. Back inside, he emptied his backpack of the bulkiest stuff and crammed in a fresh set of clothing. Bailey was roaming the yard on the return trip but ignored him as he stashed his backpack out of sight but where he could reach it. *There. All set, I hope.*

Once back inside, with the door left open for Bailey, Alex sat and leaned against his bed, certain that he had a good plan set. As the sun continued to rise and fill his room with light, he thought back to his roam of the neighborhood, and the officer's speech. *How many attacks have there been?* He gave his computer a single glance before getting up and then booting it up.

The SLPD website was the first place he went. While there was a warning about the animal attacks, it offered no records of them. *Damn. Where else?* He knew of a couple newspapers and news channels that reported for the city, but returned to the site that reported on the calf first. Starting his search with animal attacks, he got the calf story again, but no others. Repeating the story with a local news channel, he got the same story plus one more.

There has to be more than that. Alex then thought about some other terms he could use. The officer had said attack, but that meant no deaths. *Animal killings. That might work.* After changing the words in the search bars, he again got the calf story but this time, three new stories between both sites came up.

He opened each one in a new tab and read them over for any details or patterns. Though none mentioned a sighting, in all cases, the affected animals had turned up partially eaten, and some ways from where they were snagged. The sudden grumbling of his stomach as he read the articles urged a paw to be placed against it, which slid up towards his heart after the noise stopped.

How hungry he had been after the shift slipped into mind. With how fast he seemed to burn off food, if he didn't change back soon... But he still had plenty of things to eat besides snacks and pre-made stuff.

* * *

As the morning hours continued to go by, Alex tried to stay occupied while listening for the doorbell or the front door unlocking. Thanks to his trek the night before, the house was slowly feeling more like a giant, self-imposed cage that he couldn't wait to get away from. Opening his windows for the morning breezes, and catching whiffs of the numerous scents outside, helped ease his mood some.

When he heard his phone ring around eleven, he jumped at the sound before retrieving it. The caller ID showed Blue Moon Comics, and he set the phone back down after the voicemail had answered for him. *Sorry, boss. Can't come in today.* He then smirked a bit thinking about how it would look if he went to work as he was. *Someone would finger me as The Astounding Wolf-Man, I bet.*

Taking the next few hours to game on his XBOX, keeping the volume down as he did so, the size of his paws and presence of his claws made anything besides rough trigger-pulling tricky. Every so often, he paused to rehearse his hiding and escape plans, getting a feel of how he had to move the window and considering what he could afford to leave lying around. Opening the window too fast made the metal parts scrape, but the guest room door was often closed.

When his phone rang again that afternoon, he checked it to find his dad calling him. Seeing the name didn't unnerve as much as before, but not willing to risk getting caught, he headed for the guest room. After closing the door and checking the window, he sat near the closet door, ready to huddle inside if he needed. His phone soon rang again, the noise muffled by the door. Certain it was his dad trying again to reach him, the thought of leaving his phone in such an obvious place gave him a few seconds pause before he got back up and returned to his room.

With it in his paws, Alex glanced around his room. *Would they suspect that much if I just left it on the bed? If I change back soon...but it's been almost twenty-four hours.* As the thought of being a werewolf for another day came to mind, Alex was quick to remind himself that the full moon would be waning by midnight.

If it's lasting this long... Does it last nine hours before and after the day of the full moon? He covered his face and breathed an uneasy sigh, noticing scents of old sweat as he did. If that was true, no matter what he did tonight, he would be facing his parents by dawn.

More minutes went by without hint of his parents, leaving Alex hopeful that they had listened to his suggestion. It was already early afternoon, a good sign if they were still gone. As he settled on what, if anything, to tell Nathan about his absence, he headed for his bookshelf to grab a magazine to read.

That was when he heard wheels coming up the driveway, and the rumbling of a truck engine he knew belonged his father.

Immediately his pulse rocketed, and the magazine slipped from his paws. His legs, though trembling, stuck him in place until the click of the front door's deadbolt got him to move. He got one glance at his phone before reaching the guest room door, his nerves and shaky limbs making him swing it shut almost too fast.

As it closed, and he heard his dad's boots against tile, Alex gripped the door handle until his fears of the situation won over. He let the knob reset as his parents greeted Bailey, and then ducked into the closet, huddling in the back and shaking like mad. How fast his heart was beating, and how hot he felt, left him panting.

His eyes soon closed, and he focused on the sounds outside the door. He heard his parents coming closer, his father's boots making the most noise. They stopped outside the guest room door, and Alex curled up, clamping his muzzle shut.

His father spoke first. "So, his motorcycle's still here and he left his phone. Where is he?"

"He has class right now, doesn't he?"

"Unless it got canceled, I believe so."

A pause came, and then the guest room door opened. "He's probably not far."

Alex shook his head lightly, trying not to shed tears or make a single noise. He heard Bailey coming closer, and then sniff near the door. *Bailey, don't. Stay away, please.*

"Bailey. You need to go out?" His mother came close. Alex tried to take solace from anything he could. "C'mon. Outside." Bailey snorted and walked away with her. Alex didn't relax until he heard his parents walk into their room and close their door. He could barely breathe once they did. He felt trapped, like one sound would give him away.

With no way to gauge the time, he listened to his parents move around the house, sticking mostly within their room, but then the hunger pangs returned. He tried breathing slowly, keeping food out of his mind. When Bailey came back in, he heard him settle on the futon cushions, but not make any noise. *Good boy, Bailey. Stay quiet.*

He soon heard his mother speak. "We going anywhere tonight?"

"Up to you, dear."

"There's a new Italian restaurant in Town Square. Looked nice."

"Sure, why not? Italian sounds good. Let's go before rush hour, though."

"That's not for another two hours."

"If this place is new, they'll fill up quickly."

Alex swallowed once as the urge to lick his lips came.

"At four, then. That'll give us enough time."

Alex couldn't help smiling after hearing that.

* * *

As he continued to huddle in darkness, Alex's hunger steadily grew. Not thinking about the meat left in the fridge became harder by the minute, and when he heard the first gurgle from his stomach, it came as a prolonged churning that lasted multiple seconds. Alex placed a paw over his stomach, hoping four was close, and that his parents wouldn't hear his protesting stomach before then.

Another gurgle came soon after, and he felt his stomach move behind his skin. *I can't be that hungry.* Thinking his body had started absorbing food faster than usual, Alex leaned back and tried to relax.

"Bye, Bailey," he heard his mother say some time later. "Guard the house."

By that point, Alex's arms had started quivering. He listened for the front door closing, and then after a period of silence, heard a truck engine turn over. The closet door was then opened, his eyes squinting at the light as he stood up.

First Colony... So I've got two or three hours at best...but then what? Alex looked back inside the closet. It had worked once already. *Just need to sneak outside next time.*

Once in the kitchen, he found the rest of the patties and hot dogs, fixing one of each and starting with the patty once it had cooled. The quivering of his limbs weakened with each piece he ate, but with those same pieces, the ground beef was becoming less appealing and filling. After a few bites of the hot dog, the same thing happened with it.

What's going on? Setting aside his half-eaten meal, Alex went for some water. The liquid cooled him and filled his stomach, but the hunger persisted. When he tried to eat another bite of both meats, they seemed to do nothing for him.

Panic began to surface as Alex walked back to the guest room to think, catching the aerial scents his parents had left along the way. He couldn't help picturing them in the house, or remembering how close they'd come to discovering him. If his hunger persisted until they returned...

Stay calm. Maybe I'm about to change back. He sat down by the window, waiting for any change in how he felt or a sign of change on his body. Instead, he was treated to a continually growing sense of emptiness in his abdomen, and his stomach rumbling under his paw. The feeling of his blood being redirected to serve that one organ fueled his doubts about turning back, as did Bailey's woofing at the grumbling.

More minutes passed with no sign of change, and Alex covered his face with his paws. His thoughts drifted around, from his half-eaten meal, to his first shift, to how hungry he felt after it. Refusing food made sense if he was about to lose body mass—possibly stomach volume—from the change, but feeling like he was being starved of something beforehand?

Shaking his head lightly, one paw reached for and laid over his necklace. As he held it, he thought of the calf, of the were that attacked him, and then of himself eating from such a kill. The image of that stuck in his head longer than he wanted, his pulse rising as it continued to refuse to vanish. *No. That can't be.*

Alex shot up and made for the kitchen, his uneven breaths enhancing his unintentional growling as he ate the rest of the hot dog. It was no use; it still tasted unappealing and his stomach didn't quiet.

When the calf had been killed snapped into his thoughts: August 13th. August had thirty calendar days, versus twenty-nine of the lunar cycle.

No. Oh fuck, no.

Alex's eyes welled with tears and his blood turned to ice as the pieces fell into place. August 13th was the previous full moon. The police were suspecting wolves from the partially consumed carcass. The sudden severity of his hunger, and how unwilling his body was to accept meat he'd been eating since the change stripped the last of his doubt away.

As he wiped his eyes and tried to take a relaxed breath, his fears of going feral returned. The hour that followed of him sitting in his room, staying lost in thoughts and listening for noises, let the emptiness spread to his limbs. No shakiness came with it, but memories of the last couple animals he'd helped put down did.

When 5:30 came with no sign of his parents, Alex made for the guest room and let himself out, unwilling to risk getting trapped again. Inside the garage, scents of cooking meat and burning charcoal kept drifting in through the open door. Feeling his abdomen, and then his necklace, he wished he could simply sleep through the hunger. Do something besides kill and eat an innocent animal. Meanwhile, the question of what he was risking if he did nothing continued to test his emotions.

Just one. That's it. I can make it quick. As the sun continued to set and his parents continued to remain gone from the house, Alex focused on that line of reasoning to try and calm his nerves. When he felt it was dark enough, he followed his route to the creek from the night before, taking every cautious step with limbs that felt loaded with lead.

He saw the police only once as he approached the road leading to his high school, causing him to duck out of sight until the SUV drove away. When a south-bound breeze brought with it the scents of animals and stable equipment, Alex felt a surge go through him that he didn't want. Sticking close to clumps of trees and grasses as he made his way north, he followed the scents through the school's baseball field, going behind it and the football stadium to bring him close to the stable.

He sat a distance away in the tall grass and looked over the enclosures. A young doe was alone in the central enclosure, a cow in another, and a foal and mare in another. With his sights on the doe, Alex hesitated and lightly shook his head. The scents of the animals, and how close he was to them, continued to make his hunger worse, how wrong this all felt rooting him to the spot. The bit of confidence he'd manufactured back at home crumbled, leaving him feeling shaky for a length of time he couldn't gauge.

When he forced himself to move, he felt tears come on again. The doe would be fast, but the easiest for him to grab.

He was over the railing easily, but before he landed the doe tried to bolt backwards, running into the locked door and throwing the padlock around. Alex's dominant claws found its neck as it tried to run past him, pinning it to the wall before his other arm wrapped around its chest. The thrashing animal tested his hold as fear and panic rushed in.

The doe bayed in fear, making him wince and leaving his ears ringing at the noise. His grip on the animal's ribs tightened before he let go of its neck and wrapped his freed paw around its muzzle. Around him, the other animals were panicking and crying out.

Alex froze, unable to move beyond holding the doe, but as it kicked against the floor and walls, his grip on its ribs gave way to a sound of tearing and warmth flowing over his digits. The animal frenzied, throwing its head around, thrashing its hooves against the ground near his paws. His grip on the doe's muzzle loosened, risking release. Clamping down as hard as he could, he hoisted it and bent its neck back until it laid against his abdomen.

Holding back a swear, he closed his eyes and parted his jaws. The point of no return was already past.

Alex felt his fangs punch through the muscle and tissue of the doe's neck as he bit down. The iron taste of blood was in his mouth a second later and his jaws released, his tongue lapping the fluid almost on instinct. He lost track of how many seconds passed as he tried not to listen to the sound of tearing flesh that came with almost every jerking movement the doe made. The feeling of warm muscle and bone against the digits of his left paw heightened the sick feeling rising in his stomach.

As the doe's kicking and squirming weakened, Alex held on to be sure it wouldn't jerk free at the last second. It never came; the animal was too weak. As it went limp in his arms, he opened his eyes. Splatters of red gore were all around the enclosure floor, and the fur of his hind paws and legs. His heart was pounding from adrenaline and fear, but he couldn't move. Every second he stood still, the shakier he felt.

When he at last looked toward the railing of the enclosure, the space between the bars looked large enough to slip the body through. Once he got moving, that was proven true, and he was soon back over the railing himself.

With his arms once again holding up the doe's limp head and chest, his destination was anywhere out of the range of the stable lights. He reached that quickly, despite the weight of the carcass, but didn't stop until he reached the far end of the soccer fields.

As he laid the body down and sat in the grass to catch his breath, he heard no sirens in the distance, much to his relief. When his attention was drawn to the doe's head however, he was quickly reminded of what he'd just done. Despite the massive puncture wounds on its neck, and open gashes in its chest, it was still, if weakly, trying to move its head and its legs, the sounds it attempted to make sounding just as weak.

Swallowing once with a paw near his muzzle, Alex's empty stomach and the taste of blood on his fangs clashed with his cocktail of emotions. For a while, he only stared at the doe and his blood-stained paws, unable to bring himself any closer to it. When he at last did, he didn't feel a heartbeat. Whether his fear of going feral and attacking others for food was founded or not no longer mattered then.

With his first nip of flesh and muscle from the spots he'd already torn open, Alex's conscience was wrenched in every direction. His body tensed and relaxed in uneven patterns, well into the next few pieces he took. The slowly laxing feeling of emptiness in his stomach and limbs, and the strangely good taste of the animal meat, barely compensated for how he felt overall, but as he continued to eat from his kill, the mix of conflicting emotions began to gel with and weaken each other. Not enough to where he could feel pleasure at what he was doing, but enough that it didn't make him feel as disturbed for continuing to do it.

As his hunger lost the last of its influence, Alex forced himself to take a few more bites before breaking his attention away. Somewhere among the nearby tree-line, among the dense vegetation and branches lining the ground, seemed the best place to toss the carcass. He licked his blood-stained muzzle before taking the carcass by the legs and hauling it to the closest spot that caught his eye.

After a few steps further back, Alex let it drop, tearing his eyes away from the remains the second he had the chance. A forced swallow and a weak sigh came as he emerged from the tree-line and began the trek home.

Chapter 12 – Human Once Again

Monday, September 12th, 2011
Moon Phase – Full

When he returned, unsure of what time it was or if his folks were asleep, he scaled the fence behind the garage, careful not to make much noise, and hid near the guest room window. Their room light was off, and Bailey was nowhere in sight when he looked inside. An ear pressed to the glass was met with silence.

The lingering scent of drying blood in his fur got him to retreat from the spot after a moment. With a weak stream of water from the backyard hose, he washed the stains from his fur as best he could. The doe, and what he'd done to it, refused to leave his thoughts as his white and grey fur lost the tints of red, his throat tightening between each forced swallow.

The deed was done. He'd done it for a good reason, not because he'd felt like it. It was either that or risk whatever that hunger would've caused otherwise. He kept telling himself all of that as he massaged his throat and wrestled with the emotions he'd been holding back.

Once back near the window, Alex waited until he felt he could sneak inside without risking getting emotional and giving himself away. His picking at the window once that happened eventually released the air and scents inside the house, his first whiff of them calming him a touch. As the air conditioning turned on, and the nearby blades whirred up, he hurried inside, a rush of relief and safety hitting him once the window was closed. He then paused once again to listen for movement and activity, dropping to all fours and making for his room when nothing came to him.

Bailey, asleep in his dog bed, barely moved as Alex snuck past him, into the gap between his bed and the wall by his bookshelf. After he dropped to the floor and curled his legs up, the thought of what to do if his parents found him like this delayed sleep from taking over.

Tuesday, September 13th, 2011
Moon Phase – Waning Gibbous

When he awoke, Alex noticed his increased heartrate before anything else. His shoulders felt tight, as did his chest, like his muscles had been tensing up. As he clasped his muzzle to halt any panting breaths, the numbness and lack of claws on his digits stole his attention. *How long have those been gone?*

As he tried to put a time to the question, the tightening of his muscles spread to his abdomen, and then his arms and legs. Hints of the puppeting that had happened before became more noticeable by the second, how close he still was to his parent's bedroom getting him to rethink staying where he was.

After a roll onto his chest, he picked himself up, the tension around his body and shrinking of his muscle structure slowing his ascent and the steps he took to get out of his room. Once out of the hall, the kitchen pantry became his goal, how ready he was to leave his werewolf form behind helping to dampen the discomfort of the pressure building on his bones.

As he made it inside and back to his knees, he got only seconds of relief before the tension intensified from tightening to bone-crushing, forcing him down and on his side against the tiled floor. His clamped muzzle barely held back his gasps at the shock, his breaths puffing past his gritted teeth and out his nose.

And then he heard his bones cracking.

Hoping the noise wasn't carrying, Alex felt his metatarsals gave first, the lengthened bones reworking themselves back to their old human shape, along with his fore and hind paws. When the same noises sounded from his skull and jaw, he released them, leaving him open to gasp as his bones snapped, went slack, and shrunk back into his human jawline.

Until his tail receded and his ears shrunk back to their human shape, his ribs and sternum were all that remained unchanged. Alex had since dropped to his back in preparation for it, but the compression of his chest when it happened, the feeling of his ribs pushing his organs back into a smaller frame, made him reach for and cover his face. Only when he felt his breaths relax from the last of the compressions of his skeleton and muscles did Alex release his mouth.

With sweat pooling under his fur, he gripped his chest to feel his heart. As weak as his grip felt, it pulled a tuft loose from his skin with barely an itch or a sting. More strands came loose as he brushed his face, pushing him to get to his knees to remove the rest. The temptation to shake himself free of the many shed strands was there, but as the pile of fur around him grew, so did how cold he felt without it all coating him.

With his arms wrapped around his chest to fight the house's chill, the soreness of his bones and the strained feelings of his muscles kept him kneeling until he heard claws clicking on the tile behind him. Turning around to see Bailey rounding the corner, his pet paused briefly before rushing towards him.

The rabid licking and jumping that followed his approach Alex didn't bother stopping. "Yeah, good boy," he whispered, his throat lumping as he rubbed his dog's pelt.

After Bailey stopped licking him and turned his attention to the fur pile, Alex let him be and looked around for the stuff he needed to sweep it up, seeing nothing but benefits to letting his dog note the scents of his fur. How much there was to clean up stunned him; the pile reached nearly a foot tall in places, and filled the trash bag he found to the brim.

Sweeping the few strands he couldn't get into a corner under the pantry shelves, Alex tied off and hoisted the bag before sneaking back to his room and stashing it in one of his closets. With no noise coming from his parent's room, he found a fresh set of clothes, warming up with each article he put on, and climbed back into bed once he was fully dressed.

Despite the time on his phone saying 4:03, how wide awake he felt with the reverse shift behind him made the thought of going back to sleep so soon more unlikely by the minute. Soon, he began fingering through the messages he'd received since he'd shifted. Aside from the call from Blue Moon, which had been from Trevor about a shift he could take, his father had called the night they left to warn him about the curfew, but also to call him back when possible. Nathan had also tried to reach him while he'd been hiding in the closet, leaving a text and then a voicemail asking if something happened.

Until he heard his parents rousing around an hour later, Alex passed the time with a handful of videos and book chapters. His father was the first to leave the bedroom, his attention locking on him as soon as he saw him.

"Morning, Son."

Hearing some suspicion in the grogginess of his voice, Alex kept his tone as even as he could. "Hey, Dad."

"You're up early."

"Yeah. Just got up."

"Where were you yesterday?"

"Around the neighborhood, mostly."

"You got the message I left you on Sunday, I hope."

Alex nodded. "Not until later. Didn't realize I'd forgotten my phone for quite a while, and I figured you guys were asleep by the time I saw it."

His father didn't respond immediately. "You had us worried, not calling back for so long and then not coming home until late at night."

Alex felt a rise in his pulse and fought the surfacing of his emotions. "Sorry. Didn't mean for that." As his father walked off, Alex squeezed his face and breathed out in relief. He couldn't help feeling that his folks knew something was going on, and that stuck in his head as he headed to the bathroom for a shower and bladder relief.

Once both of his parents had left for work, Alex recovered the bag of discarded fur, only to hesitate at the door to the backyard. A few moments of consideration were all he needed to shake his head and get moving. It was a lot of fur, but no one could seriously consider him a werewolf on that alone, much less try and stalk him in a city like this without looking suspicious, or him catching their scent.

Outside, despite his denim jacket, he shivered at how much cooler it was without any fur coating him. His stashed backpack was then recovered, the contents emptied out onto his bed as he looked back on the time he'd spent as a werewolf.

The doe was still heavy on his mind, as was how hostile Bailey had been at first. The close calls, real and self-imposed, he'd had with his parents slowly overshadowed those two things until the guilt he hadn't felt from before everything happened surfaced. If he'd worked up the guts to tell them before... But then, all that aside, his first full moon hadn't been as unbearable as he'd been fearing. The shift coming out of nowhere had been a shock, but learning to work with his canine-ish body and heightened senses had been simple enough, and an interesting experience. That he'd kept his sanity after the shift had been a welcome discovery too.

It was when he began questioning if it would be any easier if his parents, maybe his friends, knew what was happening that he had to take a moment to compose himself. Sane or not, he'd been lucky so far. Would that even last for all of the next twenty-nine days?

Egh, get a grip. I still have time.

* * *

Hours later, when Alex arrived at campus, his still strong feeling of relief and pleasure from being human again and being able to move freely in broad daylight proved effective at keeping him from feeling too uneasy. Heading upstairs to a spot he knew was quiet, and his phone blaring his metal soundtrack through his headphones, helped as well.

As his first class approached, his phone sounded the IM received tone. Nathan had sent it.

Nathan T.: Are you OK? You're being a
bit too quiet.

Alex paced the typing of his response.

Alex S.: Yeah, I'm fine. Didn't feel
good yesterday.

Nathan T.: I thought so. What happened?

Alex S.: Headaches and nausea. No
idea what caused it.

Nathan T.: Those bites, maybe?

Alex felt a chill at that.

Alex S.: Don't think so. Would've happened
weeks ago, if that was the reason.

Nathan T.: I guess. Anyway, glad to
hear it. Catch you later.

Alex S.: You too, man.

As his classes began, Alex was left wondering why Nathan had questioned the bites, but nothing else. He saw no reason to believe his friend suspected lycanthropy, but how quickly he'd responded left him unable to shake the feeling that it was possible. Halfway into his second class, whether because of time or his questioning of his friend's knowledge, his anxiety recovered its strength. Despite the whiffs of the tennis ball, he felt urged to leave the room as soon as he was able.

He was nearing the stairwell when Catherine's voice reached him and stopped him. After spotting her, he waited for her to come closer, managing a quick greeting before a lump formed in his throat.

"Hey. You feeling better?"

Figuring Nathan had told her, Alex responded first with a nod. "Yeah."

"That's good." Though she stopped talking, she looked like she was trying to recall something.

"Something up?" Alex asked.

"There was something... Oh, that curfew that's going on. I meant to text you about that the other day."

"Oh. Yeah, Dad told me about it on Sunday. Why? You and Marcus get stopped?"

"No. Heard about it on the news. Thought you'd know something about it."

"A bit. It's in place because these animal attacks are all happening at night."

"I figured. Did your dad say if it was a stay-inside-after-dark curfew?"

"No, but I think it's more of a no-public-places-after-this-time one."

"Makes sense."

"Yeah. This city's too big for a lock-down kind of curfew."

Hearing a blip from Catherine's phone, he watched her answer the text she got. "Oh, wow."

"What?"

She gestured him closer. "Another dead animal at our high school."

Alex skimmed what he could see before gesturing for her phone. The article had gone live four hours ago. As he scrolled down and read over the description of the discovery, it read like hadn't bothered to hide the carcass.

He didn't notice Catherine wrinkle her nose before she made the same gesture for her phone back. "That makes five, and one person."

"Five?"

The surprise in Catherine's tone was Alex's signal to continue. "Yeah. That calf from last month, this doe, and three others between them." She kept quiet after his response, as though lost in thought or processing what she'd been told. "I didn't know either until the other day."

"Still, that many?"

"Not a comforting thought, I know."

"No kidding." Both Alex and Catherine went silent until he asked if there was something else on her mind. "No. Glad to know you're feeling better, though."

"Thanks. Appreciate it."

When they reached the first floor and began to split up, Catherine called for Alex to wait. "You remember what the thirtieth is, right?"

"Marcus's birthday. I haven't forgotten." As Catherine smiled, nodded, and then resumed her walk, Alex waved goodbye to her, then went straight home.

With Bailey by his side, he looked up the article Catherine had shown him. His first thought after a second read of it was the carcass had been moved after he left it, and that possibility made him shiver. Had he been followed? And if he had been, was it the were that bit him? Or another one?

He stood up from the chair he'd been sitting in before second guessing the idea of going near the location. Weekdays meant school activities, and active bodies. Sniffing at the grass like an animal was the last thing he needed to be doing around others. *Nighttime might work better...if there's even a trace to find by that point.* He pictured shifting only his nose and muzzle to help with such a search, the question of if such a thing was possible following.

When his mother returned home around four, it wasn't long before she stopped by his door.

"Hey, Mom," Alex said after pausing the game he'd been playing.

"Do you know what happened to those patties and hot dogs we bought last week?"

Alex almost facepalmed at hearing that. "Yeah. The patties were starting to smell, so I tossed them out. The hot dogs I ate."

"They went bad that quickly?"

"Smelled like it."

"Huh." His mother's pause hinted at the loss of the receipt for the patties, which relieved him. "In that case, I'll get some more when we go shopping tonight."

As his parents prepared to leave once his father returned home, Alex felt spurred to go with them. Had it not been the day that he'd shifted back to his human form, he would've stayed home. The ride saw a few questions asked of him before they arrived, if he had any money with him being one.

"I've got some. Wednesday's our pay-day." Alex pulled two twenties from his wallet as they parked.

Glancing over to the Blue Moon storefront before following his folks inside the grocer, he split off and stocked up on the foods he wanted, his mind on next month as he tried to filter out, and not get disoriented by, the store's ocean of scents. Within ten minutes, he had everything he could afford and rejoined his folks.

Although thankful they didn't ask too many questions about his haul of meats and similar snacks, as they found and entered one of the shorter lines, which to Alex's surprise was being run by Cameron, a sudden high-pitched tone made him clamp his eyes shut, grit his teeth, and nod his head, one hand reaching towards his right ear.

"Son, you okay?" his father asked.

"Yeah," Alex quickly lied as he opened his eyes and faked stroking his chin. *The hell's making that noise?* His glances around gave him no clue about what was making it, and how easily it pierced his skull made it seem like it was coming from all around him.

Alex stood less than a second more of it before he took a step back; his folks would buy that he'd suddenly felt dizzy. With his next two steps the noise weakened, giving him an idea of where it was coming from, but then, just as quickly as it came, it ceased.

With a wipe of his eyes, he looked back towards the registers, but still saw nothing that could've caused the sound. The looks on the faces of his parents, as well as his still ringing ears, made him hope the sound didn't happen again before they left.

Though Cameron was giving him a similar look, Alex flashed him a thumbs-up, which was returned in kind. That was when the customer Cameron was checking out loudly asked if he was done. Alex's urge to say something at that conflicted with his fears of drawing the attention of so many strangers. With a loud huff, he bit his tongue and waited for his folks to pay for their stuff.

Something that smelled of alcohol got his attention as he walked near where the loud customer had recently stood, the sharp and fresh scents drifting with it shaping his outlook. *Lovely.*

"So, this is where you work."

"For now, yeah. How's things?" Cameron asked as he started ringing the items.

"Alright, more or less." Alex glanced aside and spotted the customer skimming his receipt, thumbing his direction before continuing. "That guy give you grief?"

Cameron shrugged. "Yeah. Quite a few of those in here tonight."

"Any as drunk as he is?"

"No. Least I don't think so."

"Hope not."

Cameron chuckled at that, only for the drunk customer to come back and once again get loud, his outburst aimed at him. Alex caught more of the alcohol scent from his breath and shook his head as his annoyance built, his response coming only when his fear of attention was fully supplanted by it.

"Hey, shut up and calm down." He licked his teeth as the drunk customer looked at him.

"Does this involve you?"

"Does you being drunk and disorderly involve us?"

"What?"

"You heard me." The customer almost took a step forward before his eyes widened in shock as if he'd just been slapped. With his order still unpaid, Alex glanced back at Cameron and slipped him the bills he needed. The tension in his gut had begun to resurface by the time he'd slipped past and towards his parents, hopefully away from the attention he knew he'd drawn.

Outside, his father was the first to speak. "Alex, why did you do that?"

Alex shrugged. "Eh. Had to say something."

"That he was drunk?"

Alex almost blurted out that he'd smelled alcohol. "He was acting that way to me."

"That's still not a smart thing to do, Son."

His mother then chimed in. "Good thing you walked away. I thought he was going to hit you."

While trying not to show that his limbs were shaking, Alex huffed again, his father easing him forward after a second. During the ride home, the look on the customer's face didn't leave his thoughts. How frightened he'd looked versus insulted.

Chapter 13 - Reflections

Wednesday, September 13th, 2011
Moon Phase – Waning Gibbous
1:35 p.m.

The next day, despite the nearby tennis ball and constant assurances that only the professors truly cared about his absences, Alex found fighting the onset of anxiety throughout his first class more difficult. After class was over and he was alone upstairs, the feelings settled to a marginally more comfortable threshold, freeing up his mind to wonder about the doe and why the carcass had been moved.

After checking the dates of the killings against his lunar calendar, he found that all of them had happened within a week of him being bitten, leaving a ten-day gap between them and the recent full moon.

Two crescents and the new moon... So, it's smart enough to kill on dark nights. Then again, the calf wasn't that well-hidden either.

It took Alex recalling hearing back to back sirens during his trek home for a theory to form. That after he'd left, the other werewolf had come in, eaten its fill, and then tried to haul the carcass away, only to be scared into dropping it and then running off. How much time had separated them, if any, was Alex's next concern. For all he knew, the werewolf had been hiding downwind of him the whole time.

His concern and the accompanying chill in his skin hung around until Nathan arrived for his next class. Aside from the document he had open and was pecking away at on his laptop, there was a PDF open with 'Character Sheet' in the header.

"You look busy," Alex said as the professor arrived.

"Yeah. Paper for my Professional Writing class," Nathan replied, continuing once he stopped typing. "Think I may have to spend tonight getting it done. You feeling better, though?"

Alex nodded. "I felt better after some water, so guess it was dehydration."

"Good to know."

Hearing no hint of suspicion in his friend's tone, Alex relaxed a bit.

* * *

Once class let out and he began to stand up, Alex felt Nathan tap his shoulder.

"Question," he began. "That skatepark you told me about? What's their policy on filming?"

"Haven't asked the owner about that yet. Thanks for reminding me, though."

"Let me know once you do, though these next few weeks are gonna be pretty crammed for me," Nathan said as he too stood up.

"How so? More homework than you expected?"

"Not yet, thankfully. You remember the campaign I was running for Mage last year?" Nathan asked, pointing at Alex as he did so.

"Yeah. You starting a new one?"

Nathan nodded. "I'm two players short, so if you're interested..."

"No joke I'm interested," Alex replied with a growing grin. "Anything noteworthy about the campaign, though?"

"It's set in Iowa, so expect lots of fields, exploring, and maybe a few Fae or Garou."

"Changelings, werewolves, and magicians. That should be fun." After a final word from Nathan about when he expected word from a potential third player, Alex shook his hand and the two parted ways once back on the first floor.

* * *

Back at home, with a steak sub ready for his lunch, Alex let Bailey out before sneaking a taste when his pet was distracted. With it, his memory of the doe returned, of how soft and warm the animal's muscle and viscera was compared to how stringy and tough the roasted meat was. His heart beat faster in response, and the sight of the rest of his meal suddenly felt like an unpleasant reminder of his actions.

Even after the sub was stashed in the fridge, the memory continued to prod him as dinner approached, the lingering tension in his throat getting him to retreat to the bathroom.

The resulting dip in his appetite soon got his mother's attention. "How come you're not eating?"

Alex snuck a glance up at her. "Just thinking about something."

"Like what?"

Alex stalled too long on an answer, and then saw his dad looking over him.

"You look a bit upset. Did something happen?"

Feeling like he was being pulled back into the motions from before the full moon, but with his pool of lies dying up, Alex continued to stall.

When he forced out a 'No', a weak shake of his head accompanying his answer, his father continued. "C'mon, Son. What's going on?"

Alex didn't reply until a third look at his meal elicited a lick of his teeth. "It's nothing. I'll get over it."

"Get over what?" Alex tried to keep his hands away from his face upon hearing the concern in his mother's voice, but found no courage to respond in turn.

"Alex, if something's bothering you, tell us." His father's tone stayed firm as he spoke, and Alex's hope of keeping the truth from his folks for another week, much less another month, vanished.

"Trying not to let it," he finally said.

"That's admirable, but you've been behaving strangely as of late, and I get the feeling you're holding a lot in about something."

"You feel like talking about it?" his mother asked after a brief pause.

Alex slowed his breathing to relax. "Not right now." The lack of questioning following that statement helped even more, though he still ate slowly for a time.

When he scratched at his chest to get a hand close to his necklace, his silver theory was brought into question. Was the metal really keeping him sane if a hunger for animal meat could affect him as it had? Or was it helping him stay sane in the face of it? Recalling how long he'd stayed inside after it surfaced, despite how quickly it had worsened, the latter felt more plausible.

Friday, September 16th, 2011
Moon Phase – Waning Gibbous

For the rest of the night, and most of Thursday, Alex kept an eye on his parents' interest in his mood and actions. Though they didn't directly question his readiness to talk, which he was thankful for, how frequently he felt under observation, even when doing innocuous things, clawed at his insides.

With plans set to spend as much of Friday as he could skating to get his mind off it all, while sitting outside his first class that morning, he heard a text come through.

Nathan T.: Hey, man. Good news.
Found our last player.

> *Alex S.*: Nice. What's our start date?

Nathan T.: Next Monday. We'll be
setting up characters for the first
session or two.

I'll tell you more in class, though.

> *Alex S.*: Got it. Thanks.
>
> Oh, I asked Walter about filming
> in the park. It's perfectly fine by him.

Several minutes passed before Alex got a reply.

Nathan T.: In that case, I've got four
to eight tonight free. After that, I have
the campaign and classwork to focus on.

> *Alex S.*: Understandable.

Alex's eagerness to hear more about the first session did little to counter the increase in anxiety his first class faced him with. His first test of the semester had arrived, and along with having to take copies from the stack his professor held and hand them out, both actions that drew eyes and attention his way, the tennis ball, along with his backpack, had to be left on the floor. How fast his heartbeat remained throughout the test duration, along with his refusal to take his jacket off at the risk of attracting more attention, left him sweating by the time he was done.

* * *

Until Nathan arrived at the shop around 4:00, Alex killed the time that he wasn't riding around the park chatting up Cameron and Walter. By 6:15, the camcorder's battery was on its last legs.

"Should have enough for a few more minutes," Nathan said as Alex rolled to a stop nearby.

"That's fine. Just one more trick and I'll call it a day." Alex then eyed a rail he'd used a few times and directed Nathan towards it. "That's perfect," he said once his friend was in position.

"Then...recording." Alex pushed off at that statement, towards the quarterpipe ahead of him. The incline he rolled down added enough speed to let him reach and grind its lip with both trucks. After dropping back in, he aimed for the rail, his initial grind shifting into a Tailslide before he slid himself off.

"Nice, man. Looks great," Alex said as the low battery icon continued to flash on the camcorder's preview screen.

"You hoping to impress the owner with any of this?" Nathan asked as he gave Alex the SD card with the footage.

"I think just being social will do that, but it never hurts."

As Alex pulled out his phone to check for messages, Nathan slipped him a suggestion. "Hey, you feel like heading over to Half-Price Books for a while?"

"Yeah, sure. Might go get something to eat first, though."

* * *

Alex chose a place halfway down the strip center from the bookstore, leaving him more than enough time to consume half of his meal and most of his drink during the return walk. Inside the store, as he cut between two entrance displays, heading towards the rows of shelves along the store's right side, a casual breath brought with it the skin scent of the werewolf that bit him.

He noticed it again with another sniff, and his pulse jumped in turn. After backing up into a more open position, he glanced around and counted seven other people in the store: five customers, one employee at the main register, and Catherine behind the trade-in counter. She gave him a wave as the two of them matched each other's gaze, Alex returning the gesture, but turning away immediately after. *Shit, is it still here?*

At first thinking he needed to walk closer to where Catherine was to be sure, Alex instead circled the shelving he was near. The scent was nowhere in the air around the side closest to the shop entrance. *Which way did it go?* He doubled back and headed into the aisle dividing the rows of bookshelves, picking up the trail within a step and then losing it as he approached the end of the collection of rows, the draft behind him sweeping the scent near his nose when he stopped moving.

He stepped back and inched into the nearby aisles until he found the scent again. It trailed towards the back wall, then forked left. Alex followed it towards the trade-in counter, now wishing he was invisible and had his more sensitive werewolf nose.

As he came close to the counter, the scent became scattered and interspersed with others who'd walked by. A collection of scents like decayed spice and chemicals filtered through sweat glands made him exhale through his nose and shake his head.

"Yeah," Catherine said. Alex looked aside to see her waving a makeshift paper fan near her face. "That last guy was a special kind of ripe."

"Uh huh." Masking his worry as best he could, Alex quickly continued. "I'll be back in a sec." After Catherine nodded, he stepped away and huffed to clear his nose, before locating a strengthening trail a few aisles away from where Nathan was standing.

As he got back to following it, the opening of the store's door got him to stop and rush left down the nearest aisle, only to see two people coming in, but no one leaving. *Gotta be over here somewhere.* When that crossed his mind, he was left wondering just what he could do if he did find the werewolf. He could observe it, but without looking suspicious himself? *Probably need some stuff in my hands...look more like a customer.*

With a walk past the gaming aisle, and Nathan, to be sure the trail was still there, Alex doubled back and went for two easy-to-hold game cases, spotting the aquamarine-colored rulebook of the Mage game his friend was working on.

"They just brought that out," Nathan said after a brief glance up from the book he had. "Already looked through it. It's in good shape."

Perfect. "Thanks, man," Alex said before opening the book to a random page. He then stepped out of the aisle and resumed his trek.

The scent stayed strong for one more aisle before the doors opened once again. This time, Alex reached the end of the closest aisle to find three people leaving, one holding the door for the first two. The path he took in turn—a beeline towards the south wall, then a few steps into each aisle he had passed—didn't see him walk through any trails the werewolf had left. A check of the area close to the doors gave him the same result, but as he walked past the single operating register, the scent became noticeable again, only for it to weaken before he reached the closest shelf.

Alex walked a wider sweep of the entrance and nearby aisles in turn, finding only the weakened remnants of the trail he'd walked through after entering the store. Now torn between relief and worry, he stopped walking near the trade-in counter to collect his thoughts. How fresh had the scents been? Had the werewolf come and gone while he'd been out getting his meal? Did it know about his friendships with two of the people in the store?

Catherine snuck up on him while the latter question was on his mind. "Hey."

Alex jumped in response, and then looked back at her as cold pinpricks formed under his skin. "Thanks for that."

"You okay?" Although Alex was quick to respond with a nod, the expression of concern that remained on his face was the stronger signal to his friend. "You sure? Doesn't look like it."

"Just thinking about something." When Catherine didn't respond, Alex glanced over to find her looking at something beyond him. Figuring it was Nathan, he turned his direction to find him coming closer, a stack of books and game cases held in one arm.

The resultant small talk between them slowly tempered Alex's unease, despite the werewolf remaining on mind.

"Yeah, we should probably move." Catherine said after he glanced around a few times.

"It's not that busy in here," Nathan said.

"Eh, just in case." Once they'd relocated to the gaming aisle, Catherine continued. "Oh, while I've got you guys here, question: Do you think we should go somewhere nice to eat for Marcus's birthday?"

Alex shrugged at first. "Like where?"

Nathan jumped in as Catherine tried to think of an answer. "Hang on. Shouldn't we plan on doing all of this earlier in the day?"

"What fo—" Catherine began, before finishing with, "oh, right. The curfew."

Alex spoke up after a second. "So long as we don't hang around a park or someplace really open like that after eight, we'll be fine."

"Good to know," Nathan said.

Alex nodded and then thumbed towards Catherine before he spoke. "Like I told her the other day, there's no way a city this big can go under lockdown for a curfew."

"Makes me wonder though. How long will it go on?"

"No idea. Dad's only getting animal attack reports in relation to this thing, so…"

"No sightings?" Catherine asked, to which Alex shook his head. "Have you told him you saw it?"

Alex almost stalled too long. "Never told him, or mom."

Catherine raised an eyebrow at that. "You probably should. They're going to find out at some point, I'm sure."

When Alex stayed silent beyond a sigh and then looked away, his pulse rising a few beats at that sentence, Nathan took over. "Speaking of those wolves, something just occurred to me." Alex glanced up at him, only to see his attention turn towards his right arm. "How did you get bitten on your arm?"

Alex fought his urge to walk away. He could feel Nathan and Catherine's eyes on him, expecting an answer. Too much wayward information… But too much deception or unwillingness… *Don't make me do this, guys.*

It took him until he reigned in his emotions to say anything, a length of time that felt close to a minute.

"It snapped at me, I backed up and tripped, and then it went for me." The crack in his voice and the pause after prompted Catherine to ask if he was okay, to which Alex nodded. "I guess I have kept it from my folks too long."

After Alex's head and gaze tilted down, Catherine's look of worry towards Nathan was met with him mouthing, 'Something's up', before he tilted his head to the left.

"Well, just tell them you freaked and kept it to yourself because you didn't get sick," Catherine said. "I'd believe that. They probably would."

"Maybe," Alex replied, squeezing his forehead as he spoke.

Chapter 14 – Trust and Risk

Saturday, September 17th, 2011
Moon Phase – Waning Gibbous
6:02 p.m.

Alex spent the morning and afternoon of Saturday waiting for what he thought was the right moment to make the first move. The thought of what his parents would say, the shrinking of his gut when he stayed near them for longer than a minute, and every hint of them watching him all worked against him the few times he felt the moment coming close. Shortly before six in the evening, he wrote the day off as a loss and headed outside to clear his head.

A south-bound cold front began to blow through as he got to practicing on his grind-box, the chill biting through the denim of his jacket. When the thought of growing a bit of fur to counter the chill returned, a shake of his head swept the idea away. For all he knew, if he tried to pull off something like that, he'd fully turn.

The thought stuck around as he set up his board for another run at his grindbox. Though not a horrifying prospect initially, the next question across his mind made it one: was there something, or some situation, that would make him change when he didn't want to?

Alex felt ready to smack himself for not thinking about that sooner, until a few seconds of consideration had passed. He didn't have anger issues or a tendency to stay angry at things, both things he figured were likely to trigger a shift. The discomfort and apprehension he was feeling around strangers hadn't caused a shift yet, and likely wouldn't. He gave the idea a little longer to stew, but couldn't see a reason for an involuntary shift beyond his life being threatened.

That just left voluntary shifts, and if and how he could cause one. The pain and soreness he could handle, and he had enough food to counter the hunger he'd have once it was over, but what overshadowed those facts was what the point would be in shifting outside of the full moon. He paced around the garage once before something about his first time struck him: how nervous Bailey had been with him in that form.

He's not used to me being like that. If I did it more often...

Though he didn't finish the thought, one reason a voluntary shift could be to his benefit soon came to him. He'd made a lot of noise and had to rush around when it happened the first time because he hadn't seen any of it coming, and then he'd ended up recovering from the resulting soreness for hours. And his parents. If he couldn't keep or convince them to stay away when it had to happen next, they'd be hearing everything he went through, or possibly seeing him half-shifted. If every noise out of him was a pained growl or a pant, or he was caught in the wrong place when his bones started breaking...

Alex shook aside the image of his parents reacting to that, and the roaring screams he'd made when it had happened, his arms briefly wrapping around his body. He knew already what would change and when, and a glass or two of water would help if he got dehydrated again, but if more shifting would make it easier on his body, that would be a plus overall. And if he did shift, that would mean he had to find a way to turn back, something that would be a huge benefit to know if the worst ever did happen and a shift came when he didn't want it.

Maybe I should consider it.

He gave the idea one more minute of consideration before pulling his phone out and checking the lunar calendar against the coming dates. The Last Quarter phase was coming up on the twentieth, and the New on the twenty-seventh, but with school and work factored in, the only days he truly had free were Sundays.

The twenty-fourth might work best... Wait a sec. Isn't campus closed for a day next week? Heading inside to check his class syllabuses, Wednesday, the date of the Last Quarter, was that date. *Mom's home at five usually... If I wake up early enough, I'll have nine or so hours to myself.*

Hoping that would be enough time, Alex pocketed his phone and sat back in his desk chair to continue to think on things.

Monday, September 19th, 2011
Moon Phase - Waning Gibbous

As the start of his second class drew closer, Alex kept his attention buried in his Mage rulebook, noting some aspects of the character he wished to build. Nathan took the seat next to him when he arrived and was quick to ask about it.

"Got an Acanthus character in mind this time," Alex said as he dug his class papers out of his backpack.

"Nice. Everyone's meeting in the commons at four, but I think we'll just be spending today making characters."

Alex nodded in response. "Can't wait, man." His enthusiasm held throughout the first fifteen minutes of class, before taking a dip when the professor started calling out students to answer questions on the homework from the weekend. Hoping he wouldn't be called, Alex kept his head down, pencil in hand to fake taking notes.

"Actually, you should've gotten three as your answer," the professor said after a student two seats behind him had given her answer. "Don't leave these looking like fractions if possible. Okay…Alex? Question number nine, please."

Despite his head already turned down, towards the answer he'd logged, hearing his name shot Alex's pulse up by almost twenty beats, his breathing quickening to compensate.

He moved his paper around, for what reason he didn't know. *Shit. Say six. That's it.* He couldn't. He wanted everyone's eyes off him. On someone else.

"Do you have the homework for today?" the professor asked.

Damn it. When he forced out a 'Yes', embarrassment rushed in to mix with his cresting fear, and he balled a fist under the desk. Although the professor didn't coax him, when he noticed Nathan lean over, his friend was quick to answer for him. "Six is what he got." Alex grimaced at that, the fingers of his right hand squeezing his face for nearly a minute.

Once class was at last over, Nathan stuck close to him as they left the room, easing him aside after they'd covered some distance. "That was new," he said.

With the old emotions still simmering, Alex went with the first thought he had. "Second-guessed my answer at the last second."

"That's not what it looked like to me," Nathan replied, his tone showing hints of worry. "It looked like you were verging on a panic attack."

Great. Alex bit his tongue, unable to think of a way to defuse that outlook or to stop thinking about what would happen the next time.

"That's never happened before?"

"No. Never has." Although his friend didn't reply to that, the location his eyes drifted to—his right arm—was enough of a hint to what he was thinking. He kept quiet as he noticed another student coming their way.

As they passed, the draft that followed pulled whiffs of Nathan's scent near Alex's nose. Punctuating the familiar makeup was a pungent smell he didn't recognize, one that, instead of being repulsive, was calming.

As he wondered what the scent was, Alex adjusted his jacket and then spoke up. "I still haven't told Dad yet, if you're wondering."

"Hmm... If you don't mind my asking then, how come?"

At that question, just like with his parents the day after he was bitten, Alex struggled to think of a response. Several seconds went by as he tried, his friend's continued silence pushing him towards and then past several answers. What he eventually settled on came only after Nathan said, "I don't think he'll stay angry with you if you tell him and give a good description."

"I know he won't, but I freaked out back then, fibbed my way out of it... I know he'll grill me for it, but even if I tell him, what good will it do?"

"What do you mean?"

Alex took a breath to focus. "Every officer's already watching for large canines, but like I said before, no sightings. And if the precinct hasn't seen that thing yet, and there's a curfew in place, what use would telling the truth and giving a description be?"

Nathan once again didn't respond to that, but the length of his silence, and what Alex once again saw when he glanced at him—his eyes darting between his arm, his face, and someplace behind him—made his heart speed up and his skin tighten.

"I get what you're saying, but...can I be frank with you for a minute?"

Alex felt a shiver come on at that. "Sure."

Nathan then pointed at his arm. "I think something happened beyond you getting bitten. You've never been shy about telling me or Marcus or Catherine when these things happen, and less than two weeks to heal? That can't be possible for a bite that large." He paused for a moment, and then sighed. "I know it's not my place to pry, but after that near panic episode you had... Whatever's going on with you, it's starting to scare me."

Alex bit his tongue as Nathan stopped talking, trying not to show that he felt cornered or that sadness was building in his chest. His friend's tone had been thick with unease, but he saw only bad outcomes from telling his friend of so many years the truth.

Nothing was stopping him from distancing himself from him for any number of resulting fears, and if he was already noticing this much wrong with him, Marcus and Catherine would also. With his heart still racing, the idea of one or more of his longtime friends never speaking to him again crossed Alex's mind. His throat knotted in effect, and his free hand soon reached up to massage it.

"You need a minute?" Alex nodded and swallowed. He saw no way out of this, aside from more delaying. Looking over the Mage rulebook cover didn't help, but it did get Nathan to talk. "Tell you what. After the session, if you want to tell me something, I'll stick around and listen."

A single word of thanks was all Alex got out, his voice showing signs of cracking. After a few seconds to compose himself, he let Nathan leave first, detouring to the nearest bathroom afterwards to check how red his face was.

* * *

The session began a few minutes after 4:00. As it progressed, between the periods of building his character, Alex kept questioning what, if anything, he could trust his friend with without giving him cause to keep away.

He didn't bring up last Monday...but he did question the healing speed. Alex rubbed his chin as he looked over his character sheet. *Is he thinking werewolf? How could he?* That concern stuck in Alex's head the longest. Even if his friends knew nothing now, if something happened that revealed what he was, or put them in danger... *Hope it's difficult to shift on my own.*

The session began to wrap up around 8:30, and as Alex waited for the other players to leave, he kept an eye on his friend. The last few hours of role-playing and dice-rolling was keeping his attention the most, as were the other players asking him questions. Once they had all gone and his friend was looking his direction, Alex tilted his head to the side.

Most of the commons was empty by then, but he still led his friend toward where he felt the safest from curious, passing ears. With how much each step felt like a move towards a threshold he could never walk back across, Alex came to a stop with the idea of walking away, of saying it wasn't worth it, fighting for control of his legs.

"I'm ready when you are," Nathan said after he stopped walking.

Alex closed his eyes and took a slow breath, bringing his hand near his mouth before he spoke. "When's the next time you're off work?"

"Without class on the same day? Sunday."

So that would be three of us...

"How come? Did you have something in mind?"

"Just a hangout at my place. For a few hours."

"I'd be up for it."

Alex questioned for a moment how laid-back his friend's response was, brushing it off after figuring he was trying not to pry as he'd said before. "Then I'll see if Catherine and Marcus can make it as well."

"I don't think she has Sunday as a work day..."

"I'll ask. I want all four of us to be there, though."

"How come?"

"To get something off my chest. I'd rather not talk about it until we can all hear the same thing."

"I get you."

Alex let out a sigh, his tense chest laxing in turn. "Thanks, man. And thanks for being up front with me before."

"Anytime. That's what I'm here for."

After exchanging a handshake with his friend, Alex departed from the campus main building, confidence building in his mind in stark contrast to just minutes before, and what thoughts remained that he was making another huge mistake.

Wednesday, September 21st, 2011
Moon Phase - Last Quarter

When he awoke Wednesday morning, Alex paced the house, locking all the major windows and doors, closing all the blinds and curtains, and then did a second walk to be sure he hadn't missed anything. *Alright. Eight or so hours to myself. Should be plenty of time.*

After a quick stroking of Bailey's pelt, he went for a shower to think on things. Exhaustion was a given if he pulled it off, but if he did, would he be able to change back before his folks came home? Unable to see enough reason to believe he could, even with the passing of several minutes, Alex moved his thoughts to planning an escape and where to hide.

I could use the closet again... He tossed that idea upon remembering how claustrophobic and burglarish it had felt hiding in there. His room felt a touch more secure and safe, if he kept the door shut and muted his phone, but if he 'didn't come home' again, or his parents heard him changing back...

Catherine's warning about his folks finding out at some point started replaying in his head, even after a light shake of it. If he warned them ahead of time... But how could he without sounding like he was putting them in danger, or giving them reason to question him even more?

He let that question, and the possible answers, cycle through his thoughts as he got a soda and sipped it. A short time later, with his dad's number dialed, Alex felt his chest tighten as each ring went unanswered until the third one.

"Hey, Son."

"Hey, Dad."

"Something going on?"

"No. Just wanted to say that...that I've got something to tell you and Mom tonight."

"I see." His father's response was calming, despite sounding inquisitive.

"I didn't do anything bad. It's just about what happened last week."

"Okay."

"Then...I guess I'll see you later."

"You too, Son. See you later."

Alex inhaled and then sighed as he hung up, dialing his mother's number as soon as he felt composed enough. She noticed the unease in his tone within the first sentence, but sounded pleased at hearing he wanted to talk.

Chapter 15 – Do They Know?

Wednesday, September 21st, 2011
Moon Phase – Last Quarter

After saying goodbye and hanging up, Alex checked the time. 9:31. Seven hours left to find out at least one way he could shift on his own, or to prepare for a talk with his folks.

Anger was his first thought for starting a shift, but along with feeling more mentally drained than angry over the last week, he had no idea if that kind of trigger, if it was one at all, would cost him his sanity, or something else. Hunger was out of the question in that respect as well. *What else could do it?* Pain was a possibility, but he'd hurt himself plenty while skateboarding over the last week. The idea of purposefully hurting himself was quickly brushed aside with a head shake.

Hmm... Maybe I can imagine it and start it that way? After Alex shuddered at the thought of being caught in the wrong position again, he left his room and got a glass of water and ice.

Bailey followed him back, keeping silent, though staring at him with a slight wag to his tail. "C'mon, boy." Alex said before leading his pet into the backyard. He slipped back inside after a few strokes of Bailey's neck and body, then removed his tee and jeans once he was back in his room.

After checking his necklace, Alex leaned against his bed, shut his eyes, and started recalling how he'd felt exploring the house as a werewolf, his learning how to move with animal-like legs, and how much he'd enjoyed exploring once outside. A minute passed with no change in how he felt, prompting a change in his tactic. This time, he pictured himself once again going through the change. Though his breathing picked up speed as he became more absorbed in the thought, his memory soon flipped to the intense pain that followed being on his feet when his metatarsals snapped, and then what he thought it would look like from someone else's perspective. From his parent's.

His concentration broke. *Damnit... They're not here. They won't see it.* As he gave it another shot, he succeeded in ignoring that image, but couldn't get as absorbed into the idea anymore. Bailey's sudden barking only made it harder.

After redressing and letting his dog back inside, Alex retrieved his skateboard and headed out front, sticking to casually coasting up and down the driveway to keep his mind freed. Despite that, he couldn't come up with any new ideas, and tried to refocus to what he would tell his folks when they came home.

Several minutes later, he readied for a handplant, slapping his hand against the pavement and then pulling his weight up and over it. Near the apex of the trick, Alex misjudged how far forward he placed his weight and began to fall towards his back.

He tucked his head and reached out to try and catch himself, to no avail. He hit the ground on his back, his right wrist bending back sharply before whipping free of the pavement, the concrete scraping off some of his skin.

As he held his wrist with his free hand, his pulse and breathing shot up. Before he could think to massage the area, or even get up, Alex felt the first of many tinglings and quiverings under the skin around his wrist, with cricking noises reaching his ears as he brought his breathing under control. As the ligaments of his injured wrist then stretched and contracted, pulling his fingers in ways he was certain he wasn't choosing, the intensity of the pain weakened. When everything stopped, only a moderate level of soreness was left.

Alex then pulled himself to his feet and went inside, the event putting his mind back on the first time he'd shifted. He recalled the image of his hands turning to paws, the shock he'd felt from seeing that, and the sudden, wrenching changes to his body, getting in only one flex of his injured hand before the nerves in his fingers began to give out. *Oh, shit.* His pulse stayed elevated as he looked down at them, and within seconds, his fingernails popped up. Underneath them were the tips of his claws, the bone-white color untouched by any red.

Torn between fear and pride at what he was seeing, Alex wasted no time racing to his room and stripping his clothes off, leaving only his necklace. With Bailey elsewhere, he shut his bedroom door, tasting blood as his teeth shaped into fangs, his hands continuing their change into paws as the puppeting moved into the muscles of his arms, legs, and chest.

Saliva welled in his mouth as he held it open, making him tilt his head up to swallow. The best drink he could get from the glass he'd prepared washed away the blood, though the taste remained. As he leaned against his desk to let his muscles continue to flex and grow, the pitch of his breathing and groaning dropped. Only when he felt in full control of his legs did he lower himself to the floor, one paw keeping near the closest leg of his bed in prep for what was next.

The Charlie-horse sensation of rods being shoved into his leg muscles left him gasping and massaging his legs, only for his paws to be urged away to rub at the skin under his emerging pelt. As his tail formed and his ears changed their shapes, the hints of bones cracking grew loud enough for him to hear. His ribs and sternum gave way first, his expanding chest cavity once again leaving him worried about panting or breathing in or out too long. The last pair of them set just before the cracking of his skull and jaw made them both go slack. With his lengthening muzzle pointed up, Alex held off trying to swallow until it was fully formed, his first chance coming a second before his legs and feet began to change.

When he could no longer hear his bones breaking, he gave everything a second, and then let his limbs drop to the floor. His eyes then opened, but immediately closed again to clear them of stored tears.

As the only sound in the room continued to be his quivering, growl-laced breathing, he couldn't help feeling accomplished, and a bit horrified. *What time is it?* Once Alex pulled himself onto all fours, he fished his phone from his jeans pocket and waited for the screen to adjust.

10:19. Good, I still have a few hours. Phone still in-hand, Alex propped himself against his bed's headrest to relax some more. Though his muscles weren't as sore nor his skin as tingly as they had been after his first shift, the aching of his bones and how soggy his undercoat felt kept him standing in the draft from the AC vent.

When he was interrupted by the grumbling of his stomach, he raided the kitchen, costing him two of the hot dog packages and one double pack of patties. Several times throughout, the sodium-laced, meat filler offerings were compared against the warmth of the doe's muscle and viscera, his head shaking after the second time. 10:53 was what the stove clock read when he finished, and once back in his room, he stretched out onto his bed to think.

How long did he have to wait before he could change back? An hour? Until his bones and joints no longer ached? Or could he change back at any time, if he found the right means? Though the last possibility seemed the most likely, Alex saw little reason to think he could do it just by imagining it happening. He'd managed this shift thanks to his memories of his first one, and the shot of adrenaline from being hurt. Would it take something as drastic to turn him back?

And if he couldn't find a way in time, would his past escape route still work?

He gave himself some time to consider it all, massaging a few sore spots around his legs and face in the meantime. When Bailey appeared outside of his room, Alex dangled his right arm over the side of his bed.

"It's me, boy," he said, hoping his pet would come closer. Although his posture wasn't in line with being afraid, Bailey kept his distance and did little beyond stare. *Guess he's still nervous.*

Alex looked over his paw as he withdrew it, noting the claws and how he easily had twice the bulk of his human form like this. He had been considering fear as a possible way to reverse the shift, but if his mere presence was unsettling to others, being in this form was too advantageous to bring on that emotion—or so it seemed at first. His still-present fears of being discovered in this form, of what could result from it, was much different than that of fearing for his life.

But if that was a possible means to shift back, he would be cutting it very close with his folks. Possibly so close that he'd give them enough time, and enough audio signals, to find him changing forms anyway.

As 11:30 approached, Alex slid off his bed and leaned against the head of it. For the last few minutes, he'd been attempting to work himself up about being found, but every time it strengthened, something would calm him back down. How many hours he still had to himself; his budding hope that his folks would understand and not be as scared as Bailey when he told them; his mental recapping of his escape route; and how safe he felt being inside with Bailey around, nervous disposition or otherwise.

His unease grew over the next hour, and the next, as he continued to fail at triggering the reverse shift. He then switched thoughts to what it had felt like going through his first reverse shift. How tightly his muscles contracted before crushing his bones, bit by bit, back into a smaller frame. He felt no change to his body as a result, only a different kind of unease about going through a shift again so soon. His resulting sigh of frustration came with a rumbling growl.

When Catherine and then Nathan attempted to reach him via phone awhile later, Alex tried to use the surprise the sudden ringing had sparked to fuel another attempt at changing back, to no avail. The failed attempt was followed up with another check of his escape route.

Then came 2:30. After a quick snack, Alex kept sneaking peeks outside until a bus from his high school stopped near the front yard and dropped off nearly ten students. After five minutes they'd all left, though he was quick to start fearing what he would have to do if his folks came home around rush hour.

Another hour passed sooner than he expected, by which time he'd reconsidered using the guest room closet to hide versus dashing for the vacant, wooded lot. Bailey had led his folks right to him last time. He couldn't afford that again.

When he checked on the room and found Bailey resting on the futon, Alex glanced between him and the window. "Stay calm, boy," Alex said before he took a step into the room.

That was when he heard the first rumblings of a car's engine, and then the closing of a door, all from the driveway. *Oh, no.* His attempt at focusing on turning back, despite his quickly rising pulse, was interrupted by Bailey bumping his leg as he rushed past.

"Bailey, get..." The sound of the doorbell cut him off. *Shit.*

As his limbs began to tremble, Alex rushed into the room and shut the door. The window was halfway opened before he heard the click of the front door's deadbolt, and then the hint of whimpering from his dog after it opened. He forced himself outside as his mother called for him, the scents from miles around assaulting his olfactory sense as the window was slid shut.

Now cut off from his feeling of safety, the unhindered sunlight washed a nasty, nagging feeling of being watched over him, which he didn't bother to fight. If he didn't hurry, Bailey would corner him, or possibly his mother would see him.

At the fence behind the garage, Alex vaulted over the wooden planks before going to all fours on the other side. With no one in sight, he continued towards the driveway. His mother had parked on the right side, too far from the fence, but close enough to the garage should a car start coming his way. None did as he took a minute to catch his breath, and then continued towards the porch's bush.

Once near it, he lowered his body and peered around the edge, spotting three people down the street, one walking his direction. They were four houses away, but as his route was gauged, he heard the glass door of his parent's room slide open behind him, sending a chill through his nerves.

His limbs refused to move for several seconds before he forced his stance to break, taking his first step, then the next, and the next, with increasing speed. The sole glance he made to his right as he reached a near trot showed the walker now three houses away, but also stopped and possibly staring. The muscle-tightening, autonomous feeling that shot throughout his limbs at that sight held until he was near the trees, his body gaining what felt like double its weight as he ducked behind a nearby fence and came to a stop halfway down its length.

Alex didn't dare move from the spot as he clutched his chest and worked to catch his breath again, even when a fear of the police showing up started clawing into his mind. He gave that fear several minutes to be justified, staying ready to run or leap the fence he was next to if he had to. That whole time he heard cars driving by, but none coming to a stop nearby and no doors opening.

When he finally worked up the courage to inch back towards the edge of the fence, only civilian vehicles were on the street, with one or two walkers otherwise. Unwilling to risk getting spotted, Alex backed away and circled wide into the patch of trees and brush, finding a spot far enough back where he could see the house, but also duck behind something or retreat if he needed to.

* * *

By the time his father returned home, only one police cruiser had driven near the lot, the officer inside only slowing down as they passed versus stopping. The north-bound direction of the breezes had let Alex catch another canine unit scent coming from it, which kept him huddled behind cover.

That same breeze direction brought the scent of spent gunpowder to him shortly after his dad left his truck. Hoping it was because of shooting range practice, when his father allowed the front door to stay open too long, he saw Bailey rush past him and put his nose to the ground near the front porch bushes.

Before his pet got much further, his collar was grabbed, and he was commanded to sit and stay. He didn't listen in favor of fighting the hold until he was rearing on his hind legs, barking as he lost some of his gained distance.

"Bailey, sit. Now." It wasn't until his father forced his hip down that Bailey listened and did just that.

Alex barely heard his dog whine in response and lowered his body. *C'mon, boy. Be good. Don't follow me.* As a new scent akin to used leather reached his nose, along with one that reminded him of work, Alex waited for his family to all be inside and the street to clear before inching toward the source.

What he found was a drawstring leather bag half the size of his paw, with four ten-sided dice inside. *Huh. Where'd this come from?* He sniffed it again to find not only more scents in line with the many stagnant ones from work, but another from the bag's pocket that sparked a familiar shudder.

This is Nathan's? Not even a second after that realization, Alex's blood went cold. The spot where he'd jumped the fence was visible from here. He sniffed at the ground around the bag's location, but despite no further trace of his friend's scent, his unease grew. *He couldn't have. I didn't tell him that much.* Recalling his friend's suspicions about his behavior and his statement of how fast he'd healed, the only conclusion Alex could draw was he had guessed something was up, and then fled the area when he was proven right.

The question of how and why he'd been near his place today of all days escaped him until he remembered both he and Catherine had tried to reach him hours ago. *No. No, that can't be.* As much as Alex wanted to believe it wasn't possible that a single ignored call was enough to tip his friend off, to encourage him to act, the chance was there. All he could do then was hope his friend would not think any less of him after this.

* * *

As the sun came closer to setting completely, Alex noticed the backyard lights turn on. When the carbonized wood scent of charcoal and the sodium-laced ones of freshly exposed meat reached his nose, even though he wasn't too hungry, a twinge of alienation built in his chest. *They've got to be waiting for me by now.*

When he saw his chance to cross the road a few minutes later, he stalled after his first step. He'd had no success with changing back over the last eight or so hours. Even if he got inside without his parents hearing him, he'd be gambling against them finding him like this. Or, if he somehow managed to start a shift back, them finding him mid-revert.

Glancing between his forepaws and the house as another opportunity presented itself, Alex went on the move. As the grass and dirt under his paws changed to concrete, and his muscles again tightened and went autonomous, he felt the idea of revealing his were form to his parents becoming more of an inevitability.

Once up on the porch, he changed his mind about going inside and moved toward his father's truck, being careful not to let his claws click despite his father speaking. "Why would he call us to say he wants to tell us something and then vanish without his phone?"

Alex gauged how much room he had to slip under the truck as his mother replied. "He might not be willing to talk just yet."

Truer than you think. Once he figured he had enough space, Alex slid underneath the truck, glad to be so close to his parents and yet in a spot where he wouldn't be seen.

"I don't know. Being so evasive like this..."

"You think he's doing something he shouldn't be?"

"No. He is not telling us something, though." With the image of his friend fleeing in fear still playing in his head, Alex took some relief from what his father said next. "Maybe it's about that night he was mugged, or why he wasn't home all day Monday, I don't know."

"Well, if that's what he wants to talk about, I'm sure he will."

The conversation trailed off after that into the subject of counseling. Alex put a paw over his face and grimaced when it came up. *Like any counselor could help with this.*

A few minutes later, Bailey's scratching at the door interrupted his folks. "Silly dog," his father said before sliding the glass door open. Once it was, the clicking of claws moved toward the yard, but then stopped and came back toward the side gate. Alex inched aside as his dog came straight for him, his sniffing at the gap in the wood planks of the fence followed up by scratching of the wood and whining.

"Bailey, what is wrong with you tonight?" With his father's boots sounding closer with each step, Alex shuffled fully from under the truck, his pulse racing. The bullet on his necklace audibly clinked against the concrete as his fur snagged the sharp bits of pavement.

His father stopped his walk for over a second. Alex felt his heart start hammering his ribs.

Chapter 16 – The First Talks

Wednesday, September 21st, 2011
Moon Phase – Last Quarter

As he got back to all fours, his broadened ribcage and back made him bump into his mother's sedan. He turned his head in shock, almost smacking his muzzle against it as well.

"What's making that noise?" his mother asked.

"No idea."

Hearing a clunk from the grabbing of metal holstered in leather, panic rushed Alex's head. He heard his father command Bailey to sit and stay as he moved toward the garage, a whine sounding from his pet as a result.

And then the side gate opened.

Alex heard a click, saw a hint of light on the garage door, and ducked. Keeping vehicles between him and his father, the flashlight spot swept near his head until his father stopped walking. Certain he was about to crouch, Alex bolted into the grass, eyeing a spot in the bushes to run through.

As he threw himself into the shrubbery, the rustling of leaves drowned out the finer sounds behind him. Bits of his fur were pulled from his skin and his momentum broke twigs and a few large branches free as he made it to the other side. Now in a darkened part of his neighbor's yard, Alex dropped back to his chest and let his ears do the tracking.

The flashlight beam lit up the bushes he ran through until he heard bootsteps on concrete again, moving away from him. The opening and closing of the side gate afterward was his signal to return to the yard, his courage towards revealing himself having taken a hit. What he heard next impacted it further.

"Didn't see what it was. Sounded like it was huge, though."

"Then we should get inside as soon as these are done."

Alex felt the muscles around his chest tighten and weight come into his frame. How many minutes did he have? Could he still set things up on his own terms? With the gate closed again, sneaking to the front door wouldn't be hard, but if the door was locked… How could he convince his parents it was him in the first place, without giving the wrong impression or scaring them?

At the corner of the garage, he listened to make sure everyone was outside before making any moves. The crickets around him helped mask his steps until he was at the front door. He inched the door's latch down until a soft click sounded, and then nudged the door with his shoulder. It didn't stop him from moving.

As he slipped inside and closed the door, the wood squeaking into place before he let the latch go, how quiet the house was made his initial idea of waiting for his parents to come inside before saying anything look more foolish by the second. One stray sound they weren't expecting and he'd be caught, but speaking first, even if it gave him an upper hand, meant gambling on how suspicious his growl-laced voice would sound to them.

Alex held his arms with his paws as he worked up the guts to start the walk towards his room. His first step came after a lengthy exhale, none of his unease going with it, and once at the doorframe, the void that had started building behind his ribs and lungs had crested. His breathing had taken on a noticeable shiver by then, the growling undertone amplified because of it.

As he grabbed the drawstring of the blinds and pulled them up, he didn't let his eyes sway from his parents or Bailey. The grill was out of sight, but both his mother and father were standing up and focusing on the fence and gate. His father had his phone by his ear, and Alex's heart knotted as he thought of what he could be doing.

After a few deep breaths to try and calm himself, Alex reached for the nearest window latches. The pop from the first unlock got Bailey's attention, his head turning towards him with the second. *Stay calm, boy.* His initial nudge of the window to open it didn't go quietly, which he expected, and the sound tipped off his father, who turned his head in response.

"Alex, that you?"

His words froze in his throat as he heard that. His arms started to tremble and his heart beat faster, made no better when Bailey started sniffing at the air. *C'mon, don't stall. Say something.* Taking a breath as his father repeated his name, he forced out an acknowledgement. It came out no louder than a mumble, the low pitch enhancing the growling.

"Is something wrong? Did you hurt yourself?" his mother asked.

"Not…really."

"Then why is your voice so hoarse?"

Alex glanced at Bailey before he responded. His dog was now standing and staring in his direction. "About that, I need to tell you both something."

"Mark, I'll call you back," his father said before hanging up the phone. Alex recognized the name; he was an SLPD sergeant. "Then come out here and do it. Get yourself some dinner."

Despite licking his muzzle at that offer and the smell of cooking meat, Alex didn't budge. "Actually, could you both...come inside for a minute?"

"What for?" Alex froze again. "What's going on, Son?"

He forced himself to speak when he saw his father's hand reach for his service pistol. "No one's in here. I'm fine."

"Then stay there."

Though his mother protested the idea of his father pulling his gun, Alex felt the blood drain from his head and bolted to the kitchen as soon as he heard the glass door slide open. Bailey stayed right on their tails, a brief warning growl sent towards him before his father told him to be quiet. Once out of the hall and past the living room, Alex found the kitchen light switch and killed the lights, leaving only the final bits of sunlight streaming through the nearby windows.

After taking a position by the corner of the wall, he listened for the opening of the door to his parent's room. It was followed by a click, then of a beam of light shone into the living room. The hallway lights were turned on afterward, and then he heard metal rubbing against leather.

"Dad, wait," Alex pleaded as the two pairs of footsteps reached the end of the hallway.

"Son, this isn't funny."

"Why did you turn the lights off?" his mother asked.

Alex licked his fangs, his words again stalled in his throat. This was it. He had nowhere to go. Swallowing once, feeling his racing heart, he spoke up. "Just...don't come any closer yet."

Hearing a pair of footsteps nearby, he suspected his father wasn't listening. "For what reason?"

"I just need to say something...before you see me like this."

"Like this? What are you talking about?" his mother asked.

"Remember that night I came home without my stuff?" Both of his parents acknowledged it. "I lied about what came after me."

"I had a feeling you were." The reply from his father was a semi-expected gut punch on top of everything already piled on him. "What really happened?"

Instead of replying, Alex prepped himself. Words wouldn't do it. He had to show them.

As he took his first step, towards the stream of light coming from the hallway lights, he heard Bailey's paws against the carpet. He was quick to enter his line of sight, and upon seeing him, shirked back into a defensive posture and growled.

"Bailey?"

The nervous tone from his mother was all Alex needed to make his move. "It's me, boy. Calm down." Despite his body trembling and his eyes watering over, he took the edge of the wall in his left paw and inched himself beyond its corner. He saw his father first, his right hand still near his pistol and his left holding his flashlight. He pointed the beam up and into his eyes, getting him to wince and raise a paw to shield them.

The gasp from his mother preceded her turning on the living room ceiling fan lights, and when his eyes adjusted, Alex found her clasping a hand over her mouth, her eyes wide with horror as though she'd just watched him get shot. He could almost swear she'd taken a step back too. His father, by contrast, his free hand still resting on his service pistol, did little beyond stare at the towering wolf-man in front of him, his expression a hybrid of shock, inquisition, and determination.

All of them stood in silence for many minutes, with Alex trying and failing to think of something to say and muster the courage to say it. His urge to flee clashed with how scared he was to move, keeping him rooted to a spot where he could do little beyond study the shock and fright on the faces of his parents. Even though he hadn't made one move or said one word since the lights came on, both of their postures screamed 'keep still and keep away'.

When the AC turned on, the draft from the hallway swept a pair of raw scents by his muzzle, making his nose twitch. The feeling he got from noticing them reminded him of his talk with Nathan two days before, and it didn't take long for him to realize that, back then and right now, he was literally smelling the fear of those around him.

"A werewolf came after me that night," Alex finally said. His folks still didn't speak, although his father looked like he was trying to bring himself to do it.

His mother beat him to it, though it took several seconds for her to speak. "How long...have you known about this?"

"Since that same night."

His father then pulled his hand away from his pistol and placed it over his forehead, looking back to his mother and then to him. "I don't believe this." His tone juggled disappointment and fear.

Alex diverted his view to his mother while working out what to say next. "I wanted to tell you both sooner..." Even though he froze once again, his parents didn't reply, giving him time to recover. "I didn't know how, or what would happen to me." The silence resumed once he finished talking. With his parents either too scared or too lost in their thoughts, Alex broke eye contact with them to check on Bailey. He'd been inching closer to his leg, his nose pointed at it, but the first hint of movement made him inch back, pull his ears back some and growl.

Alex let him react as he wanted, taking a glance back at his parents to see if their attention had diverted as well. Only his mother's had.

"I didn't..." Alex paused when she looked his direction, "mean to scare you both like that."

His father replied after a stretch of more silence. "This certainly explains a few things."

Alex gave a slow nod as the pressure on his chest lifted a bit. "A lot, I know." When he was met with silence again, he brought up the burgers still on the grill to try and break the uneasy feeling in the room. Although his stomach wasn't begging to be filled, he figured the patties were close to done by then anyway.

It took a minute for either of his parents to want to move, but as he followed them to the back door and then outside into the backyard, their fear scents began to lose potency. Despite that, as he prepared his meal, the few glances he made towards them showed that they were still unsure of what to think of him. At least one time each, they looked away when he laid eyes on them. His first few nips of hamburger and attempts to chew drew more attention from them, which he tried to defuse by slowing down his eating, to no avail.

"How long will you stay like that?"

Alex looked over at his mother, not wanted to say what he did next. "I don't know. I've been trying to turn back all day, and nothing's working."

"Then, did this just...happen?"

Alex felt his chest tighten before he shook his head. "I messed up a trick, sprained my wrist, and then imagined it happening, and it did."

"Wait a minute," his father began, his tone full of surprise. "You caused this? Just like that?"

"Not 'just like that'. It didn't work until after I got hurt."

"You were trying to do it on purpose?"

Alex took another nip of his burger. "Just to find out what could cause it when the moon's not full." Both of his parents looked at him in disbelief. "Nothing's happened to me since then."

"But you can't change yourself back?"

Alex shook his head. "I'm sure it's possible. Maybe I'm not doing something right."

"But, if it's not possible..." His father paused. "How long did you stay like this before?"

"Thirty-six hours." Alex caught sight of his mother's eyes widening at that.

"So, for all you know, you could stay like this for that long again."

"Maybe, but..." Alex pulled his meal away from his muzzle. "I wouldn't mind if that ends up being true."

"I would think you'd want to change back more than anything," his father said after a moment.

"I do, but if I can't, or I have to wait, I can live with it."

His parents didn't speak after that, giving him time to finish his burger and go for a second one. Picking one that was coated in cheese, he took a bite before sitting back down.

His mother was next to break the silence with a question. "What happened to you while we were gone?"

Alex felt a creeping of emotions come on as he remembered the doe. *It was the full moon that night...* "Just this."

"That's it?"

From his father's tone, Alex knew he wasn't buying that claim. "I got hungry faster than normal, but I stayed in control."

"Stayed in control?" his mother asked.

"I mean I didn't start doing things I had no control over," Alex clarified. "Like I was afraid I would."

"So, you have a good idea of what to expect when you're like that?"

"I still have doubts, but yes."

"Doubts...about what?"

The shift in pitch between his father's words got Alex to look down and away from him. "Never mind. Wrong word."

"So, what you meant to say is you're still unsure about some things?"

Alex nodded. "Like what else besides adrenaline could trigger this."

"Still, now that you know that's one cause, you can be more careful, right?"

"That was the plan." Several bites of food later, Alex noticed his mother looking more relaxed, while his father's excess attention towards him hadn't laxed. Pleased that things were going so well, he tried to smile for them before a shift in the breeze brought weak traces of their fear scents near his nose. The scents prompted him to speak up and try to reassure them. "I'll try to change back when I'm done eating. A full stomach might help."

"Let's hope."

Alex glanced at his father at that remark, but couldn't find the words to reply with.

"Is..." his mother began, drawing his attention, "that all that happens to you?"

Alex looked over his fur-covered arms and then back at his mother, before sighing to himself and shaking his head. "No, but everything else I've gotten used to. Mostly."

"Mostly?"

"I'm still not used to this nose, how sensitive it gets when this happens."

"Within less than a month, you've gotten used to something that made this drastic of a change to you?"

With the stern tone of his father now much clearer, Alex couldn't look at him directly. "As best I can. I didn't ask for this."

"Yet you're talking as though all of this hardly bothers you."

Alex gave himself a second. "I'm trying not to let it."

His mother took over the questioning then. "Then what made you so upset last week?"

"Bad timing, honestly."

"With what?"

Alex tried without avail to not think of the doe, of eating from its carcass. "Nothing."

"Son, listen." His father's tone got him glace at him for a moment. "If this hardly bothers you, then nothing about it should've made you that upset."

Alex swallowed to keep his emotions back. "Wasn't one thing that did it. I had a lot of things on my mind up to then."

"Sounds to me like this is affecting you more than you think."

"Maybe," Alex said, "but I can deal with it. Better that than be anxious and depressed for the rest of my life."

"Rest of your life?"

The twinge of sadness in his mother's voice caused Alex's eyes to widen. When he turned towards her, her hands were covering her face.

Of all the screw-ups he could've had tonight.

While clenching his paws, he tried to think of an optimistic response. None came to mind, and the longer he went without any words, the more he thought of kicking himself.

His father spoke up after a few seconds, trying to reassure his mother that things were fine. Though she acknowledged what he told her, to Alex it was obvious how close she was to getting emotional, and he lost his drive to speak. After he finished his meal, he sat for a minute longer, doing nothing beyond glancing between his parents.

He played with the idea of going to sleep and letting everything settle, rather than focus on shifting back, and after deciding it was the better idea, went back inside and settled on his bed.

When his folks came back inside, Alex kept still with an arm around his chest and his free paw under his muzzle as though he was thinking, glancing over when he heard one of them stop near his door—his mother as it happened. Though she did little beyond stare at him for a moment, as he drifted off to sleep shortly after, he heard both his parents stop near his door before one of them approached him and rubbed the fur of his face.

Chapter 17 – Signs of Hunger

Thursday, September 22nd, 2011
Moon Phase – Waning Crescent

When he roused the next morning, the irritated space behind his eyes and forehead was what he noticed first. How much his night vision was working to counter the darkness left him wondering what time it was and reaching for his phone.

2:57?

At first wondering what, if anything, besides the headache had woken him up, the start-up of the air conditioner against the silence of the house helped ease him out of bed.

Bailey stayed asleep in his dog bed as Alex inched his way to his bedroom door, his steps masked by the whir of the AC fans and current of air from the vents. Pausing briefly before he started down the hallway, he could just make out the sound of one of his parents snoring. *Good. If I start changing back, they shouldn't hear it.* He then made his way to the kitchen for a glass of ice water and a quick snack, his headache dulling over the next few minutes.

After prepping a spot on the pantry floor and the stuff he would need to clean up his discarded fur, Alex laid down on the couch in the study. The traces of Bailey's scent in the cushions he disturbed were sniffed lazily as his body relaxed, but even after several minutes, he felt no change in his form, and sat back up.

The presence of the calming scents, and how things had gone the night before, kept him from bothering with fear. Instead, he tried once again to recall the shift in its entirety, how it started, how it felt, how he'd reacted. Though his paws and arms wrapped around his chest as he recalled the compression of his muscles and the loss of trapped body heat, all he achieved from the attempt was an elevated breathing rate.

Damn it. Why's this so freaking hard? What am I doing wrong? He huffed in frustration at the last question, the tail end of it dipping into a rumbling growl, before remembering what his father had said last night.

That for all he knew, he'd be stuck like this for another thirty-six hours. He wouldn't be human again until ten or so tonight if that was true.

Egh, no. Something's gotta work. Alex stood back up at that, figuring a few more minutes to think was in order. He made his way to the living room's bay window and opened the curtains just enough to see outside before kneeling in front of it. He let his mind relax for a minute, then went over every failed method he'd tried since yesterday.

It had taken a jolt to his system to get him to change before... But he hadn't been awake when his claws shrank back, only when his muscles were close to compressing. Was he too comfortable to make changing back a necessity? Or was something else keeping him from doing it? He continued asking himself those questions as he stared outside, letting him spot a hint of headlights on the street directly across from the window.

When the headlight source emerged from behind the bushes of the yard, and Alex saw the color scheme and lettering of one of the SLPD's SUVs, he pulled his head back. A second later he made for the front door, and watched the cruiser come to a stop near the vacant lot.

The longer it sat there, despite the searchlight never coming on, the more his budding urge to sneak outside while it was still dark diminished. Then came his anxiousness about being stuck in the house for the rest of the day. *The backyard's nice and quiet... Wonder if just the air outside will help.*

At that, Alex slipped away from the foyer, towards the hallway. With one of his parents still snoring, he found his grip on the guest room window and nudged it until it moved, pausing as soon as he heard metal scraping. The snoring didn't break rhythm, and he found the first hints of outside scents within two feet of the crack in the window gap.

The first few familiar ones did ease his thoughts about having to stay within, or close to, the house until he changed back, but then he found hints of decaying meat and blood—weak ones in contrast to everything else, and which fluxed in intensity by the second. The numerous animal scents accompanying it made pinpointing the source near impossible, though Alex was quick to suspect the other werewolf had killed another animal.

He spent a moment watching the trees in his neighbor's yard, their sway helping him gauge north, or north-east, as the direction the scents were coming from. *Kempner's west of here... Is there another stable or something north of here?* Though he couldn't recall any, the direction the scents were coming from soon sparked a shiver. Marcus and Catherine lived in another subdivision less than two miles away in that same direction.

Wish these things worked with my phone. Alex thought as he glanced at his claws, and made a mental note to text them the first chance he got. After closing the window, he returned to his room for a bit of reading material.

The first pangs of hunger came as he flipped through one of his older skateboarding magazines, though he let it slide until the growling started. After breaking one of the leftover burgers into chunks and warming them in the microwave, his first taste of the meat saw his brain compare it to the taste and texture of the doe's muscle and viscera. Saw it urge him towards believing that, while good, this meat was not what he should be eating.

He shook his head at the thought, hoping to forget it that easily, but with more chewing and tasting, he began imagining a fresh kill in front of him that he was being denied. His jaws snapped with a sudden bite into another piece of burger. Contrasted against the near silence in the house, the sound sent another shock through him and he put his meal aside.

With his heart starting to race, Alex pulled a can of soda from the fridge, but within his first few sips of the ice-cold liquid, the makeup of the taste became unpleasant. Too sharp and too chemical-laced. Another piece of the burger was soon in his paw, this one with cheese that was no longer bubbling. Once again it felt like what he was eating was a cheap substitute for what he'd once eaten, but he forced himself to eat more, not stopping until half the burger was eaten.

His hunger only worsened.

Now trembling, Alex closed his eyes and held his arms. It wasn't the full moon tonight. He couldn't be feeling the same things now. As he worked to hold his growing panic and sense of being trapped at bay, a sickening thought came to him. Had he done this to himself? And how? By staying like this for so long?

Alex tried to calm his quickened breathing while trying not to think of his parents, his trembling legs forcing him to sit to gather his thoughts. The longer he went without an idea of what to do, the more the feeling of emptiness inched its way from his stomach out to his arms and legs, testing his concentration.

He'd put up with it for five hours before, but he didn't have that long until the sun rose. Two hours at most, and kids would be waiting for the bus to school well before then. It had taken half an hour to walk to his high school before, but it had been hit twice. The police would likely be there or have patrols in the area. On the off chance they weren't, this early in the morning, ruckus from the animals was a factor.

That scent was coming from north of here... Alex returned to his room and snatched his phone on instinct, before tossing it aside and turning on his desktop computer. The mass of his paws meant pecking at the keys with his claws until he found the site he needed. He soon found an animal farm listing just to the northwest of Catherine and Marcus's neighborhood.

His pleasure at the realization didn't last beyond the discovery. The farm was a mile and half away, and the roads leading to it would be growing busier by this hour, plus the farm itself was at the intersection of two of those busy roads. The chance that he would be spotted by car headlights along the way, or take so long getting there and catching something that he'd be out in the open by the time the sun started rising, made the location feel even less appealing.

With the location bookmarked regardless, he thought back to his high school's stable. The mare and cow were too big, and could easily crush him or leave him with a broken bone. The chance of the one young horse not being stabled with its mother by now was slim to none.

As his heart continued pounding against his ribs, a new question struck him: would changing back now stop his hunger? He hadn't felt it as a human yet.

With the hope that it would clenched in his head, he lowered himself to the floor and rolled onto his back before closing his eyes and trying to breathe easy. He stayed tense for several minutes, even with imagining a successful change, and his arms soon wrapped around his chest. As more doubts about the approach crept into his head, he imagined himself as a human, kneeling next to a dead deer, his normal hands holding disemboweled organs and muscles near his mouth, his skin caked with blood. His lungs trembled at the thought, shaking his breathing.

Until he heard his parents getting roused, Alex stayed on his back, wracking his brain for ideas. At least once he thought of dropping the idea of attempting to change back to focus on the easiest way to find a loose animal to feed on. The sounds of sheets moving, groaning, and heavy landings on carpet snapped the idea back into his head along with his fears of being trapped. As his stomach once again rumbled, he got up onto all fours and kept that posture until he was out of the hallway.

Seeing what remained of his unfinished meal in the kitchen, Alex licked his fangs before he tossed it out. With another glass of ice water down his throat, he leaned against the counter, nervous sweat seeping into his fur, his heightened pulse bringing him close to panting. 4:38, and his folks were already waking up.

They can't help with this. I can hold out until they leave. That sho—

With the sound of a door opening, he froze. As it closed, he turned his head to the right, spotting his mother rounding the corner. She gasped and covered her mouth, the silence after lasting until after the kitchen chandelier was turned on.

"Sorry." Alex got no reply beyond his mother's hand uncovering her mouth and being placed over her chest. "Been trying all morning to change back."

"Well...just give it time."

When his stomach rumbled again, Alex kept his paws away, even as the muscles in his chest and face tightened. "I have." Pushing away from the counter when no response came, as he passed his mother, he felt her hand grasp his arm and stopped.

Turning to face her, he didn't pull his arm away but didn't make eye contact either. The deeper pitch of her heartbeat, and how much faster it was than Bailey's, stood out immediately. When he noticed her scent, fear was already lacing it.

"Are you okay?"

As Alex stalled on answering, the continued presence of his mother's scent remained calming, and then grew more pleasant. In a way that didn't shrink his stomach like the scent of the burger meat. The chilling terror that built under his skin at that almost made him backpedal. Almost made it impossible to keep a straight face as he forced a reply. "Just need to think."

After pulling his arm free of his mother's grasp, and once in his room with the door closed, Alex stood quaking at what he'd experienced. He exhaled several times to cleanse his nostrils, the scents from his room overtaking what remained of his mother's, but his anxiety barely laxed. With his necklace and bullet held tightly in one paw, he sat against his bed, listening for the moment his father left the bedroom.

When he at last did, Alex heard him stop outside his door. Although hoping his father would leave him be, his door was opened. His expression displayed no extremes, which Alex was glad to see, though the initial silence and stare was still telling.

"Anything?" his father soon asked.

Alex shook his head. "Still thinking, and trying."

His father hummed in response versus saying more, and the door was left open after he departed, leaving Alex able to hear when the louder noises from the kitchen began. The grinding of coffee was first after a bit of talking, the noise lasting long enough to encourage him to move.

His door made no noise as it inched it open further, exactly what he was hoping for. Once near the door to his parent's room, Alex reached for the knob. His paw concealed the whole of it, and inched it counter-clockwise until it no longer turned. Though it made little noise, behind him, things suddenly became quieter.

Alex remained still, hoping the grinding sound would return. It didn't. He nudged the door once, moving it an inch. No sound was given off, and he nudged it further, relaxing the torque on the handle after several inches.

As he slipped into the room and approached the sliding glass door to the backyard, he heard something climbing the fence outside. Shortly after, a large raccoon wandered into his view. Alex couldn't help licking his fangs or shaking in excitement from seeing it.

Ignoring a call-out from his father, he crept closer to the door, hoping he wouldn't scare off his potential prey. The lever lock squeaked into unlocked, and each inch of the door's movement produced sounds of plastic sliding over metal. The raccoon didn't seem interested in the noises, or the light growls Alex produced as he sized up his prey and method to catch it.

When the outside air blew past his nose, it brought the raccoon's scent to him, exciting him further.

"Alex?"

How close the second callout sounded made Alex jump, his reaction causing the raccoon to bolt and his eyes to widen. He leapt to his hind legs and took off after it, the awkwardness of moving in his canine legs nearly lost to how desperate he was to end his hunger.

When it leapt towards and climbed the fence, Alex lunged. His first swipe missed, slapping its tail, but his second connected, bringing his paw around the animal's body, his grip punching his claws through its skin.

The raccoon screeched in pain, shattering the silence around him. Yanking it from the fence, its claws scraping loudly against the wood, Alex wrapped his paw around the animal's face. The screeching stopped, replaced by a muffled squealing.

His heart racing, he stood rooted to the spot, listening for any voices. From his parents or anyone else.

A minute seemed to pass. Nothing.

The raccoon scratched at his paws, its claws barely slicing his skin, but he could feel his grip loosening from it squirming around so much. When the paw over its face loosened to reposition, the raccoon went on the attack, biting into the flesh of his paw. With a dull snarl of pain, Alex pulled the raccoon off and sealed its mouth again, his paw now wrapped around its neck as well.

With it now at his mercy, how gigantic his paws were compared to its body made his pulse weaken and his blood run cold. He couldn't.

His grumbling stomach told him otherwise.

Alex shook his head with his eyes shut tight as he began to twist his clenched paws, his teeth gritting with the progression of the twisting. He kept them closed as a set of rips and a loud pop sounded, the raccoon going limp in his paws afterward. Nausea was quick to wash through his stomach and lungs, the increasing quaking of his body making holding his catch difficult. But the deed was done. He'd done it for a good reason. It was either this or leave himself at risk of something worse. Those fractured thoughts helped him refocus on his catch.

Until footsteps sounded behind him.

Chapter 18 - Aftermath

Thursday, September 22nd, 2011
Moon Phase – Waning Crescent

The terror Alex felt at being caught, and wondering how long he'd been watched, was dulled by the emotions already affecting him.

Until he was addressed, no other sounds came to him.

"Alex...what the hell?"

Recognizing his father's voice, Alex hung his head, unable to reply until he heard his father come three steps closer. "Dad...don't watch."

"Why?" Alex didn't answer. "What's going on? Or did you snap that animal's neck for no reason?"

Hearing his father say that, cold crawled through Alex's skin, and he had to force what he said next through a rapidly constricting throat. "No... None of the food we have is helping me."

Though he couldn't hear his father's heartbeat or see his face, how long he stalled on responding was all Alex needed to know that he was putting the pieces together. How laced with horror his eventual response was got his chest to tighten.

"Oh, my God."

"I didn't want to. I never did..."

"Then get it over with. I won't watch."

Alex didn't move until he heard his father go back inside, his thoughts stuck in reflection of what he'd been told. Had his father figured this out last night, or sooner?

Would he walk back into the house to hear his mother holding back tears again?

With a light shake of his head, he finally opened his eyes to see the raccoon, now lifeless in his paws. It took until his shaking was under control, an amount of time he quickly lost track of, to take his first nip. With his fangs working around the bones, he got as much of the animal as he could, his ears perked to listen for any other sounds.

As the hunger at last subsided, Alex licked his teeth and dropped the carcass behind the garage. Inside, he heard no call-outs to him, and no sounds of sadness as he headed for the bathroom, though the weight on his chest built with each step. Not wanting to approach the kitchen, nor trigger the discussion he was certain was coming, he washed his muzzle and paws free of bloodstains and then retreated to his room, shutting his door behind him.

He sat and kept quiet as his parents went through their morning routines, each pacing of steps by his door leaving him expecting it to open. Though he was left undisturbed outside of a pair of goodbyes, and his mother sounding more worried than upset, the thought of his father getting him to spill his guts, either tonight or after that, refused to sit well.

When only Bailey was left in the house, the old image of him eating from a dead deer was forgotten in favor of him eating a normal meal with his pet by his side. How badly he wanted to leave his were form after what had happened made his muscles feel heavy and tight. As he held his arms and paced his breathing, the tension didn't lax. It built, to the point where he could feel pressure against his ribs and clavicles, and further inward against his organs.

The claws of his fingers were the first to change, blunting and retracting to allow his skin and tendons to wrap around them. At the first sound of his skull and jaw cracking, he was up and out of his room, dropping to the floor again once in the bathroom. His muzzle went slack and retracted into his human jaw as his muscle structure and forepaws compressed to their old forms, and as before, the reverse shift came to an end with the compression of his ribcage.

After brushing his skin free of the shed fur, Alex followed up the loss of warmth with a shower and a fresh set of clothes. He headed out back to collect the raccoon's carcass once the fur pile was swept up, leaving the door open for Bailey. His pet homed in on the decaying carcass within a second of being outside, and rushed past him to where it had been dropped.

"No, Bailey. Stop," Alex demanded as his dog came close to where the carcass was stashed. "Sit..." He repeated the command when Bailey didn't immediately listen. "Good boy. Wait right there," he said before approaching the carcass.

Despite having eaten the animal not even two hours ago, the sight of its twisted neck and gutted abdomen made his heart tremble and hastened his tying up of the bag. As he dumped it into the bin by the street, the sound of an approaching dump truck helped relieve the tension in his chest and lungs.

* * *

The relief didn't last past his first class that day. Along with imagining the expression on his father's face at the moment he'd been caught, Alex received no response from him after texting both his parents to assure them he was fine, and human again. By the time his second class concluded, how stuck in his mind the raccoon still was made the thought of eating too unappealing, and his stomach growled and churned throughout his four-hour shift at Blue Moon that afternoon.

Back at home, Alex remained seated after his bike's engine was shut off. The living room curtains were lit, and as soon as he walked in, the questions would come. If not immediately, then before his parents went to sleep, and he knew the raccoon would be part of it.

When his stomach growled again, how hungry he was eclipsed his apprehension for a moment. Only when it happened the second time did he get off the seat and approach the front door. With the moon shrinking from its Last Quarter phase, he was able to sniff at the crack in the door without a chill running down his spine. Bailey was nowhere close by, but on the currents were hints of fettuccine and garlic bread, both of which relaxed his stomach and made him salivate.

As Alex at last reached for his keys and unlocked the door, his pulse began to climb. Bailey ran to greet him as he crossed the threshold, but even after rubbing his head for a bit, Alex couldn't manage more than a glimpse at his parents as he crossed the living room. Both of them looked relieved to see him as a human again, though his father's expression was one he knew all too well. The kind that meant, 'We need to talk'.

That expression got Alex to stall on returning to the living room, much less approaching the kitchen, until the scents of warm food won over again. Expecting to be questioned as soon as he sat down with his meal, his father instead stayed quiet, as if offering a chance for him to take the initiative.

It took less time than he thought for his mother to ask if he was okay. A weak nod of his head followed.

"Did something happen?"

As he began questioning how much his mother knew, Alex took two breaths before answering. "This morning, yeah." When he got in another glance, she was looking at him as though she expected him to walk away at any minute.

"What happened?"

Alex got in another glance. Her attention was going between him and his father.

"Give him a minute, hon."

While he struggled to think of what to say next, he heard Bailey get up from the couch and approach him. He took his 'at-attention' stance near his chair, allowing Alex's free hand to reach over and rub his head.

The stroking helped ease out the words he needed. "I kept trying to change back all morning, and…then I got hungry, but nothing we had did anything."

"Why not?"

Alex froze, and the hand stroking Bailey clenched. Saying he had eaten a living animal. Even though his father already saw him do it, imagining those words coming out of his mouth made him feel like he was about to flee his own skin in fear and his breathing sped up.

"Son, calm down. Take your time."

Alex rested his head on the tips of his fingers and closed his eyes. His throat lumped, forcing a swallow. He didn't want to say it, but he'd already brought himself within a hair of it.

"Nothing stops it except animal meat." How deathly silent things remained after that made him keep his eyes closed. Bailey had since moved to licking his hand. "I didn't want to…"

His parents said nothing, but one of their fear scents soon reached him.

As he opened his eyes and wiped them and his nose, he fought his emotions back as best he could before looking up. The lack of horror on his mother's face was at first comforting, the unease and tremors in her eventual follow-up question giving away how she really felt.

"Do you know why that happened?"

"Time…maybe. That's my best guess."

His father took over the questions then. "Then this happened to you the last time you were like that as well?"

Alex hesitated for only a second. "Yeah."

As his mother placed a hand over her chest, his father sighed and rested his face in his palms. "Why would you not tell us about that?" he asked after taking them away.

Alex rubbed his mouth, then shook his head. "I wasn't ready…and I didn't know it would happen to me this time."

"Then, is there anything else about this that we need to know?"

Alex shook his head again. "I'm picking these things up as I go, but that's all I know." The table went quiet again, and as the next few minutes passed, his emotions waned.

It was as he finished his first plate that he remembered the warning he meant to text Marcus and Catherine. Despite a news search turning up no word of new animal attacks, he couldn't shake his dread about the other werewolf moving further north to hunt.

Friday, September 23rd, 2011
Moon Phase - Waning Crescent

With his heart weighed down well into the afternoon the next day, Alex awaited the end of his classes and the moment that he could get back on his skateboard. A few laps around the campus grounds helped ease the feeling, as well as a few ollies down the stair sets.

It was as he held a grind on a concrete bench that his board hit a snag, the sudden stop throwing him forward. His resulting stumble ruined his chance to catch himself and his right knee hit the pavement first, his jeans taking most of the impact. His arms were next and not as lucky; the rough concrete scraped the skin from his palms and left elbow before his momentum was spent.

Once upright again, quivering from the fall, the damage to his arms held Alex's attention as he made for his backpack. By the time he had the gauze he needed, the bleeding on his elbow had slowed to a trickling ooze, and three pats of the area saw the end of it.

* * *

When he arrived at work an hour later, he found Marcus on-shift, in the middle of ringing up a stack of comics and trades. "Hey, man," he said as he came near the counter.

When his friend glanced up, Alex caught the wince in his expression. With how fast he'd healed before, as he clocked in, he couldn't help wondering if Marcus would notice the healing speed before his four-hour shift was done.

Half an hour later, when his friend asked if he had a minute, Alex's brain snapped to work thinking of an excuse. "Yeah, hang on." As he came up on the counter, what he'd come up with sat on his tongue, ready to go.

"Just curious. That text you sent us the other day? What gave you that impression?"

"Oh…" Alex bit his tongue as he reformed his thoughts.

"Just figured you'd tell us?" Marcus asked after a few seconds.

"Something like that." *C'mon, think.* "That thing's attacked a stable before, so…"

"I guess. If it's determined enough." Alex mumbled an agreement before Marcus continued. "That reminds me, did you tell your folks what happened?"

"Yeah," Alex said after glancing around the store. "Two days ago."

"I'm guessing it didn't go well."

"It went okay, but I was right about Dad grilling me for not saying anything for so long."

"Well, at least he knows for certain it's a wolf doing this stuff."

"Yeah. No idea how much help it'll be, though."

"What do you mean?"

"No officers have seen it, and no reports have come in. Of wolves or anything."

"With that curfew in place, I'm not surprised."

"Still, I told them, but it didn't feel like it was worth it. Dad acted like I said, and Mom almost freaked out."

"They're your parents, man. Being concerned about you is pretty much their job."

"Yeah, I know."

When the silence between him and Marcus lasted beyond two seconds, Alex headed back to where he'd been working the shelves. Though the idea of giving his friend an early hint at what was coming on Sunday floated in and out of his thoughts over the next few hours, he didn't act on it.

Chapter 19 – Those You Trust

Sunday, September 25th, 2011
Moon Phase – Waning Crescent

As his morning walk with Bailey on Sunday came to an end, Alex took a seat on the couch and coaxed him onto his lap. An hour, at best, was all he had before his friends would start arriving, and as he stroked Bailey's pelt, he continued to hope with everything he had that none of them would distance themselves from him after today.

When the sound of a running engine coming up the driveway snapped Alex's attention from his phone, Bailey rushed from his new spot at his feet for the front door. At first figuring his parents had come home for something, Alex glanced outside to find Nathan's sedan already parked.

"Bailey, stay," Alex said as he reached for the door handle. He kept the door closed until his friend was in front of it, his presence making Bailey's tail wag faster. "Hey, man."

"Hey. Your folks leave you the house today?" Nathan asked as he stepped inside, and Bailey broke his stance to greet him.

"Until five, yeah." Alex closed the door before continuing. "Got both soda and water, if you want either."

"Water's fine, thanks."

With a quick nod, Alex got two glasses ready. His friend had brought his laptop with him, and didn't take long to ask if he was interested in watching some funny videos he'd found. Alex accepted, hoping to ease the tension in his chest. His friend's choice of videos and the soft feel of Bailey's fur did just that until he heard a truck engine coming up the driveway.

Once everyone was inside and the door was closed, even though he couldn't see a violently frightful reaction coming from any of them, Alex hesitated on turning the deadbolt, and returning to the kitchen.

"You guys hungry at all?" he asked as two more glasses were handed out. He knew at least one of them would say yes, and when Marcus and Nathan did, he let them toss around ideas before they settled on pizza. The tension around his chest didn't relax, even as he called in the order.

"Should be here in about half an hour," Alex said as he hung up his phone. When no one spoke, he continued. "Hey Nathan, let's show them that video from before."

As his friend did so, Alex spent the length of its runtime working up the courage to make the first move. Near the video's conclusion, his fears of what would happen once his case was made had surged, enough to cause his throat to clench.

Out of eyeshot, the resultant change in his breathing and expression redirected Catherine's attention.

"You okay?" she asked.

Alex tried to answer, and not massage his throat. *Damn it. Get a grip.* The moment Nathan paused the video was when it was clear he'd been too slow with that. When Catherine repeated the question, he licked his lips and exhaled through his nose.

"Yeah." His friends kept silent, as did he, allowing the old feeling of eyes locking onto him to return. If he spoke up now... "Just let something get to me."

"That's been happening a lot lately, it seems."

"Yeah...and that's why I wanted you guys here." Nathan and Catherine looked at each other for a second after he spoke, a gesture that didn't escape his notice. "I just need to come clean about something."

"Okay. Like what?" Marcus asked.

Alex took a few seconds to answer. His fist clenched under the table several times as the found the words he needed. "That wolf that I said attacked me last month? That wasn't what it was."

"You could've told us that anytime else, though."

"If that was the whole story, I would've."

As Alex paused to work his emotions back, Marcus took the initiative. "Why are you being so cryptic? What was it you saw?"

"Something I didn't think was real until then. And I'm not being cryptic or trying to pull your legs here."

"Then just say what you need to."

Alex held his breath after that, the racing pace of his heart all he could feel besides the urge to back out now, even if he'd already given too much of a hint. When his next breath came, so did his clarification. "It was a werewolf that did that to me."

As if with the flick of switch, that sentence pulled the atmosphere around him down several degrees, the deathly silence intensifying Alex's feeling that he'd just made not only the wrong choice, but a damning one.

"You can't be serious." Marcus's tone was heavy with disappointment, as though he'd been sincerely concerned up until that moment.

"I believe him," Nathan said.

What? The declaration from his friend pulled Alex's head and gaze up, how dumbstruck he'd become and how devoid of being his lungs felt keeping him from talking.

"Why?" Marcus asked.

"For one, since when could a bite wound heal that fast? Without medical help, no less? And then he goes missing the day of the full moon this month." Nathan's gaze matched Alex's for a second. "I can't think of any other explanation, besides him getting some damn good acting and makeup lessons from someone."

"There's no way."

Alex fought the lock on his lungs to no avail as Catherine took over. "Maybe, but I've never seen him get so upset and defensive about a bite before."

"If something did that to me, it'd scare and upset me too."

"Yeah," Nathan began, "but since when have you known him to act like that for so long after the fact?" No one answered, and with another glance over at Alex, Nathan continued. "And then last week, when our professor called on him mid-class, he tensed up and didn't talk. Like he was nearing a panic attack."

Alex looked aside as what his friend had said back then replayed in his head. His right hand, meanwhile, fished a flashlight out of his pocket.

"You've had classes with him too," Nathan said with a gesture towards Catherine. "Since when has he behaved that way to a random call-out?"

"Never," she replied after a second to think.

Marcus responded with a lengthy sigh, his right hand covering and rubbing his mouth. Alex didn't look towards him as he pulled the flashlight above the tabletop. Once it was in view of his friends and their attention was drawn to it, the last mental barrier stopping him from talking dissolved.

"It's hard to believe, I know, but I can prove it. You know how canine eyes shine in indirect light?"

"Yours do that?" Marcus replied, one eyebrow going up.

Alex nodded before holding the flashlight out for Marcus to take. When he did so and clicked it on, Alex watched the sense of surprise gradually build in Marcus's expression when the light came near his head. He glanced over at Nathan and Catherine again, lowering the flashlight without a word and holding it out for them. Catherine took it and repeated the process, while Nathan leaned over to get a better view. Her free hand approached her mouth as her expression began to mirror Marcus's, while Nathan watched with an expression unmoved from intrigue.

The return of silence to the room, something Alex still feared despite what had just happened, prompted him to speak before he gestured for the flashlight back. "And it didn't just get me on the arm that night."

"Where else?" Catherine asked.

"On my shoulder." Alex traced the general pattern before pulling at the left side of his t-shirt collar. As half of the muzzle pattern of scars became visible, Nathan's expression went from intrigue to a wince, while Marcus's and Catherine's remained close to the same. "I'd seen it clear enough by then, but then I got home, realized how fast all of this had stopped bleeding..." His voice gained a crack as he stopped to compose. "Ah, geez."

What felt like a full minute passed before anyone spoke, Nathan taking charge. "You okay?"

Alex nodded. "Yeah. This whole thing's been eating at me all month."

"Sounds like it."

Alex sighed to compose himself further. "Sorry. Trying my best not to act like this... Frigging embarrassing."

"Can't say I blame you," Catherine said.

"So..." Marcus said after an extended silence, "what happened the first time you changed? Or, do you not remember any of it?"

With Catherine and Nathan looking towards him again, Alex's answer came quickly. "I do. I don't act feral or lose control when it happens."

"But the full moon part is true?"

"Yeah. Not nine to six true, though. It's all day, and then some."

"Really?" Nathan asked.

Alex nodded in response. "And I changed the day before the full moon."

"Holy crap."

"Yeah. Scared the hell out of me, and lucky me it was just Bailey with me that night."

"Your folks never saw you?" Catherine asked.

Alex shook his head, turning it towards his dog when he heard his claws clicking on the tile. Once his free hand had begun rubbing his pet's head, he continued. "I hid from them all day on the twelfth, and then when it was dark, snuck back inside and crashed."

Nathan exhaled noticeably. "Not a smart move, man."

"Yeah. That was when I realized I couldn't hide this much longer."

"No wonder you were so upset before," Catherine said.

Alex got in a shrug before a ring of the doorbell disrupted the conversation. Payment in hand, he headed for the front door, but instead of opening it immediately, he brought his nose close to the crack and inhaled. The scents he picked up were mostly urban with plants and vegetation until the first signs of pizza—cooked dough, cheese and marinara—leaked past.

With some food ready to go, Alex took the first few slices from his order, handing out plates to his friends as they came for theirs. For the duration of everyone's first slice there was little talking, giving him the time to reflect on the last half-hour. He couldn't help feeling thankful that this get-together was still going as planned, but in the back of his head, he was singling out many a situation or bit of news that would threaten how well his friends were taking this.

"Guys," Alex continued once everyone's attention was towards him. "Just in case it crossed your minds, I can shift outside of the full moon."

"I had a feeling," Catherine replied.

Thought so. "I've already done it once. Last Wednesday. It's harder to pull off than I thought, thankfully."

A look of question flashed across Marcus's face. "Wasn't that the day you told your folks about this?"

"Yeah. I couldn't figure out how to change back before they got home, so I had to let them see me and then explain myself."

"You told them something before then, I hope," Catherine said.

"Just that I wanted to tell them something when they came home. Nothing specific."

"So, they were expecting you…"

"But not as a werewolf."

"Then you shifting that day was an accident?" Marcus asked.

"Sort of. I was trying to do it that morning, but got nowhere with it until I messed up a handplant and hurt my wrist." The table went quiet again, and as he glanced around, Alex could see the gears turning behind the looks on his friends' faces.

"Was it the pain, or…"

"Had to be the adrenaline from the shock; the pain was dulled before I got back up."

"We'll try not to get you angry or slap you, then."

Alex raised an eyebrow at that, only to find a smirk emerging on Nathan's face that Catherine shot him a look for. Alex kept his own face from mirroring the expression, difficult as it was, as he replied.

"Uh, I doubt that'll happen."

As the smile that preceded his reply returned to his normal expression, the lack of further questioning gave him the opening he wanted to move the discussion away from his lycanthropy.

"But, anyway, I appreciate you guys coming and hearing me out on this. Means a lot."

"No problem," Catherine said, her posture relaxing a bit.

Alex gave her a nod in response, the tension around his ribs relaxing some in turn. When he stood up a minute later to refill his plate, the dice bag snapped to mind, and stayed on it until he was holding it again. If Nathan had seen him that day… But then, even when he'd made his case, he hadn't brought that up.

Was he assuming wrong and the bag had gotten there by other means?

Eh… There wasn't any of that werewolf's scent on this thing. Couldn't have been that. Alex rolled the dice in his palm for a bit, then made his way back to the kitchen, getting his friend's attention before he rounded the corner. "I think these are yours, man."

A second's glance at the dangling bag preceded Nathan's response. "I've been looking for that. Where was it?"

"In the grass across the street." Nathan casually snatched the bag out of mid-air after Alex tossed it his way. "Found it when I was hiding from my folks."

"Huh. No wonder I couldn't find it."

So he did lose it by accident. Whew.

"Not to pry or sound suspicious," Marcus began after a few seconds of silence, "but how did you know that was his?"

After a moment to consider his answer, Alex's response came with little hesitation. "Because his scent was inside the bag." When he noticed Catherine remove her hands from the table, as though she was trying to hide herself from him, a chill went down his spine. "I don't mean that in a weird way, I promise. I just have a more sensitive nose because of what happened, and…well, that's how I knew when I found it."

"How sensitive?" Nathan asked.

"Uh… I don't have a basis for comparison, but probably a real wolf's nose. Or Bailey's. Whichever one, I need much less of any one scent to notice it and what parts make it up." His friend mouthed a 'Wow' as he broke eye contact, the continued silence that followed helping spread the spinal chill over Alex's body.

With Marcus's fear scent weakened since the first hint of it, Alex remained seated, nibbling on his last pizza slice as both he and Catherine got up from the table and walked behind him. The discovery of an unfamiliar, yet pungent scent on the drafts that went by his nose kept him seated until they returned to their chairs and both his pizza and soda were finished.

"You all need to be anywhere soon?" Alex asked as he dropped his plate in the sink.

"Not for a while," Nathan said.

"Catherine and I have some plans for later tonight, so by six or so," Marcus said.

"In that case, there anything you guys want to do? Or would a movie or something suffice?" As his friends came to agree on watching something, Alex removed himself from the kitchen to look for something humorous, hoping it would sweep away the lingering mood of the last few minutes.

As the first episode of the TV series he chose played, the chuckling and commentary from everyone on and near the couch kept his eyes wandering, though his attention kept getting snagged on the gestures that hinted at his friends not being as relaxed as they sounded. Standout among them was the shuffling and repositioning of limbs. Catherine was doing it the most, with her arms folding a few seconds before they uncoiled, her hands holding the opposite forearm, or one hand covering another on her leg. Nathan's displays weren't as twitchy or evasive, with little beyond arm-folding, while Marcus simply leaned forward in his chair and interlaced his fingers.

Alex couldn't blame any of them, however. Had the roles been reversed, with one of them in his situation, he would be just as worried.

* * *

As 5:00 neared and his parents returned home, Nathan was the first to hint that he was about to leave. With Bailey pursuing him, Alex followed his friend outside.

"Thanks again for being here, man," he said as Bailey ran into the yard and Nathan unlocked his car.

"You're welcome."

"I...have to admit though," Alex began after a glance towards Bailey, "I didn't expect anyone to figure things out before I said anything."

Nathan gave a single chuckle. "It was nice to know my logic wasn't faulty, but still..."

"Yeah. Who would've thought werewolves were real?" With an offering of his hand, his friend shook it before sitting in the car. "Oh, just a sec. Did you talk to Marcus or Catherine about this before today?"

"I did tell them I had some suspicions, but nothing specific."

"Ah. Good thing I got all of us together then."

Nathan nodded before responding. "See you tomorrow in class, then?"

"Yeah. Later, man." After waving his friend off, Alex called for Bailey and coaxed him back inside. Hearing water running in the kitchen and bird chirps in the living room, he stopped at the edge of the foyer and repeated the thanks he'd given to Nathan a minute before.

"No problem," Marcus said from the kitchen.

"Glad we could help," Catherine said.

A smile worked its way onto Alex's face as his mother entered and walked through the living room. When Marcus reappeared, a fresh glass of ice-water in hand, Alex nodded to him before pulling out his phone.

How quiet his friends remained over the next minute however prompted him to speak. "Something still on your minds?"

"Yeah," Marcus said. "Given everything you told us, it sounds like this doesn't affect you beyond a monthly inconvenience."

"When I shift, yeah, but even then, I'm trying not to see it that way."

"I get you. If that's the case though, then what's the reason for all these animal killings?"

Alex's pulse rose a few beats at that, and he kept himself still despite wanting to take a step. With his free hand on his chin, he faked thinking about a possibility until Catherine spoke up.

"You said you stay in control when it happens, right?" she asked, to which Alex nodded. "Maybe that other one doesn't."

"That's possible..."

"Doesn't explain why they would do it so much, though," Marcus added.

"No, it doesn't." As he said that, Alex's thoughts returned to Angela—how badly she'd been torn up, how frightened she'd been. Several degrees of warmth were sapped from his skin in turn, and as he once again questioned why she'd been killed and he allowed to get away.

With Marcus and Catherine's departure a few minutes later, the sense of dread from his friend questioning the killings grew. That he could keep to himself, so long as he was careful, but the fact that his friend had suspicions about them, even if that was as far as it had gone for now...

Back inside, his parents were warming up a few slices of the pizza.

"How did it go?" his mother asked when he came close.

Alex's response came after a few seconds. "Okay."

"Did something happen?"

"No," Alex said with a shake of his head. "Nothing bad."

"'Bad'? What do you mean?"

"They understood, mostly."

"Did you tell them everything?" his father asked.

Alex only shook his head.

Chapter 20 – Covering the Bases

Monday, September 26th, 2011
Moon Phase – Waning Crescent

As his second class drew closer the next day, the possibility of Nathan questioning him about the animal deaths left him dreading the moment, if any, that he'd get his attention. Although Alex couldn't see him in any of the chairs when he was near the door to the room, how fidgety his hands were after walking in and sitting down spiked his anxiety.

For a moment following the gripping of his hands, Alex tried to convince himself that he was worrying over nothing. Nathan hadn't given any hints before that he was withholding something from the others or him, and when the class went by with little beyond a few glances from his friend, that feeling strengthened.

It was as his shift at the comic shop arrived that the feeling weakened. Marcus was working with him for three hours. The question from the previous day had to still be on his mind. How likely was he to be asked about that within a three-hour timespan?

For the first hour of his shift, nothing was asked of him outside of where a few products were. Despite that, Alex couldn't help glancing over at Marcus, to see if he was doing the same. Only once did he catch him doing it, within the quarter-hour before Trevor left the shop for his break.

When the store was empty of everyone but him and Marcus, his friend wasted no time calling his name.

"Yeah?" Alex replied after a second.

"Got a second?"

"Uh, yeah." He didn't continue until he was near the counter and had taken a glance outside. "What's up?"

"Just wanted your take on something that crossed my mind yesterday, after me and Catherine left." Alex felt his heart speed up at that, and as his friend took a second to speak. "These animal killings... We talked about it until I dropped her off, but what's the likelihood that these animals are food for that other werewolf?"

"Uh…" *Oh boy, stay calm.* Alex forced a 'Hmm' to disguise his stalling, and hoped that an interruption would present itself. *He didn't mention the moon…* "I'd say, pretty likely. Both times I've shifted, I've needed a lot of food afterward, but it doesn't have to be meat."

"I see." Though Marcus again went silent, before he or Alex could continue, a customer walked in, drawing their attention to the door. After welcoming them, and waiting for them to walk out of sight, he continued in a whispered tone. "Good to know. Who would make a habit of that, though?"

"No idea, man," Alex replied with a similar pitch to his voice, hoping that was enough to convince his friend. The passage of the following two hours with no other questions gave him a good feeling that it had.

Tuesday, September 27th, 2011
Moon Phase – New

The next day, as his second class reached its halfway point, the screen of his phone lit up, a text notification showing with it. It was from Catherine, asking if he was busy. Figuring she was planning on telling him something about Friday, he texted back that he'd call once out of class.

It took only one ring for her to answer when that time came. "Hey. Something going on?" Alex asked.

"Not really. Just wanted to say I hope I wasn't acting too weird the other day."

Acting weird? When what she meant by that clicked, Alex glanced around before replying. "You mean the hiding your arms and all that?"

"Yeah."

"No big deal. Everything I said to you guys freaked my folks out too."

Catherine gave a hum in response at first. "If you don't mind me asking…does it matter if you're like that or not? The better nose thing, I mean."

"It does. Considerably." Alex gave Catherine a second before continuing. "How much so, I can't tell, but it's pretty drastic."

"Okay."

For a time following that reply, neither of them said anything. While Alex was picturing what his friend's expression and train of thought could be on the other side of the call, he remembered the scent trail at her place of work.

"Oh, while I've got you on the phone, there's something I need to tell you."

"Sure."

"Remember that day a few weeks back when me and Nathan came by your work, when I bought that Mage rulebook?"

"Yeah. Why?"

"I didn't know how to tell you guys this back then, but when we came inside, I found the scent of the werewolf that bit me drifting around." Alex gave Catherine barely two seconds to think on that before continuing. "I'm not trying to freak you out. Just thought you should know."

Catherine took a few seconds to respond. "Was it the scent itself, or something else about it that made you nervous?"

"A bit of both. It was all over the store, so I couldn't tell if it was there shopping or...I hate to say it, scoping."

"Hmm. I guess my most pressing question would be, have you found that scent anywhere else? Blue Moon? Gamestop?"

"Haven't been to Nathan's work in a while, but Blue Moon, no." Recalling his mother's workplace at the library by the mall, a chill ran through him. "I guess if animals are this thing's target, it won't bother us."

"What about that girl?"

"That I still can't figure out." Alex and Catherine went quiet again for a time. "Wish I had something concrete to go on, something I could tell you guys."

"I'd say you already have. If you find that scent at Nathan's workplace, or yours, let us know."

"I will."

"And I'll keep my eyes open for anyone suspicious," Catherine offered. "Just in case."

"You sure?"

"Yeah, I don't mind."

Alex's initial negative feelings about the idea weakened over the following seconds, until he told her, "Be careful if you do."

"I will. I'll text you if I think I have something."

"Thanks, Catherine."

"No problem. Catch you later." As she hung up, Alex lightly sighed and turned around to march himself out of the building. Gamestop and the library. If his attacker's scent was in either of those places... But if it truly was interested in his friends and family, would it make it as obvious as stalking their workplaces? Almost a full month had passed since he'd been bitten as well. *Better play it safe.*

He went for the library first, snagging a parking spot close to the front doors. With his nose and eyes at the ready, he headed for the first of the airlock doors, ignoring the pocket of scents between them. Once the second door opened, he found hints of his mother's scent. Though she wasn't in sight, Alex let his eyes wander, holding one hand over his mouth and chin.

The librarians aside, already he could see nine other people in the building. The rows of shelves stretching from end to end could be hiding who knew how many more. As he began questioning the likelihood of finding a trace of his attacker, the idea of sniffing near the floor slipped into mind; the shudder that resulted shook it right back out and got him moving.

The people he passed along the way to the audiobooks shelves didn't reek of the other werewolf, nor did anyone sitting at the library desktops. After a second lap of the spots he figured were densest with past foot traffic, he continued with the aisles along the left side of the building, once again coming up empty. His confidence budding, Alex returned to the center of the building and pulled a book from the mass market displays before faking a gesture like he'd dropped something.

Of the scents that had settled to the floor, over a dozen were unique to what was already in the air, but the werewolf's was still not noticeable. He breathed a sigh as he stood back up. Nothing. Just what he was hoping for.

Chapter 21 – A Chance Encounter...

Tuesday, September 27th, 2011
Moon Phase – Waning Crescent
4:22 p.m.

Once outside and back on his motorcycle, the sight of his mother's sedan got Alex to raise his helmet's visor.

"Were you looking for me?" she asked as she pulled alongside him.

Alex shook his head. "Just stopped by for a bit. Didn't find any books I wanted."

"All right. See you at home, then. Love you."

"You too, Mom." With the visor back down, Alex revved his bike and headed for Nathan's workplace. He arrived to find it housing five window-shopping customers, with only one leaving during the minute he spent sitting on his bike. His first steps inside presented the same lack of scent as the library.

"Hey, man," Alex said, getting both Nathan's attention and the employee he was working with. After a full lap of the tiny shop, he approached the counter. "New release rush?"

"Earlier, yeah," Nathan said. "Mostly high-def collections this week, but still."

"Were you looking for something?" the other employee asked.

Marcus's upcoming birthday snapped to Alex's thoughts as he glanced around. "For a friend. No idea what to get him, but I'll look around for a minute. See if something strikes me." After filling his hands with a few game cases, Alex continued to glance around, easing up a touch when the other employee was sent on his break and left the store.

"The last game he bought was Duke Nukem Forever, if that helps," Nathan said as the front door swung shut.

"It does. Thanks." As Alex replaced the cases he had for two shooter-themed games, the front door opened again, drawing his attention. The new customer wore a red hoodie, his attention fixed on the PC section near the entrance. His hair was black, except parts of the longer strands around his forehead, which were bleached white. From the looks of him, Alex guessed he was his age, or a bit younger.

When the customer locked eyes with him after glancing away from the shelves, Alex gave him a quick nod before going back to reading the manuals he had.

"Welcome to Gamestop," Nathan said to the customer. "Looking for something?"

"No. Just browsing," the customer said. Nathan acknowledged the statement before resuming cleaning up the shelves behind the registers.

"I'm drawing a blank, man. Any suggestions?" Alex said after a minute.

"Uh…how about Metro 2033?"

The new customer chimed in before Alex found the game case. "That's a good one."

"Story-wise, or…"

"Yeah, and the gameplay too."

"Hmm." As he flipped the box around to read the back of it, and went through the manual, Alex snuck a few glances at the customer. He was now at the counter with a PC game in hand. "Looks neat. Might buy a copy for myself."

"Read the novel it's based on if you really like the game."

"I'm guessing you have already?"

"Almost done with a second read of it. Really good post-apocalypse setting."

"Makes sense, too. Using metro tunnels for shelter after shit goes south." Alex didn't get a response to that, the customer instead saying they'd pay cash for the game they had.

"There's your receipt." Nathan eventually said. "Enjoy."

"Thanks, Nathan."

Alex glanced towards the door when it opened again, catching sight of the customer looking in his direction as he departed. "He a regular?"

"No. I've only seen him in here once before," Nathan replied.

"Huh. Anyway, I think I'll go with what he suggested. You got a sealed copy of it in stock?"

"Yeah. Give me a sec."

As Alex replaced the case and walked up to the counter, he stepped into the patch of scents from the customer. Though the cleaning products were what he noticed first, before his second breath, every warning receptor in his head went off. His pulse rose, and a chill ran through him as he realized who he'd been talking to.

"Oh, shit." Alex didn't waste a second making for the door.

"What?" Nathan asked.

Alex didn't answer him and shoved the door open. As he stood at the curb of the parking lot, looking around in every direction, he didn't see the other werewolf. With some sniffs of the north-bound winds, he didn't find his scent. Standing further out, near his motorcycle, didn't reveal where it had gone, urging him back inside.

Nathan was quick to continue as the door closed. "What was that all about?"

"That was the werewolf that bit me," Alex said, glancing behind himself.

Though Nathan looked ready to ask if he was certain, he glanced towards the door and kept silent. Alex ran his hands through his hair at the same time. Several questions rushed him, the major one being if he was right about this guy stalking his friends. Even if it had been over a week since he'd caught his scent last, it couldn't have been a coincidence that he'd run into the werewolf here, or now.

"Well...we got a good look at him. So, there's that," Nathan at last said.

When he heard that, Alex's hand went for his phone. As he grabbed it, he thought of his father. Even if the police managed to find him, he could shift at will. The idea of his father being inflicted with what he had, much less ending up in the hospital for doing his job, hit his stomach like a gut punch.

His resultant shaky breathing pushed Nathan to speak up. "Dude, hey. Calm down."

With his right hand wrapped over his mouth and his face turned away from his friend, Alex replied. "Can't believe we were talking to that guy. Like it was nothing."

"Well, we didn't know until just now. Don't beat yourself up over it." Alex attempted to reign in his shaky breathing instead of responding. "Take a few minutes. Calm down."

"What about Catherine and Marcus?" Alex asked once he felt sturdy enough.

"I'll text Catherine, you let Marcus know. If the guy I sent on break comes back when he's supposed to, I'll call her."

"Alright." Alex kept his phone pressed to his ear after dialing Marcus' number. Though his friend was supposed to be off work, he didn't answer until four rings in.

"Hello?"

"Hey, man."

"Hey. What's up?"

Alex had to quietly sigh to continue talking. "Nathan and I just had a run-in with the werewolf that bit me."

The silence on the phone lines lasted for a few seconds afterward. "What happened?"

"That's the thing. Nothing. He just walked in, chatted with us, bought a game and left. I didn't realize it was him until after he left, when I walked into his scent trail."

Marcus didn't respond for a time. "That sounds to me like he didn't expect you to be there."

"I don't know, but anyway, we know what he looks like now."

"Anything that stood out?"

"His hair. It was…a bit moppy, and jet black, but the tips of a lot of the stands were bleached."

"Huh. That would make him stick out. What about the rest of him? How old was he?"

"He looked about sixteen to eighteen, I think; Nathan didn't ask for his ID for the game he bought. I couldn't tell how built he was either. He had a hoodie on."

"So, between sixteen and eighteen years old, maybe. Black and bleached hair, likely a thin build…"

"Yeah. Keep away from him if you see him. I don't trust that attitude he showed us."

"I wouldn't either." As Alex thought of something else to add, Marcus continued. "Hey, is this the first time you've smelled this guy?"

"Here, yeah."

"Where else has he shown up?"

"The Half-Price Books near here. About a week back."

"When Catherine was working?"

"As far as I could tell. The scent was still in the air when me and Nathan got there." Marcus hummed before Alex continued. "And I keep wondering, what if this guy's scoping us out?"

"What gave you that impression?"

"Me finding this guy's scent at two places where all of us work. Within one week."

"Okay, so…how would he know about any of us?" Marcus asked after a period of silence.

"What do you mean?"

"I mean, even if he can tell something by scent, like you can, how would he know we all know each other?" Alex tossed the question around until Marcus continued. "The last time we all got together was that party at Nathan's place, and I've seen no one like that before or since."

Alex strained his memory for a minute, leaning towards thinking his friend had a point before he pictured his attacker's black and tan pelt. "What about any large, black canines?"

"Seen none of those." Alex asked if he was certain. "Hundred percent."

Better ask Nathan and Catherine as well…

"If he's only shown up in those two places, I think we're fine."

"Even so, if you do see him, act normal. Don't let him know you're onto him."

"No problem."

* * *

"Something on your mind, Son?" When his father asked that question, Alex glanced up from his meal to find his parents watching him as though he'd done something. "You're being very quiet again."

Alex was hesitant to say there was. Since the encounter that afternoon, he'd thought about little else besides the werewolf, and allowed some old emotions to resurface with regards to his friends. "Just thinking."

"About?"

"Nothing specific."

"C'mon, Son," his father said after a brief silence. "Every time you've gone silent like this, something's been bothering you."

"Just talk to us," his mother added.

Alex sighed to himself before pulling his gaze down and shielding his mouth behind one hand. He spoke only after convincing himself that his parents could handle the same things his friends had, and removing that same hand.

"The werewolf that bit me? I saw him."

Immediately, shock replaced the concern on his mother's face. "Where?"

"At Nathan's workplace. Today."

"Did he threaten you?"

"No. He just walked in, bought a game, gave me his opinion on something, and left." With a glance towards his father, Alex continued, anticipating his question. "I didn't catch his name or if he had a driver's license or not; the game he bought wasn't age-restricted."

"Do you remember what he looked like?"

Alex nodded and then listed off everything he could remember.

"Huh. Aside from the hair, he'll blend into places really easily."

"Is there anything you can do about him?" his mother asked.

"Under these circumstances, no. The precinct is looking for a canine." Alex looked away when his father glanced at him. "I wish I could, but unless this kid does something unlawful, the best I can do is inform the officers I oversee to watch out for him."

"Hope that's enough," Alex said, trying to mask his disappointment and unease. Things went quiet again after that, and he noticed his mother reach for his father's hand and grip it.

After dinner, as he sat in his room with his homework in front of him, the two forms of the werewolf, and his scent, phased in and out of his thoughts. First Colony was a long way south from where he'd been attacked, as well as where the werewolf seemed to favor hunting, but that was the only area where he had shown as a human so far.

The longer Alex thought on things, the better the idea of searching for the werewolf himself seemed. The scent-tracking he'd done up to now was no different than what the police canine units did, and now that he knew what the werewolf looked like, as well as where he was likely to appear, all he needed was time to find more hints of his presence. Then he could branch out and track him down.

Chapter 22 ✦ ...Of Two Werewolves

Wednesday, September 28th, 2011
Moon Phase – Waxing Crescent

Alex spent the rest of Tuesday night marking spots on his phone's map where the werewolf had shown. Once his classes were over on Wednesday, and his stomach filled with a soda and a sub-sandwich, he drove to Gamestop again. Nathan's car wasn't there but the store was packed, keeping him seated on his bike, his held phone disguising his glances up and into the store.

Despite seeing no one with red clothing or black and bleached hair, he soon got off his bike to check inside. Within five minutes, he'd passed through every spot in the store that felt like a potential lingering spot for scents, finding none that belonged to the werewolf. Sighing quietly in relief, he made his way back outside, and then to Half-Price Books.

Once again, there was no immediate sign of the werewolf from the parking lot, and Alex found no trace of him inside around the entrance, or near the closest rows of shelves. When Catherine glanced up and saw him, he waved to her before coming closer.

Her first words to him were exactly what he was hoping to hear. "I haven't seen that guy you told us about."

"Nice. I didn't see him at Gamestop either. Just came from there." Catherine nodded with a smile, albeit one that wasn't completely uplifting. Alex lowered his voice for what he said next and stepped away as he finished. "Didn't find his scent around the front, but just in case..."

Starting from the spot where he'd found the werewolf's scent weeks ago, Alex stuck to the center aisle all the way down before double backing and weaving through the rows of shelves closest to the entrance. Despite the occasional stop and crouch, the scent wasn't among the many he found, and he moved to the other side of the building, once again finding no trace among the aisles.

He returned to find Catherine sifting through two stacks of book and DVD trade-ins. By the time she made eye contact, he was close enough to tell her the good news. "Glad to hear it," she replied before making a glance around.

"Then, catch you later?"

"Yeah. Don't forget, Friday."

"I know, I haven't. Thanks." As Catherine nodded to him, Alex returned the gesture and waved before heading outside. For a second, he thought of diverting towards the Tampa shop instead of Blue Moon, just in case the werewolf had shown up around there. Thinking it was too far out of the way, he continued to his workplace.

Daniel was working the register when he arrived, offering him a wave as he entered. Alex returned the gesture just before walking into a patch of air scrubbed of scents beyond a deodorizer and concentrated oxygen. After several feet, he was out of the scrubbed cloud, only to find it again in a few aisles, both in the air and close to the ground.

Wonder if Daniel noticed him? The closer Alex got to asking that question of his coworker, the more he hoped it wouldn't put suspicion on him in turn. When he did ask, Daniel hummed and looked aside.

"No, I haven't seen anyone with that kind of hair."

"Alright. Thanks." When his coworker returned to reading a nearby trade, Alex slipped away to breathe an easy sigh. Clear on all three fronts. At least for now.

Friday, September 30th, 2011
Moon Phase - Waxing Crescent

It was during his classes on Thursday that he got the inkling to check the skatepark he'd been attacked at. By then, he'd added the location of the kills he knew to his phone's map, with the spread of it all, an area of several square miles, making it clear how difficult it was going to be to find this guy. As his classes dragged on, he began to feel what he was certain his father did sometimes. That even though he had the information he needed, it was one guy out of thousands, over miles of space, that he was searching for.

When his scouring of the park and the fields around it that afternoon uncovered no traces of the werewolf, the location where he'd refrained from following the scent got him to question once again where the werewolf had gone that night. The houses across the street were one possibility, but so was the neighborhood down the road from his old middle school. Or was it somewhere within his own neighborhood?

* * *

The next day, during the test he was taking in his second class, Alex cursed to himself when his phone vibrated, and when Nathan glanced at the pocket that held his own phone. *Shit. Not now.* As he kept at the questions, each new vibration tested his nerves. He wanted to peek, even though he knew what would happen if the professor caught him doing it.

Shortly after Nathan turned in his test and left, another text came in. For the fifteen minutes that followed, Alex pushed through the last leg of his test, and when he finally got his chance to check the texts, how incorrect his assumptions were were laid bare.

Catherine W.: Guys, I was wondering if you all wanted to see a movie or something before we go out to eat tonight.

Happy Birthday, Marcus.

Marcus A.: Thanks, and sure.

Nathan T.: Sure. Any good ones out right now?

Marcus A.: A few.

Catherine W.: Keep them in mind, then. Let's wait for Alex.

Nathan T.: He's still in class. Shouldn't be too long.

Should've figured. Alex thought after a light sigh, and before wondering if he'd botched his test by worrying so much.

Alex S.: Yeah, that sounds good. What's showing?

His friends were quick to respond with a handful of films they wanted to see. After one was chosen, Alex left campus and headed for the theatre near

First Colony's mall. One half of the lot was almost barren of cars, leaving him plenty of space to skate around for a while, though after a few minutes, he grew curious if the theater was one of the places the werewolf frequented.

Deciding not to risk it, Alex made his way towards the building, halting near one of its corners. None of the scents from the ticket booth crowd matched the werewolf, and after getting his ticket, none that he found around the inside entryway, or the nearby men's restroom, did either.

* * *

When Marcus at last arrived, the sight of his work tee prompted Alex to ask if he'd been called in for something. He shook his head in response.

"Just grabbed a shirt and left the house. It's not that cold out." A sudden gust rushed by as he finished.

"If you say so," Alex said. "Happy Birthday."

"Thanks." Marcus took a seat inside his truck as Alex resumed skating around, though waved him back over less than a minute later. "Hey, have you found that thing's…scent at the bookstore since Tuesday?"

"No. Why?"

"Because Catherine seemed a bit fixated on keeping a lookout for it when I saw her at work yesterday."

Alex took a second to think over his response. "Was she nervous, or…"

"Didn't seem like it. More like she was distracted."

Alex hummed at first. "Okay. I wasn't trying to unnerve her. Just wanted to keep her informed and figure out if there was a pattern to this guy."

"You had any luck with that?"

"Aside from Nathan's place of work, no. This guy could be… Hang on, let me show you." Alex pulled out his phone and once the map app was open, zoomed out to show the spread of the killings and spots where the scent had been found.

"That's a pretty big area."

"No joke. Me and Nathan were lucky to even see him when we did."

Marcus studied the map for a few seconds before speaking again. "Looking at this, I think he lives around here somewhere."

"In First Colony?"

"Yeah."

"I thought so for a while too, but I don't know."

"It makes sense to me."

"This area is really packed though, plus all the killings have happened close to me and Nathan." At that, Alex noticed Marcus' expression take on some concern.

"Hope he doesn't live near us."

"Likewise, man." Alex turned his phone off and tucked it away before his friend could add more to his comment. Tonight wasn't the night for this, and with Nathan and Catherine's arrival, the subject was buried.

* * *

By the time the film finished, the four of them had decided on having dinner first, then hanging around Town Square for a while to end the night. The many scents of cooking meat at Marcus's choice of steakhouse left Alex unable to make up his mind for a while.

"So, how's it feel to be twenty-one?" Catherine asked as they waited for their meals to arrive.

"No different than twenty," Marcus said. "At least until I try a shot of whiskey."

"Got a flavor picked out?" Nathan asked.

"Nah. My folks have some ready for me. A Scottish brand, I think."

"Be careful then," Alex said. "Their stuff is potent."

"How would you know?" One side of Marcus's lips curled up as he asked the question.

Alex snorted a laugh but didn't answer.

"Because he's swiped a drink before, I'll bet," Catherine chimed in, keeping a straight face.

"It's Scottish. That says it all."

As the minutes went by, Alex began picking up the intensifying of scents related to their meals. His steak had gone to cook first, and then the three burgers his friends had ordered, as well as the four sides they'd chosen. When Catherine indirectly questioned how much longer it would take for their food to arrive, his snap answer got her and Marcus to get up and refill their drinks.

At the same time, the new arrivals to the restaurant, signaled by the tone the wooden doors set off when they opened, consistently drew Alex's attention. Between a family of three, two individuals, and what he assumed was a business manager group, only one pair of bodies left the building, freeing the table to his left.

Once their meals arrived, his side of garlic bread was pushed aside in favor of his steak until two bites were taken. By then, Catherine had pulled an envelope and a wrapped gift, likely a book from its size, from her bag. "Happy twenty-first." she said as Marcus took the items from her.

"Thank you." As Marcus wrapped an arm around her and pulled her close for a hug, Alex ducked down and began to sift through his backpack for the game and the card he'd purchased. The place he thought he'd put it was proven incorrect in seconds, and his heart rate sped up. He switched to the middle pocket, finding only his college papers at first.

Oh, crap. Did I leave it at the house? Moments later, in the back pocket, he at last felt what he knew was the wrapping paper and the edge of the card. Breathing a massive sigh to himself, he pulled them out as Nathan handed his gift over. "Enjoy your twenty-first, man."

"Thanks. Soon as we're outside, I'll open them up."

Nodding in response, Alex went back to his steak before remembering the door opening chime had sounded while his head was down. One of the families that had been there before them had left, and another had come in. No individuals otherwise. He took another bite of his steak, chewing slowly to savor the flavor, just before the door chime sounded again.

With his glance up, he saw the red hoodie first, then the person's arms wrapped around themselves. His pulse immediately jumped, a rise he could feel in his ears and neck as his body went still. The person shook their head once as they approached the order counter, and Alex continued watching as the hood was pulled down, revealing the black and bleached hair.

No. His arms began to tremble. He almost couldn't breathe. Not here. Anywhere but here. His breathing dropped in pitch, helping his lungs produce some slight growls, each one shaking his throat.

"Hey." Feeling something push his right shoulder, Alex snapped his head to the right, to which Nathan leaned back almost a foot. "Dude, the hell?"

Alex didn't answer. The other werewolf took precedence.

Turning back to see it hadn't noticed them yet—at least he hoped—his heart kept thumping, hard and strong against his ribs.

"Alex?" Catherine's voice was laced with apprehension.

"He's here," Alex replied. "The counter." None of his friends spoke after that, and when he heard the werewolf once again say he would pay in cash, he couldn't help wondering where the money was coming from. Did this guy have a job, or steal it from someone?

The idea of a family of werewolves lasted less than a second before Alex saw the werewolf turn and lock eyes with him.

His head dropped half an inch in response and another growl sounded, a louder one. He stopped making the noise only when the iron-like taste of blood hit his tongue; his canines had reshaped. And then his olfactory sense caught the first trace of fear, one he was familiar with: Nathan's.

Torn between his own feelings of fear and self-preservation, Alex tried to relax while not taking his eyes off the werewolf, to no avail. As soon as it began moving again, he inched himself up from his chair, straightening his neck and running his tongue near his fangs.

Out of the corner of his eye, he saw Marcus looking up at him, one hand reaching behind him to grab his chair. Though Nathan and Catherine were still silent, when he thought he heard a gasp from her, the realization that he was scaring his friends smacked him in the face. Gripping his hands, the tips of his claws poked one palm and scratched against the wooden table.

That realization froze him on the spot. Had anyone else seen him showcase those? Or his fangs? Or something else he wasn't aware of? *No. Don't panic. Calm down.* Despite feeling as if the eyes of the entire world were on him, Alex shook his head. This guy had seen his friends with him. If nothing else, he now knew who to look for.

Once the werewolf sat down, Alex took a step forward. Marcus shot up from his chair and stood between him and the werewolf.

"Wait..." He stopped talking.

Alex could see the fear in his eyes. Not unjustified at all.

"Stay back." He stepped around Marcus and made his way to the other werewolf. As much as he wanted to tell himself that this guy wasn't meaning them any direct harm, 'direct' was the key word. He wouldn't cause something here, with witnesses. He would do it without them. Without him knowing.

Up close, Alex's memory of the night he was attacked flashed through his head. This was the kid who had bitten into and shredded his shoulder and arm? Who had been killing so many animals for food? He shook that thought aside. Their roles were reversed here. He had the upper hand now.

"What are you doing here?" Alex's voice came out lower than normal.

"Wanted a nice meal." The werewolf's reply was neutral in tone, if not slightly agitated.

"I don't buy that, for one second," Alex said, wishing he could hear the werewolf's heartbeat. The silence he got in response went on for several seconds, until the werewolf turned his head to look back. Alex's limbs quivered harder at that sight. "If you even think about it…"

The werewolf then stood up, sliding his chair away so loudly that Alex felt every eye look their direction. No reply came after the action, just the action itself. But whether it was that, or the look in the werewolf's eyes, he shirked back an inch, narrowing his eyes. Deep down, it was like his body was recoiling on its own.

When his shoulder was grabbed, Alex glanced aside to find Marcus eying him, his expression unwavering but with fear rooted behind the surface. Alex looked back towards the werewolf, then Marcus again, lost for words. Nothing felt right enough to say.

And as he struggled to act, the shaking in his arms and shoulders continued, progressing into near spasms that went into his chest and legs, in turn testing his balance.

All Alex's thoughts, outside of panicked words to himself, froze as he corrected his stance. With one final glare at the other werewolf, he headed outside, trying not to rush his pacing and draw more attention or suspicion; the footfalls behind him told him Marcus was in pursuit.

Outside, the strengthening of his olfactory sense flooded Alex's head with new scents to process, his brain feeling a squeeze from the changes. His breathing quickened, exposing the animalistic rumbling behind each breath, only for it to be snagged by the sound of the restaurant door opening behind him. Who was following them?

As the sounds of the bones and tissue of his hands crunching began to sound, he tucked them between his jacket and T-shirt before noticing a reflection on the windshield of his friend's truck. Nathan had followed them.

"Hey, Marcus. Your keys," he demanded.

Marcus's tone was rife with fear as he spoke. "What for?"

"Your truck bed's covered." As he heard the keys change hands, Alex silently thanked him. The cover of Marcus's Ford, however, was a thin aluminum and fabric shield. Too much noise, or any screaming, would sound from behind it.

As Nathan's shaking hands got the key into the tailgate lock, Alex could feel his muscles growing and tightening behind his skin and clothing. Once it was down, the barely-illuminated cage behind it made him take a subconscious step back.

What urged him forward again was the sound of a car passing by to his left. Alex glanced towards it and once it was out of sight, climbed inside the truck bed. Nathan inched the tailgate closed right after, the clamping of the lock cutting off the outside lights and leaving him in pitch blackness.

With his T-shirt tightened around his chest and arms from how long his muscles had been bulging, he couldn't avoid tearing into the fabric as he pulled it and his jacket off, though the rest of his clothing slipped off easily. Now lying on the ice cold, and rough-surfaced, bed-liner, he grabbed his discarded shirt to cover his mouth in case he had to scream, at the same time wishing his fur would grow in to heat him up.

His first time to need it came as the bones in his feet crunched and snapped, starting the change to their canine shapes. With tears welling in his eyes, the cotton tee muffled his groaning, forcing him to breathe through his nose.

For a moment, he pictured his friends, along with the fearful expressions he'd seen them display. He'd started to shift right in front of them. Now what would they see in him?

The thought clawed at his insides as his legs finished taking shape and his tail emerged, followed by the first patches of his pelt. The progressing itching left him rubbing at his skin until he heard the bones of his jaws popping. His tee was wrapped loosely around his face as both bones went slack and pushed out to form his muzzle, only coming off as the last of his pelt grew in to coat it.

Chapter 23 – Logic and Emotion

Friday, September 30th, 2011
Moon Phase – Waxing Crescent

With the transformation over, Alex held still and reigned in his shaky breathing as best he could. He soon heard footsteps on the left of the truck, ones moving towards the restaurant before returning his way after a bit of time. Figuring it was Nathan, he then heard another set, and then a voice.

"Think he's okay?" It was Catherine.

"No idea." This time it was Nathan.

Unable to tell if they were saying those things out of fear or concern, Alex felt around for the walls of the truck bed and then, after a period of silence, tapped the liner once, then twice. Though he wanted to talk and reassure them, for now, that would work.

Shortly after the taps, the footsteps sounded again, heading towards the front of the truck. Assuming it was Catherine, how quiet she and Nathan were only added to the guilt and embarrassment coursing through his body. The second set of footsteps sounded a few seconds after, this time heading for the rear of the truck.

As he tracked them, Alex shuffled further back into the bed. For a moment they stopped, and then the telltale sound of tires rolling by came close. His pulse shot up at the thought of the police being just outside. As cornered as he was...

With a shaky reach up, he touched the cover of the truck bed. It was loose, and the tiny crack he opened let a bit of moonlight into the pitch-black space. His night-vision went to work, letting him see how much space he had before he leaned up and his back bumped the cover.

He got no further than that before the tailgate's handle clicked.

His head snapped to the side and his body recoiled into the corner. As he felt his blood rushing into his neck and ears, the tailgate came down to reveal only Nathan's torso, and then his head as he leaned down.

"You okay?"

Alex didn't respond. His friend's expression of worry, along with his trembling arms and still-present scent of fear, made trying to harder, even when he squinted to try and see further in.

When Nathan reached for his phone, the mental barrier keeping Alex silent cracked. "Yeah." Despite saying no more than that, his friend noticeably flinched.

"Not sure what Catherine's doing," Nathan said after a bit of silence and a peek over the cover.

"That guy leave?" Alex asked. He got a shake of his friend's head when he leaned back down in response.

"He hasn't said anything to us though. No looks either."

Alex smiled to himself at that. "Good." The silence after his response dragged on longer than he was comfortable with and telling himself that he had no idea this would happen didn't help. With the first quivering of his stomach, he wrapped an arm tightly around it, hoping the noise hadn't carried.

When the door of the restaurant opened again, the approaching footsteps stopped near the back of the truck. "So, what now?" Nathan asked.

"He suggested we go to the elevated lot by the mall, or the theater parking lot," Catherine replied. "Shouldn't be a lot of people there."

The uncertain reply from Nathan got Alex to chime in. "Guys?" He waited for acknowledgment before continuing, his stomach churning again as he spoke. "If it's easier, you can drop me off at my place, then come back."

"What about your bike?" Catherine asked.

"It won't get towed."

"You're sure?"

"Very, and Dad can pick it up if need be."

Catherine's eventual reply was followed by her footsteps back towards the restaurant. As he waited for her and Marcus, Alex's stomach continued to churn. The thought of his steak in his hands made him lick his lips, but even when he could smell it on the air, embarrassment and guilt kept him from asking for it.

"You sure you're okay?" Nathan asked once it sounded like everyone was ready to go.

"Yeah," Alex said as he rubbed his stomach. "Where we going?"

"Your place."

"Thanks." The tailgate went up and locked shortly after his reply.

Hoping that a drive would lessen the unease among everyone, Alex tried to relax as the truck started up and began to move, eagerly awaiting being able to get out. With the tailgate closed, the bed once again felt like a cage, the stops and turns that occurred when he couldn't see them, and the rough liner picking at his fur, not helping that feeling.

For most of the ride, he anchored himself against both sides of the bed, trying to keep a mental map of where they were going. After what felt like ten minutes, the truck slowed down and began to stop and turn more often— a good sign they were in his neighborhood.

The bumping of the tires and drive up a short incline signaled the end of the trip, with one of his friends getting out after the truck stopped.

"We're clear out here." Nathan said once the tailgate was down again.

"Thanks." His discarded clothes in paw, Alex crawled over to the opening, peeking his head out first. His folks hadn't left the porch light on, and the streetlight directly across from the driveway was out. All good signs as the scents from his steak wafted near his nose again, encouraging a lick of his lips.

As he dropped from the tailgate into a crouch, Alex glanced under the truck. Nathan was facing his way but keeping back near the rear driver side door, and his father's truck was also missing from the driveway. "You guys okay?"

"Yeah," Nathan said. "Still shaking a bit, though."

Alex sighed to himself. "I'm sorry, man. I didn't mean for this." He got no response, and in turn, took longer to make himself stand up.

As his head crested the top of the cover, he kept his focus on where Nathan was standing. The passenger door he'd exited through was ajar, and the cabin lights were on. With a glance towards Marcus and Catherine, Alex looked back in time to spot Nathan's throat bulge for a swallow before he broke eye contact to focus on the takeout box in his hands. Inside the truck, Catherine was staring at him with a curled hand near her mouth, her eyes making it clear how nervous she was.

Though Marcus didn't show any outward signs of nerves, only immense surprise, as Alex approached Nathan, his ears folded further back with each thought of what his friends might say to him. The rapid pacing heartbeats he expected to hear were muffled in turn.

"My folks reacted the same way," he said as his friend handed him the container.

"I can imagine," Nathan said, trying not to sound unnerved. "I mean...holy shit."

"Yeah." Alex attempted to look up and around before continuing. "If you all want to head out, that's fine. I'll figure something out in the meantime."

Nathan barely started his reply before Alex's stomach growled and a paw was placed over it. The noise went on for several seconds, and through several pitches, before it stopped. His friend inched back further as it did, and Alex felt his heart clench at the sight.

"You sure you're alright?" Nathan at last said.

"I will be." As Alex looked down at the container in his paw, then up and around for civilian activity, the unwavering attention his friends had on him changed his mind about separating from them. They were already here. He could invite them in, at least let things end on a semi-good note. "On second thought, I can host you guys for a while, if you want. My folks won't mind."

The hesitation he was met with put more pressure on his heart, though all three of his friends eventually agreed on it. With a nod, Alex returned to the truck bed to grab his clothes and locate his key ring. Once the front door opened, he heard Bailey's paws hit the carpet and then drop into a more paced rhythm; he'd been sleeping on his bed. With a gesture to his friends to follow, Alex held still and sealed his lips, awaiting the reaction from his pet.

The recoil through Bailey's body as he rounded the corner from the living room and spotted him was unmistakable, though it thankfully wasn't followed by any defensive posturing or growling. "Good boy," Alex said before slipping into the office to his left. Bailey didn't follow, instead keeping still until his friends came inside and Catherine began sweet-talking to him.

After closing every set of window blinds he could see, Alex slipped into the kitchen storage room and tore open the container his steak was in. His friends made their way into the dining area as he bit off the first two pieces, their continued silence getting him to ask if he could get them anything. With Marcus the only one who didn't answer 'some water', Alex bit off and chewed another piece of his steak before gathering what he needed for them.

What he found when he entered the dining area, glasses in paw, was Nathan and Catherine seated and both of their fear scents present in the air. Alex couldn't help glancing around at them in turn. The hiding of limbs or the shuffling of them into defensive gestures, things he'd seen mostly with Catherine before, were now more pronounced with Nathan as well. Hoping it wouldn't last, he set the glasses down with as toothless a smile as he could manage. "If you need more, tell me."

"Thanks," Catherine said, to which Alex nodded and returned to the storage room. As the rest of his steak was consumed, he heard Marcus come back into the dining room and take a seat. The only sounds he heard afterward were from take-home packages being moved and used, and his guilt strengthened.

"Hey, Alex?" Nathan said after several minutes.

"Yeah?" Alex's attention didn't break from the hot dogs warming up in the microwave.

"I think your folks are home. Just saw the curtains light up."

The news sent a chill through Alex's skin before a rumbling sigh escaped his lungs. He said nothing more and waited for the front door to open, all the while keeping his thoughts on what he needed to say. That him shifting was an accident.

His father was the one to call into the house after the door opened.

"Hey, Mr. Stryker," Marcus called back.

Alex felt his chest, and then his throat, as he inched into the kitchen. "Where's Alex?" his father asked.

"The uh…pantry, I think. Microwave just went off."

The silence Marcus received was broken by a question from his mother. "Did something happen? You all seem kind of quiet."

After a second more of feeling his blood pumping in his ears and neck, Alex forced himself to speak, though what came out sounded filtered through unwilling growls. "When we were out eating, yes." He got no reaction from his parents, though what he thought was happening around the corner stuck in his head until he stepped out and saw them. His mother was covering her mouth with both hands, while his father covered his forehead with one. Both of them looked horror-stricken.

"Oh, my God. How did this happen?"

With a glance around at his friends, Alex knew he'd be the only one talking for a while. Which didn't help the tightening of his chest and muscles resulting from being the center of attention. "Dad, it was an accident. I didn't mean for it."

"How could it have been an accident? Did you not notice something was wrong?"

Alex dropped his head, his new view shifting to Marcus first. "Not until it was too late. I wasn't thinking straight."

"Why not? What happened?"

The tone his father directed at him, one losing the hint of fear, helped relax his nerves. Just a straight answer. That was all he needed to give. "The werewolf I told you about? He showed up at the restaurant we went to." His parents didn't speak during his pause, and Alex continued. "I thought he was there to watch us, and…I was already changing when I confronted him."

"Did anything else happen?"

"No," Marcus said. "He got outside in time. Hid in my truck bed until we got here." Alex looked over to him again, nodding both his thanks and a confirmation.

His mother then removed her hands from her face, and placed them over her chest, before she spoke, "That's good to hear."

"It'll be a while before my heart beats that fast again, though," Nathan added, trying to sound amused.

Alex gave the silence that followed a couple seconds before he turned around and went for his meal. The dogs had cooled enough to hold by then, and half of the plate was eaten as his parents exchanged a few words with his friends. Once he heard their door close, he took what remained of his current meal and set it on the table, along with his drinks.

The second plate of eight hot dogs he brought out drew clear amazed looks from Nathan and Catherine, something that didn't go away as the first of them was eaten. Figuring it was the sight of him having to open his muzzle so much, Alex swallowed the piece he had before nibbling his next bite.

"Can't really close my mouth like this," he said between bites.

"Changing makes you that hungry?" Nathan said.

Alex nodded. "It caught me off guard the first time. Scared me a bit."

"I'm more amazed that you can still talk." Catherine said.

"I was too when I realized it." Alex said as a smile worked into his muzzle. With no response to his answer, he continued with his meal until the sound of Bailey's claws against the tile got his attention. His eye contact slowed his pet's pace before Marcus tried to call him over. A glance was all he got before Bailey continued into the kitchen, head and ears both down.

"Poor puppy." Nathan said.

"Yeah. He'll be fine once I change back," Alex said.

"How long do you think that'll take?"

The fact that the last two times he'd changed back happened after feeding on something live made Alex hesitant to answer. He could feel the sentence reach his mouth before he diverted to another train of thought.

There had to be something he wasn't considering about this, but what? "I don't know. I don't think time is a factor, but…"

Marcus picked up when Alex paused. "But nothing so far proves otherwise."

"Yeah. Relaxing doesn't do it, imagining it happening doesn't do it…"

"Well, you've only been a werewolf for…a month, right?" Catherine asked.

Alex nodded. "And I've only shifted on my own once before now."

Nathan took a second before speaking up. "Maybe it's just harder to change back."

"Maybe. Starting it isn't easy either."

"Didn't seem like it to me." Marcus said.

"My first time it was. This time…I don't know what set it off."

"Anger, probably," Nathan said. "Kind of hard to forget that look on your face and the noises you were making."

"Yeah, that was pretty scary," Catherine said.

"I don't think it was that," Alex said after several shakes of his head. "I wasn't angry, I was worried. I didn't want that guy coming near us, even if it was just a coincidence that he showed up there."

Nathan and Marcus looked at each other, then over to Catherine. "So, more like self-defense?" Marcus asked.

Alex nodded again. "If that's true though, then I really need to be careful after this."

"No joke."

As he finished off the last of his hot dogs, Alex closed his eyes and leaned on his paws. The lack of noise around the table made the heartbeats of his friends audible again. Though Marcus seemed the calmest, all three of them had elevated pulses compared to his own, a contrast that struck him as worrisome with the now lack of their fear scents.

"You look like a sleepy dog doing that," Catherine remarked after a minute.

Alex opened his eyes just as Nathan started chuckling under his breath. "Well, don't ask me to fetch something or roll over," he said, his muzzle showing a smile again.

"I'm tempted," Nathan chimed in.

"Very funny." With his eyes once again closed, Alex fingered the bullet around his neck and thought over what to do. If his friends left before he managed the reverse shift, only his parents would be an issue. If not, the bathroom was behind two doors, and he had plenty of towels to muffle any noises. The idea of going to sleep early and then trying to shift back once he woke was tossed out as soon as he thought of it. If he didn't wake hungry for live meat, he'd be that much closer to hitting that point, and likely damning himself to risk exposure.

"Um, you want some privacy?" Catherine asked.

Alex didn't open his eyes. "No, just thinking. Getting some ideas."

Marcus was first to speak after that. "Curious. Did you try to change back immediately last time?"

"Yeah, I did."

Marcus hummed at first. "Could be that you just can't until enough time passes."

"I'm not sure. It doesn't feel that way. More like I'm doing something wrong."

"But you were stuck like this all day that time, right?"

"Yeah, and..." During his pause, Alex recalled the time he'd spent sitting in his room after eating the raccoon and getting caught. The guilt he felt for letting his father see what he had, along with the rest of the emotions that had been swimming in his brain back then, began to seep back into his chest, and his free paw gripped his necklace.

"What?" Catherine asked.

Alex exhaled out his nose. The emotions clawing at his chest didn't go away. "Nothing. Just realized what Marcus was implying."

"Then," Marcus began, "what got you to change back?"

"I don't know. A lot was going on when it happened." The further questioning Alex expected as he once again paused never came, as if his friends were giving him time to answer. "Whatever it was, there's got to be something else I can try. Something that doesn't depend on emotions or things I can't control."

"Well, I'd suggest hitting the hay early, then trying something when you wake up." Nathan said. "Who knows? Maybe even a quick nap will help?"

Alex shook his head as Catherine voiced her agreement. "No, I don't think so."

"Trevor won't mind if you need to miss an hour or two of work," Marcus said. "Just come in a bit later."

"I know...but I'd rather not," Alex finally said. "Not if I could come up with something now." A short exhale went out his nose as he slowed his breathing and tried to think, his eyes closing again. For a moment, he swore the pacing of heartbeats around him was accelerating.

Nathan's next words didn't quell that assumption, nor did the creak from his chair. "Then, should we leave you alone a while?"

"No, you're fine," Alex said as he crossed his arms over the table and laid his head down over them. The scents of fear he expected to find were weaker than he thought, and reached his nose for only a handful of breaths.

When he opened his eyes, Catherine was the first he glanced at. "No luck?" she asked, to which Alex shook his head.

"I can't think of anything," he said before pulling his head back up.

"Then try to relax for a minute," Marcus offered.

Alex didn't answer in favor of taking a few deep breaths, but when he snuck a look at Marcus, he couldn't help picturing what was going through his head. He'd questioned him before about the dead animals. Had he acted out enough to put that back into his thoughts? Or was he just giving some friendly advice? Alex took a few more breaths, the blood pumping in his ears revealing when his pulse began to slow.

He then pictured holding his console's controller in his paws, watching them start to turn back into his human hands, and then making for bathroom before the rest of the reverse shift played out. His real arms had since crossed in front of his stomach, as if in prep for the reverse shift to hit him any second, and there first. When Alex then tried to imagine himself emerging from the bathroom after changing back and having a shower, what pleasure he got from the idea was short-lived, even when he followed it up with the mental image of his friends helping him clean up his discarded fur, awkward smiles all around.

I shouldn't be keeping you guys around for this, Alex said to himself before exhaling out his nose. He'd already cost them an hour of potential pleasure on an eventful day, and for all he knew Marcus was right and time was a factor working against him.

Or possibly worse.

Alex tightened the hold his arms had on his chest while his throat did the same all its own. The hunger hadn't shown until more than eighteen hours had passed last time. He had to have that much time at least, but if he didn't figure something out, he'd be forced to hunt in broad daylight—a death sentence if he was caught or followed home. And what if he had no success and the hunger was allowed to worsen?

He cursed himself for not keeping in control at that thought, only for the image of his friends keeping away from him to resurface. What if they figured it all out because an animal died the day after they saw him change? Even if he lied and said that other werewolf did it, Marcus's suspicions wouldn't be quelled, and then it was only a matter of time.

When Catherine asked if he was okay, Alex's swollen throat kept his muzzle closed, a brief glance the only reaction he gave her. At the same time, he could feel his abdomen taking the opposite action, mildly at first, but then so much so that the compression was turning painful. As his breathing quickened and grew more growl-laced in response, he heard the chairs around him slide back.

Alex did the same after freeing an arm, his eyes keeping shut until he felt his chair bump the counter behind him. Once he was sure it was braced, he leaned back to the relief of his stomach, and with a deep breath leaned forward again to get to his feet. The sole glance he got at his friends landed on Marcus and Catherine, their cautious stares, as his chest began to compress, his lips parting further at the discomfort.

But as he took his first step towards the living room, the reverse shift accelerated. The tension in his muscles shot though his limbs as the increase in pressure on his chest drew a protracted snarl. The chairs his friends were using were pushed back in response, two of them colliding with the walls and their footsteps freezing before any of them took two steps.

The noise also drew his parents, the opening of their door drawing Alex's head up enough to glance at them as he made for the bathroom. Hoping the arms around his chest were enough of a signal, he shut both bathroom doors behind him and let himself down onto the tiled floor.

As he worked to pace his breathing, and muffle the growls escaping his lungs, the pressure on his stomach was slow to lax, even as his bones began to reform. His expanded ribcage remained as the collapsing of his muscle structure began and he tilted his head to the side, just in case his stomach was forced to empty.

When he tried to move his right arm—and now clawless paw—closer to his mouth, how heavy his limb seemed set off an alarm in his head. He hadn't felt this way last time during the reverse shift, at any time. With his eyes once again open, he listened close to his breathing, his arms now folded across his stomach. As his tail and ears reverted, he kept his focus on staying awake and alert. All that was left then was his chest.

When the crunching down of his ribs and sternum at last came, Alex gasped to draw the air he needed. The loss of mass added to the lethargy he was feeling, the shrinking of his lungs forcing out as much air as he took in.

After what felt like minutes, the last of his ribs settled. With no change to how weighed down and shaky his arms felt, he slid them up towards his chest, brushing the discarded strands of his pelt off his abdomen, and then let his head fall back.

Chapter 24 – Some Time to Pause

Friday, September 30th, 2011
Moon Phase – Waxing Crescent

With everything once again quiet, the lack of voices beyond the doors he was sheltered behind left Alex with the impression that he'd scared everyone in the house into silence. The image of his friends leaving while he was changing back was quick to surface and linger in turn, adding pressure to his throat.

His parents came to mind next. Right outside the room was where he felt they were, but after turning his head to his right, his view through the door's bottom gap showed no hint of them. Although thankful that they were giving him some space, and that he'd managed to shift back so soon, Alex couldn't help feeling a bit defeated. This made it twice in a row that an emotion, and likely adrenaline, had been driving the change instead of something, or a combination of things, that he could control.

When he tried to move his arms after what felt like a few minutes, the weakness throughout his muscles had laxed, enough that he could lift them a few feet, but the soreness in his joints hadn't. How nice a cold shower would feel helped push him to get up several minutes later and start brushing off his pelt. The heat the strands had trapped vanished as more came off and the pile around him grew, the first splashes of cold water taking away what remained of both.

Once he was done, and had passed the first of the bathroom doors, the lack of voices was broken by the sound of Bailey sniffing under the second door, and Alex let him in. His pet made a beeline for the pile of discarded fur after confirming he was human again and licking at his face, leaving Alex a path to his room and a change of clothes.

It was as he entered the hallway that he spotted his parents sitting on the living room couch and halted. The look of relief from his mother pushed half a smile onto his own, though his father had a more concerned look.

"Everyone okay?" Alex asked.

"Yeah," Nathan responded from the dining room, relieving some of Alex's fears.

His father spoke next. "What about you?"

"Really sore." Alex got no response, but figured it was obvious to at least his parents and continued to his room.

The sight of his bed, and how suddenly his thoughts changed to flopping down atop it, added weight to his eyelids until a brief chuckle helped push them back open. They drooped again as he was halfway dressed, and closed for a few seconds, until he shook his head. He'd never hear the end of things if he left the pile of fur, much less his motorcycle, uncollected.

On the way back to the living room, his eyelids drooped again; the brief shake of his head got his parents to stop him as he neared the corner to the dining area.

"You sure you're okay?" his mother asked.

Alex got in a glance at his friends, and a massage of one hand and elbow, before answering. With just their postures to judge by, all three of them seemed more relaxed, though just as observant. "Yeah. It'll pass."

Silence followed until Catherine spoke up. "What about your motorcycle?"

Alex didn't get the chance to answer. "I don't think he should be driving right now," his mother said, to which his father agreed.

"Then, Dad, could you help me haul it back?" When his father agreed to the idea, Alex rubbed his eyes. Just one more hour, then he could collapse in his bed.

His friends took their leave as he found what he needed to sweep up the fur pile. Alex apologized and thanked them as much as he could before the front door was shut and he was left with his parents. Throughout the trip to and back from First Colony, despite the acceleration and turns, the rumbling of his father's truck's engine, and the lowered windows allowing in the cool night air, Alex couldn't avoid shutting his eyes and nodding off every so often.

Saturday, October 1st
Moon Phase – Waxing Crescent

He awoke early the next morning to most of his joints and muscles still aching from the shifts. With a warm shower hardly helping that feeling, he spent the following hour outside coasting the sidewalks and playing fetch with Bailey.

As noon came around and he went back inside for lunch, his mother, already seated at the dining table, got his attention while he fixed a sandwich. "Are you feeling any better?"

"Yeah."

His mother took a few seconds to respond. "Does that always happen?"

"Does what?" Alex corrected himself before she spoke. "Oh, no, just that time."

"How long were you like that yesterday?"

"Hour and a half, I think." Figuring his mother would ask how he'd pulled it off, he continued. "And I didn't do it willingly, either time."

"Then, you have no idea what changed you back?"

Alex sighed. "Some idea. Something got to me, then it happened."

"What did?"

"Doesn't matter."

His mother didn't respond immediately. "You were scared, weren't you?"

Alex glanced up, catching his mother's concerned gaze, and then hung his head. His emotions from before began pushing tears into his eyes before he tried huffing them back. "Still doesn't matter; I can't depend on that." He kept at pushing his emotions back as his mother got up and came close, what control he had over them slipping as she wrapped her arms around him.

By the time his mother spoke again, Alex had moved from pushing his emotions back to fighting the lump in his throat. "Then, can you promise me you'll be careful from now on?"

Unwilling to answer with his emotions running so strong, Alex thought over what to say. 'I'll try' was all he could agree to. The other werewolf couldn't be the only trigger for an involuntary shift, much less the only thing that would make him so worried about anyone he was close to. Thankfully, his mother kept silent until he'd bottled his emotions enough to answer on his terms. She hugged him tighter after he gave his answer.

For a while after lunch, Alex was too distracted to do anything but game. With Bailey lying by his lap, the occasional rub of his dog's head eased his mind onto other things, though for a while he couldn't stop imagining how his friends would react, or speak, to him when they next saw him. Marcus especially, and he had several shifts with him next week.

As his choice of game hit a slow point, he paused it and stroked Bailey's head some more. Eventually, the idea of taking the initiative snuck into mind.

Marcus was on shift today, and he had been the calmest before, at least on the outside.

Over the next few minutes, Alex kept reassuring himself that he hadn't done anything damning, that he didn't have anything to be nervous about with talking to a friend. He then coaxed Bailey outside for another few rounds of fetch and when 1:00 came, he started up his bike and headed for the comic shop.

Once there, he spotted Marcus working the register and parked next to his truck. As he came inside, his friend's greeting was more neutral than usual.

"Hey," Alex responded. "Trevor here?"

"No. He's on his lunch break."

Alex nodded once. "Then, you have a minute?"

"Yeah."

Alex looked aside at the door before walking towards the counter. Though he could picture well enough what he wanted to say, how long he stalled on it got Marcus to speak first. "This about yesterday?"

"Yeah," Alex said.

Marcus jumped in before he could continue. "It's fine."

Alex breathed a quiet sigh. "Thanks. I didn't expect that guy to set me off that much."

"I could tell..." Marcus began, checking the doors again, "from the growling and your eyes turning yellow."

My eyes changed color? The news didn't feel breaking to him for some reason. "I'll try not to let it happen again. Not sure how though."

"On that, mind if I ask you something?"

"Sure. What?"

"If you see this guy again..." Marcus stalled, and then restarted his sentence. "You said you were concerned about us before, so what happens if you find him again?"

Alex averted his eyes for a second. If Marcus was asking about how he would confront his attacker again, why would he add something to the thought? "I'm confused."

"When you confronted that guy, you almost stepped back when he got up."

"It caught me by surprise, if that's what you mean."

"Maybe, but as soon as he got up and stared at you, you lowered your head a bit." Marcus waited for a moment, as if for an answer or to see if Alex would add something he was missing. "That's not something I've ever seen someone do when surprised."

Alex thought on that for a time. Backing away. Lowering his head when confronted. A chill touched his skin when one explanation stood out. "I was acting submissive?"

"I have no idea man, but that really stood out to me."

Alex looked away and rubbed his forehead. "Thanks for telling me. I had no idea I did that."

"No problem."

After a few seconds, Alex continued. "To answer your question though," he paused to think about his answer, "if I do run into him again...I don't know. I guess try and keep myself calm."

"That's a given I think, but submission is a canine thing, right?"

"When there's a hierarchy in play, yes." When Alex said that, something clicked. That was what his friend was trying to say. "Oh, shit." A shiver ran through him as he ran a hand through his hair. Marcus's expression when he looked at him again made it clear he was weighing up what was said as well.

Alex then recalled how he'd behaved the night before. Taking the initiative to break his concentration before he started changing. He'd seemed more determined than angry now that he reflected on things. Had that rolled over into his attitude for the rest of the night?

"You okay?" Marcus finally asked.

"Yeah," Alex replied. He cleared his throat before speaking again. "And I know I said this last night, but thanks for everything you did for me." He held his hand out afterwards.

"You're welcome," Marcus said, returning the handshake with a firm grip. "And thanks for the game. Been enjoying it so far."

The statement drew a weak smile out of Alex. "Glad to hear it." His friend broke the handshake when a customer entered the store a second later, and Alex stepped aside to let him get back to work.

The questions came again as he found something to read. Had he acted submissive on instinct? What would that signal to his attacker if he had? That he was afraid of him no matter how he found him? The thought of acting like that subconsciously was bad enough.

It was when Alex began questioning if the werewolf noticed what Marcus had that something occurred to him. Even if he had acted that way, it was only when the werewolf stood up as if to face him, and he hadn't shirked away or acted like he wasn't a threat after that, something that he knew submissive canines would do. Whether that was due to his friends being close by or not hung in his thoughts until he was ready to leave.

Instead of heading straight home, Alex made another run of the locations his friends worked at. Neither Nathan nor Catherine were working, something he was pleased to know when he found the werewolf's scent at the bookstore once again.

As he followed it towards the right side of the store, and tested how far it went down each aisle, he soon found the strongest concentrations: down a Sci-Fi/Fantasy aisle, and around the New Age section. Seeing an influx of books on werewolves in the latter section, Alex watched for a free moment before sniffing near the spines; the werewolf's scent was on two of them.

He flipped through a few pages of one, seeing little of note or what felt true, before something crossed his mind: this guy was in the same position as him. Why was he killing so much more? Remembering how calm he had been both times he'd seen him, Alex disregarded the brief thought that this guy was weak-willed.

But then everything else started to come into question. The many killings had happened after he'd been bitten, after someone had been killed.

Was he a scapegoat?

That theory refused to leave his thoughts. He'd already made one mistake that nearly exposed him instead of the other werewolf, and if it happened again... Or if the reverse happened and the other werewolf went away...

Alex sighed deeply to try and calm himself as he put the book aside. If that was the game this guy was playing, all he had to do was be careful.

* * *

Later that night, though his father was already informed of what he'd told his mother, Alex had to elaborate on a few points for him. That it had been fear that changed him back was the first.

"What makes you think that?" his father asked.

Alex tried not to stall too long. "Because that's what I felt most before I changed back." His father only hummed in response. "I'll be more careful from now on."

"If that's the only way you can change back, I hope so."

"I don't think it is. It never felt like it."

"Then what do you think it is?"

Alex kept his gaze away from his parents as he poured over ideas.

After a minute, or what felt like it, his father continued. "Son, if you don't know, just be careful and don't tempt it."

"I know, I will. It's just…"

"Please don't," his mother interrupted. "You changed back before anything happened. What if you can't next time?"

"That's what I mean. I want to know how I can change back on my own, so I can keep from doing what I did last time."

"That's understandable," his father began, "and we do too, but listen to your mother and me here. Don't tempt it and get yourself in a rut you can't get out of, just for that."

Alex raised his head to glance at his parents, biting his tongue as his response formed. They would probably respond that it wasn't worth it if he could already keep from changing when the moon wasn't full.

"Please? For us?" his mother asked after a stretch of silence.

Alex exhaled through his nose, expecting to pick up some hint of fear from them, but none were present. "I know. I will." After his reply, when his parents came close to hug him, those very scents rushed his nose, killing his drive to retort.

Sunday, October 2nd
Moon Phase – Waxing Crescent

The next day, as he relaxed after an unbroken ride around the neighborhood park, Alex kept his phone in his hand. For the last few minutes, he'd been wondering why he wasn't hearing anything from Catherine or Nathan. He didn't want to believe he'd scared them into not talking to him again, but the idea refused to go away, pushing him to think of something to text to them.

His fear that he'd get no reply—or worse, one that confirmed his suspicions—held firm until an hour later, when he heard the IM notification tone. Slipping his phone from his pocket before the screen went dark, he noticed the message.

Catherine W.: You doing okay?

At first relieved, a niggling doubt about its sincerity crept in as Alex thought about what to say. He rewrote his text three times in turn.

Alex S.: Yeah. Joints aren't sore anymore.

When he received no reply after a few minutes, a second text was sent to her.

Alex S.: I didn't scare you that much, did I?

Though hopeful that she knew what he was trying to say, the uncertainty about what he would be told made putting his phone away difficult, more so when several minutes passed with no reply. Despite his skateboard under his foot, Alex didn't try to ride it anymore and headed home.

He was halfway there when at last his phone sounded the IM tone.

Catherine W.: For a while, yeah.

Alex kept from replying immediately, thinking she had more to say; a twinge of guilt hit him just the same.

Catherine W.: Wasn't sure what say before now.

Alex S.: I get you. No worries.

As he approached his house, another message came in.

Catherine W.: You really did look like a sleeping dog that night though. Was kind of cute. :)

The smile Alex got from that held as he typed his response.

Alex S.: :D Thanks for reminding me.

Catherine W.: Heh heh. Well, talk to you later.

Alex S.: You too, Catherine. And thanks.

Later that day, with still no word from Nathan, Alex decided to take the initiative with him as well. The text he sent went unanswered long enough for his fears to start seeping back in, though rereading Catherine's messages helped keep them at bay. When Nathan at last responded, although his initial response was as brief as hers, how much more he spoke kept any feelings of guilt from surfacing.

Monday, October 3rd, 2011
Moon Phase – First Quarter

Despite sitting next to his friend throughout their second class the next day, only quick smiles and nods were exchanged between them. Ignoring the little voice in his head nagging him to say something, Alex left campus as soon as class was over, leaving him an hour to get some lunch before starting his shift. Once there, he relished being back at work. A few hours around the shelves of gaming and comic memorabilia felt like a great way to get his mind off things.

While sitting in the back room, a few of the new scents detailed the goings on since he'd been there last. A new shipment of comics had come in, along with what he was sure was a shipment of role-playing books; the sharp binder, ink, and paper scents were unmistakable.

When his shift began, the first customer he encountered asked for help. Until Marcus came in an hour later, Alex had to work to ignore the Werewolf: The Forsaken rulebooks he'd helped the customer search through. The one that described itself as a tome on werewolf biology and physiology he found the hardest to withhold his curiosity about.

"The game should go on past my break, so I'll try and join," Alex said after he and Marcus exchanged a few words about the D&D session Trevor would be hosting.

"Hopefully I'll see you then," Marcus said before walking away and blending in among the other customers in the store. Half an hour after the game started, Gwen arrived, leaving Alex free to check on the game after getting something to drink.

In total, three people had taken the role of players at the table, Trevor acting as dungeon master. Marcus was pouring over his sheets and the cards he had, the rest of the table showing a collection of maps, cardboard character tokens, soda, and dice. A normal encounter at first glance.

"How's it going?" Alex asked.

"I'm getting my ass handed to me," Marcus said after glancing over at him.

"He's got a third of his HP left," said another player, a weak smile on his face. He seemed in his mid to early twenties.

"Says the guy who nearly blew us, and me, up earlier," Marcus retorted in jest.

"We've got no wizard. What did you expect?"

"Not using that scroll for one," said the third player as he flipped through his collection of cards.

As Alex listened to the back and forth, the attention put on him pulled a twinge of nervousness from his brain, one tempered by the familiar scents and friendly faces. "At least in Mage, that's intentional. Trying to blow someone up."

"I'm a rogue," said the player who'd 'nearly blown up' the party.

"Meaning anything magical is dangerous in your hands," Marcus said.

"Are you coming to play for a bit?" Trevor asked as the other players began talking healing. "We could use a wizard for a round or two."

"Yeah," Alex said before glancing behind him and then pulling his phone out. Just thirteen minutes to spare.

"If we're not that busy, I don't mind you taking a few more minutes for your break."

"Oh, okay." As he found his seat, Alex was handed his character sheet. Though some of the stats stood out immediately, along with what the spells he had did, when to use what stat was already causing questions. "So, what's going on?" he asked after looking over the table.

"We're in the middle of an encounter," Trevor said, "so roll for initiative."

Alex nodded in response and found the needed die. With a 16 on his roll, he was acting after their main enemy, as well as Marcus, and his character token was placed on the map. Once the game resumed, while the other players decided on their moves, he kept his attention on his character sheet, wondering what to do when his turn came. Their reactions to their rolls pulled a muffled snicker from him twice.

"Okay. You going to move or attack first?" Trevor asked after choosing what to do with the dragon the party was dueling. With his avatar risking being cornered, Alex decided to move. Showing where to on the map, Trevor continued. "Alright, that's an attack of opportunity." Trevor rolled a die behind his DM screen. "And he does hit you for..." another roll came after some silent mouthing, "seven HP."

"Ouch," Alex said as he moved his figure. With only a few minutes remaining in his break at that point, he checked the customer traffic again.

"Break almost up?" Marcus asked.

"Yeah, but I won't need long for this." After deciding to use his strongest spell, Alex pulled the card for it. "I'll use Flame Pillar on this guy."

"Okay. Roll a D20 again," Trevor said. Alex ended up with a 14. "And…you beat his reflex save, so roll for damage."

"Sweet," Alex said, rolling the dice and running the numbers in his head. "Eight damage."

"So, our friendly Wyrmling here now has his scales set on fire," Trevor said.

"That has a per-turn effect as well," said one of the players. "Five extra damage, then again per turn."

"Nice," Alex said with another look outside. This time, past the window outside, he saw a bit of bright red clothing. He was too far away to make it out clearly, but it seemed like part of a jacket. Hearing the doorbell ring soon after noticing it, Alex tried to downplay what he'd seen. He hadn't noticed a hood with the clothing.

When his gaze diverted back, Marcus locked eyes with him. As if he was taking notice of his sudden interest, he also looked out to the sales floor.

"Are we getting busy out there?" Trevor asked.

"Doesn't look like it," Marcus said. "Mostly browsers out there."

"Either way, my break's over," Alex said, getting up from the seat. "Do I need another roll, or…"

"No, you're fine," said one of the players. "We'll take over for you."

Nodding to and thanking everyone at the table, Alex headed back into the store, Marcus remarking behind him that he was getting hungry and a break felt in order, excuses that Alex quickly realized were to let his friend intercept him.

"Did you see him?" Marcus asked, his voice just above a whisper.

"Not sure," Alex said. "I just saw someone wearing red."

Marcus sighed. "Don't scare me like that."

Alex didn't respond in favor of taking another glance around the store.

"Dude," Marcus began, giving his friend a look of growing terror, "remember what happened last time."

Alex again didn't speak; Marcus's last statement summed up everything he was feeling, along with the look in his eyes. The store was packed with customers, and if he shifted again, things would get ugly, fast.

Chapter 25 – The Second Encounter

Monday, October 3rd, 2011
Moon Phase – First Quarter

With a quick tilt of his head before one of the players walked past them, Alex and Marcus followed each other out into the store. With his friend nearby, even though this guy likely knew Marcus's scent by now, he felt far more at ease. Showing this guy that neither of them were about to be rattled felt like the best way to go.

Until both of them had scoured the whole store, their gazes continually moved. There were eight customers in total, most of them college-aged. Many of them were browsing, but all had their heads and hair exposed. None were sporting black, and the person Alex had seen wearing red was in fact a woman in a windbreaker.

Relieved, but also a bit embarrassed, as Alex clocked back in, all he could say to his friend was, "Thanks, man."

"No problem."

It was as Alex began walking towards the counter that another customer entered the store. He saw their face first and didn't need to see the hair after that; his attacker had ditched his red hoodie, leaving an untucked T-shirt.

Alex's pulse rocketed, and his arms trembled as the werewolf locked eyes with him. He stopped his tongue from slipping between his teeth, though a rumbling growl still made it out.

Everything went quiet around him. Or felt like it.

"Hey." Marcus's voice came with a shaking of his shoulders, and Alex broke eye contact. He didn't speak, however. All his attention had gone to the werewolf, even though he was halfway across the store. "Relax."

"How can I?" Alex asked, clenching one hand. "He's right there."

Marcus looked around briefly. "Don't start a scene," he said before lowering his voice. "And don't shift."

Alex licked his teeth after that. No fangs. While trying to take slower breaths, he kept an eye on the werewolf. He was soon browsing the trade hardbacks, standing next to another customer. Simply having him in the store was bad enough; trying to ignore him only allowed a crushing void to open behind his ribs.

Marcus spoke up when it became clear Alex was struggling to relax, and when it was clear no one had yet noticed them. "I'll stick around and help watch this guy. Just in case."

"You sure?" Alex asked. Marcus nodded in response. "No offense, but I'd rather you don't."

"None taken, but you're on the clock. I'm not."

"I know, I know."

With the register occupied, Marcus took a lookout spot near it while Alex inched back into walking the floor and arranging the shelves, shooting glances at the werewolf every so often. Beyond reading a few trades, he didn't seem interested in things going on nearby. In the pit of his stomach however, Alex refused to believe that was all he was doing, and kept hoping for him to leave.

More customers entered the store as the minutes ticked by with no hint of that happening. All the while, Alex was considering asserting his position. He couldn't do it now, with so many around, but the crowd would eventually thin out.

Several times over the next ten minutes, Alex was forced to break his concentration on the werewolf to help someone among the crowd. One of them led him close to a spot where the werewolf had just been, letting him notice the scents he'd left behind. All of them dominated Alex's nostrils until he moved away; the few parts that were new were too unfamiliar, or weak, for him to pinpoint.

It was close to 4:00 when he noticed Marcus heading his way and looked over to the gaming room. Trevor was back in his seat, behind the dungeon master's shield. "I think we're fine, man," Marcus said after a second to look around.

Alex didn't want to agree. "Then what do I do?"

"Just stay calm. Hang around near the back if you need to."

Alex exhaled out his nose and nodded after a second to think. When he glanced aside again, the werewolf had left his line of sight. "Yeah."

Marcus stepped away a few seconds later, after asking if he was alright and getting a nod. Despite the lack of unease on his friend's face, Alex let him reach the game room and put his attention back on Trevor. It took only seconds for him to spot the werewolf again; he'd moved to the far-right side of the store, to a spot where, at most, one other person was near.

For a moment, Alex hesitated to move any closer. If he didn't hold it together... But he had so far, unlike last time, and there wasn't any doubt the werewolf had noticed both of them by now. So long as he didn't make a scene, as Marcus had said, he had no reason to wait.

After one final glance around, and a check on Marcus and his boss, Alex started approaching the werewolf. Each step closer intensified the quivering around his body, and the feeling of it pulling in underneath his skin, as if in prep for a fight. His tongue also stayed wrapped around his teeth.

Keep it together. Don't make a scene... Alex glanced around and checked on Gwen at the counter, just in case she was looking at him. As soon as he was certain she wasn't, he continued moving.

When he finally stood near the werewolf, his heart pounding, Alex leaned against the glass shelving. "Can I help you?" The statement came out with no tremors in his voice.

The werewolf only glanced at him. "No. I'm fine."

Unable to settle on an emotion, Alex tried to respond in kind. "So, what are you doing here?"

This time, the werewolf looked him in the eyes. Alex felt his jaws tighten and his head lower a bit. "Enjoying myself. Unlike you, it seems."

Alex exhaled. "Really?" He let his gaze wander when he got no immediate answer, then the werewolf did the same, turning his head and looking around before turning back.

"What exactly am I doing to make you so tense?" the werewolf asked.

The question caught Alex off guard and no words came to him, even though everything in him screamed to either be smart with this guy or give it to him straight. He was stalking his friends, and he knew it. Licking his teeth again, there were still no fangs.

With another glance up, Alex noticed Gwen looking at and gesturing for him. Even though Trevor was nowhere in sight, a chill gripped his chest. After pushing away from the shelf, he circled behind the werewolf, relieved to get some distance but hating that he'd been seen.

"Hey," Gwen began as he came close. Her tone helped reign in Alex's fears. "I gotta use the restroom. Watch the front for a minute."

"Yeah, sure." Once she was out of sight, Alex checked behind himself. The werewolf had moved somewhere else; his first assumption was closer to the gaming room. If he had, any talking from either of them would get Marcus or Trevor's attention. As soon as Gwen was back, Alex headed towards the rear of the store, glancing to his sides as he went. His assumption was proven right: the werewolf had moved to the new issue racks lining the back wall.

Damn it. Before the werewolf could notice him, he backed up, giving Marcus a nod and smile when he noticed him. *Why'd I freeze like that?* With a hand wrapped in front of his mouth, Alex tried to see some kind of positive. The only one that stuck was that the werewolf had stayed on the right side of the store since he'd come in. With just one and a half hours left in his shift, he made a sweep of the store for anything to take care of, and then continued to keep an eye on the werewolf.

It wasn't long before Alex noticed him change position, back to the trades along the right-most wall. He stopped around the DC H-K shelves, a spot where Alex felt he wouldn't be noticed. By Gwen or Marcus.

All he needed was two minutes. That was it.

Holding back his urge to rush the werewolf, he worked his way over by skimming the nearby shelves. The old pit behind his ribs didn't reopen as he closed in, and then stood next to him again.

He waited for the werewolf to notice him before speaking. "I know what you're doing." Before the werewolf could retort, he continued. "Quit stalking my friends."

The werewolf looked at him again; Alex didn't buy his look of confusion. "What gave you that idea?"

Alex tapped his nose, but didn't say anything.

"Yeah. Keep thinking that."

"Gladly, because that's what it is."

"Or you're paranoid, and in denial."

Hearing that sentence, Alex's flesh rippled, and his throat tightened. Feeling a growl reach his mouth, he tried to keep his voice down. "Don't...test me."

"How about you not accuse me of what I'm not doing?"

Seeing the werewolf's face starting to show signs of anger, Alex felt his body tighten around his chest and neck. He could feel a vein pumping as he tried to form a response, but instead of words, the growl slipped out. A low, rumbling one.

The werewolf returned the growl before locking eyes with him. A brisk, sharp one in contrast to his. Alex quaked and nearly stepped back as his head lowered again.

And then he saw the werewolf's eyes shift from green and white to amber.

His heart dropped from his chest in fear. He wouldn't shift here; everyone would see him. He kept telling himself that, if only to calm himself. He lost track of time as the werewolf continued to glare at him. His vocal cords felt locked, trapping his voices of fear, embarrassment, and anger in his lungs. It gave them time to gel, and wrench open the same void behind his ribs as before.

Even so, he didn't want this guy out of his sight. Not until he left the store. His eyes didn't change back to white and green as the growling stopped, and in his head, Alex feared the same had happened to him.

Eventually, and with a snort, the werewolf broke the stare, slapping the trade in his hands against the others on the shelf. As Alex watched him walk away, Marcus came into view. How worried he seemed made Alex curse himself, dampening the relief he felt from staying composed enough to not shift.

The werewolf was gone no more than two seconds before Marcus closed in on him. Expecting some amount of disappointment, or something similar, from his friend, Alex couldn't bring himself to look his direction, even when he began with, 'You okay?'

"Yeah," Alex said after letting out a muffled exhale.

Marcus replied a few seconds later. "Good. That scared the hell out me."

I'm sorry, man. Unable to say what he wanted, from embarrassment and otherwise, Alex kept quiet, taking slow breaths to relax. His friend didn't press him, which he was thankful for, but him not leaving the store after letting him go back to work was enough of a hint that he wanted to know what else happened.

With the end of his shift, Alex had relaxed enough to approach him first, but not speak first, opting for a nod instead once he was noticed.

"So, what did you say to him?" Marcus asked after glancing around.

"That I knew what he was doing, and to quit stalking you guys."

Marcus didn't respond immediately. "Too blunt, man. He could've gotten you fired if he told Trevor about that."

The embarrassment and guilt Alex was still feeling dug deeper into his chest at that. Admitting that he didn't consider that would've only made it worse. "I couldn't just say nothing."

"Not my point, but it's done. It's over." Marcus took a second to continue. "What else happened?"

"He asked why I thought that, I tapped my nose and then he said, 'Yeah, keep thinking that.'"

"How'd he say it?"

"Sarcastically, and angrily."

"Okay."

"I stood my ground, said that's what it is, and then he said, 'Or you're paranoid and in denial.'"

Marcus's expression shifted at that, from calm and aware to a bit uneasy. In response, Alex looked aside, only to be surprised by the increase in customer numbers since he and Marcus started talking. His friend did the same, and then gestured for him to follow him.

Until the shop's doors closed behind them, and they were standing near Marcus' truck, neither of them said a word. The darkness they walked into had Alex glancing around until then.

"You think he meant that?" Marcus asked.

"Hardly," Alex said after shaking his head. "Being concerned is nowhere near the same as being paranoid."

"Then, don't take this the wrong way, but I can't see why just having him around makes you so anxious and defensive."

"Because I only see him when one of you guys are nearby. All three times it's been that way, and that worries me."

"That is weird, I'll admit, but that can't be the only reason."

Alex sighed to calm himself. "It's not. After everything he's done, even his scent worries me." He didn't get an immediate response.

"Then, do you think there's some kind of animal mindset at work there? You said you didn't know you were acting submissive before."

Alex gave the question a minute to turn over in his head. He could see where his friend was coming from, but at the same time, he knew how little of any one scent it took to identify something about someone. How often this guy hung around the places they all worked. What he could do to someone who wasn't ready for him, and what would result from exactly that. His throat seized up the more into those thoughts he went.

It didn't take Marcus long to notice something was up. "You okay?"

Holding back from wiping his eyes, Alex took a few long breaths. "Yeah. Fine."

Marcus held up a hand as he responded. "I'm not trying to upset you, man. It just makes me nervous, seeing you behaving like this so suddenly."

"I know. I don't mean to." When his friend didn't immediately speak, Alex took a bit more time to compose, and consider how to answer. After another exhale he spoke, now with his elbows held in the opposing hands. "If he hadn't attacked and bitten me, I'd be wondering those same things too, but even then, I don't know what his deal is, so..."

"So, all of this is down to fear and uncertainty?"

Alex nodded in agreement. "Yeah."

Marcus again didn't speak immediately. "Then I wouldn't call you paranoid, by any means. Overcautious, more like."

Though the guilt dagger touched Alex's throat at that, in his head he couldn't help asking what else he was supposed to do. Doing something was better than nothing, and nothing so far was enough to show he was wrong about this guy. "Like I said, I don't know what his deal is, and his behavior doesn't help, so what else can I be but that?"

"I know, I get you. Not saying you're wrong, just saying maybe you're overthinking things. Jumping to conclusions and being too quick to act on them."

"Maybe," Alex said after a sigh.

"If it helps you relax, I have been keeping an eye out for what you described. Either this guy or a big, black canine. I've seen nothing so far, and neither has Catherine. Nathan's said nothing to us, so I doubt he has either."

Alex didn't press his friend's response, even though the urge was there. They didn't have his sense of smell, and a part of him was certain Marcus was aware of that. "It does. I just don't want him turning any of you."

"That's why we're being careful too, man. Trust me."

"I do. Not going to let my guard down, though."

"That's fine. Just be careful."

Alex nodded before taking in a few longer breaths. With his drive to chat almost drained, he said goodbye to his friend and went back inside to collect his stuff, grabbing a cheeseburger and fries on the way home. Bailey's presence and willingness to lick at him once he was home helped pull his mood back up for the rest of the night.

Tuesday, October 4th, 2011
Moon Phase – First Quarter

It was as he sat through his classes the next day that part of his talk with Marcus snuck back to mind. Without his emotions directing his thinking this time, he started to see the parallels to his nervousness around strange people and places and how he'd reacted when the werewolf was around. He could handle the former with scent-laced items, but the latter wouldn't change so easily. Not with how infrequently he saw the werewolf in person versus by scent, much less what he'd done.

As his second class wound down, Alex hadn't come close to settling on a way to handle that, or the werewolf. Part of him wanted to remain aggressive and direct, continue to drive home that he wouldn't take this guy harming his friends or family with even a bit of leniency. He'd already done so once without shifting, so it could be done. The rest of him was worried about how much it would take to make his friends start to distance themselves from him, make them see him as the greater threat.

Once he'd filled up from lunch and then began to coast around the Tampa Skateshop's park, the worst of those thoughts were whisked away. He hadn't done anything damning yet, and as long as he kept it that way, he could make things work.

Sliding out of a Backside Tailslide a while later, now warmed up and sweating from practice, he heard the tail-end of the IM message tone sound from his phone. After coming to a stop, he pulled his phone out and read the message.

Catherine W.: Hey. You busy?

Alex skated to a calmer spot and texted her back.

Alex S.: Just skating around. What's up?

Catherine W.: Not much. Just wanted to see if you were okay.

Alex S.: Marcus told you what happened?

Catherine W.: Yeah. Last night.

She continued before Alex finished his response.

Catherine W.: I figured you wanted to relax
after all that, so…

> *Alex S.:* Thanks. That did help.

Catherine W.: Glad to hear it.

The chat stopped long enough for Alex to take another drink. His water bottle was warming up, prompting an exit from the park to refill it at the water fountain. As he did so, another message came in.

Catherine W.: Almost forgot. You busy tomorrow?

> *Alex S.:* Nope. Why?

Catherine W.: Nathan and I are meeting for a study
session tomorrow, big project coming up for class,
and we're making some time afterward for him to show
me how to play that game you guys played yesterday.

Thought you might be interested, at least in that.

> *Alex S.:* Yeah, certainly. Be glad to come.

Catherine W.: Great. We'll be meeting at 2:00
in the common room on campus. See you then.

> *Alex S.:* Got it. See you then.

After his hour of park access came to an end, Alex hung around the shop for a while, debating whether to pay for another. Some play time with Bailey became more appealing with each minute he spent browsing the stuff on display until it pushed him to say goodbye to Walter.

He was halfway to the door when he was called to. He stopped and spun before answering Walter. "Yeah?"

"I meant to tell you when you arrived," Walter began once Alex was closer. "We're having a 'Family Night' event here on Friday. Think something like that would interest you, or your parents?"

"Uh...maybe. You got a sheet or something for it?"

"Right here." Walter then held up a clipboard.

As Alex read over it, taking note when the event was meant to start and end among other things, the most he could see either of his parents staying was an hour and a half. As fun as it looked, seven others, including Cameron, had signed up for the event. The number of eyes that could potentially be on him in turn already made him nervous.

"I think my folks could spare some time for this. After 6:30 or so," he said as he filled in his name.

"Alright. If it turns out they can't make it, I've got your signature so the park will cost half as much for you that night."

"Works for me. Thanks." With a shake of his hand, Alex left the shop and headed home.

Chapter 26 – Opinions...Or Facts?

Wednesday, October 5th, 2011
Moon Phase – First Quarter
Days until the Full Moon – 7

As he waited for Catherine and Nathan to show the next day, Alex kept himself busy with a fantasy novel and a few bits of homework, his dice bag laid out nearby and Bailey's tennis ball resting at the mouth of his backpack. Both of them saw him first, and Catherine gave a quick wave when he pulled his head up to look around.

"Hey guys," Alex said as they sat down. He continued after they'd both replied in kind. "What's the project?"

"A presentation," Nathan replied. "We've got the general idea down. We just need to refine a few things."

"Alright. If you guys need some input from me, let me know."

"Will do." Catherine said.

As she and Nathan began comparing notes and screens, Alex sunk back into reading and what remained of his homework. For a while, the three of them minded only the business in front of themselves, something Alex was fine with given the situation. At the same time, he couldn't help thinking Catherine wanted to talk to him about the encounter once the opportunity came. Possibly Nathan as well.

Alex continued to flip between reading and listening as the next hour passed; the pool of scents around him was rarely disturbed for that same time, and he noticed nothing of note when it was. His friends asked for his input only once, that being after he heard them start to organize their ideas. When he came closer and stood between them, although he focused mostly on their work, he was glad to see no avoidance in their gestures.

"I can't see anything to add," Alex said after looking it all over but before glancing at both of them. "Looks good."

"Then, should we call it done for now?" Catherine asked.

"I think so," Nathan said. "We've still got a week and change to add anything else."

"Alright then." Catherine gathered her notes as she continued. "How long would it take to run me though the rules of that game?"

"The basics? Not long. Probably ten minutes, tops."

"Then," Alex began, "is anyone getting hungry?"

"Not me," Nathan said.

"Me either," Catherine added.

"In that case, be back in a second." Already holding an idea of what he wanted, Alex returned to the table with the first bite of his sandwich already taken.

Nathan spoke up as he sat down and took another. "Hey, quick question. Have you seen that guy since the other day?"

Alex's immediately shook his head, though as soon as he did, he remembered yesterday. That he hadn't checked any of the places he'd found the scent before, and for a few days by now.

"Okay, good. Marcus told me what happened yesterday. When he did though, I remembered something about this guy." While Catherine only shifted her gaze Nathan's way, Alex's eyebrows rose a bit. "Remember that day he came into the store while you were there?"

"Yeah." Alex said.

"The time I saw him before that, he came in looking really upset."

"Really? Why?" Catherine asked.

Nathan shrugged. "No idea. I just kept an eye on him until he left, and didn't think much of it until yesterday."

"When was that?" Alex asked.

"Uh...a month ago, or so."

When he heard that, Alex strained his memory for reasons why. That was around the time Angela had died and he had been turned. "Hang on a sec." He dug his phone out and pulled up his calendar. "Around late August?"

"Think so. Why?"

"Here." When he was once again standing between his friends, he held out his phone and continued, though with a hushed voice to counter any eavesdropping. "That was around the same time he came after me and Angela, and when all those animals were killed."

"Yeah... Maybe that was why he was upset," Catherine asked.

"If it was, I couldn't tell. All he's been so far is evasive and angry."

Before Catherine responded, Alex noticed her remove her hands from the table. "From what Marcus told me, he wasn't doing anything when you confronted him."

"No, but I couldn't just stand there and say nothing. Like I told him, he only shows up when you guys are around." No one spoke for a few seconds. "I'm assuming he told you both what this guy accused me of being."

"Yeah." Nathan said.

Alex than glanced towards Catherine, who nodded instead of speaking. "Thought so." He took a second before continuing. "Maybe I am being overprotective, but the way this guy behaves and when I see him... It doesn't help."

"Marcus told you we're keeping an eye out as well, right?"

"He did, but you guys can't smell this guy like I can."

Alex's response made the table go quiet for a few seconds. "Completely forgot about that," Catherine said.

"I doubt he's being a werewolf more than me at this point though, so..."

"So, because we haven't seen him outside of the last few times, we should be fine?" Catherine asked.

Alex glanced at her at that. Just as with Marcus, he didn't want to fully agree, and couldn't think of an answer he felt satisfied with in turn. At Nathan's suggestion, he left his choice of words to stew until they were done with the practice session, which went on for upwards of half-an-hour.

"Thanks, guys. That was fun," Catherine said as the three of them gathered their stuff. "If the store has another session when we're both off work, I'll tag along."

"Glad to hear it," Alex said with a smile. Seconds later, something he wanted to say before came to mind. "Actually, about before... If you've not seen this guy without me around, great. Just don't write him off on that alone."

"We're not," Nathan said.

After Alex nodded to his friend, the three of them got up from their seats and exchanged a few handshakes and words. Before they parted, Catherine got his attention. "You be careful with this guy too. Alright?" Certain of what the concerned look on her face was implying, Alex nodded again.

On his way back home, with the talk with his friends still fresh in mind, he detoured into First Colony and parked near Nathan's workplace. As soon as he walked in, his nostrils were flooded with cleaning solution and air purifier scents. How dark the normally washed out floor looked told him everything: the place had been steam-cleaned recently. Catherine's place of work hadn't had the same treatment, but the lack of the werewolf's scent put Alex's mind at ease and he resumed his drive home.

Thursday, October 6th, 2011
Moon Phase – First Quarter
Days until the Full Moon – 6
3:49 p.m.

"C'mon, boy. Time for a walk," Alex said as he put his XBOX controller aside. Bailey stood up with him, his tail already slapping anything it was close to, and barked as his leash was found. "I know, boy. Calm down."

Outside, Alex took Bailey southward, the northwestern breezes rushing hundreds of scents from the nearby houses, and a bit beyond, by his face. With no one but him walking the street, he started hearing a vehicle approaching the intersection ahead of him. The black front, white middle, and word 'POLICE' on the SUV were what he saw before it turned onto the street he was walking.

As Bailey left his scent on a nearby tree, the cruiser came closer, and Alex soon lifted a hand to offer a wave. The officer inside returned the gesture just before Alex noticed the phrase "K-9 Unit" on the SUV's back end. The wave of scents and air that hit him as the vehicle passed made sure he caught not only the heat and exhaust from the engine, but the scent of the canine riding in the back. Despite not being in his werewolf form, his pulse went up a few beats when it registered, more so when the thought of fighting off such a trained animal entered his head.

With his phone removed from his pocket, Alex pretended to check his calls before glancing back at the SUV. Though he expected it to slow at the curve onto his street, it came to stop just before he lost sight of it.

He stayed rooted to the spot even as Bailey wanted to keep going. Why was it stopping near his house? While trying not to assume anything, he tugged at Bailey's leash and headed back up the street.

The officer stayed put until Alex was halfway down his own street. The most he could see him doing before then was checking the cruiser's laptop. Once the SUV drove past, Alex waited for it to leave his sight before turning around and returning to the wooded lot. His pet kept his nose down, scouring the area for scents, while Alex began questioning what to do if the police were to start keeping tabs on similar areas.

This spot goes all the way to the next street... He pulled his phone out at that thought to check if the creek he'd used before did so too. After seeing that it did, and while questioning if such a route would be stealthier and less risky, he started hearing faint, grassy footsteps to his left. A wooden fence, and the still northbound breezes, kept who it was a mystery until, after calling Bailey back for a head rub, he looked up and in their direction.

Once again, the werewolf lacked his red hoodie in favor of a T-shirt. Alex cursed to himself when he saw him, his attention not wavering as he came closer.

"I thought that was you," was the first thing the werewolf said.

Alex didn't respond. Already, fear and anger were pulling at him. What did this guy want, and why was he here?

When he checked on Bailey, he was staring at the werewolf and wagging his tail, but not lolling his tongue. Hoping the breeze wouldn't shift and direct the werewolf's scent towards him, a slight smile appeared on the werewolf and he took a few steps closer. Alex reached down and rubbed Bailey's head in response.

"Gotta love German shepherds," the werewolf said. Nothing about his tone felt sinister, but Alex didn't buy it. "How long have you had him?"

"Since he was a puppy," Alex replied. He then shook his head lightly. What was he doing? "Look, what do you want?"

"Nothing. Was just walking around."

"Yeah, sure."

The werewolf sighed. "What is your problem?" Alex didn't answer. "Are you that convinced that I'm planning something or stalking your friends?"

"Since when have you given me a reason not to think that?"

"I don't see why I need to. I'm not doing anything," the werewolf said. "You, on the other hand, driving all over town and leaving your scent around those three so often? How possessive of them are you?"

Possessive? That word in Alex's mind stuck out the most from everything the werewolf was saying. "They're not possessions; they're my friends."

"And yet I can't be anywhere near them without you getting angry and confronting me."

Alex took a second of pause before responding. No more beating around the bush. He had to make his position clear, now. "Do not...turn them, or come after them."

"I'm not trying to. Haven't you noticed that yet?"

"And yet lately I keep bumping into you with them around."

"So, to you, that means I'm stalking them and or thinking of turning them?" The werewolf awaited a response. Alex again didn't give one. "That's your view. Besides, the first time I talked to Nathan with you around, you seemed perfectly happy with it."

Recalling the encounter at Gamestop, Alex refrained from lashing back, as much as he wanted to. In that case, he was right, but only in one respect. "You never spoke to or approached me before then, so yeah, it did seem that way."

The werewolf broke eye contact for a second before he replied. "I don't see how that would've helped." He then thrust an arm forward and back. "If this is any hint, you would've been at my throat regardless."

As Alex paused to think of a response, he remembered Marcus' chat with him, and the suggestion he had made back then. "Then, enlighten me a bit. How do you see my friends?"

"They're still hanging out with you, so I guess they're trustworthy enough to keep a secret. And they don't seem distrustful of me, yet."

"You say that like you want to get close to them."

"No, I say that because I don't know what ideas you've put in their heads about me."

The response Alex wanted to give, that it was all the dead animals, along with Angela, that was causing concern with them, never left his mouth. By the time he stopped thinking about it, his dormant fear of his friends figuring out what he had to do come the full moon had returned. "They've seen as much of you as me. What else is there to know?"

"Maybe the fact that I didn't mean to kill her? That she was threatening my livelihood and the things that mattered to me before we started fighting?"

Alex refrained from scoffing at that statement. "She's still dead."

"I don't see you being passive about things you care about. Why should I be?"

"So that's it? She's dead, and you just don't care?"

"I would've, if she hadn't been a werewolf and doing what I said she was." Alex's eyes widened halfway through that sentence. "Don't believe me?"

Alex was torn on what to say as his memories of that night came rushing back. Angela's behavior and words, her wanting to avoid a hospital in favor of healing on her own, now made more sense, but he'd sustained injuries that were just as bad, and he'd survived. That was the train of thought that focused his next words. "That you didn't mean to kill her? No."

"Why?"

"Because you attacked me and let me go."

"I let her go too. You didn't keep throwing swipes at me after I did so."

By this point, Alex's body heat was bleeding through his skin. With his pulse elevated, he licked his teeth and found no fangs. "So why did you come after me?" He continued before the werewolf could respond. "At least tell me that, and while you're at it, your name too."

"Fine. It's Shane." Alex repeated the name in his head. Finally, he had some kind of info. "And before you get any ideas, I didn't come after you because I'm an asshole or because you two tried to help her."

"Really?" Alex growled, his eyebrows lowered into a scowl. "After what you just said?"

"How about you calm down for a second?"

Alex huffed at that, only for Bailey to nudge his leg. When he looked down, his dog was staring up at him, his tail still. When Alex brought his hand close, his dog sniffed it before licking it, and did so for longer than normal.

"No, I didn't try to help her that night, or when you guys showed up. Know why? Because you and Nathan would've freaked the fuck out if you saw me."

He shifted before we got there? Alex wanted to believe he was lying, but couldn't fully bring himself to. The bite that was on Angela's shoulder, the canine shape of it, made sure of that. "You didn't answer me. Why did you bite me?"

Shane held off for a second. "I may not have had to..."

Alex cut him off when the delay in his response came. "But you said 'Screw it', and did it anyway?"

A second later, Shane sounded a protracted, guttural growl, his tongue sticking between his closed jaws. Bailey stepped back and tucked his tail and ears in fear. Alex did the same with his neck, watching Shane's eyes. They remained green and white until the growling stopped.

"She coughed blood on you that night. You got more of it on your skin when you tried to help her. If you're so smart, how about thinking about that for a second."

While he comforted Bailey, Alex tried to do just that. The cough he remembered; the spray had caused him to close his eyes and recoil. His hands had stayed mostly clean thanks to his shirt, but his arms...

"You want the truth?" Shane continued, bringing his tone back to normal. "I bit you to make sure you knew what was coming, instead of letting you run loose with no clue about it."

"Just me?" Alex asked after a moment.

Shane's agitated sigh preceded a covering of his face with his hands. "For fuck's sake, just drop it, will you?" he said as he took them away. "Nathan I'm not touching, or your other friends, or your family. All they would be is more risk and more mouths to feed."

Alex wanted to say something in response. Call Shane a liar, or something. He could call him a murderer, but at that moment, he didn't feel right enough to truly let all his hatred out. Maybe it was some semblance of relief that was making it so. "So long as that's true, fine."

"Good," Shane said, "and keep that in mind from now on. I'm getting sick of you treating me like this."

As Alex watched Shane go back the way he came, his trembling limbs almost saw him fall onto Bailey. Though his pet's ears and tail were no longer laid back and tucked, on the way home he kept so close to him that his paws were at risk of being stepped on.

Once they were inside and Bailey was off his leash, Alex felt relieved, and immensely so. A few things still tugged at his mind though. Most of all, Shane's assertion that what he did was warranted and meant as a warning.

Chapter 27 – Second Opinions

Friday, October 7th, 2011
Moon Phase – Waxing Gibbous
Days until the Full Moon – 5

As Thursday night wore on and Friday arrived, that point stayed on Alex's mind. The rest of the encounter was drawn out as his second class began and progressed, Nathan's presence pushing him to not forget any details. As soon as it was over, he waited for half the class to leave and then directed his friend to a spot in the nearby hallway far enough, he felt, away from any foot traffic.

"What's up?" Nathan asked.

"I ran into that guy again."

Nathan's eyebrows rose a bit. "When? Yesterday?"

"Yeah." Alex stalled for a second. "Across the way from my house."

"Oh, crap," Nathan said, covering his mouth with curved fingers.

"Yeah. Freaked me out a bit when I saw him."

"So, what did he do?"

"Nothing besides talk, thankfully."

"Really?" Alex nodded, and Nathan continued. "About what?"

"Angela, why he came after me… He kept saying he's not interested in turning anyone else."

Nathan's reserved look stayed after he spoke a few seconds later. "You believe him?"

"So long as none of you get the sense that he's lying about that. He was getting agitated every time I brought it up."

"I see. What about Angela, and him attacking you?"

"He said she was a werewolf too, and that he came after me because she bled on me that night."

Nathan's expression, which began as one of interest, shifted to surprise, and then confusion at that answer.

"She did say she'd heal, but I don't remember her bleeding on me *that* much that night."

"Neither do I. Was that all he said about that?"

"No. He said he 'let her go' like he did with me, but that she kept fighting with him." Alex shrugged. "For all I know, he was telling the truth, but I couldn't believe how little remorse he had for the whole thing."

Nathan glanced aside, keeping quiet for a while. "Then, what made him so upset back then?"

"No idea, man. If it was that, I couldn't see it."

"So, he gets in a fight with her... I'm guessing he said why."

"Because she was threatening the things he cared about. He didn't say what they were." For a moment after he spoke, Alex recalled Shane's words about him not being passive with what he cared about. What had happened the first time he let that get the best of him.

Nathan gave a lengthy exhale; Alex figured he was thinking this entire thing over. "So, all that happens, then he comes after you... That kind of makes sense, but is werewolf blood really that potent?"

"No idea, but blood is a biohazard and can transmit diseases through skin contact. First thing they teach you at any first-aid class, and what I was taught at the vet. Plus, I didn't wash it off until after I got home, after it was dried out."

"Yeah... Actually, if that was true, why would he wait for and bite you instead of looking for and talking to you?"

"I asked him about that as well. He said he did it to make sure I knew what to expect."

Nathan's response, after a scrunching of his eyebrows, was the opposite of what Alex expected. "Yeah, I call bullshit on that. If he knew her blood could do that, he should have warned you. If he'd done that, and if somehow it wasn't enough, you wouldn't be a werewolf at all."

Any response Alex could've given evaporated the second he stopped to think about that. The bites caused a breaking of his skin and direct fluid transfers. Blood in contact with skin wasn't as capable of that.

As the realizations clicked, his eyes started to water and his chest tightened. Why hadn't he realized that the day before? It was right in front of his face. Trying not to swear in anger, Alex swallowed hard. Maybe Shane was correct? But then, Nathan was also. He would've had no reason to bite him if that was true.

Had he made that up to cover for what he'd done?

Had he been expecting him to not ask more questions after that?

More and more thoughts and assumptions ran through Alex's head over the next few seconds, all of them possible explanations in his eyes.

"I can't believe this guy," Nathan finally said with a groan. "He attacks you, and then explains it like that?"

Despite his friend channeling what felt like the same anger he was feeling, Alex couldn't speak; he could only breathe and attempt to hold back tears. When he was asked if he was okay, he shook his head.

"Can't believe I missed that," he eventually said. The crack in his voice then caused his breathing to rumble, close to what sounded like a growl.

As Nathan grabbed his shoulder and told him to calm down, his fear scent reached his nostrils. With his tongue laying against his teeth, Alex did his best to do just that, even as it made his lungs and throat feel hot and clogged.

"You okay?" Nathan asked again after what seemed like a full minute.

"I will be," Alex said with his breathing and pulse still elevated.

Nathan continued after a brief pause. "You want me to fill Marcus and Catherine in about all that?"

Alex again shook his head. "No, I'll tell them. Thanks, though."

Nathan patted his shoulder. "You're welcome, man. Anytime."

Wiping his eyes free of tears, and hoping his face hadn't turned too red, Alex headed for the closest restroom on the same floor after Nathan departed. Though it wasn't too apparent he'd gotten upset, a splash of cold water and a toweling wiped away what evidence was left on the outside. With some of the anger from the realizations lingering, he retired to a nearby stall to let it dissipate. A combination of listening to some music, testing the spin of his skateboard's bearings, and deep, lengthy breaths, all for several minutes, helped, but didn't eliminate it.

As he pushed his thoughts onto the upcoming event at the skateshop, some time with Bailey and some practice beforehand began to feel like better stress relievers.

* * *

Once his stuff was tossed onto his bed back home, he found a tennis ball and coaxed Bailey outside. After a few rounds of fetch, he started glancing at the wooded area. Had Shane always been wandering and loitering around the neighborhood, watching him? It wasn't difficult to imagine, given what he'd said.

Around 2:00, as he tossed the ball again, Alex's phone started ringing. His father was on the line. "Hello, Son. You back home?" he asked.

"Yeah. Just playing with Bailey," Alex said as his pet came running back his direction.

"OK. About tonight, what time was this event starting again?"

"Five-thirty. Are you off shift around then?"

"I'll be off at six, so around seven or so I'll be there."

"That's fine, and you don't need to worry about coming in your uniform," Alex said, hoping his dad would get the joke.

"We'll see. I gotta get back on my beat—" A radio call for assistance in a traffic stop interrupted him. "I'll talk to you later, Son."

"You too, Dad. See you later." After hanging up, Alex recovered the ball from Bailey and led him back inside before tossing it into the living room, his pet chasing it down before dropping it from his mouth and then going for a drink. Until he started feeling hungry a while later, the novel he'd been reading and his choice of shooter occupied his time, the gore sprays and gunfire bringing a smile back to his face.

* * *

When he arrived at the shop around 4:00, the presence of two sets of parents kept him from approaching the main desk and Walter, who was talking to all four of them. While the other two employees in the shop kept busy with cleaning, Alex watched from the T-shirt racks for the opening he wanted. So far he'd found no trace of Cameron's scent, but from the noises had figured on at least three skaters already in the park.

"Something going on?" Walter asked when Alex eventually approached him.

The question went unanswered for a moment. "Sort of."

"I had a feeling," Walter said as he took what Alex handed him. "You looked kind of down."

"It's nothing. Just something I'm mulling over," Alex replied before asking for a soda from the nearby refrigerator.

"I see. Are your folks on their way?"

"Not yet," Alex said as he fished some change from his back pocket. "Mom's got a meeting at work until eight, so it's only my dad who's coming. Around seven or so."

"You're here pretty early, then."

"Yeah, but I've got something to read if I need a break."

As Alex's talk with Walter progressed into books, and then the stories Walter had enjoyed in his favored genres, how similar the conversation was to his interview with Trevor let the time slip by. When the parents from before asked for help, Alex checked the time and paid for an hour of park access.

For the first five minutes he hung around the observation deck, his headphones in and some music playing, watching the others ride around and attempt some tricks. All of them were focused on the nearby funboxes and quarterpipes, pushing him to start on the halfpipe, or just coast around for a while. The latter became his decision as his soda was finished.

He casually took in the scents around him he coasted around the park, finding none that made him consider slowing down and looking around for the source. Once his coasting progressed into grinding the copings of the quarterpipes, Alex paid less attention to things beyond the other skaters and the sweat streaming from under his hair until he stopped for a drink. Another pair of parents had taken a spot on the observation deck since he'd last looked, and the store was now packed with as many bodies as the park.

Right away, the realization got his nerves to rile. Once he was out of the park and in front of the store's water fountain, he glanced aside. Walter and Cameron were holding the attention of several kids and sets of parents, leaving Alex hoping they wouldn't enter the park for some time.

Though he did his best not to keep glancing at the park entrance once he'd returned to skating, he soon spotted half a dozen more people entering and retired to spot underneath the observation deck. As his nerves relaxed, he heard his phone start to ring, and with it out of his pocket, he saw 'Dad' on the caller ID.

With a feeling of what he was calling about, Alex answered after walking to a quieter corner.

"Hey, Son. I may not be able to make it for a little while longer, I'm afraid."

"Let me guess," Alex said, his voice lacking disappointment. "You need to respond to something?"

"Yeah. Dispatch is asking for several officers from this beat."

Several? "That's unusual. What for?"

"An animal disturbance call."

When he heard that sentence, a hint of worry gripped Alex's head. "Was it near a ranch?"

His father didn't answer for a second, but he could hear keyboard keys clicking in the background. "Not from what I'm seeing. It's more of a small stable."

"Dad," Alex began before turning his head, "be careful around there."

"It'll be fine, Son. I'll have a few officers on site with me."

"Not that." Alex lowered his voice. "That other werewolf could be around that place."

"I haven't forgotten what you've told me about him, but until I know more, I can't jump to that conclusion."

Breathing a slight sigh at first, Alex then raised an eyebrow as he comprehended the rest of the reply. "'Until you know more'? Did the caller not give any information?"

"He told dispatch that he didn't see anything, just that he heard a noise... Hang on."

"What?"

"Just a minute, Son. I need to hear this."

Alex didn't reply and listened intently. His father didn't put him on hold, letting him hear the radio make another announcement.

All units en-route, the caller is reporting two of his animals missing. Report back any suspicious findings.

"That is him," Alex blurted out, causing his father to shush him. Despite that, his heart was thundering. His dad was going straight to where this guy could still be. Nathan's words replayed in his head, making him await the end of the radio call.

"The MO does sound really similar." His father paused for a second. "Once I get there, I'll give you a call back and let you know if I see something."

"Dad, I don't like that idea."

"Then what would you suggest instead of that?"

Alex had to stop and think. What else could he do? The police were already en-route, and if one of them pissed this guy off or found him as a werewolf... After what felt like a full minute, Alex replied. "Give me the street address of the call. I'll figure something out on the way and meet you there."

"Are you sure about that?"

"Yeah."

"Alright. The call came from Industrial Blvd. You know where that is?"

"Let me check." Putting the call in the background and opening his GPS, Alex typed in the street name. A few seconds passed before the bird's eye view came up with the location. Seeing it made him feel silly for not checking someplace like that long before this point. It was sandwiched between the locations of the animal attacks, and where he had found this guy in human form. "Yeah, I got it," Alex said as he pulled the call back up.

"Alright. I'll see you there, Son."

"You too, Dad." After hanging up, Alex's thoughts went blank until he sighed once. He could take some comfort in knowing that his dad was willing to meet him and talk about what they could do.

Though the store was still packed, and he once again felt uneasy at seeing so many bodies, Alex zeroed in on Walter, his expression kept as close to neutral as he could manage. As soon as he was greeted, he replied, "I gotta go. Something came up with my dad."

"Nothing serious, I hope." Alex shook his head. "Just a second, then." Walter soon returned with his backpack and helmet.

"Thanks. If you do another one of these, let me know. I really want to support this shop if I can."

"Will do. Have a good one."

Nodding as he attached his skateboard to his backpack, Alex left the shop into the muggy afternoon and low-angle sunbeams, readying his keys, sunglasses, and helmet as he did so. That was when his phone once again rang, and again it was his father.

"Hey, Dad."

"Alex, on second thought, don't come."

A feeling akin to sudden pressure on his guts hit Alex at those words. "Wait a second. Why?"

"I'd rather you not be near the scene."

"I won't get in the way."

"Not the point, Son."

"What is, then?"

"That I'm more concerned about you than this guy right now, and I can't help feeling you'll put yourself at risk if you come here."

"I won't."

"Alex, please. Leave it to me and the other officers. We'll be fine."

Alex couldn't answer, and his father hung up. After a moment to compose himself, he threw on his helmet and cranked the ignition of his bike. With the first gap that came in the traffic, he punched the accelerator, his rear tire peeling out before it gripped the ground. Fifteen minutes at least stood between him and the location of the ranch, more than enough time for Shane to flee the area, if he filled his stomach that fast.

He could already see his father beating him there and readying the officers to comb the scene, a thought that produced an uneasy sigh. The bit of faith he could muster about Shane not attacking someone, much less armed officers in broad daylight, redirected his worries to the canine units tracking his scent and the police finding him post or mid-shift.

As he drew closer to First Colony, and the first street where he could take a shortcut to the next highway, the density of the traffic kept him from switching lanes to recover lost speed. Torn between hoping he'd find nothing once there, and what to do if he did, he kept still at the next intersection to gauge the wind direction. It was coming from behind him and favoring the right side, making it a westward or northwest wind.

With the direction in mind, he kept driving towards the street he was looking for, now with his thoughts on the satellite images he'd seen on his maps app. They had been within a month of a year old, but the area surrounding the ranch had shown a lot of green and grass. Most of it had to still be there, and if the grass was tall enough, or the brush and tree density thick enough...

Would let him hide pretty easy for a while. Alex continued north with that thought in mind until something else came to him. The street he was thinking of driving down was upwind of where Shane could be hiding. If he drove along a downwind street instead... Or was Shane keeping ready to flee at the first hint of nearby bodies, let alone someone approaching him from that direction?

The light Alex was waiting on turned green as that question ran through his head. The closer he got to the next light, his last chance to decide on a direction to take, the more his head turned side to side.

He was halfway across the highway when he turned his bike's handlebars to steer him left.

Chapter 28 – Out With It

Friday, October 7th, 2011
Moon Phase – Waxing Gibbous
Days until the Full Moon – 5

After crossing over the railroad tracks several intersections along, Alex slowed down and nudged his visor open by one notch. With the scents around him strengthened, he inched his bike's tires closer to the curb, in case he needed to stop.

Fresh or drying blood; warm animal meat; Shane's fur. Any of those scents or parts of them would do. As the southern edge of the wooded area drew closer, one of the vehicles behind him passed on his left, the draft sweeping air around him and mixing the scents he'd begun noticing with ones of exhaust. He pulled over to let the rest pass, keeping an eye on the intersection behind him for when no more vehicles were coming. The lights he could see turning red were his cue to get moving again.

As he resumed facing forward, the sight of a police SUV at the intersection ahead got him to resume going the speed limit versus half of it. When it began to move, and then turn his direction, Alex kept watch for who the driver was.

It slowed down as it drew closer, letting him see his father through the windshield before he stopped the cruiser. Alex did the same with his bike, his heart beating even faster as his father rolled down the window.

"What are you doing here, Son?" Alex couldn't speak. "Stay there. I need to talk to you."

Damn it. Though his father left the flashing lights off until he'd turned around and approached his bike from behind, his tone of voice wasn't what Alex wanted to hear. With the sound of the cruiser door opening and closing followed up by bootsteps, he turned off his bike's engine, and thought of a quick excuse.

His father stopped by his side before he spoke. "Why didn't you listen to me?"

Alex took several seconds to answer. "I was worried."

"I know you were, but I told you not to come here and put yourself at risk."

"I'm just trying to find out if this guy's in there or not."

This time, his father didn't speak immediately. Alex noticed him look over the edge of the wooded area. "How?"

"Drive up the road, see if his scent's on the breeze."

"'Scent's on the breeze'... Oh, right. You did tell us about that."

Alex nodded. "If he is in there, I'll know." When his father again didn't respond right away, Alex took a few more sniffs of the air.

"And then what?"

The first answer that formed in Alex's head was the easy one: encourage Shane to leave the scene, clear the air of the possibility of an officer being hurt, and leave it at that. The idea that he'd be interfering with police investigations surfaced just before he glanced up at his father, who matched his gaze shortly after. How calm he looked help brush his worry aside.

But then Alex remembered the story Shane had told him the day before. That he'd bitten him to make sure he knew what was coming. Stuck him with this when it was possible he could've avoided being a werewolf in the first place. As his talk with Nathan flashed through his head, pressure built in his throat and water welled in his eyes.

When his name was spoken, he snapped back to the present and responded. "I don't know what I can do besides that."

The crack in his voice got his father's attention. "You okay?"

"Yeah."

"Sounds more like you're upset." Alex swallowed and didn't respond fast enough. "Alex, what's going on?"

Shaking his head, Alex breathed out. "Something yesterday." A call from his father's radio distracted both of them, relieving his expression slightly.

"What kind of something?"

Feeling his pulse slowing down over a series of seconds, Alex soon spoke up, glad to hear the crack in his voice from before was gone. "This guy... He told me something about what he did to me." He shook his head once. "I didn't catch it then."

"I don't like where this is going, Alex." His father's tone was one in line with understanding, yet clear suspicion of his motives.

"If I can, I'll try and make him leave. At least that."

"But that's not the only thing you're considering doing, is it?" Again, Alex shook his head; it was no use lying. "What else? Question him?"

"If I can." He heard his father sigh before he walked back to his cruiser. Figuring he was doing it to check for incoming reports, and to continue the act of having him pulled over, Alex readied for his return.

His father was quick to speak once he was close enough. "And if what happened to you last time happens again, then what?"

Not expecting that question, Alex stumbled on an answer, and his father continued.

"That's why I'm more concerned about you than this guy right now. Why I didn't want you coming here."

"He caught me by surprise that time. It hasn't happened since."

Another pause came from his father. "Alright, tell you what." He ripped a blank ticket report from the pad he was carrying, continuing after Alex stuffed it into his jacket pocket. "Go ahead and drive up the road. If you smell him, stop and wave for me."

Alex nodded and took a few more sniffs before cranking his bike's engine again. With his visor in the same cracked position as before, he took to the road doing half the speed limit.

Halfway to the next intersection, nothing. Only the scents of the animals from the ranch, and those of two canines.

It was when he passed the intersection that the scent of blood, and then Shane's fur, slowed him down. Alex snapped his head to the right, but saw nothing through the thick brush and grass. A wave for his father was quick to follow.

He pulled alongside him and spoke out the open window. "Alex."

"Yeah?"

His father waited until he was looking his way before continuing. "I'll trust that you know what you're doing, but if you insist on going in there, do your mother and me a favor. Don't push your luck and let something happen."

"I won't."

"Alright. Stay safe, Son."

Until his father was down the road and out of sight, Alex kept his bike's engine running. Once it and his helmet were off, he parked it close to a nearby utility gate and stashed his gear behind a bush near the road. Although not expecting anything to happen, a lighter load would help if anything did. His phone was then muted and the GPS pulled up. He'd smelled Shane with the breezes going northwest, and the area he was facing had nearly a square quarter-mile of space between him and the ranch.

The initial rhythm of his feet crunching against the grasses and dropped leaves as he began walking was subtly soothing to his ears. At the same time, he felt a poke at his back like someone was watching him, despite hearing nothing of note.

Shane's scent continued to drift along with the others on the breeze until it shifted to a more northern direction. When he lost it, Alex stopped and checked his GPS. He'd covered almost thirty-five yards going southeast so far. He changed his direction east, then again to south when hints of Shane's scent returned to the breeze.

As he came near an old maple tree, several noises he wasn't producing got his attention. A rustling of grasses and dropped leaves, and a rubbing, abrasive sound from something heavy being dragged along the grass, all in the distance. With the brush and trees around him obscuring much of the ground, he gave the noises a few seconds to continue, to allow him to gauge their direction.

He covered less than half of what he thought the distance was to them before the dragging sounds stopped. What replaced them were impacts in the grass, the frequency in line with an animal's walking pace, and their direction circling to the north of him.

When they slowed down, and then started coming his way, it didn't take long for Shane to appear, his dark gray, black, and tan pelt coming in sharp contrast to the greens and browns around him. His stalking pace, unwavering stare and all fours gait got Alex's pulse up before a chill ran through him. What if he was asked how he'd found him? If this guy knew he had connections with the police, what would he try and do? Or what if he already knew from watching his neighborhood?

"I thought that was you." Shane's growl-laced sentence was followed up by him glancing to the southwest.

"Any reason why you're a werewolf in broad daylight?" Alex asked before he could continue.

"I was hungry, and there was easy prey nearby," Shane replied after a lick of his fangs.

"Figures," Alex said, trying to keep his tone casual. "You going to change back?"

"Not right now. Why should I?"

"What, you can't smell the gun lubricant? Or the canines?" Shane's scoff in response to that sounded like a mix between a forced exhale and a snarl. Alex let his eyes pull his head to the right briefly.

"They're not here yet," Shane said, his tone confident.

"No, but they are doing their jobs."

This time Shane kept quiet, as though he expected more to be said. Instead of talking, Alex's gaze went in the supposed direction of the police again.

Shane sighed aloud in response, the growl-backed noise drawing Alex's attention back to him. "I know your dad is a cop." Despite having considered that possibility, Alex felt his heart sink. How long had he known? "But you already know I'm not interested in turning him, or anyone else."

"I'm aware of that..." Alex felt the rest of his sentence freeze in his throat.

"Then can you let that idea go?"

"I would," Alex began, "but something's bothering me."

"What?"

"What if you were wrong about what Angela did to me?"

"You think I never considered that?"

Alex held back from saying he didn't know. "How sure were you?"

"Enough to risk being seen that night."

"Then why didn't you just warn me?"

"Because you wouldn't have believed me if all I did was speak to you. Don't try to pretend like you would've."

"I'm just saying."

"Alright, then how would you have done something like that? Besides go through a full shift in front of someone you barely know and has no reason to trust a word you say." Alex stalled too long. "That's what I thought."

The rising pitch and underlying annoyance, possibly anger, in Shane's voice pulled a reply from Alex as soon as he finished. "Everyone I told handled it well enough."

"Of course they would. They're your friends, and your family. But even then, none of them believed you at first, did they?"

"One did."

"Exception, not the rule. And I bet they've tried not to act scared of you after that, haven't they?"

Recalling the barrage of fear scents from his friends the night he shifted in front of them, and from his parents when they found out, Alex licked his teeth and a swallow slipped by. "Alright, fine. Still, how do I know that what you told me is true? I only have your word for it. No one else's."

Shane narrowed his eyes a bit. "What are you getting at?" When Alex didn't answer, thanks to his now-quivering chest, Shane's next few breaths became backed by the rumbles of growls. "You think I'm lying to you, is that it?"

"For all I know."

The next growl from Shane held for more than a second, to which Alex barely flinched, though he felt his flesh tighten. His quivering tongue rubbed a part of his teeth again, this time to check for his fangs. None so far.

"Then what do you think I'm getting out of doing that to you?"

Alex tried to think of a response, but none came beyond a turning of his head away from Shane's gaze.

Shane continued when he kept silent again. "Are you just acting like this because of someone else's views?"

Shit. Alex ran off the first thought that formed from his sudden worry. "I said your explanation bothers me, and it does."

"Then why so suddenly assume that I'm lying?"

Taking a second, Alex gathered his thoughts. Something was up with Shane's reactions. Was he giving responses that were too easily countered? Or was this guy really that convinced that he'd hardly done anything wrong?

"If you don't want to believe what I told you, that's your problem."

"And you think that's the end of it?"

"No." Shane then began to stand back on all fours instead of crouching as he had been. Alex leaned back slightly. "Because now you're dead set on thinking of me as a liar, aren't you?"

"I wouldn't be if your idea wasn't so full of holes. Biting me instead of waiting or warning me."

"You really think I would risk something like that? Leave someone like you with no idea what you were in for with only weeks to figure it out? Nothing good happens with that."

"Nothing good happened after you bit me either." Alex's arms were trembling then, his emotions rushing and boiling over. "At least there was that chance..."

The lock-up of Alex's throat gave Shane the time to speak. "And yet you've managed, and no one left you out to dry when they found out, did they?"

"Wasn't worth it."

"Having no clue and keeping your life at risk, that would have been better?"

"Then this all boils down to 'He's screwed either way. Just do it and leave no question'."

Within a second of that sentence leaving Alex's mouth, Shane was up on his legs and had closed the gap between them, staring into his opponent's eyes with his own squinted in anger and insult. His muzzle hung slightly open, letting his snarls sound freely.

The adrenaline rushing through Alex's veins by then was gearing him to run. His legs wouldn't cooperate. They trembled. They froze him in place. In a spot where he was at Shane's mercy. How much taller Shane was than him, his massive fangs, his murderous gaze, all those things vice-gripped Alex's attention, the guttural noises from Shane's lungs shaking his chest.

Alex felt more than a shirk away from Shane at that moment. He felt his whole leg step back, and then his stomach shrink, pulling him into a slight crouch. He felt a jab in his throat that didn't come from any physical claws. He couldn't speak. He could only behave in ways that involved moving away. Making himself smaller. Less threatening.

When the snarling stopped in favor of growl-laced breaths, Alex let his gaze break. Shane's paws were curled at the digits, and his claws now held his attention. When Shane crouched as well, Alex felt his growl-laced breaths brush his neck. Ones laced with the rusted iron scent of blood.

They stopped just before Shane spoke. "You really think it was that easy a decision for me?"

Alex remained silent. His eye contact remained broken.

As though the gestures were a signal, the guttural snarls sounded again before a snapping of jaws happened behind his head. Alex crouched as low as he could. That distance was instantly closed again, and he felt Shane's hot breath against his neck. His pulse rose even more and his eyes watered even more.

Then came Shane's gigantic paw pressing against his back. His claws arched, and Alex felt the stings of them through his denim jacket. He was trapped. Everything around him faded to the sounds of snarling and the smell of blood. Keeping his mouth shut and cowering as he was made his chest feel empty; it was begging to be filled with anger, which didn't seem to come.

"How the fuck can you believe that?" Shane demanded at last, his voice approaching a roaring pitch. The pause after his sentence was nothing but angry growls. "Fine. Don't believe me. I don't give a shit anymore."

Alex didn't dare reply as the swishes of hot breath continued to brush his neck. It was already taking everything he had not to pull his arms up to cover his head.

When Shane continued, Alex noticed his tone losing the tinge of disgust and sadness. "I could've let you flounder after what you did. Let you find out the hard way what you were in for, maybe let it cost you your livelihood or a few of your friends." He paused. "I didn't, and yet you're even worse of a rogue than I thought you would be."

Alex lost track of how long it was that Shane stayed quiet after that, but even as the growling breaths behind his neck began to lose their ferocity, he still didn't dare say anything. He checked his teeth again. No fangs.

"I'm watching you from now on."

Alex felt his heart stop when that sentence was spoken. What had he done? "Just me then." he pleaded.

"Not a chance."

"Dad's not talking. No one is."

"I don't expect them to. You losing it will do that just as easily."

Alex didn't know how to feel right then. Emotions of many kinds pulled at him.

When Shane's breaths against his neck eventually stopped, his ears were freed from the constant processing of growling. With the noise no longer flooding his ears, he heard what sounded like footfalls crunching leaves and wood, and chatter from a radio from somewhere behind him.

"When I let you go, wait until I start moving, then run to your left," Shane said, his tone not wavering much. "Not at first. Go slow, and then run."

Alex then felt the claws retract from his back, freeing his muscles from the risk of being torn. He backed up a step, barely getting up as he did.

After Shane took another glance around the area, he turned his attention back to him. "If they or your dad find me or start shooting, you better believe I'll defend myself."

Alex felt a growl reach his mouth, but before he could let it out, Shane had taken off, running on all fours with barely a break in his stride. With one more glance in the direction he'd taken interest in, Alex stepped aside, keeping slow as he'd been told. And that let him hear something, a command from the police.

"I heard something. Up ahead."

Alex crouched a bit to try and muffle his footsteps. It only made them louder to his ears. He had to flee to the areas lacking leaf-covered ground, and at that thought, picked up his pace.

As the last few yards of brush and vegetation were passed through and left behind, Alex swept up his backpack. He couldn't stop thinking about Shane's warning to him. Much less everything else he'd been told.

He needed to sit. To think over what had happened. Shaking, out of breath, his back stinging and his eyes ready to leak, he sat on his bike to do just that. He had no idea what he'd accomplished by tracking Shane down, if he'd accomplished anything at all besides make things worse.

And then he'd cowered from him. Acted submissive—the very thing he didn't want to do, at any moment of the encounter. Swearing loudly, multiple times, before remembering the Blue Moon encounter, Alex looked into one of his motorcycle's rear-view mirrors.

Ignoring how red his face was, half of what was supposed to be his blue irises were yellow. Taking deep breaths to quell his emotional cocktail, the yellow soon faded and his eyes were blue again. While wondering how close he'd once again come to shifting, he felt for his phone through his jeans. As much as he wanted to get away from the scene, the obligation to call his dad first overshadowed it, if only so he could let him know what had happened and hopefully keep him and the officers away from Shane.

With his phone freed from his pocket, he dialed his father's number. Far to his right, he could hear the canine units barking.

Two rings in, the call went unanswered. *C'mon Dad, please pick up.* The third ring, then the fourth went unanswered, and his voicemail came up. Alex hung up and tried again, to no avail. *Damn it. Did he mute his phone?* He sent a message to call him back, but as the seconds dragged on after it was sent, the continued barking of the canine units drove his fears of Shane being found.

He must have covered a lot of ground by now. Though that thought started as an easy boost of confidence, Alex turned it over a few times until something came to him. Was his father keeping near the ranch, or was he among the officers doing the search? He hadn't hinted at helping with the latter before.

As he settled on one of the two possibilities, Alex slipped his helmet back on. The ranch itself he could check much more easily, and without risking looking suspicious. *I'll just play it calm when I get close.*

Epilogue – A Return to the Scene

Friday, October 7th, 2011
Moon Phase – Waxing Gibbous
Days until the Full Moon – 5

With another long breath to steady his nerves, Alex cranked his bike's engine. The road his father had driven down before came to a four-way, which he couldn't help looking down in case he saw Shane dash across the street. With his helmet's visor open one notch, he could just smell him on the wind, along with the police dogs, and as the lights changed to green, he steered right.

He never saw him cross, and his scent was lost the further east Alex drove. Not even his rearview mirrors showed him crossing.

Speeding up in turn, he blew though the corner ahead before taking the nearby south route towards Industrial Blvd, the street where he expected to find his father.

The distant flashing of police lights grabbed his attention as he passed the trees and fence lining the right edge of the road. Hoping his face hadn't remained red, he slowed down and pulled his visor up more. There was some left, but enough was gone, he felt, to hide what had happened, and after a check behind him, he looked ahead to try and spot his father.

It didn't take long. He emerged from behind one SUV cruiser, notebook in hand, while the other officers looked busy with who Alex assumed was the owner of the place. His father glanced aside once, then locked his gaze on him as he came closer. Beyond him, one and then both of the officers turned and saw him approach as well.

Before he stopped and fully opened his visor, the movement of Alex's helmet became his father's cue to turn his head. "It's my son," he said to them, one of whom gave a noncommittal response. He then turned back and said, "Can you wait here for a minute?"

Alex quickly glanced around the scene. He could still hear the dogs barking. A good sign, but given how Bailey had reacted to him the first time, and how little he was assured that Shane would completely flee the scene, warning his father was priority one. "I found him, as a werewolf."

His father's calm and intent expression shifted to horrified within a second. "You're..." He cut himself off before looking out towards the trees and brush, and then reaching for his shoulder radio. "Units 203 and K79, do you copy?"

Despite Shane having fled from the police and telling him to do likewise, Alex breathed an easy sigh as one of the two officers responded. "This is K79. We copy."

"What's your situation?"

The response came a few seconds later. "Found something. Looks like one of the animals." They continued after a few more seconds. "No sign of the other one."

Alex's father gave a standard police acknowledgment, along with a reminder to the officers to let him know of any developments, before looking back at him. "Alright, can you wait here for a minute?"

Though he wanted to say more, and right then instead of later, Alex nodded after a few seconds. His bike's engine was turned off, and he kept seated as his thoughts went to the officers on the search, and then back to everything Shane had said to him. Some of it still carved a void in his chest, making the reprieve his father had given him all the more worthwhile. The less he let off his chest in front of him, around the other officers, the better.

Yet the more Alex repeated Shane's words about him losing it, the more his emotions swelled back up to test him. He wasn't the only one who could potentially get caught, and the increased police presence wasn't something he caused.

Like you're in any position to talk about restraint, Alex growled to himself as he pictured the encounter again. If Shane's carelessness kept up, more police would get involved and one of them was bound to get caught or make a damning mistake.

And if it happened, which one of them would take the brunt of it?

Bonus Short Story

Wednesday, October 31st, 2012 – Sugar Land, Texas
Moon Phase - Waning Gibbous
9:09 p.m.

Digging his claws into the carpet as his body entered the final stage of transformation, Alex Stryker tried to keep himself from screaming as his face and jaws shifted into a wolf's muzzle and his legs into more canine-like limbs. With his folks off enjoying a party with his father's police colleagues, the house was empty except for himself and Bailey. Meaning the only sounds he had heard over the last four agonizing minutes were coming from him, and inside him, but he knew this would soon be over. It wasn't like he hadn't been expecting this.

It had been over a year since he first became a werewolf, and over that time he had grown used to some of the pain that came with transforming. Mostly the subtle changes that occurred before the very worst parts. Yet no matter how well he tried to prepare himself for the three nights of the full moon each month, the sickening sounds of his bones cracking under his own skin and the feeling of that same skin stretching to mold to his emerging wolf-like skeleton and body were things he would never be used to. When the change was at last over, his body was sore from top to bottom and his heart was thundering in his chest as he tried to catch his breath, each one making his body tremble like he was shivering.

Looking over to where Bailey had taken to hiding as he underwent the change, Alex saw him trying to maneuver around him, nearly rubbing himself against the foot of the bed as he did so. Although Bailey was a German Shepard, much less one who had protected him from harm several times before in his human form, all it took was seeing the were form of his master to make him cower and avoid his presence. Despite Alex laying on his back, which he knew was a sign of submission among dogs and wolves, Bailey refused to come near him and left as soon as he was able.

Sorry, boy. There's nothing I can do. Alex thought as his hind paws found some footing and he got back to his feet. Although still trembling a bit from the recent change, he made his way to the living room to get away from the now cramped space of his room. He had closed every window and curtain in the house well before he felt the change coming, so no one would see him walking around. Still, of all the nights that one of the three nights of the full moon could fall on, one of them had to be Halloween. The night he had been looking forward to since July that year, until he looked ahead on his calendar.

Peeking out though the curtains of the living room, parts of his neighborhood were brightly illuminated by the still low hanging full moon. All the houses he could see had their doorway lights on, and the crowds of kids walking the neighborhood were just as numerous as they had been an hour prior. It was the first time in months when he truly felt depressed about having to keep himself away from others. Any other time, he wouldn't have cared.

"And Nathan's throwing a costume party tonight." His vocal grumbling came as a low, growl-laced voice versus his normal radio announcer deep voice. He knew at least one of his friends would be at the party, and with Bailey so afraid of him in this form, the idea of sneaking out of the house and going several streets over was much more appealing than just staying inside all night like he had done in the past. *I would fit in just fine over there...if everyone was half drunk.*

Alex tossed the idea around in his head for a while longer, torn between completely forgetting the idea and just saying, 'Damn the consequences.' Eventually, he asked himself the most important question relating to the matter: What was he afraid of? It was Halloween night, when just about everyone was running around in a costume of some kind.

Even if he was seen briefly, as long as he wasn't causing any trouble or making himself look suspicious, no one would bat an eye or even have second thoughts about him. Looking at the now humanish clawed paws he sported in his were form, he was sure he could make it that far without much difficulty. *Aw hell, why not? It beats doing nothing until tomorrow.*

Heading for the guest bedroom opposite from his, which was his usual way of getting inside and out when all the doors in the house were locked, he slid the glass window open, feeling the evening cold sweep over his fur as the AC blew outside. Even if he did end up changing his mind about this, he could lounge around outside for a while.

Climbing outside and into a small stretch of the backyard, Alex slid the window closed behind him and quickly took off for the patio. He could hear the sounds of kids laughing and teens talking among each other as he came close to the backyard gate, as well as one of his favorite parts of the holiday: the opening of candy wrappers. He could already smell some faint traces of chocolate and caramel in the air, making him lick his lips in response before he reminded himself that his goal was getting to Nathan's place. Not acting like he was in costume to get some of those treats, however tasty they smelled.

Working his way through the neighborhood after leaping the fence around his house, Alex did his best to stay a good distance away from anybody walking the streets and on all four limbs as he went along. Barely three minutes later however, he came close to encountering a small group of kids who were trick or treating on their own. With his heart pounding in fear, but his nose focusing on the scents from the candy they had opened, he made himself scarce from the group's location.

Hearing one of the kids trying to get him to come back by saying they wouldn't hurt him didn't get him to change his mind. He knew what they were trying to achieve with that sentence: the chance to pet him. He wasn't about to let himself be stroked and petted like a dog, but for now it was either act like one and let others believe he was one or turn back altogether.

A few streets further, he could hear even more trick or treaters walking the streets and ducked behind a thick bush to wait for their numbers to decrease. The sweet smells of candy accompanied them and wafted over him as the evening breezes began again. Everything from chocolate bars to gummy worms, white chocolate and even older candies he could barely recall. All of them made him salivate the more he sniffed at the air, and not being able to sample any of it was making him twitch.

Seeing a few lone kids pass by his temporary hiding spot, for a second he thought to run up to them and snatch one of the buckets they were carrying in his jaws. He could dump it out, grab a few pieces of candy and run for it to enjoy them. Even if one of them lost some candy, they could make it up and as long as he stayed on four legs, they'd easily mistake him for a dog. No harm would be done and no one would be the wiser.

With a quick check of the area around him, Alex got into position for a running start, aiming his body in the direction of the two kids. He was ready to make his move, but then hesitated on executing it. If he missed the handles of the buckets and bit into their hands by accident...

Shaking his head and turning away he instantly dropped the thought of trying to steal some candy for himself, frightened that he had even considered it knowing his bite would infect others. *OK, calm down. I remembered in time. Nothing happened and nothing will happen, so just move on.* Taking some comfort in the fact that he stopped himself from potentially making a huge mistake like that, Alex waited for another gap in the traffic of trick or treaters then continued towards Nathan's street a few blocks over.

When he got there, he saw that the exterior was littered with decorations of all kinds; some painted, some store bought, and a selection of orange and black lights that ran around the perimeter of the front yard. He was sure Nathan's parents had helped with much of the set-up, but he could definitely see some of the handiwork of his friend in this; he had been into crafts since he first met him in middle school, and enjoyed set design as a hobby throughout high school.

It was enough to make Alex reveal a fanged smile as he scoped out a good hiding spot and crossed the final street separating him from his goal. Between Nathan's place and his neighbor to the west, there was a darkened gap that looked quite appealing, and the bushes that ran nearby could also help him stay out of sight. Settling into the new hiding place and hearing the music blaring through the windows, he started to feel much more at ease and upbeat than before when he was alone with Bailey. Like he was involved in something fun and social, despite not taking a direct part in it.

Laying the grass with his legs folded and his head resting on his paws, Alex listened in on the playlist of songs from the stereo inside; the lyrics of "Animal I Have Become" he found ironic listening to it now. Every so often, he could hear more kids walking by and talking, and each time he opened his eyes to watch where they went. Most of them seemed to avoid the house even though the lights were on, which he found odd but welcome.

A while later, he heard a group of teenaged kids heading down the street. This time instead of walking past, they turned onto the sidewalk leading to the house. Although he wasn't terribly worried that they would see him, Alex backed up a bit anyway just in case. As he did so, hearing the teens talking amongst each other, he suddenly found an urge to have some fun with these guys. Standing up on all fours, he slowly crept around the side of the building as the teens made their way to the front door and rang the bell. The music inside was so loud that he was sure the greeter wouldn't be able to respond for a bit.

"So, who's the host of this party?" asked one of the group.

"His name's Nathan Travers, a good friend of mine." Hearing the voice of Catherine, Alex suddenly felt worried. She, Nathan, and Marcus all knew about his lycanthropy, and the fact that he was completely sentient as a werewolf. If he pulled a stunt like this with her nearby, what would she think of him?

Shaking his head and assuring himself that he was worrying too much about the situation, Alex decided to go for it and hopefully get some joy out of the experience. He drew a slow, rumbling growl from his lungs, enough to get the attention of the group as he continued to approach them. "Was that growling I just heard?" asked the second male of the group.

"God, I hope not," Catherine replied. Alex fought back the last worry he had about what he was about to do. This wasn't a 'damn the consequences' moment like his choice to come here. It was just a joke and the moment was right for it anyway. Growling again, this time more loudly than before, he got on his hind legs and prepared to make his move.

"Uh, guys. Maybe we should get inside?" Hearing that request and the truly worried tone it presented, Alex knew the time was right and made his move. With one motion, he grabbed the bricks on the side of the house and with a loud snarl and his jaws apart, he revealed himself to the group of four teens. Both of the girls present, Catherine in her cat-girl costume and the other in a US Army jumpsuit, screamed and took a step backwards in response to seeing him. Meanwhile, the two guys looked like they were about to jump completely out of their costumes, a vampire and Green Lantern costume respectfully, at the sight of him snarling at them.

As quickly as the event started however, it ended when the front door of the house opened, revealing Nathan in the Jason Vorhees costume he was wearing for the night. Looking in Alex's direction, he jumped a bit as well before addressing him directly. "Damnit, Alex. What are you doing?" he said, despite the music blaring behind him.

"You know this guy?" asked the teen in the vampire costume.

"Sure do." Catherine said, sounding quite pissed off.

While Alex was turning red under his fur in embarrassment from hearing how much distaste was being leveled his way by his friends, the other three teens were starting to smile again and soon began laughing. "Did you make that costume?" asked the teen in the Green Lantern outfit. "Looks awesome."

"I'll say. Nice work on the fur," said the Army girl before she put her hands over her chest. Alex nodded his thanks to the two compliments from the teens then backed out of sight with a final glance at Catherine and Nathan. Now that things had happened and he heard how his friends reacted to the stunt, he started to feel terrible at doing the deed. Despite hearing one last compliment about good luck in scaring more people that night, his throat began to feel like someone had shoved a lump of flesh down it.

Leaning against the side of the house to collect his thoughts, he soon heard Nathan and Catherine coming his way; the looks on their faces when they saw him were as if he'd just disrespected them in front of their parents.

"What are you doing here, and what was the reason for that?" Nathan's tone was rife with frustration and a bit of fear.

"It's Halloween, and what exactly did I do beyond scare them?" Alex protested in his growling voice, trying to dodge the question.

Shaking her head, Catherine spoke in response. "You said you had to stay inside because it's a full moon."

"I know that and I intended to," Alex said, turning his head back towards Nathan. "but you saw how they reacted. They loved that jump scare."

"That's not the point." Catherine replied. "What if one of them attacked you and got what you have?"

"I'm not that careless, and I have to bite someone to pass lycanthropy."

"Just answer the question, Alex." Nathan demanded, now sounding annoyed. "What...are you doing here?"

Biting his tongue for a second, Alex struggled to answer without sounding like a wimp. "I didn't want to be stuck in the house all night without some good company. That's why I came."

"And the idea of calling us never crossed your mind?" Catherine asked.

"No." Alex answered, his ears dropping and his head dipping a bit. "Look, I'm sorry. I was just trying to have some fun, and those three got a kick out of it anyway, so there's no harm done here."

"Fair enough." Nathan replied, his tone now less incensed than before. "You said you were looking for some company, though. That mean you're going to stick around?"

"Looking like that?" Catherine protested, her hand flying in Alex's direction.

Alex growled a bit in response to Catherine's remark, getting both her attention and Nathan's. "That a bit cold, don't you think?"

"Maybe, but seriously..."

"Use the backyard then." Nathan said, thumbing over towards it. "It's unoccupied and the lights are off, so I'll unlock the gate and make sure no one goes out there."

While Alex could easily jump the six-foot barrier and save Nathan the trouble, he didn't want to test the generosity he was shown. "I appreciate it, Nathan. Anything's better than being by myself tonight."

With a plan set, his friends went back into the house, Catherine still sounding a bit miffed. Despite how angry his friends had sounded towards him, they had all known each other for years. Something like this was nothing to agonize over. Just a bump in the road.

As the night went on into the hours around midnight, the party remained strong while Alex laid back and listened to the music inside. Every so often, Nathan stepped outside to make sure he was still there and while he wanted the chance to chat with him during those times, he was the host of the party. The person all the guests would want to thank for his time and effort in throwing it.

Around 1:10, the festivities had calmed to a point where Alex felt secure about heading home. Rolling onto his stomach, he heard the backdoor slide open again. "You still here, man?"

"In the shadows and watching you." Alex said in deeper growl, trying to make some kind of joke.

"I figured." Nathan replied, stepping outside and closing the door. "The last few guests left, just in case you wanted to know."

"Then I should go too." Alex said, getting to his feet while still in the shadows. "Thanks for letting me hang out here."

"You're welcome, but before you leave, I've got something for you." Wondering what his friend was talking about, he quickly found out when he returned with a candy filled bucket. "Happy Halloween, dude. We had enough left over, and I figured you'd like some."

Alex took the bucket in his paws, despite feeling somewhat guilty about taking what he probably didn't deserve. "Thanks. By the way..."

"It's fine. Just take them," Nathan replied with one hand held up, "and don't worry about Catherine. She and I talked for a while before she left, and she doesn't have any hard feelings about what happened."

Alex was relieved to hear those words, and his muzzle revealed a smile again. "Glad to hear it. Happy Halloween." Placing the bucket's handle between his jaws, he returned home to the same empty house he had left before, now with Bailey awaiting his return. As he took to sampling one of the mini-bars in the bucket, he proudly howled into the empty house. Despite the few bumps in the road he ran into, this Halloween night had turned out to be even more enjoyable than he'd hoped.